A DEADLY
EDUCATION

A DEADLY EDUCATION

A
EDUCATION

+ *Lesson One of The Scholomance* +

NAOMI NOVIK

1 3 5 7 9 10 8 6 4 2

Del Rey

20 Vauxhall Bridge Road,

London SW1V 2SA

Penguin
Random House
UK

Del Rey is part of the Penguin Random House group of companies
whose addresses can be found at global.penguinrandomhouse.com

www.penguin.co.uk

A CIP catalogue record for this book is available from
the British Library

Hardback ISBN 9781529100853
Trade Paperback ISBN 9781529100860

Book design by Simon M. Sullivan

Printed and bound in Great Britain by Clays Ltd, Elcograf S.p.A.

Penguin Random House is committed to a sustainable future
for our business, our readers and our planet. This book is made
from Forest Stewardship Council® certified paper

For lim, a bringer of light in dark place

A DEADLY EDUCATION

Chapter 1
SOUL-EATER

I DECIDED that Orion needed to die after the second time he saved my life. I hadn't really cared much about him before then one way or another, but I had limits. It would've been all right if he'd saved my life some really extraordinary number of times, ten or thirteen or so—thirteen is a number with distinction. Orion Lake, my personal bodyguard; I could have lived with that. But we'd been in the Scholomance almost three years by then, and he hadn't shown any previous inclination to single me out for special treatment.

Selfish of me, you'll say, to be contemplating with murderous intent the hero responsible for the continued survival of a quarter of our class. Well, too bad for the losers who couldn't stay afloat without his help. We're not *meant* to all survive, anyway. The school has to be fed somehow.

Ah, but what about me, you ask, since I'd needed him to save me? Twice, even? And that's exactly why he had to go. *He* set off the explosion in the alchemy lab last year, fighting that chimaera. I had to dig myself out of the rubble while he ran around in circles whacking at its fire-breathing tail. And that soul-eater hadn't been in my room for five seconds before he came through the door: he must have been right on its heels, probably chasing it down the hall. The thing had only swerved in here looking to escape.

But who's going to let me explain any of that? The chimaera might not have stuck to me, there were more than thirty kids in the lab that day, but a dramatic rescue in my bedchamber is on another level. As far as the rest of the school is concerned, I've just fallen into the general mass of hapless warts that Orion Lake has saved in the course of his brilliant progress, and that was intolerable.

Our rooms aren't very big. He was only a few steps from my desk chair, still hunched panting over the bubbling purplish smear of the soul-eater that was now steadily oozing into the narrow cracks between the floor tiles, the better to spread all over my room. The fading incandescence on his hands was illuminating his face, not an extraordinary face or anything: he had a big beaky nose that would maybe be dramatic one day when the rest of his face caught up, but for now was just too large, and his forehead was dripping sweat and plastered with his silver-grey hair that he hadn't cut for three weeks too long. He spends most of his time behind an impenetrable shell of devoted admirers, so it was the closest I'd ever been to him. He straightened and wiped an arm across the sweat. "You okay—Gal, right?" he said to me, just to put some salt on the wound. We'd been in the same lab section for three years.

"No thanks to you and your boundless fascination for every dark thing creeping through the place," I said icily. "And it is *not* Gal, it has never been *Gal*, it's *Galadriel*"—the name wasn't my idea, don't look at me—"and if that's too many syllables for you to manage all in one go, El will do."

His head had jerked up and he was blinking at me in a sort

of open-mouthed way. "Oh. Uh. I—I'm sorry?" he said, voice rising on the words, as if he didn't understand what was going on.

"No, no," I said. "I'm sorry. Clearly I'm not performing my role up to standard." I threw a melodramatic hand up against my forehead. "Orion, I was so terrified," I gasped, and flung myself onto him. He tottered a bit: we were the same height. "Thank *goodness* you were here to *save* me, I could never have managed a soul-eater all on my own," and I hiccuped a pathetically fake sob against his chest.

Would you believe, he actually tried to put his arm round me and give my shoulder a pat, that's how automatic it was for him. I jammed my elbow into his stomach to shove him off. He made a noise like a whoofing dog and staggered back to gawk at me. "I don't need your help, you insufferable lurker," I said. "Keep away from me or you'll be sorry." I shoved him back one more step and slammed the door shut between us, clearing the end of that beaky nose by bare centimeters. I had the brief satisfaction of seeing a look of perfect confusion on his face before it vanished away, and then I was left with only the bare metal door, with the big melted hole where the doorknob and lock used to be. Thanks, hero. I glared at it and turned back to my desk just as the blob of soul-eater collapsed the rest of the way, hissing like a leaky steam pipe, and a truly putrescent stink filled the room.

I was so angry that it took me six tries to get a spell for cleaning it up. After the fourth attempt, I stood up and hurled the latest crumbling ancient scroll back into the impenetrable dark on the other side of my desk and yelled furiously, "I don't *want* to summon an army of scuvara! I don't *want* to conjure walls of mortal flame! I want my bloody room *clean!*"

What came flying out of the void in answer was a horrible tome encased in some kind of pale crackly leather with spiked corners that scraped unpleasantly as it skidded to me across the metal of the desk. The leather had probably come off a pig, but someone had clearly wanted you to think it had been flayed from a person, which was almost as bad, and it flipped itself open to a page with instructions for enslaving an entire mob of people to do your bidding. I suppose they *would* have cleaned my room if I told them to.

I had to actually take out one of my mother's stupid crystals and sit down on my narrow squeaky bed and meditate for ten minutes, with the stench of the soul-eater all around me and getting into my clothes and sheets and papers. You'd think that any smell would clear out quickly, since one whole wall of the room is open to the scenic view of a mystical void of darkness, so delightfully like living in a spaceship aimed directly into a black hole, but you'd be wrong. After I finally managed to walk myself back from the incoherent kicking levels of anger, I pushed the pigskin book off the far edge of my desk back into the void—using a pen to touch it, just in case—and said as calmly as I could manage, "I want a simple household spell for cleaning away an unwanted mess with a bad smell."

Sullenly down came—*thump*—a gigantic volume titled *Amunan Hamwerod* packed completely full of spells written in Old English—my weakest dead language—and it didn't open to any particular page, either.

That sort of thing is always happening to me. Some sorcerers get an affinity for weather magic, or transformation spells, or fantastic combat magics like dear Orion. I got an affinity for mass destruction. It's all my mum's fault, of course, just like my stupid name. She's one of those flowers and beads and crystals sorts, dancing to the Goddess under the moon. Everyone's a lovely person and anyone who does anything wrong is misunderstood or unhappy.

She even does massage therapy for mundanes, because "it's so relaxing to make people feel better, love." Most wizards don't bother with mundane work—it's considered a bit low—or if they do, they hunt themselves out an empty sack of a job. The person who retires from the firm after forty-six years and no one quite remembers what they were doing, the befuddled librarian that you occasionally glimpse wandering the stacks without seeming to do anything, the third vice president of marketing who shows up only for meetings with senior management; that sort of thing. There're spells to find those jobs or coax them into existence, and then you've provided yourself with the necessities of life and kept your time free to build mana and make your cheap flat into a twelve-room mansion on the inside. But not Mum. She charges almost nothing, and that little mostly because if you offer to do professional massage for free, people will look at you sideways, as well they should.

Naturally I came out designed to be the exact opposite of this paragon, as anyone with a basic understanding of the balancing principle might have expected, and when I want to straighten my room, I get instructions on how to kill it with fire. Not that I can actually *use* any of these delightful cataclysmic spells the school is so eager to hand out to me. Funnily enough, you can't actually whip up an entire army of demons on just a wink. It takes power and lots of it. And no one is going to help you build mana to summon a personal demon army, so let's be real, it takes malia.

Everyone—almost everyone—uses a bit of malia here and there, stuff they don't even think of as wicked. Magic a slice of bread into cake without gathering the mana for it first, that sort of thing, which everyone thinks is just harmless cheating. Well, the power's got to come from *somewhere*, and if you haven't gathered it yourself, then it's probably coming from something living, because it's easier to get power out of something that's already alive and moving around. So you get your cake and meanwhile a colony of ants in your back garden stiffen and die and disintegrate.

Mum won't so much as keep her tea hot with malia. But if you're less of a stickler, as most people are, you can make yourself a three-tier cake out of dirt and ants every day of your life, and still live to 150 and die peacefully in your bed, assuming you don't die of cholesterol poisoning first. But if you start using malia on a grander scale than that, for example to raze a city or slaughter a whole army or any of the thousand other useless things that I know exactly how to do, you can't get enough of it except by sucking in mana—or life force or arcane energy or pixie dust or whatever you want to call it; mana's just the current trend—from things complicated enough to have feelings about it and resist you. Then the power gets tainted and you're getting psychically clawed as you try and yank away their mana, and often enough they win.

That wouldn't be a problem for me, though. I'd be brilliant at pulling malia, if I was stupid or desperate enough to try it. I do have to give Mum credit there: she did that attachment parenting nonsense, which in my case meant her lovely sparkling-clean aura enveloped mine enough to keep me from getting into malia too early. When I brought home small frogs in order to mess with their intestines it was all supremely gentle, "No, my love, we don't hurt living creatures," and she would take me to our corner shop in the village and buy me an ice cream to make up for taking them away. I was five, ice cream was my only motivation for wanting power anyway, so as you can imagine I brought all my little finds to her. And by the time I was old enough that she couldn't have stopped me, I was old enough to understand what happens to sorcerers who use malia.

Mostly it's seniors who start, with graduation staring them in the face, but there're a few in our year who've gone for it already. Sometimes if Yi Liu looks at you too quickly, her eyes are all white for a moment. Her nails have gone solid black, too, and I can tell it's not polish. Jack Westing looks all right, all blond smiling American boy, most people think he's a delight, but if you go past his room and take a deep breath in, you get a faint smell of the charnel house. If you're me, anyway. Luisa three doors down from him vanished early this year, nobody knows what happened to her—not unusual, but I'm reasonably sure what's left of her is in his room. I have a good sense for this sort of thing even when I'd rather not know.

If I *did* give in and start using malia, I'd be sailing through here borne on—admittedly—the hideous leathery bat wings of demonic beasts, but at least there'd be *some* kind of wings. The Scholomance loves to let maleficers out into the world; it almost never kills any of them. It's the rest of us who get soul-eaters popping under our doors in the middle of the afternoon and wauria slithering up out of the drain to latch on to our ankles while we're trying to take a shower and reading assignments that dissolve away our eyeballs. Not even Orion's been able to save all of us. Most of the time less than a quarter of the class makes it all the way through graduation, and eighteen years ago—which I'm sure was not coincidentally near when Orion was conceived—only a dozen students came out, and they were *all* gone dark. They'd banded into a pack and taken out all the rest of the seniors in their year for a massive dose of power.

Of course, the families of all the other students realized

what had happened—because it was stupidly obvious; the idiots hadn't let the enclave kids escape first—and hunted the dozen maleficers down. The last one of them was dead by the time Mum graduated the following year, and that was that for the Hands of Death or whatever they called themselves.

But even when you're a sneaky little fly-by-night maliasucker who picks his targets wisely and makes it out unnoticed, there's nowhere to go but further down. Darling Jack's already stealing life force from human beings, so he's going to start rotting on the inside within the first five years after he graduates. I'm sure he's got grandiose plans for how to stave off his disintegration, maleficers always do, but I don't think he's really got what it takes. Unless he comes up with something special, in ten years, fifteen at the outside, he'll cave in on himself in a nice final grotesque rush. Then they'll dig up his cellar and find a hundred corpses and everyone will tut and say good lord, he seemed like such a nice young man.

At the moment, though, while fighting through one page after another of extremely specific Old English household charms in crabbed handwriting, I felt strongly I could have gone for a nice big helping of malia myself. If my unshucked oats were ever being eaten by leapwinks—your guess is good as mine—I'd be ready. Meanwhile the puddle of soul-eater kept letting out soft flaring pops of gas behind me, each one like a distant flash of lightning before the horrible eruption of stink reached my nose.

I'd already spent the whole day in a deep slog, studying for finals. There were only three weeks left in the term: when you put your hand on the wall in the bathrooms, you could already feel the faint *chunk-chunk* noises of the middle-sized gears starting to engage, getting ready to ratchet us all down another turn. The classrooms stay in one place in the school core, and our dorms start up at the cafeteria level and rotate down each year, like some enormous metal nut whirling round the shaft of a screw, until down all the way we go for graduation. Next year is our turn on the lowest floor, not something to look forward to. I very much don't want to fail any exams and saddle myself with remedial work on top of it.

Thanks to my afternoon's diligence, my back and my bum and my neck were all sore, and my desk light was starting to sputter and go dim while I hunched over the tome, squinting to make out the letters and my arm going numb holding my Old English dictionary in the other hand. Summoning a wall of mortal flame and incinerating the soul-eater, the spellbook, the dictionary, my desk, et cetera, had rapidly increasing appeal.

It's not *completely* impossible to be a long-term maleficer. Liu's going to be all right; she's being a lot more careful about it than Jack. I'd bet she used almost her whole weight allocation to bring a sack of hamsters or something in with her and she's been sacrificing them on a planned schedule. She's sneaking a couple of cigarettes a week, not chain-smoking four packets a day. But she can afford to do that because she's not completely on her own. Her family's big—not big enough to set up an enclave of their own yet, but getting into throwing distance—and rumor has it they've had a lot of maleficers: it's a strategy, for them. She's got a pair of twin cousins who'll be turning up next year, and thanks to using malia, she'll have the power to protect them through their first year. And after Liu graduates, she'll have options. If she wants to quit, she could put spells aside entirely, get one of those dull mundane jobs to pay the bills, and rely on the rest of her family to protect her and cast for her. In ten years or so, she'll have psychically healed up enough that she'll be able to start using mana again. Or she could become a professional maleficer, the kind of witch that gets paid handsomely by enclavers to do heavy work for them with no questions asked about where the power comes from. As long as she doesn't go for anything too excessive—as in, my kind of spells—she'll probably be fine.

But I don't have family, not aside from my mum, and I certainly don't have an enclave ready to support me. We live in the Radiant Mind commune near Cardigan in Wales, which also boasts a shaman, two spirit healers, a Wiccan circle, and a troupe of Morris dancers, all of whom have roughly the same amount of real power, which is to say none whatsoever, and all of whom would fall over in horror if they saw Mum or me doing real magic. Well, me. Mum does magic by dancing up mana with a group of willing volunteers—I've told her she ought to charge people, but no—and then she spreads it out again freely in sparkles and happiness, tra la. People let us eat at their table because they love her, who wouldn't, and they built her a yurt when she came to them, straight from the Scholomance and three months pregnant with me, but none of them could help me do magic or defend me against roving maleficaria. Even if they could, they wouldn't. They don't like me. No one does, except Mum.

Dad died here, during graduation, getting Mum out. We call it graduation because that's what the Americans call it, and they've been carrying the lion's share of the cost of the school for the last seventy years or so. Those who pay the piper call the tune, et cetera. But it's hardly a celebratory occasion or anything. It's just the moment when the seniors all get dumped into the graduation hall, far below at the very bottom of the school, and try to fight their way out through all the hungry maleficaria lying in wait. About half the senior class—that is, half of the ones who've managed to survive that long—makes it. Dad didn't.

He did have family; they live near Mumbai. Mum managed to track them down, but only when I was already five.
She and Dad hadn't exchanged any real-world information or
made any plan for after they graduated and got turfed back
out to their respective homes. That would've been too sensible. They'd been together on the inside for only four months
or something, but they were soulmates and love would lead
the way. Of course, probably it *would* have, for Mum.

Anyway, when she did find them, it turned out his family
was rich, palaces and jewels and djinn servants rich, and more
important by my mum's standards, they came from an ancient strict-mana Hindu enclave that was destroyed during
the Raj, and they're still sticking to the rules. They won't eat
meat, much less pull malia. She was happy to move in with
them, and they were all excited to take us in, too. They hadn't
even known what had happened to Dad. The last time they'd
heard from him was at term-end of his junior year. The seniors collect notes from the rest of us, the week before graduation. I've already written mine for this year and given
copies to some of the London enclave kids, short and sweet:
still alive, doing all right in classes. I had to keep it so small that
no one could reasonably refuse to just add it to their envelope, because otherwise they would.

Dad sent one of those same notes to his family, so they'd
known he'd survived that long. Then he just never came out.
Another of the hundreds of kids thrown on the rubbish heap
of this place. When Mum finally unearthed his family and
told them about me, it felt to them like getting a bit of Dad
back after all. They sent us one-way plane tickets and Mum
said bye to everyone in the commune and packed me up with
all our worldly goods.

But when we got there, my great-grandmother took one
look at me and fell down in a visionary fit and said I was a

burdened soul and would bring death and destruction to all the enclaves in the world if I wasn't stopped. My grandfather and his brothers tried to do the stopping, actually. That's the only time Mum's ever really opened the pipes. I vaguely remember it, Mum standing in our bedroom with four men awkwardly trying to make her step out of the way and hand me over. I don't know what they were planning to do with me—none of them had ever deliberately hurt so much as a fly—but I guess the fit was a really alarming one.

They argued it over a bit and then all of a sudden the whole place went full of this terrible light that hurt my eyes to look at, and Mum was scooping me up with my blanket. She walked directly out of the family compound, barefoot in her nightie, and they stood around looking miserable and didn't try to touch her. She got to the nearest road and stuck out her thumb, and a passing driver picked her up and took us all the way to the airport. Then a tech billionaire about to board his private jet to London saw her standing in the airport vestibule with me and offered to take her along. He still comes to the commune for a weeklong spiritual cleanse once a year.

That's my mum for you. But it's not me. My great-grandmother was just the first in a long line of people who meet me, smile, and then stop smiling, before I've even said a word. No one's ever going to offer me a lift, or dance in a woodland circle to help me raise power, or put food on my table, or—far more to the point—stand with me against all the nasty things that routinely come after wizards, looking for a meal. If it weren't for Mum, I wouldn't have been welcome in my own home. You wouldn't believe the number of *nice* people at the commune—the kind who write long sincere letters to politicians and regularly turn out to protest for everything from social justice to the preservation of bats—

who said brightly to fourteen-year-old me how excited I must be about going away to school—ha ha—and how much I must want to strike out on my own afterwards, see more of the world, et cetera.

Not that I want to go back to the commune. I don't know if anyone who hasn't tried it can properly appreciate just how horrible it is to be constantly surrounded by people who believe in absolutely everything, from leprechauns to sweat lodges to Christmas carols, but who won't believe that you can do actual magic. I've literally shown people to their faces—or tried to; it takes loads of extra mana to cast even a little spell for starting a fire when a mundane is watching you, firmly convinced that you're a silly kid with a lighter up your sleeve and you'll probably fumble the sleight-of-hand. But even if you do get some sufficiently dramatic spell to work in front of them, then they all say wow and how amazing and then the next day it's all, *man, those mushrooms were really good.* And then they avoid me even more. I don't want to be *here,* but I don't want to be there, either.

Oh, that's a lie, of course. I constantly daydream about going home. I ration it to five minutes a day where I go and stand in front of the vent in the wall, as safely far away as I can get from it and still feel the air moving, and I shut my eyes and press my hands over my face to block the smell of burnt oil and finely aged sweat, pretending that instead I'm breathing damp earth and dried rosemary and roasted carrots in butter, and it's the wind moving through the trees, and if I just open my eyes I'll be lying on my back in a clearing and the sun has just gone behind a cloud. I would instantly trade in my room for the yurt in the woods, even after two full weeks of rain when everything I own is growing mildew. It's an improvement over the sweet fragrance of soul-eater. I even miss the people, which I'd have refused to believe if you'd told me, but after three years in here, I'd ask even Philippa Wax for a cwtch if I saw her sour, hard-mouthed face.

All right, no, I wouldn't, and I'm pretty sure that all my sentiments will revert within a week after I get back. Anyway, it's been made very clear I'm not welcome, except on sufferance. And maybe not even that, if I try to settle in again once I'm out of here. The commune council—Philippa's the secretary—will probably come up with some excuse to throw me out. *Negativity of spirit* has already been mentioned more than a few times just at the limits of my hearing, or well within them. And then I'll just have wrecked Mum's life, because she'd walk away without a second thought to stay with me.

I've known even before I came to the Scholomance that my only chance for a halfway decent life—assuming I get out of here to have one at all—is to get into an enclave. That's me and everyone else, then, but at least most independent wizards can find friends to club together and watch each other's backs, build mana, collaborate a bit. Even if people liked me enough to keep me, which no one ever has, I wouldn't be any use to them. Ordinary people want a mop in the cupboard, not a rocket launcher, and here I am struggling desperately for two hours just to turn up a spell to wash the floor.

But if you're in a lush enclave of a few hundred wizards, and a death wyrm crawls out of the depths of the nearest cavern, or another enclave decides to declare war, you really would like somebody around who can slit a cow's throat and unleash all the fires of hell in your defense. Having someone with a reputation for that kind of power in your enclave usually means you don't *get* attacked in the first place, and then no cows have to be sacrificed, and I don't ever have to take a psychic pummeling and lose five years off my life, and worse yet make my mother *cry*.

But that all depends on my having the reputation. No one's going to invite me into an enclave or even a graduation alliance if they think I'm actually some sort of pathetic damsel in distress who needs rescuing by the local hero. They certainly won't do it because they *like* me. And meanwhile Orion doesn't need to impress anybody at all. He's not even just an enclaver. His mother is one of the top candidates to be the next Domina of New York, which is probably still the single most powerful enclave in the world right now, and his father's a master artificer. He could just keep half an eye out, do the bare minimum of coursework, and walk out and spend the rest of his life in luxury and safety, surrounded by the finest wizards and the most wonderful artifice in the world.

Instead, he's been spending his school years making a massive spectacle of himself. The soul-eater behind me was probably his fourth heroic deed of the week. He's saving every dullard and weakling in the place, and not a thought given to who's going to have to pay the price. Because there's absolutely going to *be* a price. For all that I want to go home every minute of every day in here, I know perfectly well it's actually unbelievably good luck to be here. The only reason I've had that luck myself is because the school was largely built by Manchester enclave, back in the mists of the Edwardian era, and the current UK enclaves have managed to hang on to a disproportionate number of the spare seats to hand out. That might change in the next few years—the Shanghai and Jaipur enclaves have been making threatening noises about building a new school from scratch in Asia if there isn't a significant reallocation soon—but at least for the moment, any indie kid in the UK still automatically goes on the induction list.

Mum offered to get me taken off, but I wasn't insane enough to let her. The enclaves built the school because outside is *worse*. All those maleficaria creeping through the vents and the pipes and under the doors, they don't come from the Scholomance—they come *to* the Scholomance because all of us are in here, tender young wizards newly bursting with mana we're still falling over ourselves learning to use. Thanks to my freshman-year Maleficaria Studies textbook, I know that our deliciousness goes up another order of magnitude every six months between thirteen and eighteen, all wrapped up inside a thin and easy-to-break sugar shell instead of the tough chewy hide of a grown wizard. That's not a metaphor I made up myself: it's straight out of the book, which took a lot of pleasure telling us in loads of detail just how badly the maleficaria want to eat us: really, really badly.

So back in the mists of the late 1800s, the renowned artificer Sir Alfred Cooper Browning—it's hard to avoid picking up his name in here, it's plastered all over the place—came up with the Scholomance. As much as I roll my eyes at the placards everywhere, the design's really effective. The school is only just barely connected to the actual world, in one single place: the graduation gates. Which are surrounded by layers on layers of magical wards and artifice barriers. When some enterprising mal does wriggle through, it's only got inside the graduation hall, which isn't connected to the rest of the school except for the absolute minimum of pipes and air shafts required to supply the place, and all of *those* are loaded up with wards and barriers, too.

So the mals get bottled up and spend loads of time struggling to get in and get up, and fighting and devouring each other while they're at it, and the biggest and most dangerous ones can't actually squeeze their way up at all. They just have to hang around the graduation hall all year long, snacking on other mals, and wait for graduation to gorge themselves. We're a lot harder to get at in here than if we were living out in the wide open, in a yurt for instance. Even enclave kids were getting eaten more often than not before the school was built, and if you're an indie kid who doesn't get into the Scholomance, these days your odds of making it to the far side of puberty are one in twenty. One in four is plenty decent odds compared to that.

But we have to *pay* for that protection. We pay with our work, and we pay with our misery and our terror, which all build the mana that fuels the school. And we pay, most of all, with *the ones who don't make it,* so what good exactly does Orion think he's doing, what does anyone think he's doing, saving people? The bill has to come due eventually.

Except nobody thinks that way. Less than twenty juniors have died so far this year—the usual rate is a hundred plus—and everyone in the whole school thinks he hung the moon, and is wonderful, and the New York enclave's going to have five times as many applicants as they've had before. I can forget about getting in there, and the enclave in London isn't looking very good, either. It's maddening, especially when I ought to be news. I already know ten times more spells for destruction and dominion than the entire graduating class of seniors put together. You would too if you got five of them every time you wanted to mop the bloody floor.

On the bright side, today I've learned ninety-eight useful household charms in Old English, as I had to slog through to number ninety-nine to reach the one that would wipe out the stink, and the book couldn't vanish on me until I'd got to it. Every now and again, the school does shoot itself in the foot that way, usually when it's being its most awful and annoying and petty. The misery of translating ninety-nine charms with a stinking, dead soul-eater gurbling behind me was good enough to buy me the extra useful ones.

I'll be grateful in a week or two. At the moment, what I have to do is stand up and do five hundred jumping jacks in a row, in perfect form, keeping my focus tightly on my current-storing crystal the whole time, to build enough mana so I could wash my floor without accidentally killing anything. I don't dare cheat at all, not even a little. There're no ants and cockroaches in here to suck dry, and I'm getting more powerful by the day, like we all are. With my particular gift, if I tried to cheat on a cleaning spell, it's entirely possible I'd take out three of my neighbors to either side and this entire hall would end up the horrible gleaming clean of a newly sanitized morgue. I've got mana saved up, of course: Mum loaded me up with crystals she'd primed with her circle, so I could store mana for later, and I put some away every chance I get. But I wasn't going to use one of those to clean up my room. The crystals are for emergencies, when I really need power right away, and to stockpile for graduation.

After the floor came clean, I added on fifty push-ups—I've got in really good shape over the last three years—and did my mum's favorite smudging spell. It left my whole cell smelling of burnt sage, but at least that was an improvement. It was nearly dinnertime by then. A shower was more than called for, except I really didn't feel like having to fight off anything that might come out of the drains in the bathroom, which meant that something was almost sure to come if I went. Instead I changed my shirt and plaited my hair again and wiped my face with water out of my jug. I rinsed my T-shirt in the last of the water, too, and hung it up so it would dry. I had only the two tops, and they were getting threadbare. I'd had to burn half my clothes my first year when a nameless shadow crawled out from under the bed, the second night I was here, and I didn't have anywhere else to pull mana from. Sacrificing my clothes gave me enough power to fry the shadow without drawing life force from anywhere. I hadn't needed Orion Lake to save me from *that*, had I?

Even after my best efforts, I still looked wonderful enough that when I came out to the meeting point at dinnertime—we walk to the cafeteria in groups, of course, it's just stupidly asking for trouble if you go alone—Liu took one look at me and asked, "What happened to you, El?"

"Our glorious savior Lake decided to melt a soul-eater in my cell today, and left me to clean up the mess," I said.

"*Melt*? Ew," she said. Liu may be a dark witch, but at least she doesn't genuflect at Orion's throne. I like her, maleficer or not: she's one of the few people here who doesn't mind hanging out with me. She's got more social options than I do, but she's always polite.

But Ibrahim was there, too—carefully keeping his back to us while waiting for some of his own friends, making clear we weren't welcome to walk with his group—and he was already turning around in high excitement. "Orion saved you from a soul-eater!" he said. *Squealed*, really. Orion's saved his life three times—and he *needed* it to be saved.

"Orion ran a soul-eater into my room and sludged it all over my floor," I said, through my teeth, but it was no use. By the time Aadhya and Jack joined us and we had a group of five to go upstairs, Orion had heroically saved me from a soul-eater, and of course by the end of dinnertime—only two people in our year vomiting today, we were getting better at our protective charms and antidotes—everyone in the school knew about it.

Most types of maleficaria don't even have names; there are so many varieties of them, and they come and go. But soul-eaters are a big deal: a single one has taken out a dozen students in other years, and it's an extremely bad way to go, complete with dramatic light show (from the soul-eater) and shrieking wails (from the victims). It would've made my reputation to take one out by myself, and I could have. I've got twenty-six fully loaded crystals in the hand-carved little sandalwood box under my pillow, saved for exactly a situation like this, and six months ago, when I was trying to patch up my fraying sweater without resorting to the horrors of crochet, I got an incantation to unravel souls. It would've taken a soul-eater apart from the inside out—with *no* stinking residue—and even left an empty glowing wisp behind. Then I could have made a deal with Aadhya, who's artificer-track and has an affinity for using weird materials: we could have had it patrolling between our doors all night. Most of the maleficaria don't like light. That's the kind of advantage that can get you all the way to graduation. Instead all I had was the unwanted pleasure of being one more notch on Orion's belt.

My not-very-near-death experience did at least get me a good seat at dinner. Usually I have to sit alone at the far end of the half-filled table of whoever else is being most socially rejected at the time, or else people change tables away from me in groups until I'm sitting completely alone, which is worse. Today I ended up at one of the central tables right under the sunlamps—more vitamin D than I'd got, apart from a pill, in months—with Ibrahim and Aadhya and half a dozen other reasonably popular kids: there was even one girl from the smallish Maui enclave who sat with us. But I only got angrier, hearing them talking reverently about all the wonderful things Orion had done. A few of them even asked me to describe the fight. "Well, first he chased it into my room, and then he blasted open my door, and then he incandensed it before I could say boo and left a stinking mess on my floor," I snapped, but you can guess how well that went. Everyone wants to believe he's a magnificent hero who's going to save them all. Ugh.

Chapter 2
MIMICS

AFTER DINNER, I had to try and get someone to come with me to the workshop, so I could get some materials to patch up my door. It's an extremely bad idea to leave your door unlocked at night, much less with a gaping hole in it. I tried to make it casual, "Does anyone need anything from the shop?" But no one was buying. After hearing my story, they could all guess that I needed to go down, and we're all alive to the main chance in here. You don't make it out unless you use every advantage you can get, and nobody likes me enough to do me favors without payment in advance.

"I could come," Jack said, leaning forward and smiling at me with all his shiny white teeth.

I wouldn't need anything to crawl out of a dark corner if he went with me. I looked him straight in the eye and said hard, "Oh really?"

He paused and had a moment of being wary, and then he shrugged. "Wait, sorry, just remembered I've got to finish my new divining rod," he said cheerfully, but his eyes had narrowed. I hadn't really wanted him to know that I knew about him. I'd have to make him pay me for my silence now, or else he'd think he had to come after me to shut me up, and he might bet on that anyway. Yet another thing Orion had now cocked up for me.

"What's it worth to you?" Aadhya said. She's the sharp and pragmatic sort; she's one of the few people in here willing to make deals with me. One of the few people in here willing to talk to me at all, really. But she was also brutally hard-nosed about this sort of thing. I normally appreciated that she didn't beat about the bush, but knowing I was hard up, she wasn't going to put herself on the line for anything less than twice the going value of a trip down, and she also would certainly make sure I took all the significant risk. I scowled.

"I'll go with you," Orion said from the table next to ours, where the New York kids were sitting. He'd kept his head down all dinner even while everyone at our table talked loudly about how massively wonderful he was. I'd seen him do the same after his other notable rescues, and had never quite decided if he was making a pretense of modesty, was actually modest to the point of pathology, or was just so horribly awkward he had nothing to say to people complimenting him. He didn't even lift his head now, just spoke out from under his shaggy overhang of hair, staring down at his cleared plate.

So that was nice. Obviously I wasn't going to turn down free company to the shop, but it was going to look like more of the same, Orion protecting me. "Let's go, then," I said tightly, and got up at once. Here at school, you're always better off going as soon as you've got a plan, if your plan is to do something unusual.

The Scholomance isn't precisely a real place. There are perfectly real walls and floors and ceilings and pipes, all of which were made in the real world out of real iron and steel and copper and glass and so forth, and assembled according to elaborate blueprints that are on display all over the school, but if you tried to duplicate the building in the middle of London, I'm reasonably sure it wouldn't even go up for long enough to fall over. It only works because it was built into the void. I'd explain what the void is, but I haven't any idea. If you've ever wondered what it was like to live in the days when our cave-dwelling ancestors stared up at this black thing full of twinkly bits of light with no idea whatsoever what was up there and what it all meant, well, I imagine that it was similar to sitting in a Scholomance dorm room staring out at the pitch-black surroundings. I'm happy to be able to report that it's not pleasant or comfortable at all.

But thanks to being almost completely inside the void, the school doesn't have to fight boring old physics. That made it much easier for the artificers who built it to persuade it to work according to the way they wanted it to work. The blueprints are posted so that when we look at them, our belief reinforces the original construction, and so does all our trudging along the endless stairs and the endless corridors, expecting our classrooms to be where we last saw them and for water to come out of the faucets and for us all to continue breathing, even though if you asked an engineer to look at the plumbing and the ventilation, probably it's not actually sufficient to handle the needs of several thousand kids.

Which is all very well and good and extremely clever of Sir Alfred et al., but the problem with living in a *persuadable* space is, it's persuadable in all sorts of ways. When you end up on the stairs with six people rushing to the same class-room as you, it somehow takes you all half the time to cover the distance. But the creepy anxious feeling you get if you have to go down into a damp unlit basement full of cobwebs, where you become convinced there's something horrible about to jump out at you, that works on it, too. The mals are *more* than happy to cooperate with that particular kind of belief. Anytime you do anything out of the routine, like for instance going to the shop alone after dinner when nobody else is down there if they can help it, the stairs or the corridor might end up taking you somewhere that doesn't actually appear on the blueprints. And you really won't want to meet whatever is waiting there for you.

So once you've decided that you're going somewhere out of the ordinary, you're better off going as fast as you can, before you or anyone else can think about it too much. I headed straight for the nearest landing, and waited until Orion and I were far enough down the stairs that nobody else was in earshot before snapping at him. "What part of *leave me alone* didn't you understand?"

He'd been walking along next to me with his hands shoved in his pockets, slouched: he jerked his head up. "But—you just said, let's go—"

"I should've told you off in front of everyone, then, after they've all decided you saved my life?"

He actually stopped right there in the middle of the staircase and started saying, "Should I . . ." We were between floors with no landing visible, and the nearest light that wasn't completely burnt out was a sputtering gaslight twenty steps back, so our shadows darkened the stairs below us. Pausing for as much as a millisecond was a grand invitation for something to go wrong up ahead.

I'd kept going, because I wasn't an idiot, so I was two steps down before I realized he hadn't. I had to stretch out and grab him by the wrist and tug him onwards. "Not *now*. What is it with you, are you actively trying to meet new and exciting mals?" He went really red and fell back in with me, staring at the floor even harder, as if I'd scored an actual hit, no matter how stupid that was. "The ones that come your way in the ordinary course of things aren't enough?"

"They don't," he said shortly.

"What?"

"They don't come my way! They never have."

"What, you just don't get attacked?" I said, outraged. He shrugged a shoulder. "Where'd that soul-eater come from, then?"

"Huh? I'd just come out of the bathroom. I saw the tail end of it going under your door."

So he had actually come to my rescue. That was even worse. I stewed over his revelation as we kept going. Of course, it made some sense: if you were a monster, why would you attack the blinding hero who could blast you to pieces without half trying? What didn't make sense was his side of it. "So you reckon you might as well make a name for yourself, saving the rest of us?" He shrugged again, not looking up, so that wasn't it. "Do you just *like* fighting mals or something?" I prodded, and he flushed up again. "You're unbelievably odd."

"Don't *you* like practicing your affinity?" he said, defensive.

"My affinity is laying waste to multitudes, so I haven't had much opportunity to try the experience," I said.

He snorted, as though I were joking. I didn't try to persuade him. It's easy to claim to be a massively powerful dark sorceress; no one's going to believe me until I prove it, preferably with hard evidence. "Where do you get all the power, anyway?" I asked him instead. I'd often wondered. An affinity makes certain spells considerably easier to cast, but it doesn't make them free.

"From them. From the mals, I mean. I kill one, then I save

that power to fire off the next spell. Or if I'm low, I borrow some from Magnus or Chloe or David . . ."

I ground my teeth. "I get the idea." He was naming off all the other students from the New York enclave. Of course they did power-sharing, and of course they had their own power sink to boot, like my crystals, except some enormous one that every student from New York had been feeding into for the last century. He literally had a battery to pull on for his heroics, and if he could pull mana from killing maleficaria—*how?*—he probably didn't even need it.

We reached the landing for the shop level then. The senior hall was still further below, and there was a faint glow of light coming up the stairs from there. But the archway opening onto the classroom corridor itself was pitch black; the lights had gone out. I stared at the open maw of it grimly as we came down the last steps: that was what his moment of hesitation had netted us. And if mals never went for him, that meant whatever was lurking around down there was going to go for *me.*

"I'll take the lead," he offered.

"You'd better believe you're going to take the lead. And you're holding the light, too."

He didn't even argue, just nodded and put out his left hand and lit it up using a minor version of the same incandensing spell he'd used on the soul-eater. It made my eyes itch. He was all set to just march straight into the corridor; I had to yank him back and inspect the ceiling and floor and prod the nearby walls myself. Digesters that haven't eaten in a while are translucent, and if they spread themselves out thinly enough over a flat surface, you can look straight at them and never realize they're there until they flap themselves around you. The landing is a high-traffic area, so it's especially popular with them. Earlier this year, one of the sophomore boys rushing to get to class on time got caught, and he lost a leg and most of his left arm. He didn't last for long after that, obviously.

But the whole area round the landing was clear. The only thing I did turn up was an agglo hiding under one of the gas lamps, shorter than my pinky and not worth trying to harvest even for me: only two screws, half a lozenge, and a pen cap stuck onto its shell so far. It scuttled away over the wall in a panic before diving into a vent. Nothing reacted to its passage. At night, in a dark corridor on the shop level, that wasn't a good sign. There should have been *something*. Unless there was something especially bad up ahead that had scared the others away.

I put a hand spread out on the back of Orion's shoulder and kept my head turned to look behind us as we headed onwards to the main workshop entrance, the best way for a pair to walk together when there's an imminent threat. Most of the classroom doors were standing ajar just enough that we wouldn't get the warning of a doorknob turning, but not enough for us to get a good look into any of the rooms as we passed, dozens of them: aside from the workshop and the gym, most of the bottom level is taken up with small classrooms where seniors take specialized seminars. But those all end after the first half of the year; at this point all the seniors are spending all their time doing practice runs for graduation, meaning the seminar rooms are the perfect place for mals to snooze in.

I hated having to trust Orion to watch where we were going. He walked so casually, even through an unlit hallway, and when he got to the shop doors, he just pulled one open and walked on inside before I realized what he was doing. Then I had to follow him or else be stuck out in the dark corridor alone.

As soon as I stepped through the door, I grabbed a fistful of his shirt to stop him going on further. We halted just inside, the shining light in his hand reflecting off all the gleaming saw-blade teeth and the dull iron of the vises and the glossy obsidian black of the hammers, and the dull stainless steel of the shop tables and chairs lined up in neat rows filling the massive space. The gas lamps had all been turned down to tiny blue pilot dots. The squat furnaces at the end of each row had tiny flickers of orange and green glowing through the vent slits, the only sickly light. It felt weirdly crowded despite having not a single person in it. The furniture took up too much room, as if the chairs had multiplied. We all hated the workshop more than anything. Even the alchemy labs are better.

We stood still for a long moment in which nothing whatsoever happened, and then finally I deliberately stepped on the back of Orion's heel just to pay him back. "Ow!" he said.

"Oh, sorry," I said insincerely.

He glared at me, not entirely a doormat. "Will you just get the stuff and let's go," he said, like it was that easy, just go wild and start rummaging through the bins and so forth, what could go wrong. He turned to the wall and flipped the light switch. Nothing came on, of course.

"Follow me," I said, and crossed to the scrap metal bins. I picked up the long tongs hanging by the side and cautiously used them to flip open the lid. Then I reached in and took out four big flat pieces, shaking them thoroughly and banging them violently against the side of the nearest table. I wouldn't have tried to carry that many myself, but I'd make Orion carry them, and then I'd have extra to trade someone another time.

After getting the scrap, I didn't go for the wire, because that would've been an obvious choice; instead I had him reach into one of the other bins for a double handful of screws and nuts and bolts, which wouldn't be much use for repairing my door, but were worth more, so I could trade them to Aadhya for some of the wire I knew she had and even have some left over. I put them into the zip pockets of my combats. Then there wasn't any help for it: I had to have a pair of pliers.

The tool chests are large squat containers the size of a body, which they have in fact contained on at least two occasions since I've been here. You can't keep the tools you take out during class time—if you try, it'll come after you—so the only time you can get a tool for private use is after hours, and it's one of the best ways to die, since the kind of mals that climb into the tool chests are the smart ones. If you open one incautiously—

Orion reached out and lifted the lid while I was still debating strategy. Inside, there was absolutely nothing but several neat rows of hammers, screwdrivers of all sizes, spanners, hacksaws, pliers, even a *drill*. Not a one of them leapt up to smash him in the head or rip off one of his fingers or poke out his eyes. "Get a pair of pliers and the drill," I said, swallowing my seething envy in favor of maximizing the value of the situation. A drill. No one in our entire hall had a drill. I hadn't heard of anyone other than a senior artificer even seeing them more than once or twice.

Instead he grabbed a hammer and in one smooth motion whirled and smashed it down right over my shoulder, directly into the forehead of the thing that the dull metal chair behind me had turned into: a molten grey-colored blob with a maw full of jagged silver teeth opening along the seam where the seat met the back. I ducked under his arm and behind him and slammed the lid down on the tool chest and got it locked before anything else could come out of it, and then I turned round and saw four more chairs had pulled up their legs and were coming at us. There *had* been too many of them.

Orion was chanting a metal-forging spell. The nearest mimic started glowing red-hot, and he hit it with the hammer again, beating a huge hole into its side. It made a grating shrieking noise out of its sawtooth mouth and fell over. But meanwhile the others had all sprouted knife-blade limbs and charged—at *me.*

"Look out!" Orion shouted, uselessly: seeing them was not the problem. I knew a terrific spell for liquefying the bones of my enemies, which would have done nicely in the given circumstances if I'd wanted to blow a tankful of mana and if there hadn't been any Orion around to be liquefied right alongside the more immediate enemies. There was only one spell I could afford to cast. I shouted out the Old English floor-washing charm, and jumped aside as all four of the chair-mimics skidded on the wet soapy slick and shot past me straight at Orion. I grabbed two of the pieces of scrap and ran for the door while he fought them. I'd use my bare hands to wrap on the wire if I had to.

I didn't have to. Orion caught up to me on the stairs, panting, carrying two more pieces of scrap, and the pliers, *and the* drill. "Thanks a lot!" he said, indignantly. He had a thin bloody slice across one forearm and no other damage.

"I knew you had them," I said, bitterly.

The climb up the stairs to our res hall took fifteen solid minutes of trudging. We didn't talk, and nothing pestered us. I knocked on Aadhya's door on the way back to my room, swapped for wire and also let her know I had a drill now— a lot of people who wouldn't trade with me would trade with her, and if I had something she didn't, she would usually broker for a cut—and then had Orion keep watch while I fixed my door. It wasn't fun. I laboriously drilled holes in one piece of scrap and wired it in place over the hole he had left in the door, securing it thoroughly. I then sat there and wove some of the thinner wire around four thick strands to make a wider band, and I used it to wire the dented remains of my door-knob and lock roughly back in place. Then I pulled the door shut and did the same on the inside with a second piece of scrap.

"Why don't you just use the mending charm?" Orion ventured tentatively, about halfway through the agonizingly boring process, after he looked round to see what was taking me so long.

"I *am* using the mending charm," I said through my teeth. Even with the pliers and the drilled holes, my hands were throbbing. Orion kept watching with increasing confusion until I finally twisted down the last ragged end of wire. Then I put my hands flat on either side of the double-layered hole and shut my eyes. A basic version of mend-and-make is one of the spells we all learn, in shop class. The classes are the only way to get the most critical general spells. Mending is pretty obviously on that list, as you can't get anything into the school but what little you're allowed to bring in at induction. And mending is one of the most difficult spells, too, with dozens of variations depending on the materials you're working with and the complexity of what you're trying to fix. Only artificers really master it completely, and even then only within a specialized range of materials.

But at least you can usually do it in your own bloody vernacular. "Make and mend, to my will bend, iron thrust and steel extend," I said—we all knew a lot of rhymes for *mend* and *make*—and mapped in seventeen knocks around the words, somewhere between the twenty-three you use for sheet metal and the nine for wire. Then I tapped into the mana I'd built up by doing all that excessively nitpicky hand work. The charm grudgingly went churning through the materials. The pieces of scrap slagged into something like a thick metallic putty, which I pushed into place to fill the gaping hole in the door, and as the surface went smooth and hardened under my hands, the doorknobs on either side made a rude noise like a belch and finally hooked themselves back together, the dead bolt shooting back into place with a solid *thunk*. I dropped my hands, panting, and turned round.

Orion was standing in the middle of my bedroom staring like I was an exotic zoological specimen. "You're *strict mana?*"

He made it sound like I was a member of a cult or something. I glared at him. "Not all of us can pull from maleficaria."

"But—why don't you pull from—the air, or the furniture—everyone's got holes in their bedposts—"

He wasn't wrong. Cheating is a lot harder in here because there're no small living things to pull from, no ants or cockroaches or mice unless you bring them in with you, which is awkward since the only stuff you can bring is what's physically on you at the moment of induction. But most people can pull small amounts of mana from the inanimate stuff around instead: leach heat from the air or disintegrate a bit of wood. It's a lot easier to do that than to pull mana from a living human being, much less another sorcerer. For most people.

"If I pull, it won't come from there," I said.

Orion was eyeing me with a growing frown. "Er, Galadriel," he said, a bit gently, as if he was starting to think I was a lunatic, one of the ones who'd just gone crazy inside. I'd had a wildly horrible day anyway, thanks to him, and that was the final straw. I reached out and grabbed at him. Not with my hands—I grabbed at his mana, at his life force, and gave it a hard deliberate yank.

Most wizards have to work at it to steal power from a living thing. There are rituals, exercises of will, voodoo dolls, blood sacrifices. Lots of blood sacrifices. I barely have to try. Orion's life force came away from his spirit as easily as a fish on a line, being tugged out of the water. All I needed to do was keep pulling and it would end up in my hands, all that juicy power he'd built up. In fact, I could probably have followed his power-sharing lines to pull mana from all his enclave friends. I could have drained them all.

Even as Orion's face went wide with appalled shock, I let go again, so the mana went snapping back into him like a rubber band. He staggered back a full pace, his hands coming up defensively like he was ready for a fight. But I ignored him and sat down with a hard *thump* on my bed, trying not to cry. Whenever I let my temper get away from me like that, I always feel rotten afterwards. It's rubbing my own face in how easy everything would be if I just gave in.

He went on standing there, hands raised, looking a bit silly when I didn't do anything. "You're a maleficer!" he said after a moment, like he thought he was prodding me into doing something.

"I know this is going to be a challenge for you," I said through my teeth, still fighting back the sniffles, "but try not being an idiot for five minutes. If I was a maleficer, I'd have sucked you dry downstairs and told everyone you died in the workshop. It's not like anyone would've been suspicious." He didn't look like he'd found that particularly comforting. I rubbed the back of my sooty hand across my face. "Anyway," I added desolately, "if I was a maleficer, I'd just suck all of you dry and have the whole school to myself."

"Who'd want it?" Orion said after a moment.

I snorted a laugh up into my nose; all right, he had a point. "A maleficer!"

"Not even a maleficer," he said positively. He did lower his hands then, still warily, only to take another step back again when I stood up. I rolled my eyes and made a little jump at him with my hands raised like claws and squeaked, *"Boo!"*

He glared at me. I went over to where he'd put the rest of the supplies on the floor. The rest of the scrap pieces got shoved under my mattress where they couldn't be replaced by something unpleasant during the night without my noticing. The drill and pliers got strapped securely down to the lid of my storage chest next to my two knives and my one precious small screwdriver. If you keep things strapped to the underside of the lid, then if they've come loose, you can see the straps dangling when you crack it a bit. I'm really systematic about checking, so I haven't had a tool go bad for a long time: the Scholomance doesn't waste its time.

I went to the basin and rinsed off my hands and face again as well as I could: I was down to just a tiny bit left in my jug. "If you're waiting for a thank-you, you'll be here a while," I told Orion after I finished drying off. He was still standing in the corner eyeing me.

"Yeah, I noticed," he said with a huff. "You weren't kidding about your affinity, were you. So you're—what, a strict-mana maleficer?"

"That doesn't even make sense. I'm not a maleficer at all, and as long as I'm trying to not turn into one, maybe you'd better *go away*," I said, spelling it out since that was evidently necessary. "It's got to be nearly curfew by now, anyway."

Bad things happen if you're in someone else's cell past curfew. Otherwise, of course, we'd all double and triple up and take shifts on watch, not to mention that seniors would be en masse shoving freshmen out of their rooms on the top floor and postponing graduation for a year or two. Apparently there was a rash of incidents like that early on, after people started to realize there was a gigantic horde of mals waiting down in the graduation hall. I don't know exactly what the builders did about it, but I do know that having two or more kids in a room makes you a horrible magnet. And forget about running out into the corridor trying to get back to your room once you realize what trouble you're in. Two girls just down the way from me tried it in our first year. One of them spent a long time screaming outside my door before she stopped. The other one didn't make it out of the room at all. It's not the sort of thing anyone sane wants to risk.

Orion just kept staring at me. Abruptly he said, "What happened to Luisa?"

I frowned at him, wondering why he was asking me, and then I realized—"You think *I* did for her?"

"It wasn't one of the mals," he said. "My room's next to hers, and she disappeared overnight. I'd have known. I stopped mals going in after her twice."

I thought it over fast. If I told him, he was going to go after Jack. On one hand, that meant Jack would probably cease to be a problem for me. On the other hand, if Jack denied it, which wasn't unlikely, I could end up with him *and* Orion as problems together. It wasn't worth the risk when I didn't have any proof. "Well, it wasn't me," I said. "There are practicing maleficers in here, you know. Four in the senior class at least." There were six, actually, but three of them were openly practicing, so saying four would hopefully make me look like I had a tiny bit of inside knowledge, believable but not enough to be worth interrogating. "Why don't you pester one of them if you don't have enough to do looking out for the sad and gormless."

His face went set and hard. "You know, considering I've saved *your* life twice," he began.

"*Three* times," I said coldly.

It threw him off. "Uh—"

"The chimaera, end of last term," I supplied even more coldly. Since I was obviously going to stick in his head now, he was at least going to remember me correctly.

"Fine, so three times, then! You might at least—"

"No, I mightn't."

He stopped, flushing. I don't think I'd ever seen him angry before; it was always just *aw-shucks* hunching and resolution.

"I didn't ask you for your help, and I don't want it," I said. "There're more than a thousand students still left in our year and all of them gagging to swoon over you. Go and find one of them if you want some adoration." The bells rang in the hallway: five minutes to curfew. "And if you don't, go anyway!" I grabbed my door and flipped the shiny new—well, dull new—bolt and opened it.

He obviously wanted to leave on a snappy comeback, but couldn't think of one. I suppose he wasn't ever called on to produce them in the ordinary course of things. After a moment of struggle, he just scowled and stalked out.

I'm delighted to report my repaired door slammed shut on his heels beautifully.

Chapter 3
MALEFICER

I WAS EXHAUSTED, but I spent another half hour doing sit-ups in my room and built up the mana to cast a protective barrier over my bed. I can't afford to do it every night, but tonight I was shattered, and I needed something to keep me from being the lowest-hanging fruit on the vine. Once I had it up, I crawled into bed and slept like a rock, barring the three times I woke with warning jabs from the trip wires round my door: par for the course, and nothing actually tried to come in.

The next morning Aadhya knocked to get me for showers and breakfast company, which was nice of her. I wondered why. A drill was valuable, but not that valuable. Thanks to her company, I was able to take my first shower in a week and refill my water jug before we headed to the cafeteria. She didn't even try to charge me for it, except watching in turn-about while she did it, too.

All became clear as we started down the hallway. "So, you and Orion did all right in the shop last night," she said, in an overly casual, making-conversation way.

I didn't stop short, but I wanted to. "It wasn't a date!"

"Did he ask you for anything? Even a fair share?" Aadhya darted her eyes at me.

I ground my teeth. That *was* the usual rule for distinguishing between a date and an alliance, but it hardly applied. "He was paying a debt."

"Oh, right," Aadhya said. "Orion, are you going to breakfast?" she called—he was just closing his door behind him, and then I realized she must've put a trip wire on *his* door this morning, so she'd got a warning when he went to brush his teeth. She was trying to get in with him through *me*, which would have been funny if it hadn't made me want to punch her in the head. The last thing I needed was for people to get even more of an idea that I needed him to look out for me. "Walk together?"

He threw a look at me—I glared back, trying to hint him off—and said, "Sure," inexplicably. It wasn't as though he needed company, so evidently he was just doing it to spite me. He fell in on Aadhya's other side while I contemplated various forms of retribution. I couldn't just fall out, either: there wasn't anyone else waiting for a group, and then I'd be vulnerable. Breakfast isn't half as dangerous as dinner, but it's still never good to walk alone. Hope in your heart doesn't count.

"Anything unusual down in the shop last night?" she asked him. "I've got metalwork this morning."

"Um, nothing much, really," he said.

"What's wrong with you!" I said. You're not obliged to go out of your way to warn others, we all have to look out for ourselves, but if you start misleading people and setting them up, you're really in for it. That's a long step down from maleficer in most students' opinions. "There were five mimics hanging about as chairs," I told her.

"They're dead!" he said defensively.

"Doesn't mean there aren't more of them who were wait-ing for leftovers." I shook my head in disgust.

Aadhya didn't look happy about it. I wouldn't have either, if I was going to be first into the shop with a potential mimic or two lingering. But at least with the information she'd be able to make sure she wasn't literally first in, and possibly put a shield on her back or something.

"I'll hold us a table if you'll get the trays," she said as we came into the cafeteria, being too clever for my own good. I couldn't blame her, really. It wasn't stupid to want to be pals with Orion if that looked like a real possibility. Aadhya's fam-ily live in New Jersey: if she got into the New York enclave, she could probably pull them all inside. And I couldn't afford to alienate one of the vanishing few people who are willing to deal with me. Sullenly I got on the line and loaded up a tray for myself and for her, hoping faintly that Orion would spot one of his enclave friends and ditch us. Instead he put a couple of apples on the extra tray, and then reached ahead of me and said, "C'est temps dissoudre par coup de foudre," and fried a tentacle just beginning to poke out from under the steam tray of excessively inviting scrambled eggs. It dissolved with a horrible gagging smell, and a wafting green cloud leaked up from all around the tray and settled immediately over the eggs.

"That's the stupidest spell I've ever heard, and your pro-nunciation is terrible," I said, nasally. I skipped the now-stinking egg tray and went on to the porridge.

"'Thanks, Orion, I didn't see that blood-clinger about to grab me,'" he said. "Don't mention it, Galadriel, really, no problem."

"I did see it, and because there was only half an inch out, there was enough time that I could've got a helping of eggs if you hadn't shoved in front of me. And if I was still stupid enough at the tail end of junior year to go for a tray full of freshly cooked scrambled eggs without checking the perimeter, not even your undivided attention would get me out of this school alive. Are you a masochist or something? Why are you still doing favors for me?" I grabbed the raisin bowl, covered it with a small side plate, and shook it until two dozen of them had come out one at a time. I poked them all thoroughly with my fork and went on to the cinnamon shaker, but one distant sniff was enough to tell me that was no-go today. The cream was also a loss: if you tilted it to the light, there was a faint blue slick over the surface. At least the brown sugar was all right.

I took a quick look both ways after coming off the line and then carried the two trays back over to where Aadhya had set us up at a good table, three in from the door: close enough to get out if they started to shut us in, and far enough not to be in the front lines if something came in through them. She'd laid a perimeter and done a safety charm on the cutlery and even got us one of the safer water jugs, the clear ones. "No eggs, thanks to Mr. Fantastic here," I told her, putting down the trays.

"Was it the clinger? One of them got a senior pretty badly before we got here," Aadhya said, nodding over at a table where an older boy was leaning half conscious between two of his friends with a series of huge bloody sucker-marks wrapped around his arm twice like a twining bracelet. They were trying to give him something to drink, but he had a clammy going-into-shock look, and they were already trading resigned anxious glances across him. I don't think anyone ever gets used to it, but only the most sensitive flowers still burst into tears over losses by the time they're staring graduation in the face. By then they've got to be locking down alliances and planning strategy, and however critical he'd been to theirs, they were going to have to find a way to patch it—tough with only three weeks to end of term.

Sure enough, the first bell rang for seniors—we leave meals at staggered intervals, oldest kids first, and if you think that it's worse to go first, you're right—and the two of them gently eased him down slumped onto the table. Ibrahim was sitting at the end of the neighboring table with Yaakov—his best friend here in our goldfish bowl, although they both know they'll never speak to each other again if they live to get out of it—and one of the seniors turned to them and said something, probably bribing them to stay with their friend to the end. They must have had a time slot down in the gym they couldn't afford to lose: it was going to be bad enough for them losing a member of their team this close to graduation. Ibrahim and Yaakov traded looks and then nodded and switched tables, taking the gamble. It's not safe to skive off this close to finals, but lessons aren't as important as graduation practice.

"Still sorry I took it out?" Orion said to me. His face was unhappy and wrenched, looking at them, although I'd have given any odds you like that he hadn't even known the boy. No one else was looking anywhere in that direction. You have to ration sympathy and grief in here the way you ration your school supplies, unless you're a heroic enclaver with a vat of mana.

"Still sorry I was done out of my scrambled eggs," I said coolly, and started eating my porridge.

Ibrahim's deal turned out okay: the senior died before our first bell rang. Ibrahim and Yaakov left his body there, arms folded on the table and head pillowed facedown, like he'd just drifted off for a nap. It wouldn't be here by the time we came in for lunch. I marked off the table mentally, along with the ones surrounding it. Some of the things that clean up messes like that will stay around hoping for another meal.

I have languages every morning: I'm studying five of them. That sounds like I'm some mad linguistics fiend, but there're only three academic tracks here: incantations, alchemy, or artifice. And of those three, incantations is the only one you can practice in your own cell without having to go to the lab or the shop more than the minimum. Alchemy or artifice tracks only make strategic sense if you're someone like Aadhya, with a related affinity, and then you get the double advantage of playing to your own strengths and the relatively smaller number of people going for it. If she does get out of here alive, a smart, trained artificer with an affinity for unusual materials and a lot of good alliances, she might even be able to get into New York. If not, she's got good odds for New Orleans or Atlanta. The better the enclave you get into, the more power you have to draw on. The artificers in New York and London had the power to build the Trans-Atlantic Gateway, which means if I did get into New York, I could be back in Birmingham New Street, an easy train trip from home, just by walking through a door.

Of course, getting into New York wasn't on the cards for me unless I pulled off something really amazing, and probably not at all given that I was with increasing passion contemplating the murder of their darling star, but there're plenty of solid enclaves in Europe. None of them will take me, either, though, unless I come out of here with a substantial reputation and a substantial spell-list. If you're doing incantation, either you have to go languages-track to build yourself a really good collection of spells, or go creative writing and invent your own. I tried the creative writing track, but my affinity's too strong. If I sit down to write modestly useful spells, they don't work. In fact, more often than not they blow up in my face in dangerous ways. And the one and only time I let loose on the page instead, stream of consciousness the way Mum writes hers, I came up with a highly effective spell to set off a supervolcano. I burnt it straight away, but once you've invented a spell, it's out there, and who knows, someone else might get it. Hopefully there's no one garbage enough to ask the school for a spell to set off a supervolcano, but no more inventing spells for me.

So that means my main source of unique spells is whatever I get out of the void. Technically I could ask for spells nonstop, but if you don't at least read over the ones you've got, by the time you do go back, they'll all be rubbish or not what you asked for or just blank. And if you read too many spells without learning them well enough to cast them, you'll start mixing them up in your head, and then you're sure to blast yourself to bits. Yes, I can learn a hundred closely related cleaning cantrips in a row, but my limit for useful spells is somewhere around nine or ten a day.

I haven't found a limit for spells of mass destruction. I can learn a hundred of those just by glancing at them, and I never forget any of them. Which is lucky, I suppose, because I have to go through a hundred of those before I ever get one of the useful ones.

If you're collecting spells instead of writing your own, languages are absolutely critical. The school will give you spells only in languages you at least theoretically know, but as previously demonstrated, it's not particularly invested in meeting your needs. If you know a dozen languages and you leave the choice up to the school, you're more likely to get the actual kind of spell you want. And the more languages you know, the easier it is to trade spells with others to get ones you can't wheedle out of the void.

The big ones are Mandarin and English: you've got to have one of those two to come at all, since the common lessons are taught in only those two. If you're lucky enough to have both, you can probably use at least half of the spells in wide circulation at the school, and you can schedule all your required lessons to suit. Liu's taking history and maths in English to count for her language requirement; she uses the room in her schedule to take writing workshop in both languages. As you can imagine, most wizard parents start their kids with a private tutor for one or the other the minute they're born. Of course, Mum put me on Marathi instead, because of Dad. Thanks, Mum. If only all the kids from Mumbai didn't treat me like a leper because they've heard whispers about my great-grandmother's prophecy.

To be fair to Mum, I was two when she started me on the language, and she still had hopes of going to live with Dad's family. Her own family were right out. Just before she went off to school—we don't talk about it much, but I'm fairly certain that's why *she* went to the Scholomance—she acquired an evil stepdad, literally: one of those cautious professional maleficers, on the edge of shriveling. He almost certainly poisoned her dad—no proof, but the timing was extremely coincidental—in order to glom on to her mum, who was also a really good healer, through her grief. Any spell that attacks only one person at a time is a bit beneath me, but I know the type. She spent the rest of her life taking care of him, then died of an unexpected heart attack when I was around three.

The stepdad is still doing all right last we heard, but we're not what you'd call close. He used to send sad wistful letters once in a while, hidden inside innocuous envelopes, trying to catch Mum in turn, but when I was six, I opened one by accident, felt the mind-tugging spell, and instinctively snapped it straight back at him. It probably felt like having a splinter jammed directly into your eye. He hasn't tried since.

After things didn't work out very well with Dad's family either, Mum still clung to the idea that the language would give me a sense of connection to him, at some unspecified future date. At the time, it was just another thing that made me different, and even as a kid, I already felt really strongly I didn't need any more of those. We don't live in Cardiff or anything; my primary school wasn't what you'd call a hotbed of multiculturalism. One of the girls once told me I was the color of upsettingly weak tea, which isn't even true but has occupied a niche in my head ever since, as persistent as a vil-haunt. And the commune isn't exactly better. No one there will whisper a racist insult at you in the playground; instead I had grown adults wanting ten-year-old me to sign off on their decolonized yoga practice and help them translate bits of Hindi, which I didn't know.

Of course, I should be grateful to them: that's what woke me up to the idea that Hindi was more popular. When I got old enough to understand that languages were going to keep me alive, I stopped moaning about going and demanded lessons in that, too, just in time to get reasonably fluent before induction. Hindi isn't as good for flexibility, because most of the kids who speak it also have English, so they usually ask for spells in English to have better trading material. But you want languages across the spectrum. In rare or dead languages, it's a lot harder to find anyone else to barter with, but you're also more likely to get really unique spells, or a better match for the rest of your request, like my stupid Old English cleaning spells. Hindi is common enough that you can find lots of people to trade with, and as it's not one of the big two, people don't *ask* for spells in Hindi, they just get them that

way, so the spells are a bit better on average. I got to know
Aadhya by trading Hindi spells.

At the moment, I'm studying Sanskrit, Latin, German, and
Middle and Old English. The last three overlap nicely. I did
French and Spanish last year, but I've got enough of those to
muddle through the spells I get now, and they're on the same
popularity scale as Hindi, so I moved to Latin instead, which
has the benefit of a really big backlist. I've been thinking of
adding Old Norse for something really unusual. It's just as
well I hadn't, yet, because I'd probably have been handed a
book of ancient Viking cleaning incantations yesterday, even
if I'd just tried a single exercise on the subject, and then I'd be
blocked until I managed to beat my way through it. The
school takes a lot of liberties with the definition of "knowing" a language. It's safer to start new ones over the first quarter so you don't end up stuck on something near finals.

Orion walked me to my classroom. I didn't notice him
doing it at first because I was too busy keeping an eye out for
the group I usually walk with in the mornings: Nkoyo and
her best friends Jowani and Cora. They're all doing heavy
language like me, so we're on almost the same schedule.
We're not friends, but they'll let me walk to class with them
to have a fourth at their back, if I leave at the same time they
do. Good enough for me.

When I spotted them at the tables, they were already halfway through breakfast, so I had to wolf down the rest of
mine to catch up. "Got to go in five," I told Aadhya, to give
her fair warning. She waved over a couple of her friends
from the artificer track who were just coming out with trays:
given my report about the shop, she wasn't in any rush to get
to class early, anyway.

I managed to get out of the cafeteria with Cora, who
grudgingly let me catch up with her before going through

the doors—so generous—and we were outside the doors before Nkoyo did a double-take over my shoulder and I realized Orion was *right behind me.*

"We're going to languages!" I hissed at him. He's in alchemy track. In fact, alchemy track was twice as big as usual in our year, because kids were trying to stick close to him even if they didn't have an affinity. In my opinion, it wasn't nearly worth the additional lab time. He did still have language class sometimes, just like we all have to do some alchemy—we do get to ask for schedule changes on the first day of the year, but if you ask for too many easy classes or try to go too single-track, the school will put you in classes other kids have avoided. But only languages-track kids get the language hall first thing on a Monday: it's one of the big perks, being this high up when you're a junior and senior.

He looked at me mulishly. "I'm going to the supply room." We get building materials down in the workshop and alchemy supplies in the labs, but for everything less exotic, like pencils and notebooks, you have to forage in the big stockroom at the far end of the language hall.

"Can we come with you?" Nkoyo asked instantly. Cora and Jowani were both just gawking, but she's sharp. And it was obviously worth getting to class towards the late end to have a big group for company going for supplies, even leaving aside Orion himself—if only I could have left him aside—so I went along, stewing. I grabbed paper and ink and took some mercury for trading and a hole puncher, and I even found a vast ring binder for my increasing pile of spells. I spotted three eyes peering out at us from a crack in the ceiling, but it was probably just a flinger, and there were too many of us for one of those to make a try.

Afterwards, Orion walked us all back to the nearest language hall, even though there wasn't any reason. The narrow

stairwell next to the stockroom does disappear sometimes—
it's not on the blueprints, it got added belatedly when they
realized it was inconvenient to have to go a quarter mile back
to the next nearest stair—but today it wasn't just present, the
door was actually standing wide open and the light inside
was working.

"What are you doing?" I demanded, taking a risk to stay in
the corridor: the others had already dashed in to claim decent
booths. "Please tell me you *aren't* trying to go out with me."

It didn't seem likely: no one ever has. It's not that I'm ugly;
on the contrary, I've been growing increasingly beautiful in a
tall and alarming way, as befits the terrible dark sorceress I'm
meant to be, at least until I presumably collapse into a grotesque crone. Boys often think for about ten seconds that
they might want to go out with me, and then they look into
my eyes or talk to me and I suppose get the strong impression
I'm likely to devour their souls or something. Also, in Orion's
case, I'd been aggressively rude to him and nearly got him
killed by mimics.

He snorted. "Want to date a maleficer?"

I had a moment of indignation over that, about to snarl at
him yet again that I wasn't, and then I got it. "You're keeping
an eye on me? In case I start doing evil things and—what, you
need to *kill* me?"

He folded his arms across his chest and regarded me with
a cool, righteous expression: enough of an answer. I was violently tempted to kick him in the goolies. One of the things
people do believe in at the commune is about seventeen different forms of Westernized martial arts, and though they're
surrounded with a huge pile of mumbo jumbo about your
inner center and finding your balance and channeling your
spiritual force, the actual kicking and punching gets taught,
too. I wasn't an expert, but I could definitely have made Orion

Lake extremely unhappy right then, given the wide-open way he was standing.

But there was a classroom full of kids behind me watching us, most of whom would have been glad for any decent excuse to completely ostracize me, and the first late bell was about to ring, at which point the door would swing shut and leave me stuck in the hallway for the whole class period. Nobody would let me in. So I had to just stalk away from him seething and take one of the empty language booths.

There aren't any teachers at the Scholomance. The place is filled to capacity with kids; there are two applicants for every spot as it is, and our dorm rooms are less than seven feet across. Anyone who gets in doesn't need external motivation. Knowing how to make a potion that will heal the lining of your stomach after you've accidentally drunk some lyesmoke-infused apple juice is its own reward, really. Even maths becomes pretty necessary for a lot of advanced arcana, and history research brings you loads of useful spells and recipes that you won't be handed in your other courses.

So in language class, you just go to any one of the eight language halls arranged around the third floor and put yourself into one of the booths. Choose wisely; if you try the ones closest to the loo, or the really good one next to the stairs so you can get to lunch in under ten minutes, you'll have a harder time getting a decent booth, or a booth at all. Assuming you do get one, you sit inside the soundproofed cocoon, hoping you aren't missing the footsteps of something coming at your back, and read textbooks or work on exercise sheets while disembodied voices whisper to you in whatever language you're studying that day. Usually they tell me horrible gory stories or describe my death in loving detail. I had meant to work on my Old English, to try and get more use out of the spells I had learned from the household charms book, but I didn't make much progress. I just hunched over the same single page of my notebook, boiling with resentment, while my whisper tenderly recited an epic alliterative poem all about how Orion Lake, "hero of the shadowed halls," was going to murder me in my sleep.

Which would make it self-defense when I killed him, which I gave some newly serious thought to doing: it was starting to seem like I might really have to. People seem to have no trouble convincing themselves that I'm dangerous and evil even when they aren't actively looking for reasons. Of course, I could have killed him just by draining his mana, but I didn't want to actually become a maleficer and then go bursting out of this place like some monstrous butterfly hatching from a gigantic chrysalis of doom to lay waste and sow sorrow across the world as per the prophecy.

The problem was Luisa, I realized abruptly. He hadn't bought my answer about her. Just like I have a good sense of who's using malia, what they're doing, he's almost certainly got a sense for—I don't even know. Justice? Mercy? The pathetic and vulnerable? Anyway, he knew I was lying to him about Luisa, without knowing exactly how I was lying, so he'd probably decided that I really had killed her. I'd taken his question about her as a minor point, but he hadn't. I didn't know much about her, except that she'd been one of the deeply unlucky few who don't have wizard parents. The ability to hold mana does pop up in mundanes every so often, but usually they don't get in here, they just get eaten. Probably a kid who lived near her was slated to come, got eaten before induction, and she got sucked up instead because the parents didn't bother notifying the school, I can't imagine why. So in some sense she was lucky, but from her perspective, one morning she just found herself sucked up out of her ordinary life and dumped without warning into a black hole of a boarding school, surrounded by strangers, no way to get in touch with her family, no way out, and a horde of maleficaria coming to kill her. I'm sure her plight was calculated to pull on every one of Orion's finely tuned heartstrings.

And thanks to my own fit of temper the other night, he's also just discovered I'm a potential dark witch of apocalyptic proportions. Put all of that together, probably every instinct he had was now going wild with the desire to put a stop to my not-yet-begun reign of terror.

Naturally that made me want to go and launch said reign of terror immediately, but first I had to sit through two hours of language and one of Maleficaria Studies, everyone's favorite, which is held in a massive hall on the cafeteria level. We all get lumped into the room together regardless of language, as there's no lecture. The walls are covered with a huge and vividly detailed mural of the graduation ceremony, set in the moment when the senior hall rotates down. The landing is just coming into view, and the marble hall is crammed full of the various delightful creatures waiting ravenous for the buffet to begin. We each get a textbook in our mother tongue, and read along while the current mal we're studying comes alive off the walls and prowls around the stage demonstrating all the ways it might kill us. Occasionally the animated version will try to upgrade itself from being a temporary construct by actually killing someone in the front rows and consuming their mana.

I almost always have to sit in the front rows. It keeps my attention remarkably focused.

Today, though, I was able to get a seat about halfway up, and no one around it said *oh sorry, that one's saved*. It helped me to calm down to sullen irritation before lunch. The initial damage was already done, in terms of people thinking Orion was saving me, so it was time to take a deep breath and find a way to rescue the situation. And as soon as I'd forced myself to do that, my revised strategy became obvious.

So at lunchtime I made a point of sitting down next to Aadhya and whispering to her, "He walked me to class!" and followed it up with, "He can't *really* like me, though," just before he came out of the line, spotted me, and came over to our table and sat down across from me with narrowed eyes.

Orion's never dated anyone, or so I concluded from the fact that I hadn't heard about him dating anyone. Unsurprisingly, the news that he was apparently gone on me bolted through the entire school at even more lightning speed than the story of his rescuing me in the first place. By the time I had to go down to the alchemy labs for my last session of the day, a boy named Mika, whom I've never even spoken to—I think he's Finnish—had saved two seats at a prime table, and when I came in, he called, "El, El," and pointed to the one next to him.

That certainly was a change. I always rush to get to lab early despite the higher risk of being one of the few there while the room's mostly empty, because if I don't arrive while there's still a decent table open, everyone will have saved the good seats for their friends, and then I've got to sit at one of the bad tables, the ones directly underneath the air vents or closest to the door. I can't wheedle for a spot, it makes me too angry, and threatening makes me feel equally terrible, just in the opposite way. So it was very nice to walk right into a half-full room and still get a seat at the best table, without having to barter for it.

Of course, this happy state of affairs was dependent on Orion playing his part, but he came in just before the bell, looked round the room, and came straight to the seat next to mine. Mika craned his head around me to peer at him and smile hopefully. Too bad for him the gesture was lost on

Orion, who was too busy studying all my ingredients and the reaction I was working on.

Most people get alchemy assignments to produce antidotes and preventive elixirs, or the good old standby of producing gold out of cheaper elements. I'm never set recipes for anything that useful; I've got to trade for them. I had already rejected several assignments this week—turning lead into radioactive palladium, producing a deadly contact poison, and converting flesh into stone—before I got my current assignment to produce a jet of superheated plasma, which might be useful under at least some circumstances. For example, it would be absolutely ideal for charring bones into ash, which you wouldn't think would be the first thing that would jump to a person's mind, except Orion looked at it and said immediately, "That's hot enough to disintegrate bone," with hard suspicion.

"Oh, have you done this one already?" I said, insincerely. "Don't tell me, I want to learn it for myself."

He spent most of the class watching me instead of doing his own work. It made me angry, but being angry's always good for my work. My ingredients were iron, gold, water, a chunk of polished lapis lazuli, and half a teaspoon of salt, which had to be arranged at distances proportional to their relative quantities. Woe if you're off by a millimeter. But I got them lined up properly on the first go. I could hardly embark on an exercise routine in the middle of my class, so instead I softly sang three long complicated songs to raise the mana, two in English and one in Marathi. The sparking-flame bloomed inside my cupped palms, and I managed to edge my ritual tray nearer to Orion before I tipped the spark over the ingredients and jumped back. The thin blue flame swallowed them all in a gulp and roared up mightily, so hot that a sweltering wave rolled out through the entire classroom. There were even a few alarmed shrieks from inside the air ducts, and scrabbling noises went overhead.

Everyone instinctively ducked under their desks, except Orion. The paper twists he was using to hold his own ingredients had all caught on fire just from proximity, and he was desperately dousing flames. It made me feel much better.

So did having Nkoyo invite me to dinner on the way out of the lesson. "We usually meet at thirteen minutes to six, if you want to join us," she said. I didn't bother making sure Orion was overhearing; she'd have made sure of that herself.

"If I can bring Yi Liu." Hopefully Orion would get bored with my lack of actual evildoing at some point, and I didn't trust all my new friends not to ditch me as soon as that happened. But Liu would be happy to broaden her circles—she doesn't have the same effect on people that I do, but she's still not a popularity queen like Jack; you have to really go the whole hog before the malia starts to cover up—and she'd remember I'd done her a favor when I had a chance.

I caught Liu in our hall going back to her room after class and told her; she'd been at an afternoon workshop section herself. She nodded and looked at me thoughtfully and volunteered, "Orion was asking questions about Luisa in writing workshop after lunch."

"Of course he was." I grimaced. Jack would definitely blame me for that, what with Orion following me around. "Thanks. I'll see you at thirteen to six."

I didn't see Jack anywhere around, but I checked for any malicious spells on my cell door and did an especially thorough look over the room before I went inside, just in case he'd got ambitious. But there wasn't anything, so I buckled down to my mana-storing exercise routine until dinnertime.

My plan has been to fill crystals throughout this year unless an emergency or a really golden opportunity presents itself—like that soul-eater could have been!—and then use a few of them judiciously to establish my reputation just before the end of term, so I can get into a solid graduation alliance early next year. We all stockpile mana as much as we can in between near-death experiences; even enclavers. It's about the one thing you can't bring in with you, even stored tidily in a power sink like Mum's crystals.

Or rather, you're very welcome to bring all the filled-up power sinks you want, but they'll get sucked completely dry by the induction spell that lands us all in here, which is massively mana-hungry. In fact, you get extra weight allowance in exchange. Not much extra, so it's not worth it unless you're an enclaver and can casually throw away thirty filled power sinks for an extra quarter-kilo. But Mum's never had more than ten filled crystals round in my life, and the last few years we had less. I came in with my one small knapsack and my empties instead.

And I'm ahead of the game at that. Most power sinks are a lot bigger and heavier than Mum's crystals, so lots of kids can't afford to bring empties in, and most of them don't work nearly as well, especially when they've been built in the shop by a fourteen-year-old. I'm in a decent position, but it's really hard to get on when I'm constantly having mals flung at my head. And it gets harder and harder to fill them with exercise, because the older I get and the better shape I get in, the easier the same exercise gets. Mana's annoying that way. The physical labor isn't what counts. What turns it into mana is how much effort it costs me.

Next year I desperately need people watching my back and helping me fill more. If I can only make it to graduation with fifty full crystals, I'm confident I can single-handedly blaze a path for me and my allies straight to the gates and out, no more clever strategy required. It's one of the few situations in which a wall of mortal flame might actually be called for: in fact that's how the school cleans out the cafeteria and does the twice-yearly scouring of the halls. But I'm not going to get there unless I stick to my pace. Which currently means, drumroll, two hundred push-ups before dinner.

I'd like to say I didn't give Orion a thought, but actually I lost a good chunk of my push-up time pointlessly calculating the odds that he'd follow me to dinner. I settled on sixty–forty, but I admit I would have been disappointed if I hadn't seen the flash of his silver-grey hair at the meeting point when I came out. He was waiting for me. Nkoyo and Cora were both waiting, too, failing not to stare at him. There was a wild struggle between jealousy and confusion going on on Cora's face, and Nkoyo just looked woodenly blank. Liu joined me halfway down the hall, and Jowani came out of his room and hurried to meet us just in time for the walk. "Any of you know anyone else studying Old English?" I asked as we set out.

"There's a soph, isn't there?" Nkoyo said. "I don't remember his name. Anything good?"

"Ninety-nine household cleaning charms," I said, and the trio all made noises of sympathy. I was probably the only student in the place who'd gladly have traded a major combat spell for a decent water calling. Of course, no one else can *cast* the combat spells I get.

"Geoff Linds," Orion said unexpectedly. "He's from New York," he added when we looked at him.

"Well, if he wants ninety-nine ways to clean his cell in Old English, send him my way," I said sweetly. Orion frowned at me.

He frowned more through dinner, during which I was excessively nice to him. I even offered him the pudding I'd snagged, a treacle tart—not much loss there, I hate treacle tart—and he obviously wanted to turn it down, but he's also a sixteen-year-old boy who has to inspect every calorie he can get for potential contamination. All the heroic power in the world won't save you from dysentery or a charming bit of strychnine in the sauce, and it's not like he swaps his rescues for anything useful in return, like an extra helping or something. So after a moment he grudgingly said, "Thanks," and took the tart and ate it without meeting my eyes.

Afterwards he followed close on my heels as we took our trays over to the conveyor belt under the enormous sign saying BUS YOUR TRAYS, which even after three years I still think is a mad phrase that makes no sense. Admittedly, that's less of a concern than the actual busing process, which involves shoving your dirty tray into one dark slot of a massive metal rack that is slowly rotating while the conveyor belt carries it along. The safest place to do it is towards the far end, as the dishes and trays are all cleaned using jets of mortal flame, which scares off the mals, but it's almost impossible to find an empty slot at that point, and an extra minute exposed and hunting around the busing area isn't worth it. I usually aim for just short of the midpoint area, which has the benefit of a shorter line.

Orion considered this a perfect place for private conversation. "Nice try," he said over my shoulder, "but it's too late. I'm not going to forget about it just because you started pretending to be friendly. Want to try again telling me what really happened to Luisa?"

He hadn't even realized that he'd convinced everyone in school that we were dating. I rolled my eyes—metaphorically only; I wasn't fool enough to look away from the rack for even a moment. "Yes, I'm passionately excited to share more information with you. Your demonstrated sense and good judgment just fill me with confidence."

"What's that supposed to mean?" he demanded, but right then a six-armed thing vaguely like the offspring of an octopus and an iguana burst off the empty busing rack that had just rotated in, aiming right at the head of a sad-eyed freshman girl, and Orion whipped round and went for it, grabbing a knife off the girl's tray even as he hurled a spell of engorgement. I saw the writing on the wall, and also an empty slot, so I got rid of my tray and dived clear before the thing swelled up like a bloating corpse and burst all over everyone in range.

I went back to my room unbesmirched, with plans to have breakfast with three kids from the London enclave—they've completely ignored me before now—and an offer from Nkoyo to trade Latin spells in language lab tomorrow. Orion slunk off to the showers, wafting a putrid stench. I didn't feel quite even with him yet, but it was coming on nicely. So when he knocked ten minutes later with the lingering miasma wafting under the door, I felt magnanimous enough to open up and say, "Oh, all right, what will you give me for the information?"

I didn't get past *Oh*, though, because it wasn't Orion: it was Jack, smeared with a handful of the octopus thing's guts for the smell—clever of him—and he shoved a sharpened table knife right into my gut. He pushed me collapsing backwards onto the floor and slid the door shut behind him, smiling with all his white teeth while I gasped around the shock of agony, yelling *stupid stupid stupid* at myself in my head. I'd already got ready for bed; I'd hung my mana crystal over the bedpost, where I could reach it in the night and where it was uselessly out of reach right now. He knelt down over me and brushed my hair away from my face with both hands, cupping my cheeks. "Galadriel," he crooned.

My hands were wrapped around the hilt of the knife, involuntarily, trying to keep it from moving, but I made myself let go with one hand and tried to fumble it towards the other mana crystal, the half-full one I'd been working on this afternoon. It was hanging from the side of my bed right where my head went when I was doing push-ups, a few inches above the floor. If I could just reach it, I could connect to all my stored mana. I'd have absolutely no regret liquefying *Jack's* bones.

It was just out of reach. My fingers were straining. I tried to shift my body over just a little, but it hurt a really huge amount, and Jack was stroking my face with his fingertips. It irritated me almost as much as the knife. "Stop that, you colossal dick," I whispered, my voice thready with effort.

"Why don't you make me?" he whispered back. "Come on, Galadriel, just do it. You're so beautiful. You could be so beautiful. I'll help you, I'll do anything for you. We'll have so much *fun*," and I found my whole face crumpling like a sheet of cheap tinfoil. I couldn't bear it. I didn't want to know that I was going to say no. I didn't want to know that I was going to refuse, even with this sack of putrescence crawling his fingers down my ribcage towards the knife he'd jammed into my guts so he could get on with butchering me like a hog.

I'd told myself it was just common sense—going maleficer meant dying young, grotesquely. But that still ought to beat dying right now, only it didn't. It didn't, and if it wasn't an option now, it was never going to be an option, and even if I survived this, I wouldn't survive the next thing, or the one after that. There'd always been a safety valve in the back of my head: I'd always told myself *if all else fails,* but all else had failed, and I wasn't going to do it anyway.

"Fuck you, Great-Grandmother," I whispered, so angry I could have cried, and got ready to shove myself up onto the knife so I could reach the mana crystal. And then I heard the knock on the door. A knock on a school night, with everyone else sane in their own cells and study groups by then—

Talking was difficult. I pointed a finger at the door and thought, *Open sesame.* A stupid kid spell, but it was my own door, and I hadn't locked it for the night yet, so it shot open, and Orion was standing in the doorway. Jack whirled round, his hands wet and red with my blood. He'd even smeared some on his mouth to make the finishing gruesome touch.

I laid my head back down and let the mighty hero get on with it.

Chapter 4
THINGS THAT GO BUMP IN THE NIGHT

THE AWKWARDLY APPEALING SMELL of roasted flesh was filling the room when Orion dropped to his knees beside me. "Are you—" he started, and stopped at the obvious negative.

"Tool chest," I said. "Down the left side. Packet."

He dug into my tool chest—didn't even spare a glance to check the innards after he opened it—and got out the white envelope. He ripped it open and pulled out the thin linen patch. Mum had made it for me, beginning to end: she tilled the field, planted the flax, harvested it by hand, spun and wove it herself, and she chanted healing spells into it and over it the whole time. "Wipe up my blood with one side," I whispered. His face was tight with alarm, but he looked at the floor, doubtfully. "Okay if it gets dirty. Take out the knife, put the other side on the wound."

Thankfully, I sort of blacked out when he pulled the knife, the next ten minutes gone to confusion, and when I surfaced, the patch was on. Jack's knife hadn't been long enough to go all the way through me, so there was only the entry wound, and it wasn't too wide. The healing patch was glowing faintly white, hurting my eyes, but I could feel it working on my abused innards. In ten minutes more, I was ready to let Orion help me move onto the bed.

After Orion settled me there, he heaved Jack's charred corpse out into the corridor. Then he went to my basin and washed the blood off. When he sat back down on the bed, his hands were shaking. He was staring down at them. "Who—who was that?" He looked more shocky than I felt.

"You haven't bothered to learn *anyone's* names, have you," I said. "That was Jack Westing. And he's the one who ate Luisa, if it makes you feel better. You can look in his room and you'll probably find something left behind if you don't believe me."

That brought his head up. "What? Why didn't you tell me?"

"Because I was leery of getting shivved by a sociopathic maleficer, as I would think might be obvious under the circumstances," I said. "Thanks for going round loudly asking questions about Luisa, by the way, that didn't at all set him off."

"You know, it's almost impressive," he said after a moment, sounding less wobbly. "You're nearly dead and you're still the rudest person I've ever met. You're welcome *again,* by the way."

"Given that you're at least half responsible for this situation, I refuse to thank you," I said. I closed my eyes for a moment, and suddenly the five-minute warning bell was ringing for curfew. It hadn't felt like that much time had gone by. I put my hands down and touched the patch gently, testing. Sitting up was not going to appeal for a long time. The blood had gone back into me, so I felt much better, but not even Mum's top work could make a ragged gut wound disappear instantly.

I reached out for the mana crystal and hung it back round my neck. I could forget about sleep tonight, and I was going to have to use some real power. Not only hadn't I given in, Jack was dead, for a net loss of malice in the world. The maleficaria would probably go on a rampage.

Orion was still sitting on the edge of my bed as though he'd been there the whole time, and he didn't make any move to get up. "What are you doing?" I said irritably.

"What?"

"Did you not hear the warning bell?"

"I'm not leaving you," he said, as if that were obvious.

I eyed him. "Do you not understand the principle of balance at all?"

"It's a theory, first of all, and even if it's true, I'm not going to live by it!"

"You're one of those," I said, with heartfelt disgust.

"Yeah, sorry. Do you *mind* my staying, or should I leave you alone with a gut wound to be attacked all night?" I'd evidently pushed him so far he'd found some sarcasm himself.

"Of course I don't mind." It wasn't going to make things any worse for me, after all. There's a practical limit on how many maleficaria can come into your room at once, and I was already on the menu as tonight's special offer. Having Orion around could only help. It's very roughly the same principle that makes being inside the school during puberty better than being on the outside.

Curfew rang on schedule a few minutes later. Whatever kept the maleficaria from attacking Orion usually, it couldn't overcome the scent of blood in the water that I was obviously giving off, not to mention the temptation of two students doubled up in a cell. There was a squabble outside the door over Jack's body to start off the festivities, a sound of things wrestling and gnawing horribly. Orion stood there in the middle of the room with his hands flexing restlessly, listening to them.

"Why are you wasting energy? Just lie down until they come in," I muttered.

"I'm fine."

The noises outside finally stopped. The first rattle of my door came shortly after. Then a glistening black ooze began to seep under the door, thick as tar. Orion let it come halfway through and then framed it with his hands held up, making a diamond-shaped opening between them. He chanted a one-line water-spout spell in French and then blew a whistling breath through his hands. A torrent of water gushed out the other side, firehose-strong, and dissolved the ooze into a thin slick that ran along the cracks between the floor tiles and slurped down the round drain in the middle of the cell floor.

"If you'd frozen it, you could have blocked the opening," I said after a moment.

He threw an annoyed look at me, but before he could answer, there was a sudden hard vacuum-popping sensation in my ears: something big had come through the air vent. He jumped in front of my bed and threw a shielding spell over us just in time as an honest-to-goodness incarnated flame erupted at the dark end of the room, inches away from the void. It bashed my desk out of the way and started lashing blows at us with a huge thrashing whip-coil tentacle of fire that splashed gouts of flame over the surface of the shield.

I grabbed Orion's arm as he swiped a streak of dust off the top of my headboard, about to use a dust-devil spell. He yelled at me, "I'm going to kill you myself at this rate!"

"Shut up, this is actually important! You can't smother it, you have to burn it hotter to burn it out."

"You've seen one of these before?"

"I've got a summoning spell that raises a dozen of them," I said. "It was used to burn down the Library of Alexandria."

"Why would you ask for a spell like that!"

"What I asked for was a spell to light my room, you twat, that's what I *got*." To be fair, the incarnate flame was in fact doing a magnificent job of lighting the room. My room went double-height after the sophomore-year reshuffle—at term-end the school gets rid of any rooms that aren't being used anymore—and I hadn't seen the upper corners of the wall above my bed since. A whole bunch of agglo grubs up there were humping around in blind circles trying to get away from the light and getting vaporized in flaring-blue pops by the vermin stripe I'd tacked on the wall as high as I could previously see. "Do you want to keep arguing with me until it smashes through?"

He actually snarled wordlessly and then hit the incarnate with a magnificent incineration spell, barely four words long—all his spells seemed to be like that, ideal for combat—and it shrieked and went up into a towering pillar of flame that burnt out along with the spell. He sat back down on my bed breathing in hard gulps, but there was almost a static-electricity crackle coming off his skin: he was bursting with mana.

He didn't break a sweat killing the next five things that made it in, including a disembodied wight that floated through the opening he hadn't blocked under the door and a horde of little squeaking fleshy things like naked mole rats that appeared from under the bed apparently hoping to nibble us to death. He was almost glowing by the time he disposed of the last ones.

"If you have more mana than you can handle, you could put some in my crystals," I said, as a way of fighting the urge to just claw his and my own faces off with envy.

He did actually pick up the half-empty crystal dangling from my bed, gave it a double-take, then stared at the one I was wearing. "Wait—I thought—what enclave are you from?"

"I'm not in any enclave."

"Then how did you get your hands on Radiant Mind crystals? You've got *two*."

I compressed my lips, regretting I'd got us on this conversational road. Mum will give her crystals to other wizards sometimes, if she gets a good feeling from them, and since Mum's judgment on that sort of thing is fairly unerring, her crystals have developed a bit of a side reputation, out of proportion to the mana they can hold. "I've got fifty," I said shortly. The crystals were what I packed instead of more clothes, supplies, tools; anything I could live without. "They're my mum's."

He gaped at me. "Gwen Higgins is your *mother*?"

"Yes, and I don't mind the massive incredulity at all, really, it's why I make a point of telling everyone." Mum is classic English rose, small and pink and blond and going gently plump in middle age. Dad—Mum's got one photo of him that his mum gave her, from before he went to school—was six feet tall already even at fourteen, gangly with coal-black hair and serious dark eyes and a nose with just a bit of an interesting hook. She tells me earnestly all the time how wonderful it is I take after him so strongly, because she gets to still see him in me. From my perspective, it meant no one ever realized I belonged to her unless they were told. Once someone visiting our yurt spent a solid hour hinting that I might go away and stop pestering the great spiritual healer, as if I didn't live there.

But that wasn't why Orion was incredulous. Wizards tend to mix a lot more, since we all get jumbled in here together during our formative years, and the distinction that matters is between the enclavers and the rest of us have-nots. Orion was just shocked that the great spiritual healer had produced creepy proto-maleficer me, exactly the way everyone else in here would be, which is why in fact I make a point of not telling anyone.

"Oh," Orion said awkwardly, and then jumped and reflexively blasted a shadow-thing that didn't even have a chance to take enough form for me to recognize which variety it was. But he really did put some mana into my crystal afterwards, possibly as some sort of apology, or just because he was about to come apart at the seams: he filled it the rest of the way in a single go and gave a small gasp of relief after. I restrained my feelings and put it into my chest with the others and fished out a new empty one.

I managed to sleep a bit, towards the end of the night. Either the maleficaria had got discouraged, or Orion had exterminated all of the ones in range of my room; there were half-hour stretches where nothing came in. He also filled two more crystals for me. I gave him one of them, grudgingly. I'd started to feel irritatingly guilty about it, even though he hadn't asked for anything in return like a normal person would have.

I woke up the last time to my alarm going off. It was morning, and we weren't dead. Orion hadn't slept at all, and he was looking faded; I gritted my teeth and then painfully shuffled myself upright and out of the way. "Lie down, I'll fix it," I told him.

"Fix what?" he said, and yawned massively.

"That," I said. You can't actually replace sleep, but my mum's got a technique she uses on really bad insomniacs to get their third eye to close—yes, well, it's not scientific or anything—and it usually makes them feel better. I can't do most of my mum's spells very well, but this one's simple enough that I can manage it. He lay down on my bed and I had him hold the crystal I'd given him, then I put my hands over his eyes and my thumbs between his eyebrows and chanted her "inner eye lullabye" seven times over him. It worked, the way all Mum's ridiculous stuff works. He fell asleep instantly.

I let him keep sleeping for the twenty minutes until the breakfast bell rang, and he sat up looking at least five hours better. "Help me up," I said. There's no such thing as a sick day in here. Staying in the residential halls all day just means that whatever things are making their way up from below for the nighttime feasting get a midday snack. No one stays in unless they're all but dead anyway. We catch endless colds and flu, as you might imagine. There're more than four thousand of us in here, and the incoming freshmen bring along a delightful assortment of viruses and infectious diseases from around the world at the start of every year. And even after those have made the rounds, new things crop up inexplicably. Possibly they're just smaller maleficaria; isn't that a lovely thought.

As I was in fact exhausted and overwhelmed, I wasn't calculating the effect of me and Orion coming out of my room together looking exhausted and overwhelmed. But a couple of other kids who had also slept in until the bell came out the same time we did, and naturally it was everywhere by the time we arrived at the cafeteria. The scale of the gossip reached such elevated levels that one of the girls from the New York enclave dragged Orion aside after breakfast to demand to know what he was thinking.

"Orion, she's a *maleficer*," I overheard her saying. "Jack

Westing disappeared last night, people found bits of his shoes outside her door. She probably killed him."

"*I* killed him, Chloe," Orion said. "He was the maleficer. He killed Luisa."

That news distracted her enough for her to abandon her lecture on his terrible dating choices, so by the end of the day Orion was the only person in the school who didn't know we were now unquestionably an item, and for that matter an insane, spending-the-night-together item. It was almost entertaining to see the effects. The New York enclave kids all got immediately anxious: I saw the ones from our year taking time during lunch to go and tell the seniors about it, and meanwhile enough kids from the London enclave began saying nice things to me that it became clear there was a concerted effort under way on their side.

The point being, of course, if Orion was really sold on me, I had just become a chance to poach him. And I'd previously made clear to the London crowd that I'd be interested in an invitation. Not asking openly, of course, since I didn't want the scornful rejection that would have ensued, but I'd told people my mum lived nearish London, and mentioned I was thinking of applying to the enclave myself. Just enough to plant a seed for the future, once graduation started looming and I'd demonstrated some firepower. People are always more likely to make an offer if they think it's going to be accepted.

Of course, it was absolutely ridiculous for anyone involved to start either panicking or courting me over a junior-year relationship of two days' supposed standing, but that was the degree of everyone's idiocy over Orion for you. I would have been more amused if it weren't a repeated reminder of how little anyone valued me for my own sake. And if I didn't still have a barely healed gut wound, which soured my mood considerably.

I didn't let it stop me from taking advantage of everyone offering me good seats and minor bits of help all day. I needed every one to get through. I'd managed to get a bit ahead of my work over the course of the term, meaning to use the banked time to review for my final exams, but instead I had to blow it all just resting quietly while everyone else made themselves slightly more appealing targets around me. I didn't even try to get any classwork done; I just saved my energy, and that night I spent some power out of my crystal on some very heavy-duty shielding before I fell into bed and slept the sleep of those with the Aegis Ward on their door.

The next morning, the healing patch fell off, leaving me with a very faint scar, a lingering ache, and several calculated thoughts about my looming deadline in shop class. If you don't complete a shop assignment on time, your unfinished work will animate on the due date and come after you with whatever power you've put into it. And if you try and get around that by not putting anything into it, or doing it wrong, the raw materials you should have used will all animate separately and come at you. It's quite a solid teaching technique. We get a new assignment every six weeks. My final one this year was a choice of either a mesmeric orb that could be used to turn a group of people into a frenzied mob who'd tear each other apart, or a really lovely clockwork worm that would wriggle into someone's imagination and dredge up their worst nightmares one after another every night until they went mad, or a magic mirror that would give you advice and glimpses of the possible future.

If you can guess the sort of advice the mirror would offer me, well, so could I. Also, the mirror was at least ten times more complicated to make than the other two. But if I made one of the others, they'd end up getting used for definite. If not by me, by someone else.

I had already forged the frame in plain iron, and made the backing plate that the enchanted silver would go on. But it was a fair bet that the silver pour would go completely wrong the first dozen times I tried it. That was going to involve alchemy and incantation on top of the artifice, and whenever you try and cross two or more of the disciplines, it's loads more difficult, unless of course you can get a specialist from each discipline to help you. Which I couldn't.

Except today, Aadhya voluntarily walked down to the shop with me from breakfast, and took the seat next to me at one of the long benches. "I'm too tired to get anything done today, but I can't afford to fall behind on this one," I told her, and showed her my assignment.

"Ouf. That's the one you went with?" she said. "Magic mirrors are for artificer-track seniors."

"The others I got were worse," I said, not specifying how. I could have whipped up that frenzy orb in one session with a handful of broken glass. Oh, I'd probably also have needed the life's blood of one of my fellow students, but who's being picky? "What are you working on?"

Her assignment was a personal shield holder—that's an amulet you put round your neck or bind onto your wrist. You cast a shield through it, and then you can cast other things with both hands instead of holding the shield up with one. Enormously useful, and relatively quick work; looking at her workbox, I could see she was making half a dozen of them, the spares of which she'd undoubtedly trade to maximum effect. Of course, she was specializing in artifice, but even so.

She looked at me narrowly and said, "The pour would go a lot easier with an artificer and an alchemist."

"I hate to ask anyone for help," I said. That was certainly true. "It's not three weeks to the end of term, everyone's busy."

"I could maybe spare a bit of time, if you found an alchemist," Aadhya said, of course thinking of having a chance to work with Orion. "If you'd be willing to let me use it."

"Anytime you like," I said. That was a magnificent deal, and in fact I'd probably have to find some other way to compensate her, or have her angry with me, as she almost certainly wouldn't like using the mirror after the first go, unless it came out as the kind of mirror that encouraged you to think all your plans were the most brilliant and you were dazzlingly clever and beautiful all the way until you walked yourself into total ruin.

Of course, that still left me to ask Orion for help, which I grudgingly did at lunchtime. I thought I'd best take advantage of my brief window of opportunity before he finally worked out that we were supposedly dating and started avoiding me instead of pulling his continuing white-knight routine: he'd checked in on me at every meal yesterday in a muttering way, and he'd allowed himself to be pulled into a table with me by Aadhya and Ibrahim in turn. It was massively irritating, to the point that I almost let Ibrahim pester him all during dinner—it was nonstop "I still can't believe you killed a soul-eater all by yourself," and "Do you like silver or gold better as an agonist? I'd really appreciate your advice," et cetera—except the hero-worshipping was even more irritating, so I finally snapped and told Ibrahim to shut it and stop behaving like a celebrity stalker, or find another place to sit. He did shut it, and looked embarrassed, and also tried to glare at me, but I just stared back and I'm fairly sure he got the strong sense that a monstrous and terrible fate awaited any who stirred my wrath. He flinched and pretended he'd actually just been staring into space past me.

Anyway, at lunchtime I made sure to touch my abdomen with a visible wince as I queued up in the cafeteria, and sure enough Orion pushed in—if you can call it that when the girls behind me immediately let him do it, all brightly, "Go ahead, Orion, it's fine!" when he asked them—and said to me, "You all right?"

"Improving, now," I said, which was true and would also stand in for flirtation, for the avid eavesdroppers. "I've fallen behind in shop class, though. Aadhya said she'd help me, but we need an alchemist, too—it's a three-discipline project."

If that sounds like a painfully bald invitation to you, well, it did to me, too, but subtlety didn't seem called for, and indeed it wasn't. "I'll help," he said instantly.

"Great," I said. "After dinner tonight?" He nodded, and yet again didn't ask for anything back, helpfully providing more grist for the mill. I felt simultaneously aggravated and magnanimous, so I added, "The rice pud isn't, by the way," and he jerked his head round and promptly went after the glutinous maggots waiting in the tray—if you put a spoon in them they'll go boiling up it and get half your fingers to the bone unless you fling it away quick enough, in which case usually they land on a dozen different students in the line and promptly start eating whatever flesh they land on and dividing into new swarms.

Orion emerged ten minutes after I had made it out with my tray, faint blue-grey smoke following him out and his tray half empty. Everyone else behind him was also coming out with fairly minimal selections, so exterminating the maggots had evidently taken out most of the line. It wouldn't be refilled until after the last kids from our year went through and the sophomores got their turn. I privately rolled my eyes and put my spare milk carton and second bread roll on his tray when he came over and sat down next to me: the noise and confusion behind me had made it easy to nab extras for once.

Sarah and Alfie had invited me to sit with them at the London enclave table. I wasn't stupid enough to throw over Liu and Aadhya for them, though, so they'd actually had a quick private word and then had come with me, instead—a massive concession, which meant I was suddenly sitting at a surprisingly powerful table. Nkoyo with Cora and Jowani are networked with a lot of the other West and South African students, and Aadhya has a solid lineup of allies from the artificer track. They're about as well positioned as you get aside from the actual enclave kids, and now I had pulled in a pair of those.

And then Orion sat down next to me again—Aadhya had carefully left herself enough room on the bench to scoot over quickly as soon as he got close enough for his intentions to be clear—and took things to a completely new level. By far the most obvious explanation to anyone looking on was that I'd thoroughly hooked Orion, and now I was using that to build myself a power base among the people who'd tolerated me on their fringes before, likely with the intention to leverage him to get us all into a major enclave. And London was actively displaying interest. That *would* have been a magnificent bit of strategy on my hypothetical scheming self's part.

Chloe and Magnus—from New York—came off the line just a minute later. They had half a dozen of their usual tagalongs surrounding them, and another four holding a prime table and waiting for them, but their plans clearly changed when they saw Orion sitting with me again. They traded a quick whisper and then they came past and took the four end seats still left at our table—two tagalongs went on the outside edge, of course—leaving the rest of their uncertain crew to straggle on to the other table without them.

"Pass the salt, would you, Sarah?" Chloe said, very sweetly, by which she meant die in a fire, we're not letting London steal Orion, and followed it up by asking me, "Galadriel, are you feeling better? Orion said Jack nearly killed you."

I couldn't have asked for better. Except actually what I wanted to do was dump my tray over Orion's undeserving head, tell off Sarah and Alfie and Chloe and Magnus, and possibly set them all on fire. None of them were here for me. Chloe must have had to ask someone my name. Even Aadhya and Nkoyo and Liu—I was pretty sure they would at least have me at their tables after this; I'd demonstrated to them that when I did get an advantage, I paid my debts, and they were all bright enough to value proven reliability more than almost anything else. But as soon as Orion moved on to greener and less-likely-to-turn-violently-evil pastures, even they would relegate me back to bare tolerance. And the enclavers would make clear that I was dirt under their feet and had been lucky to have a minute when I'd imagined otherwise.

"Doing splendidly, thanks very," I said, icily. "It's Chloe, isn't it? Sorry, I don't think we've met."

Nkoyo darted a look at me across the table, incredulous—you didn't snub enclave kids, and we all knew their names—but Orion jerked his head up and said, "Sorry—this is Chloe Rasmussen and Magnus Tebow, they're from New York," exactly as if he felt he should introduce me to his friends. "Guys, this is Galadriel."

"Charmed," I said.

Alfie evidently took that as an indication that I preferred

London to New York, and leaned in smiling. "You live near London, El, don't you? Any chance we'd know your family?"

"I'm out in the back of beyond," I said, and left it woodenly right there. They'd have recognized Mum's name, of course, if I told them. All of them would have. I wanted to trade on her name even less than I wanted to trade on being Orion's not-girlfriend. Anyone who wanted to be friends with Gwen Higgins's daughter very much didn't want to be friends with *me*.

So instead I spent the meal being rude to some of the most popular and powerful kids in the entire school, ignoring them to discuss the mirror artifice with Aadhya and Orion, and talk Latin with Nkoyo. We'd had a really good spell-trade the other day. I'd given her a copy of the mortal flame spell. That might sound extreme, but it's not explicitly a spell to conjure *mortal* flame, it's a sliding-scale spell to conjure magical fire. Most people love those spells, because virtually anyone can cast them successfully and you just get different results depending on your affinity and how much mana you put into it. Even if you're a fumbling child, you can use it to light a match, and get better at casting it. Or if you're me, you can suck the life force out of a dozen kids and then incinerate half the school with you inside it. So helpful!

But for Nkoyo, it would probably be a fantastically useful wall-of-flame spell, and she felt she had to make equal return—I didn't argue—so she gave me a choice of two in exchange. I picked two minors she had that needed almost no mana at all: a spell for distilling clean water from dirty, so I won't have to go to the bathroom for water as often, and another that pulls in a bunch of spare electrons from the environment around you to deliver a good heavy electrical shock. As soon as I looked at the first line, I could tell it lined up with my affinity—I imagine it would've been very handy for purposes of torture—and it'll give me some breathing room in a fight, either to run away or to do a major casting.

I'm about the only kid in the school who'd swap major arcana for minor. The division is sort of vague, it's not actually anything real we learn in class, it's just what we think of as more or less powerful. You can argue yourself blue about whether one modestly powerful spell is major or minor. And people do! But walls of flame are very decidedly major, and distilling water and mana-cheap electric shock spells are very decidedly minor, so after I picked them, Nkoyo even threw in a few grooming cantrips—hair-plaiting, a bit of glamour, and a deodorant spell, which I suppose was a polite way of hinting that I could stand to wash more often than I do. I didn't need the hint, I already knew, but if it's a choice between stinking and survival, I'll choose to stink. I've never had a shower more than once a week in here, and often it's been longer.

If you're thinking that's why I don't have friends, it's a bit chicken-and-egg: anyone who doesn't have enough friends to watch their back can't afford to be well groomed, and that lets people know you don't have enough friends to watch your back, which makes them less likely to think you're a valuable ally. However, none of us spends loads of time showering, and when you want a shower, generally you ask someone who visibly needs one themselves, and it all ends up leveling out. But no one ever asks me. Anyway, I wasn't sorry to have a few more options for putting myself together, although I don't dare try that glamour cantrip or I expect I'll end up with a dozen of the more weak-minded trailing me around with hopeless eyes, whining that they long only to be allowed to serve me.

We'd both come out of the negotiation satisfied, and

agreeing to trade again. But Nkoyo wasn't in any hurry to piss off London and New York, and neither was Aadhya. When I ignored the others and talked to them instead, they kept darting anxious looks around at the enclave kids. Who themselves pretty clearly didn't know what to make of me not fawning all over them. Naturally they didn't like it, but there was Orion sitting next to me with his shaggy head bent over his plate as he shoveled in the extra food I'd given him.

Sarah and Alfie both decided to fall back on being British and posh, which meant talking in a self-deprecating way about how difficult they were finding the work in all their subjects and how hopeless they were, when actually they were both as top-tier as you'd expect given they'd been trained from birth in one of the most powerful enclaves in the world. Meanwhile Chloe decided to play defense and kept trying to have conversations with Orion all about fun things they'd apparently done in New York. He only absently responded between bites.

Magnus didn't talk at all. He obviously didn't have nearly as much cultural training in the art of being woodenly polite in the face of someone behaving all wrong, and I'm sure he also didn't enjoy always being second fiddle in his own social group: if it hadn't been for Orion, he'd have been prime candidate to dominate our year himself. I did notice him seething, but I was too busy seething myself to care. My anger's a bad guest, my mother likes to say: comes without warning and stays a long time. I was just starting to deep-breaths-and-center myself back to a state of more rational civility, telling myself I really had to say something polite to each one of the enclavers at the table, when Magnus hit his own limit and leaned in. "So, Galadriel," he said, "I'm really *dying* to know— how did you keep the mals out all night?"

He was implying that the way I'd hooked Orion was by

finding some shielding spell that let me turn my room into a sanctuary for all-night shagging, which I'd offered up in trade for Orion bestowing the favor of his attentions on me. That was a completely reasonable assumption, of course. Which didn't endear the remark to me any more, especially as it was loud enough to be overheard at the nearby tables. I got angry all over again, and I looked at him straight-on and hissed— when I'm really angry, it's a hiss, even if there're no actual sibilants involved—"We *didn't*."

Which had the power of being perfectly true, but coming out of my mouth conveyed the strong implication that we'd been cavorting *with* maleficaria. Which I suppose Orion had been doing, in a way, so even that was also true. Everyone instinctively leaned away from me, and Magnus, who'd just received a full-on dose of angry me right between the eyes, actually turned faintly pale.

It was a really lovely meal.

Chapter 5

SIRENSPIDERS

AFTER MY PERFORMANCE at lunch, it was a sure bet that Orion's enclave pals were going to pull him aside as soon as possible and give him two earfuls about why he needed to stop dating me, which would probably awaken him to the realization that we were dating. Even as irritated as I was, I recognized that my window of opportunity was closing, so as we cleared our trays, I got Aadhya aside and said, "Could we do the silver pour right now, during work time?" I think she mostly agreed because she felt she should humor an obvious lunatic. Orion just said, "Yeah, sure," with a shrug, so we headed straight downstairs to the shop before anyone from New York could intercept him.

In the middle of the school day, the trip downstairs is loads better. Most kids still try to avoid the workshop this near to end of term, but the stairs and corridors on the way are at least lit up, and we weren't the only ones when we got there: a trio of seniors at the back had skipped lunch entirely to keep working rather frantically on some kind of weapon they were likely counting on for graduation. We settled on a

bench towards the front and Orion came with me to my project locker—I handed him the key and let him open it; that's
always a bad moment—and after nothing whatsoever jumped
on us, I took out my mirror frame and we carried the rest of
the supplies back to where Aadhya had already got the small
gas burner going, a process that normally took me ten minutes each time.

She'd never bestirred herself to show off for me, but Orion's presence was all the incentive she needed to put on a
display, and it became clear she was even better than I'd realized. She wasn't going to do the actual enchantments, which
would've required her to invest mana out of her own stockpile, not something you do for just a favor in return, but she'd
volunteered to hold the perimeter, which was a tricky bit of
the pour. She set up the barrier around the edge, and Orion
mixed the silver with comfortable sureness, even while working with an enormous array of painfully hard-to-get and expensive ingredients that I'd spent most of the last few weeks
carefully collecting from the supply cabinets in the alchemy
labs—roughly as much fun as getting anything from the shop
supply—which he handled as if he could just get a jar of
moon-grown tansy and a sack of platinum shavings off the
shelf anytime he needed. He probably could.

"All right, Orion, please pour it right into the middle, from
as high up as you can reach," Aadhya said, and added to me
in lecturing tones, which I swallowed resentfully, "and make
sure you don't tilt the surface more than twenty degrees, El.
You want to keep the flow going into the middle, and just
gently spiral it out. I'll tell you when it's ready for the incantation."

Forcing an incantation into a physical material—which
then preserves the incantation's magic and makes it ongoing
instead of something ephemeral—is the hard part of making

artifice for most people, because the physical reality of the stuff resists you trying to muck with it, and you have to put a lot of power behind it. That wasn't a problem for me, but the devil was in the details. As soon as my spell hit the silver, it was going to start bubbling. And if the silver hardened with the bubbles in it, there wouldn't be much of a mirror after. I'd have to scrape the frame clean, gather new materials, and try again without all this lovely help. The proper way to do it is to ease the enchantment into the material seamlessly; that's what good artificers do. But you've got to have a sense for how the substances are reacting, and the ability to coax them along. Coaxing anything isn't my strong suit.

So instead, I was going to be throwing power at the problem—specifically a delightful spell that some Roman maleficer had worked up for crushing an entire pit's worth of living victims into pulp. He'd obviously had a harder time getting life force out of people than I did. On the other hand, his spell was the best option I had found for creating anything like a pressure chamber. It was a hefty 120 lines of ancient Latin and took an outrageous amount of mana, but I had to make the mirror somehow, and for Aadhya's benefit, I was determined to make it look absolutely effortless.

When Orion finally got round to dumping me, I wanted to come out of this mess with something more than a school-wide reputation for being a bit of a slapper. Getting Aadhya on board as a core ally would do nicely. She had a big network of friends across the school, an eclectic bunch of Americans, Hindi and Bengali speakers, and fellow artificers, and she'd built that into a still-larger network of people who were glad to work with her, as a trader or an artificer. Last year she'd brokered a big deal between some alchemy-track enclavers and a group of artificers she knew and the kids on the maintenance track: that's why the ceiling in the big alchemy lab had actually been fixed in less than a year after Orion and the chimaera had pulled it down on our heads. If I showed her that I could be a ticket straight through graduation, and she agreed to ally and talked me up, enough other people would know she wasn't either a fool or desperate and lying. We'd get invitations to join a bigger team for definite.

As Orion let the stream go, I tilted the mirror in a circling motion, keeping the silver flowing evenly all round. Aadhya held the perimeter really clean and tight, not a single drip running out, and as soon as the last bit of red vanished—I'd painted the surface red to make it easier to see when everything was covered—Aadhya said, "It's ready!" I put the mirror back down on the platform, recited the mirror enchantment itself—there went half a crystal just on that—and then I put my hands on either end of the mirror, defining the space between them, and cleared my throat, getting ready to cast the crushing spell.

Which of course is when the clear tinkling noise, like melancholy wind chimes, went off behind me: a sirenspider dropping onto one of the metal benches. The seniors at the back must have seen it coming down: they were already heading out of the door, carrying their project with them. Sensible of them not to warn us. Aadhya sucked in a breath and said, "Oh shit!" as a second clangy burst of wind chimes went off, not in harmony. *Two* sirenspiders. That was almost absurdly bad luck: normally we didn't even see sirenspiders the whole second half of the year, after their third or fourth molting; by now they were usually down in the graduation hall, spinning webs and eating the smaller maleficaria, getting ready for the big feast.

I got ready to turn around and change my target—I'd take having to redo the mirror in exchange for not being frozen into paralyzed horror by sirensong and having my blood delicately and slowly sucked out of me—and then Orion grabbed a sledgehammer someone had left on a nearby bench, vaulted over the table behind us, and charged them, because of course he did. Aadhya gave a shriek and dived underneath the table, covering her ears. I just gritted my teeth and dived into my incantation while Orion and the sirenspiders chimed and clanged around behind me like six pipe organs collapsing.

The surface of the mirror shimmered like hot oil, and I crushed it perfectly smooth, not a single break in my chanting even when a large sirenspider leg came flying over my head, slammed into the wall, and bounced off to land on the worktable right next to me, still twitching and chiming broken bits of a song of unearthly horrors et cetera. By the time Orion finished up and staggered back, panting, to ask, "You girls okay?" it was all over, and the silver had solidified without a single bubble into a glossy greenish-black pool, just aching to spit out dark prophecies by the dozen.

Aadhya crawled out shakily from under the table and performed her own ritual thanks to Orion with complete sincerity while I wrapped the useless rubbishy mirror. If she didn't cling to his arm as we went out of the shop, it wasn't because she didn't want to. To give her credit, she pulled herself together halfway up the stairs, at which point she asked me, "Can you still get credit? How bad did it warp?" I took the cover off the mirror long enough to show her the surface, and I knew what was coming even before she opened her mouth and said, admiring, "I can't even believe it. Orion, what'd you do with the silver to get it to set that smooth?"

I took the mirror back to my room and hung it over a particularly bad scorched spot the incarnate flame had left on the wall. The wrappings fell off as I put it up, and before I could drape it again, a ghastly fluorescing face appeared partway from the churning depths as if emerging from a pool of bubbling tar, and told me in sepulchral tones, "Hail, Galadriel, bringer of death! You shall sow wrath and reap destruction, cast down enclaves and level the sheltering walls, cast children from their homes and—"

"Right, yeah, old news," I said, and threw the covers back on. It muttered things from underneath all night long and occasionally burst into ghostly wailing accompanied by vividly glowing purple and neon-blue light shows. My gut was aching enough to keep me awake for it all. I glared at the tiny scuttling mals revealed up on the ceiling and felt extremely put upon. By morning I was stewing so violently that I got all the way through toothbrushing, breakfast, and my language classes of the day before I snapped at something Orion said to me in history and only then noticed he was *still there*. I stopped biting his head off long enough to side-eye him. There was no way that his friends hadn't yet found an opportunity and begged him at length to dump me. What was he even doing?

"In case it makes you feel better," I told him irritably as we walked to lunch—he'd even stayed with me after class—"if I ever do go maleficer, I promise you'll be the absolute first to know."

"If you were going to go evil, you'd have done it by now just to avoid letting me help you," he said, with a huff, which was—spot-on, actually, and I laughed before I meant to. Chloe and Magnus were coming to the lunchroom from the opposite direction just then, and both of them eyed me with the grim and resentful expressions you'd normally reserve for a really vicious final exam.

"Orion, I was hoping to catch you," Chloe said. "I'm having some trouble with my focusing potion. Would you look at the recipe over lunch?"

"Sure," Orion said. Neatly done, and it left me the choice

to tag along after Orion to their table like a trailing girlfriend, or what I actually did, which was take my tray to an empty table of my own. He'd distracted me enough I'd forgotten to pay attention, too, so I was early, and there wasn't anyone for me to even tentatively try joining. I put my tray down in the middle of the empty table—at least it was a relatively good one—and checked the underside of the table and all the chairs, did a quick cleaning charm on the table surface—there were a few suspicious stains, probably just from some senior's lunch, but if the cleaning charm hadn't worked on them, they could've been a sign of something worse—and burned a small smudge of incense, which would probably nudge along anything lurking in the ceiling overhead. By the time I was done and sitting down, more people were starting to come off the line, all of them seeing Orion over at the New York enclave table and me alone at mine.

I was sitting with my back to the queue. That's the safer way to sit—if you're friendless—since it puts you that much closer to the mass of moving students, with a better view of the doors. I resolutely started eating with my Latin book open on the table in front of me. I wasn't going to watch for any of the people I'd waved over to sit with me and Orion, the last few days. They'd decide for themselves what they wanted to do. It was just as well he wasn't sitting with me today: I'd find out where I stood. I was glad of it.

I almost managed to convince myself. Almost. I didn't want Orion's help and I didn't want him to sit with me and I didn't want any fair-weather tagalongs sitting with me, I didn't, but—I didn't want to die, either. I didn't want a clinger to jump me and I didn't want anoxienta spores to erupt out of the floor beneath me and I didn't want some slithering mess to drop on my head from the ceiling tiles, and that's what happens to people who sit alone. For the last three years, I've had to think and plan and strategize how I'm going to survive every single meal in here, and I'm so tired of it, and I'm tired of all of them, hating me for no reason, nothing I've ever done. I've never hurt any of them. I've been tying myself in knots and working myself to exhaustion just to avoid hurting any of them. It's so hard, it's so hard in here all the time, and what I was really glad of was having half an hour three times a day where I could take a breath, where I could pretend that I was just like everyone else, not some queen of popularity like an enclave girl but someone who could sit down at a good table and do a decent perimeter and people would join me instead of going out of their way in the opposite direction.

And the reason I hadn't planned my lunch out today was because Orion had been walking with me, so I'd assumed that I would get to pretend for one meal more, and that had been stupid of me. I'd been asking for this. If I'd hung back and waited, I could've joined Liu or Aadhya or Nkoyo's tables. Maybe. Or maybe they'd have done what people have always done when they see me coming towards their tables: invited the nearest loose person to sit down, to fill in any open spots before I can get there. And if they did, I'd have asked for that, too, picking a fight with the enclave kids yesterday like I thought I was as good as them. I wasn't. We're all in this shitty place together, but they're going to get out. They're loaded up with powerful artifacts and the best spells, guarding each other's backs and pumping each other full of power; they're going to survive unless they get *unlucky*. And when they get out, they'll get to go back home to their beautiful enclaves, walled round with spells and anxious new recruits for sentries, where you can just walk into your bedroom and go to sleep, not spend an hour each night helping your mum lay wards all around your one-room yurt just so nothing comes in to rip you both to shreds.

I was barely nine years old the first time something came at me. Mals don't usually come after wizards in their prime, like Mum, and they don't usually come after little ones because we don't have enough mana yet. But Mum was ill that week; she'd got a raging fever, and after she went delirious, someone at the commune took her to hospital and left me alone. I ate our cold leftovers from the night before and huddled down in our bed, trying to sing the lullabies Mum sang me every night, to pretend she was there. When the scratching started at the wards, tiny sprays of sparks going up outside the entrance like knives on steel, I got the crystal she'd been wearing with her circle that fall. I was clutching it in my hands when the scratcher started working its way in, fingers first, long jointed things with claws like the blades of paring knives.

I screamed when they poked through. Back then, I still had the idea somewhere in me that someone would come if I screamed. I was enough of an oblivious kid that I only considered whether *I* liked someone, or more often didn't, so I hadn't really noticed yet that people didn't like *me,* and I hadn't worked out that people not liking me meant they wouldn't sit at even a good table in the cafeteria with me, and they'd leave me alone and hungry in a yurt without my mum, and they wouldn't come when I screamed in the night, the way a kid would scream when something full of knives was coming at her. Nobody came even after I screamed a second time, when the scratcher's other hand squirmed in, too, knife-fingers clawing the wards open like a mouse getting into a sack. And other people heard me, I know they heard me, because through the doorway I could see the yurts on the next rise where a group of silhouettes were still up and sitting around a fire.

It was just as well that I could see them not getting up, not coming, because by the time I finished the second scream and the scratcher was inside with me, I'd understood that I was alone at my table, and there was only me to save me, because no one else cared. They were stupid not to care, though they didn't know it. It was lucky for them that I had Mum's crystal in my hands, because otherwise I would have gone grabbing at them for power instead.

Scratchers aren't hard to kill, any reasonably skilled freshman could do for one with the basic blunt-force spell we all learn in the second month of Maleficaria Studies, but I was nine, and the only spell I knew was Mum's cooking spell, which I'd picked up just because I heard it so often. It might have worked all right on a bestial-class mal, but scratchers aren't suitable for cooking: they're made almost completely of metal. That kind of mal is the work of some artificer that either deliberately or accidentally gave one of their creations enough of a brain to want to keep going; then it creeps off on its own, hunting for mana, building on armor and weapons as it goes. The average nine-year-old wizard in a panic throwing a cooking spell at a scratcher would have heated it through nicely and died on red-hot blades instead of cold ones. I used up every last drop of power in the crystal and vaporized the thing completely.

Mum got back not long afterwards. She doesn't like to use either healing magic or medicine for ordinary sickness; she thinks that being ill is part of life and you should usually just give your body rest and healthy food and respect the cycle, but in the hospital, they'd put her on an IV drip with antibiotics and she'd woken up in the middle of the night well enough to realize I was all on my own. By the time she rushed back

to the yurt, I was standing outside in a ring of little smolder-
ing flames. The metal of the scratcher had turned back into
liquid almost instantly and splattered out the entrance in a
long rectangle of muddy streaked metal that ran down the
hill like a gangway, long drips trickling away, and at all the
edges the molten metal had set the bracken on fire. I was
screaming down at the crowd of people who had finally come
after all, to keep the fire from spreading, and I was telling all
of them to go away, that I didn't care if they did all burn up, I
hoped they all died, all of them, and if anyone came near me
I'd set them on fire myself.

Mum shoved through them and took me inside. I was already as tall as she was, and she had to drag me away. She
spent a long time crying and holding me tight in her burning-
hot sweaty arms while I kicked and beat at her and fought to
get loose, until I finally gave up and burst into tears myself
and clung to her again. After I collapsed on the bed in exhaustion, she brewed a tea and made herself well, and she sang
me to sleep with a spell that made the whole thing feel like a
dream the next morning, not quite real.

But there was still a walkway outside our yurt made of
boiled scratcher. It was real, it all really happened, and it
didn't stop happening after that, because even at nine years
old, I was a good healthy snack for any hungry mal, and by
the end of the summer I turned fourteen, they were coming
at the rate of five a night. Mum wasn't looking plump and
pink anymore; the more fussy women around the commune
chided her for not getting enough rest and told me off for
being more trouble than I was worth, even though they didn't
know that I really was. When she asked to keep me out of the
Scholomance, what she was offering to do was let me watch
her get eaten before I got eaten myself.

So I don't get to be safe. I don't get to take a deep breath. I don't even get to lie to myself that after I get out of here, I'll be okay. I won't be okay, and Mum won't be okay if I stay with her, because the mals are going to keep coming for me, and people don't like me enough to help me even if I scream. So I don't bother to scream, but right then in the lunchroom I wanted to stand up on the table and scream at all of them the way I screamed at those bastards in the commune; I wanted to tell all of them I hated them and I'd set them all on fire gladly for five minutes of peace, and why shouldn't I, since they'd all stand by and watch me burn instead. I'd had that scream inside me since I was nine, knotted up with Mum's love, the only thing keeping it in, and it wasn't enough. Mum wasn't enough. She couldn't save me all on her own, not even she could do that, and for a few days of stupid pretending, I'd had other people, too, what I needed to survive, and that had been long enough for me to forget it wasn't real.

I was bent over my tray and my book, fighting not to scream, and out of the corner of my eye I could see Ibrahim sitting down with a couple of his friends and glancing over at me, and his mouth went happy for a moment. He was pleased that Orion had dumped me, and I'd asked for that, too, hadn't I? I'd asked for that smirk, because I'd told him off, only fuck him anyway. Sarah and Alfie were sitting down at a London table, carefully not even looking my way, as if I'd suddenly gone invisible.

And then Aadhya put her tray down across from me and sat down. I didn't get it for a second; I just stared at her stupidly, and she said, "Would you swap for milk? The lower tray was looking weird, I steered clear."

My throat was just shut up for a moment, choking around a solid knot like stale bread. Then I said, "Yeah, I've got spare," and held my second milk carton out to her.

"Thanks," she said, and gave me back a roll. Liu was sitting down next to me by then with a friend of hers from writing class. A couple of maintenance-track kids, English-and-Hindi-speakers from Delhi, sat down next to Aadhya, and they said a hello that didn't go out of its way to exclude me. I said hello back, and I sounded normal to my own ears, I don't know how, and a couple of the moderate-loser kids I didn't actually know, but whose table I had sat at last week—last week, had it been only one week?—were going by, and they hesitated and then tentatively came over and one said, "Taken?" pointing to the bench, and when I shook my head, they didn't slide in all the way towards me, they left some room, but they still sat down next to me. Nkoyo said, "Hey," as she went by with Cora and a couple of her other friends, on her way to another table.

I had to work hard to keep my hands from shaking while I ate the bread roll, carefully breaking it into small pieces and putting a thin scraping of cream cheese on each one. It wasn't that I didn't understand. This was exactly what I'd been aiming for when I'd made sure to ask Liu to sit with me, when I'd invited Aadhya to work on the mirror. I'd shown them I was reliable, that I'd share what good luck came my way with people who had thrown me a crumb, and now they were showing me they'd recognized it, and that they were willing to throw me more of those crumbs. And that was just good sense on their part, even without knowing that I was going equipped. It wasn't a miracle, it wasn't that they'd suddenly decided they liked me. I knew that. But I didn't want to scream anymore, I wanted to cry, like a new freshman dripping tears and snot into their food while everyone at their table pretends not to notice.

I managed to get through lunch without really embarrass-

ing myself. Aadhya asked if she could come by and look at
the mirror, and I told her she could, but I was pretty sure it
had come out cursed. "Oh, seriously?" she said.

"Yeah, sorry," I said. "It kept trying to tell me something
last night without my asking it anything." When an artifact
tries to do things for you on its own, that's a really good sign
that it doesn't have your best intentions at heart. Aadhya
knew as much, and she was looking annoyed, as well she
might, as that meant she'd nearly got killed helping me for
absolutely fuck-all. "I did get the sirenspider leg," I added; I'd
snagged it on my way out of the workshop, thinking of just
this moment. "D'you think you could get some use out of
it?"

"Yeah, that'd be great," Aadhya said, mollified: sirenspider
shells are really good for making magical instruments, if you
can figure out how to handle them, which she probably
could, with her affinity. We talked a bit about what she might
do with it, and I offered to do the incantations part for her,
too, which would make us even. Liu and I talked about our
final papers for history, as we're both in the honors track—no
one wants to be in honors classes unless they're going for
valedictorian; the school puts you in them against your will—
and we each had to write twenty pages on an ancient magical
civilization, but for a special vicious twist, one whose language we didn't know. We agreed on a swap: I'd do mine on
the two Zhou-dynasty enclaves and she'd do the Pratishthana
enclave, and we'd translate each other's primary sources.

We all paced our eating and cleared up our plates at the
same time, so nobody was left sitting on their own at the
table. I was still feeling weird and shaky inside when I went to
bus my tray. I was glad Ibrahim was right ahead of me: I
glared at the back of his head, thinking about his smirk. I

desperately wanted to be angry again, just a bit angry. But he glanced back at me as he walked away, and he didn't smirk; instead his face just fell. I stared back at him in confusion, and then Orion shoved his tray onto the rack just behind me and said, sounding irritated, "Hey, what was that about? Do you have a problem with Chloe and Magnus or something?" exactly like he'd expected me to come and sit with them.

Which he probably had. Who wouldn't sit at the New York table if they had the slightest chance; what kind of fool wouldn't take that over sitting on her own, wondering if anybody else was going to join her? "Oh, was I supposed to trot along behind you?" I snapped back. "Sorry, I didn't realize I'd attained hanger-on status; I imagined I'd have to genuflect properly first. You ought to have a badge or something to give out to people. You'd get to watch them fight over it and everything."

I felt just as mean as it sounded. Orion made a little half-twisting move away to stare at me, his face gone mad and surprised at the same time, blotchy on the cheeks under the greenish dots where he'd been spattered with something in his last lab session, probably. "Oh, go to hell," he said, a little thickly, and walked away from me fast, his shoulders hunched in.

There were about five different clusters of kids scattered between us and the doors, and they all turned towards him as he went past them, faces full of hope and calculation. Every single one of them running the same equations that were in my own head every single day, every single hour, and because they weren't stupidly stubborn morons, they were all happy to be nice to Orion Lake in exchange for getting to live; they *would* have fought over the chance to be his hangers-on. And he knew it, and instead he'd actually been making an effort to hang around with me, and if he wasn't waiting for me to turn maleficer anymore, that meant that what he wanted was—to hang out with somebody who wouldn't genuflect to him.

I hated the idea; it made him too much of a decent person, and what right did he have to be a decent person, on top of a monumentally stupid gigantic hero? But it was more or less the only thing that made sense. Just standing around in the cafeteria as everyone else pours out is a bad idea, but I did precisely that for almost a whole minute, staring after him with my fists balled up, because I was still out of my tree: angry with him, and with Chloe, and with every last person around me; I was even angry with Aadhya and Liu, because they'd made me want to cry just by deigning to sit with me.

Then I went after him. He had gone to the stairs like everyone else, but instead of going up to the library like everyone else, he was heading down, alone, to do work period in the alchemy lab or something, like a lunatic. Or like someone who'd rather be attacked by mals than be gushed at. I gritted my teeth, but there wasn't any help for it. I caught up to him halfway down the first flight. "Can I point out, not four days ago you accused me of being a serial killer," I said. "I'm *justified* in not grasping that you wanted me to sit with you for lunch."

He didn't look at me and hitched his rucksack higher up on his shoulder. "Sit wherever you want."

"I will," I said. "But as you mind so much, next time I'll tell you beforehand that I don't want to sit with your enclave mates."

He did look then, with a glare. "Why not?"

"Because they *do* want genuflection."

His shoulders were starting to stop hunching. "It's called *sitting down together,*" he said, dragging the words out exaggeratedly. "At a *table*. In *chairs*. Most people can get through lunch without turning it into an act of war."

"I'm not most people," I said. "Also, the seating arrangements *are* an act of war, and if you haven't noticed, that's just embarrassing. Do you think that everyone's always trying to sit with you for your amazing personality or something?"

"I guess you're just immune," he said.

" " I said, but he was grinning at me grown hair, tentatively, and appar-

Chapter 6
MANIFESTATION

I DON'T HAVE a very good idea of how people behave with their friends normally, because I'd never had one before, but on the bright side, Orion hadn't either, so he didn't know any more than I did. So for lack of a better idea we just went on being rude to each other, which was easy enough for me, and a refreshing and new experience for him, in both directions: being gracious to the little people had apparently been hammered into him from an early age. "I'd respond to that, but my mom's pretty big on manners," he said to me pointedly the next day after dinner as I yanked him away from the stairs down. I'd just told him he was a stupid wanker for trying to go and hide in the alchemy labs again.

"So is mine, but it didn't stick," I said, shoving him up the stairs to the library. "I don't care if you like sitting hunched alone at a lab table like a ghoul. I get enough near-death experiences in here without creating extra opportunities."

Unless you've got project work you have to do—and several friends watching your back—the library is always where you want to be: it's the safest place in the whole school. The bookcases just keep going up and up until they vanish into the same darkness that's outside our cells, so there's no place for mals to get in above. There's no plumbing on the library level at all; you have to go down to the cafeteria level if you need the loo. Even the air vents are smaller. It's musty and smells of old paper, but that's a trade-off we're all willing to accept. We'd spend every spare minute here, except there's not enough space in the reading room for everyone. Nobody gets into real fights very much in the Scholomance—it's just stupid—but enclaver groups will fight each other occasionally over a table or one of the prime reading areas with lumpy sofas big enough to kip on.

There are a handful of smaller reading rooms, up on the mezzanine level, but each of those is claimed by a consortium of two or three smaller enclaves, the ones that don't have enough firepower to claim a good section of the main reading room, but more than enough to keep out any outsiders who might want to intrude. Nkoyo gets invited to one up there fairly often, by the kids from Zanzibar and Johannesburg. If you're not invited, it's not worth going up there; on the rare occasion when no one's there, the first person who shows up—almost certainly with at least three tagalongs—will chase you, even if there's plenty of room. And for once that doesn't just mean *me*; they'll chase anyone, on principle: it's too important a resource not to police it.

The only other reasonably good place to work is one of the study carrels tucked in and around the stacks, and they don't always stay where they should. You can catch sight of one peering through a bookshelf, green lampshade like a beacon, and by the time you've got to the next aisle over, it's gone. If you do find one, and you settle in to work and then doze off over your books, you might wake up in a dim aisle full of crackling old scrolls and books in languages you can't even recognize, surrounded by dark, and good luck finding your way back before something finds you. The library is *safer*, not *safe*.

I've managed to claim one of them more or less, a scarred old monster of a desk that's probably been here as long as the school itself. It's tucked into a nook that you'd never see unless you go all the way to the end of the aisle with the Sanskrit incantations and then go around the back to the next aisle over, which has the Old English incantations. Almost no one would go that way, for good reason. The bookcases in between are full of crumbling scrolls and carved-stone tablets in some parent language so ancient that nobody knows it anymore. If you happened to look too long at a sliver of papyrus while going past, the school might decide you were now studying that language, and good luck figuring out the spells you'd get then. People can end up spell-choked that way: you get a dozen spells in a row that you can't learn well enough to cast, and suddenly you can't skip over them anymore to learn any new ones, even if you trade for them. Then the spells you've already learned are all you've got for the rest of your life. It's not really a silver lining that the rest of your life isn't likely to be very long if you're stuck working with sophomore-year spells. On top of that, the path goes underneath one of the walkways that connect the mezzanine-level areas, so a good chunk of it sits in the dark.

And that's where I found my desk. I risked the shortcut last year because I made up a special project for myself: analyzing the commonalities between spells of binding and coercion in Sanskrit, Hindi, Marathi, Old English, and Middle English. I know, charming subject, but perfectly aligned with my affinity, and it let me out of taking a final exam for languages at all. Otherwise, I'd have had five hours in a classroom full of other delicious sophomores who'd have made sure I was the one sitting in the very worst spot. The topic also near-guaranteed that I'll be assigned the Proto-Indo-European seminar next year, which always has at least ten students in it, a good healthy size for a senior languages-track seminar. But you do need a reference or two, or more accurately fifty, to get a passing mark on a project like that. Just collecting up the books from each language was going to take me a good half hour of my every work period.

I couldn't just keep them—or rather, I could; I could hide them in a dark corner or take them back to my room or set them on fire; there's no one here to stop you at the door or charge you late fees. But if you're even a little careless with a library book, it'll be gone the next time you want it, and good luck finding it on the shelves ever again. So I reshelve every time, and I have a pocket notebook I've been carrying since freshman year with the title and catalog number of every book I've used, a note about which aisle it was in, how many bookcases from the end, which shelf from the floor, how many books on either side on the shelf, and the titles of the immediate neighbors. The really valuable ones, I even do a sketch of the spine in colored pencil. Thanks to that, I can lay my hands on almost any of them, and next year I'll probably be able to sell the notebook off to a younger languages-track student right before graduation in exchange for some mana. That's the value of making loads of work for yourself.

But before I found my desk, what that meant was, anytime I had to do a paper, each day after an abbreviated lunch I dashed up here, got the books I needed, hauled them all downstairs to an empty classroom, got forty minutes of work done, hauled them back up and reshelved, and did the same thing all over again to get two hours of work done after dinner. I couldn't get a place in the reading room to save my life, even at the lousy tables in the dark corners where you have to spend your own mana to cast a light.

That was hard going for a single-subject paper where all the books were in one aisle if not in one shelf. Slogging down to Sanskrit, then all the way back through all the modern Indian languages to the main incantations aisle, and *then* going all the way to Old English, every single time I had to get some work done on the paper, would've been *too* much work. Instead I took the gamble and went round the back. As a reward, I found my desk. Yes, it's underneath the walkway, but it's got a light of its own that takes only a tiny drop of mana to start, and apart from that it's properly tidy: solid wood with a wide flat top, heavy carved legs with open sides, no drawers, no hiding places for mals to lurk in. And it's more than big enough for two. I've just never had anyone to invite.

Orion had always avoided the library like the plague, for what turned out to be the opposite reason: the moment we came into the reading room, half of the heads came up—the half facing the door—and started to smile invitations. You could just see everyone looking round at the other kids at their tables, mentally picking off the two weakest to open up a pair of seats. His shoulders hunched up. I didn't blame him for not liking it, but I gave him a hard shove on the back for being such a drip. "Stop looking like someone's about to bite your head off. I promise I'll protect you," I added, which I meant as a joke, except after we went into the stacks, three separate people tried to casually follow us, and I really did have to turn round and tell them off for being creepers. He didn't do anything about it himself.

"I'm not going to be your personal bouncer," I told him when we finally got rid of the third one, a girl who didn't quite make it all the way to suggesting that Orion might have even more fun in the dark recesses of the stacks with two girls instead of just one—obviously the only reason he could possibly want to hang out in the library with *me*—but only because I cut her off before she got that far. "You can be rude to your groupies for yourself."

"But you're so good at it," he said, and then, "No, I'm sorry, I just . . ." He trailed off, and then he said, "Luisa asked me. Three days before . . ." He stopped.

"Before Jack did for her," I supplied. He nodded. "So since then you've decided that you're under a moral obligation to bestow your magnificent favors on anyone who asks? I don't know where you're finding the time."

"No!" He glared at me. "Just, I got mad and shoved her off, and then she was dead, and I didn't even know how. And I thought that when it happened, maybe she thought I didn't come, I let whatever it was get her, because I was still mad. I know it's stupid," he added. And it *was* stupid, mainly because he was blaming himself for the completely wrong thing. Which was quite obvious to me, and he noticed. "What?" he said belligerently.

I could have considered not telling him. I suppose that would've been a kind thing to do. Instead I said, "She died because after you wouldn't go for it, she looked for somebody else who would, and Jack took her up on it." He stared at me appalled. "He would've needed some kind of consent to get power out of another wizard. Most maleficers do."

Orion looked vaguely sick. He didn't talk for the rest of the way to my desk. Nobody else popped up to bother us, and the walk was a lot shorter than usual. Normally I have to stop and read the book spines every three shelves just to make ostentatiously sure that I'm moving in the right direction, and to check the lights. That's another trick the school loves. There isn't any overhead to put a lamp on, so the aisles are lit up with glowing wispy mana lights that float around. They'll grudgingly help you read the book spines, even bob along if you fly up a shelf—or climb up it, for those of us who don't have mana to waste on floating around like giant ponces—but if you aren't actively using them, they'll go dim so carefully that you don't notice until they're about to wink out, and then you have to cast your own light, because they *will* go out if you keep going, even if you turn around. But with Orion walking alongside me, they all stayed bright enough around us that I could just glance over once in a while, to make sure we were still going in the right direction.

There was even a second chair waiting for him at my desk. Orion sat down without a first—much less a second—glance and immediately started unpacking his bag. I kicked his chair and made him help me look through the shelves at our backs and shine a light up and down the walls of the nook and over the legs of the desk and pull it away from the wall and push it back. "Okay, seriously, we're in the library," he said finally, sounding exasperated.

"I'm sorry, am I boring you with my basic precautions?" I said. "We're not all invulnerable heroes."

"Yeah, but that doesn't mean you have to be crazy paranoid, either," he said. "Come on, how many times have you gotten jumped?"

"In the last week? Do I get to count the maleficer you sicced on me?" I said, folding my arms.

"Until the end of time, obviously." He rolled his eyes. "How many times have you gotten jumped before that? Five? Six?"

I stared at him. "A *week*, maybe."

He stared back at me. "Huh?"

"I get jumped twice a week, if I'm careful," I said. "If I wasn't careful, I'd be getting jumped five times as often. I'm the class tiramisu, you spanner. The loser with a tidy bucket of mana that has to spend all her time alone. And even if I wasn't, most people get jumped once a month at least."

"They do *not*," he said, positively.

"They really do," I said.

He pulled up his sleeve to show me a piece of artifice on his wrist, a round medallion on a leather strap that looked enough like a watch to slip by at a first glance. He could have exposed it on any crowded street full of mundanes and nobody would have blinked. Then he popped it open, and it even was a watch, except through several tiny round windows cut out of the face, you could see into the interior where at least six layers of minuscule gears were turning, each in different metals, shifting through different glows of green and blue and violet. "I get buzzed if anyone from the enclave is in trouble, and there are eleven other kids from New York in this place right now."

"Oh, fine, enclave kids don't get jumped once a month," I said. "Rank and power hath their privileges. I'm shocked. Is that what you all use for power-sharing?" I peered at it as he snapped it shut again: the lid had an elaborate engraving of a cast-iron park gate with a starburst behind it, the letters *NY* looped in calligraphic script around it.

"You think the maleficaria can tell?" he said. "You think they care?"

"I think they go for the lowest-hanging fruit on the vine, and it's never one of you. Your mate Chloe has friends who offer to taste her food and get her supplies. When she does a project, she can get help for the asking from the best students in the place, and she doesn't have to help them in return. She probably has two kids walk her back to her room at night, when she finally leaves her permanently reserved place on the sofa in there." I jerked my chin towards the reading room.

"You've got power-sharers and probably—" I reached for the bottom of his shirt and lifted it up over the buckle of his belt, which—you guessed it—was absolutely a top-notch shield holder, like the ones Aadhya was making, only by comparison hers were the equivalent of a *Blue Peter* craft project done by a five-year-old.

He made a little hop with a squawk, grabbing for my hand like he thought I was making a move on him, but I was already dropping the shirt again. I snorted and flicked my fingers up towards his face to make him jump back again. "In your dreams, rich boy. I'm not one of your groupies."

"Yeah, I didn't notice," he said, even though he was blushing at the same time.

I settled down to my history paper, and the translations I was going to do for Liu's. I'm pretty locked-in when I work, and I didn't pay a lot of attention to Orion once I got going. Especially since I couldn't even cut down on the number of perimeter checks I normally do. *He* wasn't doing any. I stopped after I finished my outline and the first translation and got up to stretch: letting yourself go stiff in a chair is another bad idea. That was when I noticed he was just sitting there staring at the same page of his lab assignment. "What?"

"You really think other kids get jumped a lot more?" he said abruptly, like he'd been stewing over it the whole time.

"You aren't that bright, are you," I said, speaking from downward-dog position. "Why do you think people want to be in enclaves in the first place?"

"That's outside," he said. "We're all in here together. Everyone has the same chances—"

He turned around to look at me halfway through that sentence, at which point my upside-down stare knocked him off track and he listened to the regurgitated rubbish coming out of his own mouth. He stopped and looked unhappy again, as he deserved to. I gave him the snort he'd earned as I got up and started planking. "Right. So Luisa had the same chances as Chloe."

"Luisa was screwed!" Orion said. "She didn't know anything, she wasn't prepared for any of it. That's why I was looking out for her so much. It's not the same thing."

"Fine. You think *I* have the same chances as Chloe?"

He couldn't sell that to himself, either, and it obviously pissed him off. He looked away and said, "You're screwing up your chances all on your own."

I stood up and said, "Fuck off, then, and get away from me," my throat knotted-up around it.

He just gave a huff without even looking back at me, like he thought I was joking. "Yeah, see, like that. You'll barely talk to me and I've saved your life five times."

"*Six* times," I said.

"Whatever," he said. "Do you know that literally everybody I know has tried to tell me the last three days that I need to watch out for you because you're a maleficer? You act like one."

"I don't!" I said. "*Jack* acted like a maleficer. Maleficers are *nice to you.*"

"Okay, no one's going to accuse you of that." He bent back over his books, still frowning; he hadn't even realized I was about to punch him in the head. And I still wanted to punch him in the head, and I wanted to shout at him that I didn't have to do anything to make people assume I was evil, I never had, except—*he* hadn't assumed it. He'd only ever thought I was a maleficer when I'd given him a really good solid reason, and more to the point he was there sitting at my desk talking to me like I was a person, and I didn't want that to stop. So instead of punching him in the head, I just finished my sun salutation and then I went back to the desk and got on with my paper.

When the warning bell went off for curfew and we finally packed up, he said tentatively, "Want to come back after breakfast tomorrow?"

"Some of us can't afford to outsource our maintenance shifts," I said, but the anger had gone. "Who's doing yours?"

"I don't have one," he said, with perfect sincerity, and only looked puzzled when I gave him a look. We've all got maintenance shifts, one a week; not even being the future Domina's son from New York gets you out of being assigned. It only gets you out of doing it yourself. Enclavers generally club together in groups of ten and trade all their maintenance shifts to one kid in exchange for the promise that the kid gets to join one of their alliances at graduation time. We call that maintenance track, even though it's strictly unofficial, and it's one of the most reliable ways to get into an enclave after graduation. They're happy to let in anyone who's willing to literally do the shit work, and maintenance-track kids come out with practical experience in patching up the same kind of infrastructure that the big enclaves use.

But it's also one of the best ways to die. Maintenance-track kids end up skipping around half their lessons, so they're always on the razor's edge of failing dangerously, and they miss out on a lot of theory and advanced spells. More to the point, they're the ones who have to go into the rooms with the mysterious holes in the walls, the leaking pipes, the burned-out lights; the places where the wards are wobbly and the mals are more likely to wriggle in. And you can't sign up for maintenance track and then just skip your shifts. If you don't adequately complete your maintenance shift within the week it's due, you aren't allowed into the cafeteria again until it's done.

And if you don't do someone else's maintenance shift that you've promised to do, *they* don't get to go into the cafeteria, so enclavers keep a sharp eye on their little helpers. Most enclavers, anyway.

"Someone else from New York made the arrangements for you, didn't they, and you don't even know," I said. "That's sad, Lake. At least say thank you once in a while to the poor kid." Poor kid, ha. I'd have gone for maintenance track myself in a flash: I've already got a massive target stuck on my back. But actually the competition for it is quite stiff, and I had to give up in the first fortnight because I couldn't find an enclaver to hire me. They wouldn't even talk to me, so I didn't have much opportunity to suck up to them. To be fair, opportunity clearly wasn't my only hurdle there.

He flushed. "What are you doing for your shift?"

"Cleaning the labs," I said. Alchemy lab cleaning shifts are lousy the way any maintenance shift is lousy, but it's nothing like as bad as trying to patch a hole in a wall or mend a warding spell. Once, I had to fix a fraying ward over an air vent in one of the seminar rooms, close to the shop. The protection had worn so thin that there was literally a pack of scuttlers waiting to come through. They'd pressed the frontmost ones right squish up against it: five or six pairs of round lemur eyes staring at me full of hungry longing, drooling from their mouths full of needle-teeth. I finally got fed up and wasted a bit of mana to physically shove them back into the vent far enough so that I didn't have to look at them until I had woven the new barrier spell into place.

Cleaning's not nearly as dangerous, even in the labs. There might be a bit of acid or contact poison or some iffy alchemical substance left behind, but that's not hard to catch. Most kids don't bother, they just fill a bucket of soapy water, slap an animation spell on some rags and a mop, shove them in, and keep watch on the process from the door. But unless I'm really knackered, I do it all by hand. In the commune we all did upkeep on a rota, and my mum wouldn't let me use magic, so I know my way around a mop and bucket. I was aggrieved at the time. Now it means I actually get some mana out of the deal instead of the reverse, and I've occasionally found some usable supplies among the leftovers. It's still not a magical good time, though.

"I'll come with," Orion said.

"You'll what?" I said, and laughed when he wasn't joking: everyone would really think he was in love. "Don't let me stop you."

HIS HELP MADE short work of my shift, and we spent the rest of the weekend in the library together. I have to admit I took a lot of petty and objectively stupid satisfaction from the way the New York crew all eyed me anxiously every time we walked past their corner in the reading room, to and from meals. I knew better. I should have been chumming up with all of them. I wasn't dating Orion, but he really was my friend; that wasn't just a temporary illusion. I had an actual in at New York. If they took me in, I wouldn't need to worry about finding any other allies. I could pop on one of those power-sharers and glide all the way to the gates and right on through like I was on ice skates. I wouldn't even need to grovel, I suspected, just make myself decently polite.

But I didn't. I didn't encourage any of the enclaver kids who kept trying to make up to me; I just cold-shouldered them all. I wasn't subtle about it, either. On Saturday night, on our way to brushing our teeth, Aadhya actually said to me, tentatively, "El, have you got some kind of a plan going?"

I instantly knew what she meant. But I didn't say anything;

I didn't want to be talked sensibly out of my stupid behavior. After a pause, Aadhya said, "It is what it is. I was really popular at school outside. Soccer and gymnastics, a million friends. But my mom sat me down a year before induction and told me I was going to be a loser in here. She didn't say it like, be ready if that happens. She just told me flat-out."

"You aren't a loser," I said.

"Yeah, I am. I'm a loser because I have to think about it all the time: how am I getting out of here? We have one year left, El. You know what graduation is going to be like. The enclave kids are going to pick and choose from the best of us. They'll hand out shields and power-sharers, and cast a time-spear or light up a kettler and zoom right out the gates, and the mals will come for everybody else. We don't want to be *everybody else* in that scenario. Anyway, what are you going to do after? Go live in a hut in the Rockies?"

"A yurt in Wales," I muttered, but she was right, obviously. It was everything I'd planned on, in fact, with one crucial exception. "They don't want me, Aadhya. They want Orion."

"So what? Use it while you can," Aadhya said. "Look, I'm only saying any of this because you've done me a solid, and I think you're smart enough to hear it, so don't get mad: you know you turn people off."

"But not you?" I said, trying to sound cool about it, when I didn't feel cool at all.

"I wasn't immune or anything," she said. "But my mom also told me to be polite to rejects, because it's stupid to close doors, and suspicious of people who are too nice, because they want more from you than they're letting on. And she was right. Jacky W turns out to be Hannibal Lecter, and you turn out to be so hardcore you'd ditch New York and London to stick with me just because I didn't *completely* rip you off trading." She shrugged.

We were at the bathroom by then, so we couldn't talk anymore: I seethed the whole way through brushing my teeth and washing my face and keeping watch for Aadhya's turn. But on the way back, I burst out, "Just—why? What have I ever done that turns people off?"

I waited for her to say all the usual things: *You're rude, you're cold, you're mean, you're angry,* all the things people say to make it my fault, but she looked over at me and frowned like she was really thinking about it, and then she said with decision, "You feel like it's going to rain."

"What?"

But Aadhya was already waving her hands around and elaborating. "You know that feeling when you're a mile away from anywhere, and you didn't take your umbrella because it was sunny when you left, and you're in your good suede boots, and suddenly it gets dark and you can tell it's about to start pouring buckets, and you're like *Oh great.*" She nodded to herself, satisfied with her brilliant analogy. "That's what it feels like, whenever you show up." She paused and glanced back behind us, making sure there wasn't anyone in earshot, and then said to me abruptly, "You know, if you cheat a little too much, it can mess up your vibe. I know a kid in alchemy track who has a really good spirit cleanse recipe—"

"I *don't* cheat," I said through my teeth. "I've *never* cheated."

She gave me a dubious look. "For serious?"

So that was really helpful. Of course, it should have been. Aadhya was one hundred percent correct, and I should've listened to her and parlayed my one week of not-dating Orion into the outright invitation to join at least three separate enclaves that I could have got for the asking right then and there, setting myself up for half a dozen more to come during each further week we kept not-dating. Because I *feel like rain.*

But instead what I did the very next morning was say, "Sorry, I'm busy," with immense coldness when Sarah invited me to swap spells with her Sunday Welsh revision group. Full of UK enclave kids, each with an inherited spellbook crammed with top-notch and thoroughly tested spells, all the more valuable because the language is completely phonetic: just about anyone who can get through the full name of Llanfairpwllgwyngyll—that isn't, by the way, the full name—can pick up most of the spells without even knowing what all the words are, so you get all the benefits of a rarer language, with a bigger trading group. My own Welsh is quite solid, thanks to good old Ysgol Uwchradd Aberteifi, although I never got to use it outside of lessons. Anytime I walked into shops or the pub, they'd switch to English to talk to me without even thinking, and sometimes keep on even if I spoke Welsh back. Sarah sounded a bit dubious asking herself: "I heard you grew up in Wales, I thought perhaps," was how she phrased it. Oh, and she wanted to do this at their table in the library, after breakfast, and of course I was completely welcome to *bring a friend.*

"I don't mind," Orion actually said to me as we sat down with our trays; he'd overheard.

"I *do*," I snarled at him viciously, and if he'd said another patronizing word I'd probably have tipped my porridge over his head, but instead he went all red and stared down at his tray hard and visibly swallowed, looking on the outside roughly the way I'd felt on the inside when Aadhya had sat down with me. Like it was exactly as new an experience for him, somebody who didn't want to use him to the last drop. I nearly upended my porridge over his head anyway, but instead I ground my teeth and just shared the jug of cream I'd scrounged that morning, half full.

So the end result was, I was just as knee-deep in it as I'd

been a week ago when he'd white-knighted into my bed-room, if not worse. Apparently I wasn't going to actually use his friendship to get anywhere, and he was going to be worse than useless as help himself: it was already blindingly obvious to me that he was going to be the last one out of the gates on graduation day. Meanwhile I was well on the way to success-fully making myself violently, instead of just modestly, hate-ful to every enclave kid in the place, probably before the end of term at my current pace. And while Aadhya and Liu and Nkoyo might not actively avoid me anymore, they weren't going to choose me over survival. The alliances were going to begin forming up next year in earnest, and all three of them were sure to get scooped up early by one group of en-clavers or another. For all Aadhya wants to talk about being a loser, she has a well-polished reputation; they all do. Mine started out grimy and was in the process of being covered in the slop of my own stupid pride.

But fine: since I didn't have the self-restraint to swallow it and just make a smarmy git of myself for long enough to save my own life, the obvious answer was I had to find a way to let everyone in on the amount of power I had. Then some people would want me for myself, and then maybe I'd stop sabotaging every possible alliance offer I could get.

Anyway that's been my plan all along, to sacrifice a few crystals and establish my reputation somehow, and now was the time for it, since maleficaria activity drops off quite a bit after graduation. Loads of mals down below get killed off by the escaping seniors or eaten by each other in the feeding frenzy, and the rest are well fed and busy finding quiet cor-ners in which to make lots of little baby mals. And up here, the pest control has wiped out most of the ones living among us. The builders knew that *some* mals would wriggle their way up to us, so twice a year the halls get a good scouring. A very loud warning bell goes, we all run for our dormitory cells, shut ourselves in, and barricade our doors as thoroughly as we can. Then massive cleansing walls of mortal flame get conjured up and sent running on their merry way throughout the whole building, from top to bottom, incinerating hordes of desperate fleeing mals. It also helps warm up the machinery at graduation time, just before the dorms all rotate down to their new places.

If you're wondering why they don't also run this excellent system down in the graduation hall to clear out the mals before dumping in the seniors, the answer is they meant to, but the machinery down there has been broken since about five minutes after the school opened. No one's going down to the graduation hall to do maintenance.

Anyway, that's why induction happens literally the evening after graduation: it's the safest day of the year in the Scholomance, and the place stays relatively quiet for a good month or two afterwards. So if I can't dredge up a decent excuse for blowing a lot of power by then—like a soul-eater, not that I'm nursing a lingering bitterness or anything—I'm not going to get a better one until the end of the first quarter, and by then loads of alliances will have been formed.

I hardly got any work done the whole morning. The Zhou enclaves, which destroyed each other about three thousand years ago, had a hard time competing in my brain with the very compelling question of what I ought to do to show off. I could just make a scene in the cafeteria some morning and disintegrate a row of tables, but I writhed at the idea of wasting mana like that, and just throwing it away would make me look more than a bit thick. Or worse, people might get the idea that I had absurd amounts of power available to throw away, which I wouldn't except if I was, you guessed it, a maleficer. And they all wanted to believe that anyway.

I gave up on my own paper and started doing the translations I owed Liu for hers instead. The only Sanskrit dictionary on the shelf today was the monstrous six-kilo one, but at least slogging through its pages was mechanical, and left a considerable portion of my brain able to keep worrying the problem. I decided I'd set myself a deadline to come up with something by the end of next week. Otherwise, I'd just pretend I'd been startled by something, maybe in shop class where Aadhya would see—

My train of thought got interrupted just then as Orion turned his head to look behind us, and I realized that was the third time he'd done it. I hadn't really noticed before because that's a normal thing to do; I glance over my shoulder probably once every five minutes, automatically. But it wasn't normal for him, and before I could ask what he'd picked up on, he was up from the table, just leaving all his books and everything, and running back into the stacks towards the reading room. "What the hell, Lake!" I yelled after him, but he was already going.

I could have chased after him quickly enough to catch up, maybe, except then I'd've been running towards whatever it was at top speed, and undoubtedly the whatever was really dangerous. If he was already too far ahead, the aisles could just stretch enough to keep me from catching up, and then I'd be running full-tilt in the dark stacks all alone, which is just as brilliant an idea as it sounds.

I could also have stayed parked at the desk, except then I still wouldn't know what the whatever was, and if something really bad had made it into the library, it could just as easily flee from Orion and come for me. Anyway, I'd been looking for an excuse to show off: what more could I ask for? Taking out something big in the reading room would be a great one, as long as Orion didn't kill it before I got there. Maybe I could even save *him*.

Filled with all the hazy glory of that vision, I got up and went after him, though at a healthily cautious pace. As soon as I got into the Sanskrit aisle again, I heard the alluring song that had called him: faint screams, traveling from the reading room. I couldn't tell what was instigating the screaming, but the sheer number of voices suggested it had to be something impressive. I'd been wise to go slowly, though: I was barely in the Vedic era and Orion was already rounding the corner into the main incantations aisle far ahead, disappearing out of sight again, and the lights were dimming on his heels, making a long dark stretch of aisle ahead of me.

I stayed focused on the spine labels and stuck to my deliberate pace, the best way to keep the library from playing any tricks on me. But the aisle was already being unreasonably slow and grudging, and then it got worse: I was looking for familiar books, as landmarks, and I caught sight of two entries from my little catalog, written by the same author in the same decade, with an entire bookcase between them. I had to start deliberately reading the last label on every row out loud and letting my fingers bang into the end of each shelf to force it to let me make any real progress.

Which was extremely odd, because I could hear the screaming from the reading room getting louder. Flashes of red and violet light were appearing at the distant end of the aisle: that was Orion's combat magic going, which I was starting to be able to recognize just by the rhythm of the spell bursts. There was clearly a huge fight in the offing. Normally the school is more than happy to dump you into a mess like that if you're stupid enough to go *towards* it. Unless, it occurred to me, the maleficaria in question had a real chance of taking Orion out. I was going towards the reading room with the intent to help him, after all, and in magic, intentions matter. Of course the school would have liked to be rid of him, seeing how he's been throwing off the balance and starving the place.

I didn't like that idea at all, and I even more didn't like how much I didn't like it. Getting attached to anyone in here except on practical terms is like sending out an engraved invitation to misery, even if you don't pick out an idiot who spends all his time hurling himself into danger. But it was too late. I already didn't like it enough that I had to make a special effort to stop myself from stupidly breaking into a run. I forced myself to slow down even more instead and actively look at every single thing on the shelves. That's contrary to instinct, but it's the best way to force the library to let you get through. If an aisle is taking longer to walk, there have to be more bookcases on the same subject, and the more books the library has to dredge up out of the void to fill them. If you're going slow enough to look at all the spines, you're almost sure to find a really valuable and rare spellbook among them. So the school is almost sure to let you make progress instead.

Except what actually happened was that scads of unfamiliar books and manuscripts started appearing on the shelves. Many with numbers that I'd never seen before, and I've spent a lot of time in the Sanskrit aisle the last two years. Some of the numbers were weirdly gigantic, meaning they'd been cataloged really early on and hadn't been relabeled since. The school *really* didn't want me getting to the end of the aisle. I narrowed my eyes and looked even harder, and three shelves onward, I caught a gleam of gold off the spine of a thin volume, almost completely hidden between two heaped stacks of palm-leaf manuscripts, on a high shelf just at the limit of my arm's reach, with no label at all.

No labels means a book that has been freshly pulled from the void, never on the shelf before at all, which means it's valuable enough to hide really aggressively. And a book stuffed among palm-leaf manuscripts meant spells valuable enough that someone had copied it, centuries later, and in this case also bothered to gild the cover. I first noticed the book peeking out while I was two steps away, didn't take my eyes off it for a second as I got closer, and then I grabbed the edge of the shelf with one hand, jumped, and snagged it off. I could practically feel the whole bookcase lurch under me with resentment as I came down. I wasn't stupid enough to try and look inside, which would have made it subject to collection. I kept looking straight ahead down the aisle and got it stuffed into my bookbag without even breaking stride. But I could tell just from my fingers sliding over the cover that it was really properly good. It wasn't just the spine that was gilt, there was some sort of stamped pattern all over, and a folded-over flap to keep it closed.

The aisle did start to move quicker after that. I indulged in feeling smug for a moment, as if I'd beaten the library; I'd made it hand me something good and now it was going to have to let me go, since it didn't want me collecting any more prizes. And it didn't, of course, but I was still being an idiot. You don't ever get anything in here without paying for it. Ever.

I moved at speed through the more modern languages, until at last I got close enough that in the next flash of Orion's magic, the library couldn't keep me from getting a glimpse of the distance between me and the main incantations aisle, and I burst into a quick sprint that got me close enough I could still see the end of the aisle even after the spell-light had faded. It had taken me at least twice as long to get there as Orion. The screams were louder, and other noises too: a high-pitched shrilling, vaguely birdlike, and then a lower snarling became audible as I rounded into the main aisle. After a couple of cautious steps further on, a third sound came, like the wind whistling through dead leaves on an early-winter day.

The first two sounds could possibly have gone together. You get all sorts of ridiculous cross-breeds in the bestial or hybrid category, mals created when some excessively clever alchemist stuck together two incompatible creatures for fun and profit—if by profit you mean eventually getting eaten by your own creations, which seems to happen to almost every maleficer who goes off on that particular tangent. Crossing a wolf with a flock of sparrows might sound stupid, but it's not even unlikely. But the third sound was completely out. It wasn't precisely like the manifestation that Mum put down on Bardsey Island during the summer that she dragged me the whole width of Wales on foot along the old pilgrim way, that one had sounded more like bells ringing, but it was close enough to be unmistakable.

If a manifestation had somehow formed inside the school, the library was just the sort of place it would like. But I was surprised it had popped into the reading room. Why not stay in the nice dark stacks where it had probably been feeding off the occasional lost student for ages? And why at the same moment as something else—*two* something elses, I mentally amended, because the shrilling and the snarling were now clearly coming from different parts of the reading room, too far apart for separate heads on one creature. That made no sense, and even less after I heard Orion shout, "Magnus! Put down a slickshield!" Those are only useful against the oozes, which don't make any sound at all except squelching. That made *four* mals in the library, all at once. It would be like a pre-graduation party going in there.

And if Magnus was still in there casting defensive spells instead of running the hell away, that meant that one of the mals was keeping at least the New York corner and therefore also a heap of other kids from getting out. It was the most perfect gift-wrapped opportunity to show off that I could possibly have asked for. The main aisle was even lit the whole way down to the reading room like an airport runway.

I didn't charge down the aisle and throw myself into the beautifully visible fray. I'd been a little slow on the uptake about the book, but I'm never that slow. The library had wanted to keep me in the Sanskrit aisle, but now it wanted me in the reading room. That meant it wasn't trying to stop me saving Orion. It just didn't want me in *this* aisle. And it wanted me out of here so badly, it was even holding out everything I'd been sitting in the nook dreaming about, wanting.

So I stopped instead, right there in the corridor, and then I turned around and looked into the dark behind me.

The library air vents are in the aisles, old tarnished brass gratings set in the floor. Their edges catch the light when you're walking in the library, thin gleaming lines reflecting even when the lights are dim. I couldn't see the one that should have been behind me. I couldn't hear the annoying grate of the old grimy fans, or even the omnipresent rustle and scrape of pages shifting: as if even the books on the shelves had gone still, like sparrows when a hawk is circling. The background noise wasn't just being drowned out by the noise of the fighting behind me. I held my own breath to listen, and I heard faintly the sound of many other people breathing, soft and dark and heavy. The lights overhead were out completely, but Orion's next spell-burst was coming, another flash of light. My whole body was clenched and waiting for it, and in the next flare of deep-red light I met half a dozen human eyes watching me, scattered over the thick rolling folds of the translucent, glossy mass that was just bulging its way out of the vent, many mouths open and working for air.

Because I usually have to sit in the front rows of Maleficaria Studies, I have an especially good view of the graduation day mural centerpiece, featuring the two gigantic maw-mouths who have pride of place on either side of the gates. They're the only mals that have names: ages ago some New York enclavers started calling them Patience and Fortitude, and it stuck. They remain purely decorative, though; we don't study maw-mouths in here. There's no point. There isn't any way to stop a maw-mouth killing you. If you get out the gates quickly enough, they don't get you. Or if something else kills you first. That's the only practical advice the textbook offered about them: if you've got a choice, take the something else. But once they've got you, even a little curl of a tentacle around your ankle, you're not getting away. Not on your own.

The flaring light of Orion's spell went out behind me, and I stood there staring into the blind darkness until the next one came, a long firecracker burst of bright greens and blues. The maw-mouth was still there. It blinked back at me with some of its borrowed eyes: brown eyes in a lot of shades and shapes, occasional blue eyes and green eyes, gliding gently in opposite directions or alongside each other over the surface as it kept flowing up and out of the vent, some of them getting buried and others rolling out into the light, pupils contracting in the brightness. Some of them had wide staring expressions, others blinked rapidly, others looked glazed and dull. The half page on maw-mouths in the sophomore-year textbook also informed us in clinical prose that no one is certain what happens to those consumed by maw-mouths, and there is a substantial school of thought that believes their consciousness never actually ends and they just get exhausted into silence. For further reading, see the seminal literature by Abernathy, Kordin, and Li in the *Journal of Maleficaria Studies*, who discovered that it was possible to direct a communications spell to even a long-digested maw-mouth victim and receive back a response, albeit nothing but incoherent screaming.

I made Mum tell me how Dad died when I was nine. She didn't want to. Before then, she just said, "I'm sorry, love, I can't. I can't talk about it." But the morning after the scratcher, sitting huddled in bed with my arms around my already knobbly knees, staring at the streaked-metal walkway made out of the first hungry thing that had come out of the dark for me, I said, "Don't tell me you can't talk about it. I want to know." So Mum told me, and then she spent the rest of the day crying, in deep gulps, while she went round doing her rituals and putting things away and cooking, barefoot the way she almost always was. I could see the ring of tiny pockmarked scars around her ankle, the familiar ring. I'd liked it before; it fascinated me. I'd always try to touch it when I saw it when I was little, and I'd asked Mum about it a lot more often than I asked her about what happened to Dad. She'd always pushed off that question, too, but I hadn't realized it was the same question.

The one and only way to stop a maw-mouth is to give it indigestion. If you rush into the maw-mouth on your own, with a powerful enough shield, then you have a chance to get inside before it can start eating you. In theory, if you manage to reach the core, you can burst it apart from there. But mostly people don't get that far; there're only three known cases where that's ever been done, and by a circle of wizards. The only realistic goal for a single wizard is to distract it.

That's all Dad did. He grabbed the tentacle and pulled it away from Mum, back into the mass of the maw-mouth. He had time to turn around and tell her he loved her and loved me, the baby they'd only just realized was on the way, and then the maw-mouth got through his shield and swallowed him up.

Maybe it had even been this one. I knew it hadn't been Patience or Fortitude. Those two are so big, they don't move around anymore at all, and they rarely eat students except by accident. They spend graduation day eating up any other maw-mouths that unwarily come in reach of their tentacles, and the biggest other maleficaria. This one was clearly more energetic. There's never been a maw-mouth in the actual halls of the school before. As far as I know, of course, but they're not the kind of maleficaria where nobody escapes to tell the tale. You have lots of warning from the people screaming and thrashing as they're being swallowed. But the ones in the school have always been happy to wait down below for the annual feast.

The next flare came from the reading room as the maw-mouth finished pulling the last bit of itself out of the vent, the mass briefly keeping the boxy shape it had been squashed into, before it softened back into blob. It just sat there, its silent mouths working, taking long deep breaths, as if it was recovering from the massive effort of getting up here to hunt. I didn't run; I didn't need to. Even small maw-mouths don't eat one at a time. If it gobbled me up, it would have to sit here digesting before it moved again, and in the meantime everyone else would clear out. That was why the library had been trying to keep me away: so I wouldn't give a warning. It wanted to give the maw-mouth a good sporting chance to eat not just Orion, but everyone in the reading room. Not to mention those four powerful maleficaria that had probably come up here running away from *the maw-mouth in the first place.*

I took the first slow, careful step backwards in the dark, towards the reading room. And then another after that as Orion's next spell went off behind me, and then the maw-mouth let out a deep sighing from all its mouths and was moving—*away.* I froze, wondering if I'd seen wrong, but Orion had just cast some variety of a prisoning-dome spell, and the neon-pink glow lingered, reflecting off the glossy folds as the maw-mouth went rolling over itself with a sudden startling speed, eyes and whispering mouths coming up and going back under in waves.

It wasn't going for the reading room. It was going the other way, straight for the stairway at the end of the aisle, the one that went down from the library to the freshman dorms. Where all the youngest kids would be holed up in their rooms right now, all the ones who didn't have an enclave to get them in at one of the safe tables in the reading room, doing their homework in pairs and crowded trios. The maw-mouth would stretch itself out along the hall, blocking as many doors as it could reach, and then it would start poking tendrils inside to pull the tender oysters out of their shells.

And there was absolutely nothing I could do to save them. The quickest other way to get to the freshman dorms was to run through the reading room and down the other half of the incantations corridor to the staircase there, and I'd come out on the opposite side of the dorms. By the time I got back round, no warning would be necessary. The kids on the other side would already be screaming loudly enough.

But that was the only thing I could do, the only thing anyone could do; the only thing at all, because you can't kill maw-mouths. When a maw-mouth comes at an enclave, even their goal is defense: hunkering down, closing up entrances, driving away other mals, so the maw-mouth moves on to hunt somewhere else. The greatest wizards alive can't kill maw-mouths, and they won't even try, because if you try and you don't kill it, it eats you and it keeps eating you forever. It's worse than being killed by a soul-eater and it's worse than being grabbed by a harpy and taken to her nest to be eaten alive by her chicks and it's worse than being torn apart by kvenliks, and no one in their right mind would ever try it, no one, unless the girl you'd started dating a few months ago was going to die, her and someone you didn't even know, not even a person but just a blob of cells that had barely started dividing yet, and you stupidly cared about that enough to trade a million years of agony for theirs.

That maw-mouth wasn't going after anyone I loved. I didn't even *know* any freshmen. After it made a good meal of some dozens of them, it would settle down to digest and recover from the effort of its long climb up. It would probably stay there in their hall, riding down with it one year after another all the way to graduation. When it got hungry again, it would just creep a little way further along the corridor and eat some more freshmen who didn't have anywhere to go. At least they'd have some warning. The kids it ate today would keep begging and crying and whispering for a long time, or at least their mouths would.

And then it occurred to me, unwillingly—if I *could* somehow stop the maw-mouth, no one would even know. There wasn't a single person left in the library stacks right now, not with all the blasting and screaming in the reading room. And the freshmen wouldn't come out of their dorm rooms if they heard anything in the hallway. It was the end of freshman year, they'd learned by now to just barricade their doors, like sane people. No one but me even knew there was a maw-mouth up here, and absolutely no one would believe me if I tried to tell them I'd done for one. And I'd have to burn up who even knew how much of my hard-won mana stash. I wouldn't be *able* to show off afterwards. My reputation would be the least of my worries. I'd spend all of my senior year scrabbling desperately after every last drop of mana I could collect just to try and survive graduation.

I didn't want to realize any of that. I didn't want to realize because it mattered too much to me. You never get anything for free in here. But I'd just been handed an incredibly valuable book, and right behind me in the reading room was everything I'd been hoping for, my best chance for survival and a future. I already knew that the school wasn't holding that out to me for nothing—and here in front of me was the exact opposite. I was being offered a bribe twice over. But why would you bribe someone if you didn't have to? The school wouldn't bother trying to keep me off the maw-mouth unless the school thought—that I had a *chance*. That a sorceress designed from the ground up for slaughter and destruction might just be able to take out the one monster no one else could kill.

I looked around just in time to see Orion go flying across the corridor opening, the white flare of that top-notch shield holder of his going off as he slammed into whatever on the other side. A cloud of rilkes went boiling after him, their wings making the shrieking bird-noise, dripping blood beneath them like rain. I could run right in and vaporize all of them with a single crystal's worth of mana, just like the scratcher, and end up standing there heroically over gasping Orion, in front of a crowd of enclavers. And no one would even think twice when they heard about the maw-mouth. I wouldn't even have to pretend I hadn't seen it. I could go in there and tell everyone I'd seen it, and I'd still be a hero. Not even heroes try to stop maw-mouths.

I turned and went after the maw-mouth. I wanted to be angry, but I just felt sick. Mum would never even know what had happened to me. Nobody would see me die. Maybe some of them would hear me screaming, muffled on the other side of a door, but they wouldn't know it was me. And the kids who heard me screaming would all be screaming themselves, soon enough. Mum wouldn't know, except actually I was sure she would; she'd know the way she'd know if I ever used malia. She was probably leading a meditation circle right now, a nice summer evening in the woods, and she'd close her eyes and think about me, the way she was always thinking about me, and she'd know what had happened to me, what was happening to me. She'd have to live with it in her, along with Dad's death, for the rest of her life.

I was crying in the only way I ever let myself cry in here: with my eyes wide open, blinking hard and letting the tears just go down my face and drip off my chin so they don't blur my vision. There was a brighter light over the entrance to the staircase. I could see the glossy surface of the maw-mouth shining with iridescent reflections as it poured itself through. It didn't leave anything behind, no trail of slime or slick. It didn't even leave dust behind: I followed a smooth, clean-swept track instead, down the stairs and out the landing into the freshman hall. The light was better in there. I could see the maw-mouth clearly, already uncurling limbs out in front of the doors, like a parody of open arms. Stretched wide, it looked at me with dozens of eyes, some mouths making soft whimpering noises, others just breathing noisily. One of them said something like, "Nyeg," as if it were a word.

I gripped my crystal in my hand and linked up to all the other ones waiting back in the chest in my room, and then I walked towards the maw-mouth. I wasn't sure if I could really make myself touch it, but I didn't have to. When I got close enough, it finally did put out a tentacle just for me and wrapped it around my waist and pulled me in, a horrible feeling even through the shield: a really big sweaty man with sticky hands who had grabbed me too tight and was pulling me close against his body. The mouths near me started whispering unintelligible slurred moist words like him breathing drunk into my ear, only on both sides at once. I couldn't get away from it, this thing that *wanted* me, wanted to get inside me and open me up. I tried. I couldn't help trying. It wasn't a choice. I couldn't stop myself trying to thrash myself away from it, to twist and fight, but it didn't work. I was just helplessly in its grip.

And the only good my shield did for me was that the mawmouth couldn't quite manage to get in, yet. Like a tongue trying to push between my lips, and I was able to keep them shut, and it couldn't get my legs open. But I'd get tired eventually, I'd have to give up. I couldn't outlast it. And the terror and rage of knowing that I couldn't hold out forever was the only thing that made me able to do anything else. I pushed a little way into it, and then a wave of it rolled down over my head and it stopped being anything like being held by a person, no matter how awful. It wasn't mouths and eyes and hands, it was *intestines*, organs, and it was still trying to get in me, without limits. It wanted to open me up and make me a part of it, mash me up into itself, and it was the disgusting horrible wet inside of dying things, never quite getting to dead, rotting and still bubbling with blood. I started to scream, just from feeling it around me.

And I knew no one was coming ever, no matter how much I screamed, so I kept going at first. I pulled myself deeper into it, grabbing fistfuls of it one after another like some kind of rope that squished out of my hands almost as fast as I got it, trying to swim through meat. But I could feel my mana just going, a torrent pouring through me to hold my shielding spell up, to keep the hungry thing out of me, and I had no idea how much I was using, how much I had left, whether I'd even have enough left to destroy the thing when I got to wherever I was trying to go, and I was screaming and sobbing and blindly shoving onward without really getting anywhere, and I couldn't actually bear it lasting any longer. The textbook had been right all along, *take anything instead*, any other death, because I would rather have been dead than keep going, even with my shield.

So I didn't keep going. I stopped, and I used the best of the nineteen spells I know for killing an entire roomful of people, the shortest one; it's just three words in French, *à la mort*, but it must be cast carelessly, with a flick of the hand that most people get wrong, and if you get it even a little wrong, it kills you instead. That makes it hard to be careless. But I didn't care. Could I flick my hand properly inside here? I didn't know. It didn't matter. I was just doing something that came naturally, a spell that slipped off my tongue as easily as a breath, and I flicked my hand or maybe just thought of flicking my hand. All around me the horrible stuff went *worse*, sludging into putrescence, but that one moment of casting the spell had felt easy and good and right, so I did it again, and then again, and again, and again, just for the relief. I threw other killing spells, every one of the dozens I knew, in case any one of them would do it, would make it all stop. But it didn't stop. The rot and corruption just kept spreading wider around me, organs floating in a sloshing mass, eyes bobbing out of it to press against my shield staring at me, but at least they clouded over and shriveled up when I cursed them, so I kept going, just killing and killing until suddenly between one moment and the next the maw-mouth broke apart over my head and slithered down all around me to puddle like an emptied sack at my feet, disintegrating, the last few eyes already dead and empty before they sank in on themselves as the last of it came apart.

I thought I'd been clawing my way through it for miles, but I'd hardly gone two steps past where the maw-mouth had first grabbed me. There was a thing left on the floor a few feet away from me, a grotesque lump that looked like a deboned chicken, except a person instead, a body that had been crushed into a fetal position. Then that broke apart too into gobbets and sludge, leaving the whole hallway drenched in blood and bile and the last bits of rotting flesh.

All of it was already running away down the drains set in the floor, the carefully, thoughtfully placed drains in the slightly sloped floor that were designed for just this sort of occasion, to efficiently drain away all the evidence of any unfortunate event that might mess up the floors. They started to choke on the sheer quantity, and I thought the pipes might back up, but then the sprayers in the ceiling kicked in automatically with loud grinding thumps, and look at that, they were even up to the task of draining away the wreckage of a maw-mouth's worth of murder. I didn't know how many people I'd killed in there. I'd lost count how many times I'd cast killing spells. Of course, I'm sure they were all grateful. All of them would have taken me instead.

I had to take down my shield spell, which was still covering me up. I didn't need it anymore, and I was going to desperately need every last drop of mana it was using right now. But I couldn't make myself do it. The outer surface was drenched in rot. The sprayers had stopped, and blood and fluids were draining down, puddling red and putrid yellow around the outline of my shoes, leaving only the three-inch margin of my shield. I didn't want to put my hands out through it.

I just stood there instead, trembling, still leaking the tears that hadn't stopped, and when a line of snot dripped down my face, warm and sticky, I wanted to vomit; my whole stomach clenched up into a knot. Then I heard a voice yell, "El! Galadriel! Are you down there?" from the stairs, and it set me loose. I put my hands up through the very top of my shield and shoved it open out and down to the ground, wasting another couple seconds of mana to do it that way, so the filth just went into the last draining mess on the floor.

Orion came off the steps and into the hallway, panting and singed, half his hair burnt short on one side, and when he saw me, he stopped and heaved a deep breath like someone who's been a bit worried because you stayed out too late, and now, seeing you're fine, is annoyed. "Glad you made it out safe," he told me pointedly. "It's all over, by the way."

I burst into sobs and buried my face in my hands.

Chapter 7

MISERY

ORION HAD TO more or less carry me back to my room. Possibly less given that he couldn't actually manage my weight the whole way and had to stop and put me down a few times, and I walked for a bit before I stopped and cried some more and he picked me up again in a panic. He worked out somewhere along the way that something had happened other than me running away from a bunch of mals in the reading room, and when he got me to my room, he tried to get me to tell him about it. I suppose he would have believed me, and if he'd believed me, and told other people, wouldn't that have done it? Probably not. Everyone thought he was stupidly gone on me, after all, and they'd have asked if he saw it, and he hadn't.

I didn't find out. I didn't want to talk about it at all. I didn't answer any of his questions, except the last one; I said, "No," when he finally asked me if I wanted to be alone. He tentatively sat down on the bed next to me, and even more tentatively, after a few minutes, put his arm around my shoulders. It made me feel better, which was awful in its own way.

I fell asleep at some point. He stayed with me for the whole afternoon, even through lunch, and woke me just in time for dinner with my eyes gummy and my throat sore. I slogged through it dull and blank, taking absolutely no precautions. It was just as well that Orion never left my side. An eyestalk came up from the drains under the table I'd sat down at, which was one of the bad ones and I'd just taken it anyway; the big watery green blob of an eye swiveled around, peered at Orion's ankles, and slid quietly back under without making a full appearance. I didn't mention it.

Aadhya said, "Did she have a casting rebound or something?"

"I don't know!" Orion said, sounding frayed at the edges. "I don't think so."

"I heard you killed a manifestation in the library," Liu said. "Sometimes they can split themselves. Maybe she got partly drained."

Orion hooked a finger into the chain round my neck and fished my crystal out from under my shirt: it was dark and cracked and empty. That was because I hadn't protected it properly when I had finally yanked down the shielding spell, but it would've looked the same if I'd been shielding against a manifestation and it had broken through. But I didn't tell him Liu's guess was wrong, or say anything one way or another. The whole conversation felt like something happening on a TV screen in a program I didn't even watch, with actors I didn't recognize. "Right," Orion said, grimly. "Stay with her, would you?" and then he took off the power-sharer on his wrist and got up.

He went and grabbed one of the mops standing at the edge of the cafeteria waiting for the next maintenance shift, and went round the whole room whacking the ceiling tiles hard. People squawked complaints as mals started literally

raining down all over the place, but they were mostly the lar-
val ones who hang around waiting for leftovers; Orion ignored them until he finally hit a nest of flingers in the corner.
After he'd killed all nine of them, he came back to the table,
put his hand on my chest, and shoved what felt like a year's
worth of mana right into my not-at-all-drained body.

I've got a substantial capacity for holding mana, but it was
too much for even me. I didn't have a functional storing crystal on me, so I couldn't bleed off any of it. If I'd been properly
functional at the moment, I'd have used it for the dramatic
display I'd been planning. If I'd been a little less functional, I'd
have instinctively cast my most natural spell, which at this
particular moment was the killing spell I'd lately been casting
over and over. I was just functional enough to recognize that
I really didn't want to do that, and yet I was about to be mana-
poisoned if I didn't do something with the power. So instead
I poured it into the one completely unthinking spell I know
that doesn't involve killing people, which is the little meditation Mum had me do every morning and night, directly after
toothbrushing. She taught it to me when I was little by having me sing the Simple Gifts hymn, which is as close to the
idea as any incantation gets, but it's not really an incantation,
you don't actually need words for it at all. It's just making the
choice to put yourself right, whatever that means for you. On
the handful of occasions when I asked her whether I really
was a monster, what was wrong with me, she told me there
was nothing wrong with me that wasn't wrong with me, and
made me do the meditation until I felt right again. If that
doesn't make sense to you, you're completely welcome to go
and visit the commune and discuss it with her.

Normally the spell requires *no* mana; sitting down with
the intention to cast it is enough. I was so far from right that
I couldn't actually form that intention, but throwing so much

power into the spell was enough to force me through, rather like picking myself up by the scruff of my neck and shaking myself really hard, with a few slaps across the face from each side. I jerked up onto my feet, standing with a yowl, batting my hands at the air wildly for a moment. That only used up about one month's worth of mana; I had eleven more ready to pop my seams, and—still operating on instinct—I shoved the spell out from me, which made everyone else at the table except Orion jump and gasp just the same as I had. That took care of nine months' worth; two other random kids passing by tripped and dropped their trays as it hit them, and then it finally petered out.

I sank back down on the bench with a hard *thump*. I certainly did feel like myself again, namely violently irritated. Everyone else around the table was looking uneasily happy, their faces brighter, except Liu on the other side of the table, who was shaking violently, staring at her own hands: her fingernails had gone back to normal. She stared at Orion. "What did you *do?*" she cracked out, wobbly.

"I don't know!" Orion said. "It's never done that before!"

"Next time," I rasped out, "*ask first.*" He looked at me anxiously, and I added, "And I'm *fine,*" which I was, involuntarily, although I didn't actually *want* to be fine just yet. I've never been on board with Mum's whole schtick about letting the process run its course, but for the first time I got the idea. However, the Scholomance isn't exactly a forgiving place to do any processing, and after a moment I was more or less grateful. Well, less. "Stop hovering," I muttered, and looked away from Orion to do a quick poison check on all the food on my tray, which I hadn't actually inspected before taking. I had to chuck more than half of it, and I was starving, since I'd missed lunch.

Aadhya gave me half of her chocolate pudding and said,

"Pay me back when you have a chance," and Cora a little grudgingly gave me the apple she'd meant to save for later when Nkoyo gave her a nudge. Orion had sat down next to me slowly and was looking a little less freaked out. Liu was still staring at her own hands, tears running in two parallel lines down her face. I'd obviously been right about her carefully rationed malia use; if she'd been using more than the bare minimum, the spell wouldn't have been able to bring her true. She might have been even less happy about it than I was, though. Now she knew exactly where she was going to end up if she went back to using malia, and she'd have to do it again anyway, or completely change her entire strategy.

Orion didn't stop hovering. He walked me back to my room after dinner and obviously wanted to come inside. He'd probably have stayed with me through the night again, the wanker. "And again, I'm *fine*," I said. "Aren't you worried there's someone in need of a hero somewhere? You could always prowl the senior res hall if you're that bored."

That won me a glare, at least. "You're welcome," Orion said. "Really, no big deal, I'm up to seven times now—"

"*Six*," I said through my teeth.

"This morning?" he said pointedly.

You didn't save me from anything today, I almost said, but I wasn't completely sure that was true, and anyway I still didn't want to talk about it, so I just turned coolly on my heel and went into my room and shut the door on him.

Then, since I was in fact fine and now no longer in a nice comfortable dissociating haze, it was time to inventory the damage, which was pretty appalling. The crystal I'd used to channel to the rest of my store was also cracked. A full nineteen crystals had been completely drained. I had only eight filled ones left. And I was *alive*, after taking on a maw-mouth, which did put things into a different perspective. I sat down on the bed with the cracked crystals in my hands, staring at them. It's one thing to have the strong sense that I *could* cast any number of insanely powerful murder spells. It's another to have proven it quite that dramatically, even if the only person I'd proved it to was me.

Which was just as well, obviously. I've long entertained detailed fantasies of dramatic public rescues—several of them lately featuring a grateful and admiring Orion, to be honest—and the reaction of my fellow students, bowled over and regretful they'd never seen the real me before. But the *real me* had just single-handedly killed a maw-mouth, with liberal use of one of the most powerful and unstoppable killing spells on the books, so if my fellow students saw the real me, they wouldn't decide that after all I was a lovely person they should have been nice to all these years. No, they'd start thinking I was a violently dangerous person they should have been nice to all these years. They'd be scared of me. Of course they'd be scared of me. I could see that now with perfect clarity, despite the pathetic dreams that I'd hung on to all these years, because I was scared of me, too.

I got up and got my sophomore-year Maleficaria Studies textbook down from the upper shelf—I checked the undersides of that shelf and the one above, and ran the back of my hand across all the books before I took it down—and found the pages on maw-mouths. There was a reference for the journal article. I found it and looked up from my desk into the pitch black and said, "I want a clean, readable, English-language copy of issue seven hundred sixteen of the *Journal of Maleficaria Studies*."

I could get specific because that's the opposite of hard to get. *Journal of Maleficaria Studies* might sound academic and dusty, but it's only pretending. There's a very passionate audience for new information on the things that want to eat us.

Every enclave in the world supports the research, in exchange for a boxful of copies each month, and any independent wizard who can afford it will get a subscription; most who can't will find others and club together to get a shared copy.

This issue was quite a recent one, not twenty years old. Orion's mum was already on the board of editors: OPHELIA RHYS-LAKE, NEW YORK, eight names from the top of the masthead. She's higher up now. The article on maw-mouths took up half the contents, and the historical section went into detail on the one reputable modern account of taking one down.

A double handful of wizards in the Shanghai enclave in China were scooped up and sent away by the authorities during the Cultural Revolution—not for being wizards, they just looked suspiciously rich—and the wards on the place went downhill quite fast after the sudden loss of that many prime wizards. A maw-mouth made it through the gates and ate half the remaining inhabitants in a day; the rest ran away like sane people.

So far as that goes, it was a fairly standard story. That's how enclaves get destroyed, when they do. It's not always a maw-mouth, but a weakened enclave is always a dangerously tempting target for the really scary mals. But maybe ten years later, the prime wizards all got back, rounded up the survivors and the surviving kids, and decided to try and take back the enclave.

That was pretty insane, since at the time the only other known cases of destroying maw-mouths had *not* been reputable, but on the other hand, they were playing for high stakes. Having an enclave isn't a small thing, and it's not like you can just decide to bang one up on a whim, much less one with a thousand years of history and wards behind it.

Reading between the lines, I could also tell there had been

a case of ambition spurring the process, since "the future Do-minus of the enclave, our coauthor Li Feng," was the one who had organized the take-back. The entire group spent a year gathering mana, probably the equivalent of a thousand of my crystals. Li brought in a circle of eight really powerful independent wizards, all of them promised significant posi-tions in the enclave if it worked, and he volunteered to go into the maw-mouth himself. He linked up with the circle and did it under all their layers of shielding, powered by all the gathered mana. It took him three days to finally destroy the maw-mouth. Two of the wizards in the circle died in the process, another two days later.

I'd wanted reassurance, but the article just made it worse. I was a sixteen-year-old with twenty-nine mana crystals I'd mostly filled up by doing aerobics. It was blindingly obvious that I didn't have any business taking out a maw-mouth in a Sunday-morning jaunt. Maybe the Scholomance had known I had a chance, but I *shouldn't* have had one. I threw the jour-nal back into the dark and went to sit on my bed huddled up around my own knees, thinking about my great-grandmother's prophecy. If I ever *did* go maleficer, if I ever *did* start pulling malia out of people like toffee and tossing off those killing spells of mine left and right, I'd be unstoppable. Maybe liter-ally. Raining death and destruction on all the enclaves of the world like a maw-mouth myself, like the biggest maw-mouth ever, tearing the others apart because they were my *competi-tion.*

And everyone else seemed to just be waiting for me to get going, except for Mum, who won't even call Hitler a bad per-son. It's not that she thinks he's the product of irresistible historical forces or anything. She says it's too easy to call peo-ple evil instead of their choices, and that lets people justify making evil choices, because they convince themselves that it's okay because they're still good people overall, inside their own heads.

And yes, fine, but I think after a certain number of evil choices, it's reasonable shorthand to decide that someone's an evil person who oughtn't have the chance to make any more choices. And the more power someone has, the less slack they ought to be given. So how many chances did I get? How many had I used up? Did I get points for having gone after the maw-mouth today, or had I just given myself a taste of power that was going to lead me straight to a monstrous destiny so inevitable that it had been foreseen more than a decade ago by someone who'd wanted to *love* me?

I've been carrying that prophecy in my head my whole life. It's one of the first things I remember. It was hot that day. It would have been winter back in Wales, cold and wet; I don't remember the winter, but I remember the sun. There was a square fountain in the inner courtyard that sent up a little spray with rainbows coming through it, surrounded by small trees in pots with purple-pink flowers. The whole family gathered around us, people who looked like *me*, like the face in the mirror that the kids at school were only just starting to teach me was somehow wrong, and here was so clearly right. My father's mother got on her knees to hug me, holding me out at arm's length afterwards just to look at me, hungry tears running down her face, saying, "Oh, she looks so much like Arjun."

My great-grandmother was sitting in the shade: I just wanted to wave my hands through the rainbows and put my hands in the fountain, but they brought me over to her, and she was smiling down at me, reaching to take my wet hands with both of hers. I smiled up at her, and her whole face changed and went sagging and her eyes clouded over white and she started speaking in Marathi, which I didn't speak with anyone except my language teacher once a week, so I didn't understand the words, but I did understand everyone else around me started gasping and arguing and crying, and that Mum had to pull me away from her and carry me to another part of the courtyard and shelter me with her body and her voice from the yelling fear that ate up all the welcome.

My grandmother came and hurried us into the house, to a small, cool, quiet room where she told my mum to stay, and she threw one agonized look at me and went back out again. That was the last time I ever saw her. Someone brought us some dinner, and I forgot my own confused fear and wanted to go back to the fountain, and Mum sang me into sleep. My grandfather was one of the men who came to take me from her that night, in the dark. I know what the prophecy says because he translated it for Mum, repeated it a dozen times over trying to persuade her, because he didn't know Mum well enough to understand that the one thing she'll never go for is the lesser evil. So instead she took her greater evil back home and raised me and loved me and protected me with all her might, and now here I am, ready to begin my destined career any day I like.

I would've probably spent several more hours brooding about it, but I had too much sufficiently depressing scut work to do. I dragged myself off the bed and started the process of conditioning a new crystal to be my channel, which involved building mana by singing a bunch of long involved songs to it about open doors, flowing rivers, et cetera, while concentrating the whole time on pushing a little thread of mana in and pulling it right back out the other side. After my throat started to hurt too much to keep going, I put that one aside and got one of the emptied crystals instead and started filling it back up. But I couldn't do sit-ups or jumping jacks, thanks to my still-aching gut, so I had to crochet instead.

Words can't describe how much I hate crochet. I'd gladly do a thousand push-ups over a single line. I forced myself to learn because it's a classic mana-building option for school: all you need to bring is one tiny lightweight hook. The standard-issue blankets are made of wool that you can un-pick and put back together, no other materials required. But I'm horrible at it. I forget where I am in the pattern, how many stitches I've done, which kind of stitch I'm on, what I'm trying to make, why I haven't stabbed out my own eyes with the hook yet. It's brilliant for building a truly frothing head of rage after I've undone the last hundred stitches for the ninth time. But as a result, I do get a decent bit of mana out of it.

It took me almost an hour of mana spilling out of the crys-tal before it grudgingly started to store again. My teeth were already clenched with fury by then, with a new addition of lurking anxiety: was I starting to feel evil? Yes, now I was wor-rying I'd be turned to the dark side by too much crochet. That would be so stupid it seemed almost likely. But I had to go on and deposit at least a noticeable amount of mana, be-cause otherwise I was sure that by tomorrow the crystal would lock up again. And every single one of my drained crystals would have to be refilled the same way. I'd have to decide if I was going to invest the effort to rescue them, or cut my losses and just start filling the crystals I had left. I couldn't leave the drained ones for last; if I did, they'd go completely dead and be impossible to refill at all.

I couldn't help thinking I could ask Orion to fill some of them for me. Except if he started routinely power-sharing with me, sooner or later the rest of the New York enclave kids would block him. And that wouldn't even be unreason-able. He got to pull on them when he needed to. That was what let him go around saving people at will, instead of wor-rying about whether he had enough mana today, like me and the other losers. He had to pay for that right. Of course, I could just sign on with New York myself. With Orion run-ning around the cafeteria doing ostentatious heroics for my sake, on the heels of a weekend of what everyone else had surely assumed was serious canoodling in the library, Magnus and Chloe and the gang would probably have been relieved to lock me down at this point. And it was even more sensible on my side than it had been yesterday.

So obviously I wasn't going to do that. Instead I was going to spend the next month covering my entire blanket with a lovely and soul-destroying leaves-and-flowers pattern. If I wasn't careful, I might stitch in my rage and do the soul-destroying literally. I suppose at least then I could get shop credit for it.

The bell was ringing for curfew, but I kept going. Thanks to my long nap earlier, I could afford to stay up late. After another hour I finally let myself stop and put my hook away—I really wanted to hurl it violently into the dark, but if I did that, I'd never get it back, so instead I gritted my teeth and strapped it carefully back to the lid of my chest—and then I rewarded myself by sitting down on my bed with the one actual good thing that had happened to me all day: the book I'd got in the library off the Sanskrit shelf.

I'd been sure it was something special when I grabbed it, but I braced myself taking it out of my bag, just because the way my day—my week, my year, my life—was going, it would have really been more on brand for the book to turn out to have its contents swapped with a mundane cookbook or for the pages to be glued together with water damage or eaten by worms or something. But the cover was in beautiful shape, handmade of dark-green leather, beautifully stamped with intricate patterns in gold, even over the long flap that folded over to protect the outer side of the pages. I held it on my lap and opened it up slowly. The first page—the last page from my perspective, it was bound right to left—was written in what looked like Arabic, and my heart started pounding.

A lot of the very oldest and most powerful Sanskrit incantations in circulation, ones whose original manuscripts have been lost for ages, come from copies that were made in the Baghdad enclave a thousand years ago. The book didn't look or feel a thousand years old, but that didn't mean anything. Spellbooks wander off the shelves even in enclaves if you don't have a really good catalog and a powerful librarian keeping track of them. I don't know where they go when they're disappeared, if it's the same as the void outside our rooms or someplace different, but they don't age while they're gone. The more valuable they are, the more likely they are to slip away: they get imbued with the desire to protect themselves. This one looked so new that it had probably vanished out of the Baghdad library barely a couple of years after it had been written.

I held my breath turning the pages, and then I was looking at the first page of copied Sanskrit—annotated heavily in the margins; I was probably going to be forced to start learning Arabic, and it was going to be *worth it,* because the title page more or less said *Behold the Masterwork of the Wise One of Gandhara,* and when I saw it, I actually made a horrible squawking noise out loud and clutched the whole thing to my chest as if it was about to fly off on its own.

The Golden Stone sutras are famous because they're the first known enclave-builder spells. Before them, the only way that enclaves happened was by accident. If a community of wizards live and work together in the same place for long enough, about ten generations or so, the place starts to slip away from the world and expand in odd ways. If the wizards become systematic about going in and out from only a few places, those turn into the enclave gates, and the rest of it can be coaxed loose from the world and into the void, the same way the Scholomance is floating around in it. At which point, mals can't get at you except by finding a way through the entrances, which makes life much safer, and magic also becomes loads easier to do, which makes life much more pleasant.

There haven't been a lot of natural enclaves, though. Good luck getting ten generations with enough stability in history to let you make one. Just because you're a wizard doesn't save you from dying when your city burns down or someone sticks a sword into you. In fact, even an enclave doesn't. If you're hiding inside and your entrances get bombed, your enclave goes, too. I don't think anyone knows if you actually get blown up or if the whole thing just drops off into the void with you in it, but that's a rather academic question.

On the other hand, you'd still rather have the enclave than just be huddled in a basement. The London enclave survived the Blitz because they opened a lot of entrances all over the city, and quickly replaced any of the ones that got destroyed. That's now created a different issue for them; there's a pack of indie punk wizards in London who survive by hunting out the old lost entrances. They pry them open enough to squirm into sort of the lining of the enclave—I don't understand the technical details, and they don't, either, but it works—and they set up shop in there for themselves until the enclave council finds them and chases them out and bricks the opening back up. I know a bunch of them because they all come to Mum whenever something's wrong with them, which it often is because they're shacking up in half-real spaces and siphoning off enclave mana through old murky channels, and mostly eating food and drink they've magicked for themselves out of it.

Mum sets them right and doesn't charge them, unless you count forcing them to sit through lots of meditation and her lecturing them about how they shouldn't be hanging round the enclave and ought to go live in the woods and be spirit-whole like her. Sometimes they even listen.

But London's not a natural enclave, of course; none of the big enclaves are. They're constructed. And as far as we know, the very first enclaves anyone ever *built,* about five thousand years ago, were the Golden Stone enclaves. There were ten of them built within a century across Pakistan and Northern India; three of them are still around even after all this time. They all claim to have been built by the author of the Golden Stone sutras, this guy named Purochana who some wizard historians believe was the guy of that name who also shows up in the *Mahabharata,* more or less working for the prince of Gandhara. *The wise one of Gandhara* is how he's often referred to in medieval sources. In the *Mahabharata,* he's more or less a villain who builds a house out of wax to try and burn his prince's enemies alive, so I'm not entirely sure how that squares with him being a heroic enclave-builder, but mundane sources aren't always very kind to wizards. Or maybe he was trying to build his very flammable house and accidentally stumbled over some way to pop open an enclave instead.

Anyway, it's almost certain the ten enclaves weren't actually all founded by the same person. Once you've made yourself a tidy enclave to live in, you wouldn't really move and do it again, would you? But there was one distinct set of spells. And they've been lost for ages.

That hasn't stopped enclaves being built, obviously. Once

wizards realized you *could* build enclaves, it became a subject of enormous and sustained interest, and artificers came up with methods that let you make better and bigger ones, and the Golden Stone spells got lost over time through disuse. I don't know much about modern enclave-building, those spells are a very closely guarded secret, but I do know for definite you can't fit the process into a single book less than an inch thick, even with margin notes. It's the difference between putting together a log cabin and building the Burj Khalifa.

But despite five thousand years of refining, some of the Golden Stone building-block spells *are* still widely known, because they're such good building-block spells, especially for manipulating elements and, most famously, the phase of matter, which is a lot more important than that might sound. If you want steam, you can get some by pouring enough heat into a pot of water. But that's pretty wasteful, mana-wise. Like nine-year-old me wiping out an entire crystal to vaporize a scratcher. But if you're lucky enough to get your hands on Purochana's phase-control spell, you don't have to take the intermediate step of generating the heat and warming up all the surrounding water and the pot and the air around it and so forth. You just take the pot of liquid water and turn exactly the amount of water you want into water vapor, and you spend only exactly the amount of mana required. That kind of mana control is huge; it's what made enclave-building feasible.

And now I *had* got my hands on his phase-control spell. It was on page sixteen of the book. When I found it, my hands shaking as I turned the first pages, I had to stop reading and hold the book against my chest again, trying not to cry, because it meant I was probably going to make it out of here alive after all, which I'd been starting to doubt after seeing how badly my mana store had been wiped out. Aside from using the spell myself, I was going to be able to trade it for a *lot*.

Outside the Scholomance, buying the Golden Stone phase-control spell takes the equivalent of all the mana that a determined group of twenty wizards could put together over five years or so. And it's even harder than that sounds. You can't just store up mana for five years in a bank and then go buy the spell in a handy bookstore. The only way to get spells that valuable is to barter: find some enclave that's willing to trade it to you, negotiate a deal for something that the enclave wants but can't more easily make for themselves—generally that's because it's unpleasant or painful or dangerous—then spend five years of unpleasantness to make it and give it to them. And then hope they don't go back on the deal or tack on a few more demands, which is far from unheard of.

I didn't keep reading past the phase-control page. Instead I carefully dampened my cleanest rag and gently cleaned off every last speck of dust in every last crevice of every last pattern stamped into the cover. The whole time I talked to the book, telling it how happy I was to have it and how amazing it was and how I couldn't wait to show it to everyone and one day soon take it home to my mum and use the special handmade leather oil that one of the people at the commune makes to properly clean it and so on. I didn't even feel stupid. Mum cossets all seven of her spellbooks like that, and she's never lost one, even though she's an independent and they're all really powerful. She keeps them together in a chest with a bit of room: if she ever finds a new one in there, which happens spontaneously sometimes—only to Mum—she says it means one of the others wants to go, and she lays them all out in a circle on a blanket spread under the hole in our yurt and does a blessing on them and thanks them all for their help and says whichever of them needs to leave can go, and sure enough when she's done packing them back up, there are only seven left again.

"I'll have to make a special book chest just for you," I added, a promise. "I was planning to skive off shop class, I've finished for this term, but now I'll keep going just to get your chest begun. It's got to be perfect, so I expect it'll take a while." Then I slept with it cuddled in my arms. I wasn't taking any chances.

"Holy *shit*, El," Aadhya said, when I knocked on her door the next morning before first bell to show it to her. "What did you do for it?"

I was working really hard to forget what I'd done for it. "The library was trying really hard to keep me stuck in with the mals yesterday. It slipped the book onto an upper shelf after I started label-reading down the aisle, and I got lucky and spotted it."

"That's unbelievable." She eyed it longingly. "I don't know Sanskrit. But I'll help you run an auction for the phase-control spell, if you want?"

"An auction?" I said. I'd only meant to ask her for help trading it.

"Yeah," she said. "This is huge, you don't want to swap it for just anything. I'll collect secret bids, and the top five bidders get it, for whatever they've put up. And they have to promise that they won't trade it on themselves after. Can you put a copying curse on?"

"No," I said, flatly. The actual answer was yes, easy as winking, and it would be a good and proper curse, too, but I wasn't going to.

"You want to ask Liu to do it?"

"No curses," I said. "No one's going to be photocopying

this or anything. It's major arcana in Vedic Sanskrit. It's going to take me a week to make five clean copies, for that matter."

"You've already learned it?" Aadhya gave me a squint. "When? You were a human dishrag yesterday."

"After dinner," I said sulkily: *obviously* all thanks to that boost from Orion.

After a moment, she said, "Okay. Can you run a demo? In the shop on Wednesday, maybe? That'll give me a couple of days to pass the word. Then we can run the auction over the weekend. Seniors will really want in on this with time to get the spell down before graduation. And hey, if we're lucky, all five of the winners will be seniors and we can do a whole second auction next term after they're gone."

"Sounds great," I said. "Thanks, Aadhya. What cut do you want?"

She gnawed her lip for a moment, looking at me, then abruptly she said, "You okay with figuring it out after the auction? See what comes in and what we think is fair. Maybe there'll be enough shareable stuff I won't need anything exclusive."

I had to work at it not to squeeze the book too hard against me. "Fine with me, if you're sure," I said, casual around the lump in my throat.

Chapter 8
CRAWLER

W E WENT to the bathroom and got ready together, and met Nkoyo and Orion to walk to breakfast. "Oh, sweetness," Nkoyo said, when I showed her the book: I was keeping it on my person, possibly for the rest of my life; I'd rigged up a sling to carry it in across my chest, separate from my other books. "Are you willing to do trades? I know a couple of Somali girls doing Sanskrit."

I was so happy that when Chloe almost burst out of the girls' with her hair not quite done, obviously having hurried to catch us up, and called, "Wait for me, there in a second," I even said, "Sure," like an ordinarily civilized person, feeling magnanimous, and showed her the book, too, as we walked. She admired it appropriately, although she spoiled my five seconds of friendly feeling by darting a look at Orion that I had no trouble interpreting: she thought he'd got it for me. I couldn't kick her off our table at this point, any more than she could've shoved me when I'd been walking with Orion, that's just not on, but I would've *liked* to.

I was still looking forward to my breakfast with anticipation, though. Once Aadhya and I passed the word in the food line that I had something really good on offer, people would stop at the table just to get a quick look. It would be a good way to make more connections, especially with other students who had Sanskrit; I could get even more trades out of it in future. Except then we got to the cafeteria and I knew straightaway my book wasn't going to be the big news of the morning: a senior was sitting alone at the middle of an absolutely prime table. *Completely* alone, hunched over his tray.

Seniors don't sit alone, no matter how much the other seniors hate them. Freshmen and even sophs will fill in the spaces at their tables for the cover. Seniors get access to a lot more advanced magic, and by graduation time, they're also bursting with power, especially by comparison with the average fourteen-year-old. The kind of mals that want to hunt freshmen and sophs avoid them. But this one had been isolated so hard there weren't even any seniors sitting at the tables *around* him: they were full of hunched-over desperate loser freshmen.

I didn't recognize him, but Orion and Chloe had both frozen, staring. "Isn't he . . . New York?" Aadhya said, low, and Chloe said blankly, "That's Todd. Todd Quayle." That made it even more incomprehensible. Shunning an *enclave* kid? And Todd hadn't gone obvious whole-hog maleficer or anything; he looked totally normal.

A freshman was just making a quick dash back from the busing station, having managed to get his tray on the conveyor without problems. Orion reached out and caught him. "What did he do?" he asked, jerking his head over.

"Poached," the kid said, without really lifting his head; he darted a wary look at Orion and Chloe from under his untrimmed bangs and hurried on; Orion had dropped his arm and was looking sick. Chloe was shaking her head in denial.

"No *way*," she said. "No *fucking* way." But it was almost the only thing big enough to explain it.

Our rooms are handed out on the day we get dropped into them, and you don't get to change, even if someone dies. The empty rooms do get cleared out at the end of the year when the res halls rotate down, but the Scholomance decides how to reshuffle the walls to hand out the extra space. The only way you can deliberately change to another room is if you *take* it, and not by killing someone. You have to go into their room and push them into the void.

Nobody knows what that really means. The void isn't a vacuum or instant death or anything like that. Occasionally someone will go crazy and try to walk out into the void on their own—you can, actually, *walk* into it. It doesn't seem to matter that you can also drop things over the edge. Like that slime you can squish between your fingers or roll into an apparently solid ball: it depends how you're pushing on it, only with your will instead of your hands.

However, those people never make it very far. They panic and run back, and none of them has ever been able to describe what it's like in there. If someone's really determined and takes a running start, occasionally their momentum carries them a little further in before they can turn around, and when they do come out, those people can't talk anymore at all, at least not in any comprehensible way. They make noises like they're talking, but it's not a language anyone else knows or can understand. They mostly end up dead some other way, but a couple of them have made it out of the school alive. They've still got magic. But no one else can understand their spells, and if they're artificers or alchemists, the things they make don't work for anyone else. Like they've been shifted sideways somehow.

That's as deep as anyone can get into the void on their

own. But you can push someone else all the way in—with magic, so you get them far enough in to vanish completely, even though they don't want to go. And if you do that, if you go into someone's room after curfew and you push them all the way into the dark like a spellbook you don't want anymore, even while they're screaming and begging and trying to get back out, then after they're gone, you can spend the night in their room, and you won't get swarmed, because there's only one person in the room, and it's your room after that.

Of course, it doesn't make you very popular with, for instance, anyone else who has a room. And it's not like you can cover it up, either. As soon as people see you coming out of your new room the next morning, they know what you've done. Orion clearly wanted to go right at Todd, then and there; I had to shove him towards the food line instead. "We already missed lunch yesterday. If you want to find out more, we can go sit with him after we've got breakfast; it's not like there isn't room."

"I'm not sitting with a poacher," Orion said.

"Then endure the burning curiosity," I said. "Anyone in the school will be able to tell you all the gory details by lunchtime."

"It's a *mistake*," Chloe said again, her voice high and fraying. "There's no way Todd poached. He doesn't need to poach! He's going with Annabel and River and Jessamy, and they've got the valedictorian on board. Why would he poach?"

"It's not like we'll be with him for long. The senior bell will go five minutes after we sit down," Aadhya offered, more practically, and Orion clenched his hands and then shot off to the food line at top speed.

I'd underestimated the power of the gossip chain: we got

most of the gory details before we even got out with our trays. Todd had taken out a guy named Mika: one of the last stragglers left, the solitary kids who hadn't made it into any graduation alliance. If stragglers aren't maleficers, they pretty much don't make it out alive, and Mika wasn't a maleficer; he was just an awkward loser who couldn't manage decent social skills and wasn't talented enough for even other losers to overlook the lack. If you're thinking that doesn't sound like a crime deserving of a death sentence, I would agree with you, since I'll be in the same boat next year if I don't set myself up in time. But that's what it was, more or less. Which meant, of course, he'd been the perfect target.

Orion got out first, and he made a beeline for Todd at his table, slammed his tray down across from him, and didn't sit. "Why?" he said flatly. "You've got a team, a belt shield, a power-sharer, plenty of mana—you made a spirit glaive last quarter! But it wasn't enough? You had to have a *better room*?"

I put my own tray down next to Orion's and sat and started eating while I had the chance. Aadhya sat down next to me and did the same thing. Chloe hadn't come with us after all. After hearing the word in the line, she'd peeled off to a different New York table; all the other New York kids were sitting as far away from Todd as they could and still be in the cafeteria. She'd made the right call; I could already tell Orion wasn't going to get an answer he was going to like much, if he was going to get one at all. Todd hadn't even reacted to the question. He was hunched over his tray eating systematically, but his hands were shaking, and he was forcing the food down. He wasn't a maleficer, either; he wasn't even enough of a sociopath not to mind killing someone. I didn't know why he *had,* but he hadn't done it for malia. He'd done it in desperation.

"Where was his old room?" I asked.

"Next to the stairs," Orion said, still staring down at Todd like he could bore a hole through his skull and pull out answers. That *is* a crap room. A stairwell is for moving round the school, and the mals can use it as much as we do, so next to the stairs on the senior dorm level is the equivalent of being the first item on the food line.

But it's hardly an insurmountable threat. None of us will take the first item on the food line if there's a lid covering it, not as long as there's an easier option in the next tray along. Which there would be, because Todd's an enclaver, with more than enough mana to put up a good shield every single night, and the other enclave kids would have skipped recruiting a few of the neighboring kids, in solidarity. It didn't seem worth screwing up his alliance and maybe even his whole life—enclaves don't *openly* harbor murderers and maleficers, and literally everyone in the school knew what he'd done.

"*Answer me,*" Orion said, and reached for Todd's tray, maybe because he planned to pull it away or shove it in his face, but Todd grabbed it himself first and heaved it up, taking Orion's tray with it, throwing the whole mess all over him before reaching across the table to give him a good shove. We don't do a lot of physical fighting in here, everyone thinks of that as a mundane thing, but you don't need much practice when you're a six-foot guy who hasn't been shy about letting other people give you extras for the last four years and the kid on the other side is a shrimp of a junior. Orion staggered back, dripping milk and scrambled eggs, and nearly went over into the next table.

"*Fuck* you, Orion," Todd snarled, his voice cracking into a shrill frantic note, undermining his thug line. "You want to get in my face? Big hero on campus, clearing out the mals for everybody. Guess what, you haven't made a dent in the real crowd. They're all still down there, and thanks to you, they're starving. No little ones to snack on. So they're not waiting for dinner to be delivered this year. I've been hearing them working at the stairwell every night for a week, so loud I can't sleep. Some of them are already getting through." He pressed his clenched fists to his temples, his whole face crumpling like a toddler having a wail, tears leaking down. "A fucking *maw-mouth* went by my room yesterday. Headed upstairs. Didn't get that one, did you, hero?"

Murmurs and freaked-out gasps went out from around us like an expanding ripple as everyone at the nearby tables overheard. The whole room was absolutely agog and watching the drama unfold, some kids actually standing on benches to peer over other people's heads and see. Todd laughed a little hysterically. "Yeah, I wonder where it's gonna settle down. Keep an eye out at the supply room, everybody!" he called out, turning to the whole room and spreading his arms wide and up to take in the kids leaning over from the mezzanine, a parody of a friendly warning. "But yeah, Orion, we're so lucky to have you here protecting us. What would we do without you."

It was almost down to the letter my own thoughts about Orion's heroic campaign, and even more obviously accurate after the last week: a soul-eater in the junior res hall, mimics and sirenspiders in the shop, manifestations and maw-mouths in the library. Todd was right: there had to be a hole somewhere letting them through, a hole they'd forced through in hungry desperation.

Orion didn't say anything back. He just stood there with egg literally on his face and blobs of porridge clinging to his hair, pale and bewildered. Everyone around was darting uncertain looks at him. I stood up and said to Todd, "You'd sail right out of here, enclave boy. And let the mals eat the kid in the room next to yours instead of you. That's what *you'd* do.

But yeah, have a go at Orion. Sorry, did I miss why you have more of a right to live than anybody he's saved? More than Mika? How long did it take for him to stop screaming when you shoved him into the dark? Do you even know, or did you just plug your ears and look the other way until it was over?"

The whole room had gone so deathly quiet I could hear Todd's gulping as he stared at me bloodshot. Everyone was probably holding their breath not to miss a single nuance of this magnificent escalation of gossip. I picked up my tray and turned round to Orion, who looked back at me still shutdown, and I told him, "Come on. We're getting another table." I jerked my head to Aadhya, too, who was gawking up at me herself, and she scrambled up and grabbed her own tray and fell in with me, darting looks at my face sideways. Orion did come after us, moving a little slowly.

The only empty tables left were bad ones, far at the edges and right by the doors or under the air vents—obviously nobody had left the cafeteria a second early with this excitement going on—but as we were passing him, Ibrahim blurted into the still-total silence, "El, we have room," and waved some of the kids at his table to slide over and make space for us. The senior bell went off then, and we sat down surrounded by the sudden burst of activity and noise of all the seniors jerking into motion at once, shoveling in the last of their food and grabbing their things to rush out. Todd went out with them, weirdly separate from the rest, a ring of space left round him.

Orion sat down on the end of the bench, empty-handed. Yaakov was on the other side across from him; he picked up his napkin, hesitating, and I reached out and took it and shoved it at Orion. "You're a mess, Lake," I said, and Orion took it and started wiping himself clean. "Can anyone spare anything?" I put one of my own rolls in front of him, and then one after another every single one of the kids at the table started passing something down, even if it was just half a mini muffin or a section of orange, and a kid at the table behind us reached out and tapped me on the shoulder and handed me a carton of milk for him.

The conversation at our table was completely dead at first; with Orion right there, nobody wanted to talk about the only thing anybody wanted to talk about. Aadhya was the one who got things moving; she finished drinking the milk from the bottom of her cereal bowl—in here that's standard, not bad manners—and wiped her mouth and said, "Any of you doing Sanskrit? You're not going to believe what El got. El, you've got to show them," and I was even more grateful that I'd petted my book so much and put it in the special sling, because I'd forgotten about it completely for a few seconds, and if I'd had it in my bookbag, I am absolutely sure it would have vanished on me.

"Baghdad enclave!" Ibrahim and two others yelped in-stantly, the second I pulled it out—all the kids who know Arabic can spot books from the Baghdad enclave three shelves away—and since they couldn't talk about the real news, mine did for second-best.

I had languages after breakfast, and Orion had alchemy. He put the rubbish from his piecemeal breakfast on my tray and bused it for me, and then just as we were going out the door, he said quietly, "Thanks. But I know you didn't mean it."

"I did too mean it," I said, irritated, because now I had to work out why I did. "Someone's always got to pay, but why should Homicidal Todd get a leg up on anyone else? You're stupid for letting down your side, but you're the one who wants it to be *fair*. Go to your lesson and stop looking for a cwtch." It irritated me even more that he actually shot me a grateful look before he headed for the stairs.

Predictably, an Arabic worksheet appeared on my desk the instant I sat down that morning. There wasn't a single word of English on it; the school didn't even give me a dictionary. And judging by the cheery cartoonish illustrations next to the lines—most notably a man in a car about to mow down a couple of hapless pedestrians—I had the strong suspicion that it was modern Arabic, too. I should've got a book on Classical Arabic out of the library before going to class. When you've been exposed to a language you didn't really mean to start, you're better off giving in and just establishing some boundaries. I'd just been a bit busy yesterday.

I'd already been resigned to my fate, though, and a Saudi girl who'd been at Ibrahim's table that morning had a booth near me; she lent me her dictionary in exchange for a promise to proofread her English-language final paper. I copied out the alphabet into my notebook first and then started slogging away on the worksheet, copying out every word I looked up. And for a silver lining, I also couldn't understand a single word of the venomous tirade that the booth voice poured into my ears in between grudgingly telling me how to pronounce قتل and صرخات. I imagine it was full of particularly juicy horrors.

There was a lot of other non-magical whispering going on around me the rest of the day, among the other kids. It occurred to me, much too belatedly, that I'd just graduated from pathologically rude bitch to enclave-hater. It's not that we don't all know that it's unfair, but nobody says so, because if you say so, enclavers don't invite you to join them on the better side of the unfair. Orion's shine might have gone off, too, if enough enclave kids had decided that Todd was right. Maybe the two of us would end up sitting alone. That would be epic. My unpopularity massive enough to drag down Orion Lake himself.

It didn't look good when I first got to the cafeteria at lunchtime. None of the enclavers who'd been making up to me lately said a word; no more study group invites from Sarah today. But as I came off the food line, Aadhya got there from shop with three other artificer-track kids and waved to me on her way into the line. "Save us seats, El?" she called across the room. Nkoyo and her pals, who were a few kids behind me, heard her; I don't know if that made the difference or not, but she said, "I'll get us water if you do a perimeter," and though Jowani and Cora exchanged slightly anxious looks, they followed her lead.

By the time I'd set the perimeter and we were sitting, Aadhya and her crew were there, and they'd even got me an extra piece of cake to say thanks, the way you normally do when you ask someone to save you a place. Not that I had any personal experience before now, as people had always previously made their excuses if I asked them. Liu came, too, and sat down quietly on my other side. She was still carrying a faintly shell-shocked expression, incongruous with the actual color in her face, which had shifted at least ten degrees over on the spectrum from undead to just pale; even her hair had hints of brown in it under the sunlamp. "Did you do a UV potion, Liu?" one of Aadhya's friends said. "You look great."

"Thanks," she said, softly, and bent over her food.

There almost wasn't room when Orion and Ibrahim arrived from lab. A couple of people shifted to let him sit next to me without so much as a word. I was mostly resigned to that, too. After my performance this morning, people would now assume we were dating even if I tipped his soup over his head. If he did start actually dating someone, everybody would have us in a love triangle for the year.

Todd was in the cafeteria, too. He already wasn't being frozen out completely: a group of loser freshmen had taken seats at the end of his table. He'd probably have a new alliance in time for graduation, if his old one didn't just swallow it and take him back and leave it to the grown-ups to deal with him when they got out. Maybe they wouldn't. His parents were powerful and important if his alliance had the right to offer a guaranteed-in to the enclave, which they would've needed to get the class valedictorian. He'd tell them about the maw-mouth going past his room and they'd understand, of course he had to protect himself, and it wasn't like he'd *really* committed murder. Mika was going to die anyway in a week. It made sense to trade him for an enclave kid, a kid who had a chance, a kid who had a future. Just thinking about it made me angry enough to want to push Todd into the dark myself.

I didn't have a concrete plan for work period, but without even saying it, I'd more or less assumed Orion and I would go to the library together again. But as we were busing our trays, he said to me abruptly, "Go ahead, I'll find you."

"Suit yourself," I said shortly. There wasn't any great stroke of genius needed to guess what he was planning to do, but I didn't tell him he wasn't going to find a maw-mouth lurking anywhere in the school, or that he was a moron for trying. I just went on to the library alone.

I meant to go to my desk, but when I came in through the reading room, the place was half empty. Most of the tables and squashy chairs had been badly scorched, and there was a lingering stink of smoke mingled with something smelling a bit like the cafeteria brussels sprouts. They're the one thing that's never ever poisoned. But even taking all of that into account, the place was unusually deserted. There were freshmen with actual seats instead of just being on the floor. After a moment I realized that everyone was probably thinking—accurately, as it happened—that if you were a hungry maw-mouth, the library would be the perfect hunting ground. Probably anyone who wasn't desperate would also avoid the stockroom, exactly as Todd had suggested.

It was too good an opportunity to pass up. "Move on," I told one of the more ambitious freshmen, who'd dared to snag one of the coveted armchair-and-desk combos in the corner that was normally filled with kids from the Dubai enclave, none of whom were in evidence at the moment.

The kid gave it up without a fight; he knew he'd been reaching. "Can I sit by you?" he asked. That was new. Probably he was betting Orion might turn up.

"Suit yourself," I said, and he shifted to the open patch of floor next to the chair.

The seat back had a bad rip in the upholstery from one corner to the other, but that was why I'd wanted it. I dug the remnants of a half-scorched throw blanket out from under a sofa and got to work on it with my crochet hook. It took most of work period and a few layers of enamel off my molars, but I got the end of the blanket back into a raveled state. Then I folded it up into a pad, tied it over the rip with some stray bits of string, and sacrificed the whole thing and the mana I'd built up to do a make-and-mend on the chair back. I made sure to scribble *El* on the repaired bit. The unwritten rule is, if you fix a broken piece of school furniture, you get dibs on it for the rest of the term. The rule goes out the window often enough when there's someone more powerful on the other side, but I suspected that not even enclavers were going to pick a fight with Orion Lake's girlfriend, even if she was an enclave-hating weirdo and he turned out to be saving losers at their expense.

Afterwards, I took out the Golden Stone sutras, petted the book lovingly for a bit, then spent the rest of work period hunting up a Classical Arabic dictionary so I could start translating the first few pages. Those turned out to be just the usual foreword bits like offering acknowledgments and thanks to various important patrons—in this case senior wizards at the enclave—and talking about how hard it had been to make a precise copy. It wasn't what you'd call brilliantly productive, but I got some Arabic practice in, which was just as well since it was an absolute certainty that a quarter of my language final was going to be in Arabic.

Orion never showed. He even skipped lab that afternoon. I didn't see him again until I got to the cafeteria for dinner and he was already there alone at a table, eating like a wolf from a loaded tray: he'd clearly been first into the line, which is a great way to get plenty of food and also get eaten yourself. For most people.

I didn't ask him where he'd been, but I didn't have to. Ibrahim wasn't even in our lab section and he'd still heard that Orion had skipped class; he was asking why before he had even got into his seat.

"I didn't find it," Orion said, low, after everyone else finished making the appropriate shocked noises when he admitted he'd gone hunting the maw-mouth. It *was* insanely stupid, even for our hero. He only shrugged it off. "I checked the supply room, the shop, all over the library—"

I was eating on, determinedly ignoring his catalog, but Liu, who was next to me eating almost as mechanically, slowly began to lift her head from over her food as he talked, and when he finished up in frustration, she said, sounding a bit more like herself, "You're not going to find it." Orion looked over at her. "A maw-mouth wouldn't be hiding. If it was in the school, it would be eating. We'd all know where it was by now. So there isn't a maw-mouth in the school. Either Todd made it up, or he hallucinated it."

Everyone loved that idea, of course. "He did say he hadn't

been sleeping," one of Nkoyo's friends said, and by the end of the meal, the whole cafeteria had talked the maw-mouth out of existence and Todd into temporary insanity, to enormous and general relief.

Even mine: at least they'd all stop talking about it now. And with the maw-mouth disposed of, my find became real news at last. By the end of dinnertime, fourteen kids—eight of them seniors doing Sanskrit—had come by to take a look at the sutras, and they got so excited that some other seniors who *weren't* doing Sanskrit came over to express interest: they were mostly kids from wizard groups roughly like Liu's family, just a bit bigger, starting to get into reach of the resources to build an enclave. Getting the phase-change spell for relatively cheap would be a substantial savings.

I went back to the library after dinner pleased despite the shedload of Arabic work I still had to do. Ibrahim even volunteered to help me out with translations, in exchange for English help that he didn't really need, which was clearly meant as an apology for being a twat previously. I took it, if a little grudgingly; I'd sat down at his table, after all.

He and his pal Nadia, the girl who'd lent me the dictionary earlier, came to the library with me after dinner. The reading room was already filling up again, and the Dubai kids didn't look at all happy when I came over and said, "My chair, thanks," to the kid sitting in it. Clearly the shine was off *me*, at the very least. But I was right, they didn't try to pick a fight over it, or Ibrahim and Nadia staking out places on the floor next to it. They just shuffled themselves around so the kid who'd lost the seat got another one in the adjusted pecking order and pointedly ignored us. I didn't mind: they still talked to each other, a lot, in Arabic. I couldn't pick out words yet, but just getting the rhythm of a language helps, and getting to eavesdrop on a big group of people talking is a fair bit nicer than having to listen to whatever the Scholomance would be pouring into my ears.

I managed to slog through my Arabic worksheet and made some notes on cards for the grammar, and then I started translating the footnotes to the phase-control spell. I'd been hoping for something useful, ideally casting tips: the older a spell is, the more likely your unconscious assumptions about stance and intonation are likely to be off, and the more powerful a spell is, the more likely awful things are to happen as a result. But instead it was all nonsense about how the phase-control spell was included only for completeness's sake, as of course that particular spell had just been superseded by a new Arabic-language spell. Right. As far as I know, nobody's ever made a phase-control spell that works even half as well as Purochana's; that's why it's still in relatively popular circulation even though it's in highly antiquated Sanskrit. I had a strong suspicion that this new Arabic version had been written by a senior Baghdadi wizard that the translator had been trying to butter up.

I translated every word of the flattery, hoping that maybe there would be one useful thing hidden among the rest, but no. At least doing the work definitely helped settle the book down: I kept stroking the cover, and murmuring each word I translated out loud, and by the end of the process, it was starting to feel comfortable under my hands, like it was *mine*, instead of just something I'd come across.

Orion came in around then from making up his lab work. The Dubai kids eyed him a little hesitantly, sharing looks I could interpret perfectly well. Even if Orion was taking away some of your advantage as an enclaver in the larger scheme of things, in the *smaller* scheme of things, you as an individual still wanted him sitting in your corner just in case, for example, a grab bag of mals exploded into the library again.

After a moment, one of the seniors gave a quick jerk of her chin to a sophomore, who got up and said casually, "I'm going to bed. Orion, have my chair. Good night everyone," and took off.

The rest of them also switched to English on a dime and started in on the usual round of thanking Orion for saving their lives in the library yesterday, until I broke in and said, "Give it a rest, he doesn't need strokes. Did you manage to actually do any work today, Lake, or are you trying to be the first person to actually fail out of the Scholomance?"

He rolled his eyes as he dropped into the chair—he didn't even notice it as anything special, it must have happened to him so regularly—and said, "Thanks for the concern, I did fine. Nobody was trying to burn my face off in the lab this time."

Everyone in earshot—including Ibrahim and Nadia—eyed me in a sort of irritated and baffled way at the same time. A couple of the Dubai girls said something to each other in Arabic, which practically didn't need translation. Yes, obviously Orion was some kind of masochist nutter, dating me. I had to restrain myself severely from snarling at all of them that he *wasn't* dating me, thanks, and he should be so lucky at that.

I stayed for another hour mainly out of spite. I had crammed as much Arabic as I was going to absorb that day, and most of my other work required things that were back in my room, not to mention I needed to be doing some mana-building. But I just hung out adoring my beautiful book and sniping back and forth with Orion. I'd like to claim I couldn't bring myself to go, but I've got quite well-developed will-power when it comes to doing necessary work. I just have very little willpower when it comes to indulging petty resentment: I wanted to stay until enough of the Dubai kids finally did go to bed that there was a different chair left open, so I wasn't giving any of them anything.

But I'm more embarrassed to admit that it never crossed my mind to consider what the cozy situation looked like to someone who might be watching, for instance, from the New York corner across the reading room. As far as they could tell, I'd finally taken one of those many dangled enclave invites, Orion had in fact trotted after me, and we were now comfortably ensconced in the Dubai corner with some of those loser kids I'd recruited.

Dubai wouldn't have been a crazy choice, at that. The enclave there is relatively new and highly international. It's got a top-notch reputation for English and Hindi incantation, plus they recruit a lot of artificers and alchemists. Ibrahim also made perfect sense as a connecting point: his older half-brother was in the UAE doing work for the enclave already, and he'd probably get invited aboard, too, if Ibrahim helped them bag Orion. So it was an obvious conclusion for the New York kids to draw, and if I'd thought about it, their response would have been equally obvious. As I hadn't thought, I just sat there like a prat down the pub with my mates, and didn't pay the slightest attention when Magnus walked by to go into the alchemy aisle near us, even though he had absolutely no business going into the stacks at all when he could send any of six hangers-on to fetch him any book he wanted.

I doubt he'd have done it on his own initiative alone. They had surely been talking options amongst themselves: *How do you solve a problem like Galadriel?* And I bet Todd came into it, too. It was one thing for the New York kids to desert him, and another for a loser girl like me to rip into him in the cafeteria in front of everyone. And then to take Orion off to Dubai the very same day, after he'd already power-shared with me and—as Chloe clearly thought—got me an incredibly powerful spellbook.

I do have to give Magnus credit, the crawler was a really good one. It would absolutely have got me, too; I can't even pretend. It was made of paper, a little crumpled twist covered with what looked at a glance like math equations instead of an animating inscription. The library was full of scrap paper on a good day, much less right after a massive attack that had destroyed dozens of books and thrown kids' papers every which way, and lots of the scraps move on their own anyway. I actually noticed it moving vaguely in my direction and didn't think about it again. I didn't even have my usual baseline shield up, because I was sitting in the reading room in the library with a good line of sight and lots of other eyes watching, and I needed to save every drop of mana that I could. If I'd been sitting in an ordinary chair, or if I'd been working hard, with my feet planted on the ground, the crawler would have been able to get to the bare skin of my ankle, and one second afterwards it would have sent a heap of magic fibers corkscrewing into my flesh, and there wouldn't have been anything I could do to stop it sucking the life straight out of me.

But because I was demonstratively curled up in my nice comfy chair with my feet tucked up underneath me, it had to come up the chair leg and go over the arm. Orion happened to be looking at me in time to grab me and yank me out sprawling over the floor in front of the whole Dubai crowd, just before he disintegrated the crawler, incidentally along with three-quarters of my lovely repaired chair.

I figured out what had happened almost instantly, especially since Magnus was just sitting back down in the New York corner. Everyone was looking over at me and Orion, the way you do when something explodes into flames unexpect-

edly, but he and several other New York kids were just a bit
slow looking over. And they looked fairly grim about my visible survival. Not that I had any proof, of course, and there
was Orion smugging down at me with deliberately obnox-
ious cheer, "So that makes eight, right?"—just asking to be
told that it didn't count because it was his own arseholish
friends trying to murder me.

"Thanks loads," I said through my teeth. "On that note,
I'm going to bed." I held my sutras against my chest—
thankfully I'd been holding them in my lap—and snagged my
bookbag by the one strap it had left, and stalked directly out
of the reading room.

It wasn't my way of saying thanks or of being rude, either
one. I just had to get out of the library. I was angry at myself
for being stupid and needing my life saved, and I was angry at
the Dubai kids and everyone else, too, for thinking Orion was
a perverted loon for liking unsettling me, but most of all I
was angry at Magnus, and Todd, and every last one of the
New York enclave kids, because they had given me an excuse,
a gold-plated excuse, to do something to them. They'd deliberately tried to kill me. By Scholomance rules, that gave me a
right to do something to them. And if I didn't, then they'd
assume it was because I was afraid of them. They'd think I
was agreeing with them, telling them they were right to look
at me and see just a piece of rubbish to be kicked out of their
way. Someone who wasn't worth as much as they were.

The tears of rage were already leaking out of my eyes by
the time I got to the stairs. I was just lucky there were some
other kids going down to the dorms, and I managed to keep
at least one person in blurry sight along the way until I finally
got to my room and clanged the door shut behind me. I
started pacing the room with the sutras still clutched against
my chest. It was only five steps across and turn and go back,

over and over. I couldn't meditate, and I couldn't even try to work. If I put my hands to pen and paper right now, I knew what would happen: a spell would come out, a spell like a supervolcano.

The rotten thing about having Mum as a mum is, I know how to stop being angry. I've been taught any number of ways to manage anger, and they really work. What she's never been able to teach me is how to *want* to manage it. So I go on seething and raging and knowing the whole time that it's my own fault, because I do know how to stop.

And this time was worse, because I couldn't make excuses for them. All these years, whenever someone took advantage of me, shoved me out of the way, left me exposed, for their own benefit, at least I've been able to do that. To tell myself that they were only doing what anyone would do. We all wanted to live, and we were all doing our best to make it out of here, to end up safe, no matter how mean and awful we had to be along the way. I was doing the same thing. I'd kicked a freshman out of a chair and spent mana to fix it so I could shove myself in with a bunch of kids who didn't want me, and because I'd been sitting there being rude and mean to them, I'd scared the New York kids. They needed Orion: that little buzzer on his wrist that brought him to their rescue if they ever did get into trouble, the power he dumped into their shared power sink. What right did I have to take that for myself, eight times and counting? Why did I deserve to live more than them?

But I had an answer now: I hadn't pulled malia even with a knife in my gut, and I'd gone after a maw-mouth to save half the freshmen instead of running away, and meanwhile Magnus had tried to murder me because Orion liked me, and Todd had destroyed Mika because he was scared, and because I had that answer, I couldn't help thinking actually I did deserve to live more than them. And I know nobody gets to live or not live because they *deserve* it, deserving doesn't count for a thing, but the point was, I now felt deep in my heart that I was in fact a better human being than Magnus or Todd, and hooray, all the prizes for me, but that wasn't helpful when what I actually needed was reasons why I shouldn't just wipe them out of existence.

I went on pacing for what felt like an hour. My gut hurt, and I was wasting time and effort that could have gone into something useful like the schoolwork I should've been doing, or the mana I should've been raising. Instead I built an elaborate fantasy of how Magnus would beg my forgiveness in front of everyone and sob and plead for me not to flay him alive, especially after I tore a strip or two off just to start, and Orion would just stand by with his face angry and disappointed and his arms folded, doing nothing to help him, rejecting all his friends and his home for me. Every few minutes I veered rapidly over to feeling sick at myself and saying out loud, "Okay, I'm going to walk back and forth three more times and then I'm going to meditate," trying to commit myself, and then I walked back and forth two more times and then I started over with the fantasy from the beginning, reworking it in my head. I even talked some of the lines out under my breath.

I'm not a moron, I knew it was dangerous: I was on the edge of casting. That's all that magic is, after all. You start with a clear intention, your destination; you gather up the power; and then you send the power traveling down the road, giving the clearest directions you can, whether it's with words or goop or metal. The better the directions are, the more well-traveled the road, the easier it is for the power to get to where you want it to go; that's why most wizards can't just invent their own spells and recipes. But I can blaze a trail to

Mordor anytime I want, and I still had nine full crystals in my chest, and so what if those ran out? There was loads of power to be had. After all, if Magnus deserved to die, why shouldn't I put his life to good use?

And that thought is exactly why I knew I had to stop, I knew I had to let it all go, or else I'd become a much worse person than Magnus and Todd and Jack all put together, and no more prizes for me. But I knew it the way you know the sixth biscuit in a row isn't good for you and you'll be sorry, and they're not even really very nice, and yet you keep eating them anyway.

That's why I opened the door when Aadhya knocked. I did check it was her and kept well back this time, I wasn't getting caught the same way twice, but I let her in, even though I didn't want company at all. At least having her there would make it harder for me to keep cramming the biscuits of re-venge fantasy into my mouth. "Yeah?" I said shortly but not outright rude, my idea of self-restraint at the moment.

Aadhya came in and let me shut the door, but she didn't answer me for a moment, which was odd for her; she doesn't dither. She looked around the room: it was the first time she'd ever come over. It was the first time—apart from Jack and Orion—that I'd ever had anyone over, in fact. At most a few people have come round to swap things with me, and on those occasions they didn't come in far enough for the door to close behind them. My room's pretty spartan. I spent my freshman year turning my cupboard into wall-mounted shelves, which are massively safer than any piece of furniture that has enclosed areas and a dark underside; I got credit in shop for it. I stripped my desk drawers for the same reason, traded for metal, and reinforced the legs and top of the desk instead, which is why it survived the incarnated flame's visit.

I've got a wobbly and rusted metal rack on top for papers that I also made myself out of the easiest metal I could get. Nothing else, besides the bed and the tool chest at the foot that I use to hold anything important enough that it would probably disappear if I left it lying around. Most kids have at least a few decorative bits here and there, a photo or cards on display; people give pottery and drawings at New Year. I've never been given any, and I don't waste my own time making them.

It didn't feel bare to me, but I grew up in a one-room yurt with a couple of boxes under our bed and Mum's worktable under the one round window. Except there I had the whole green world outside the door, and here this was clearly the room of a miserable loner, somebody like Mika, who couldn't even afford the risk of cupboards. It made me even more furious, looking at it through another person's eyes. Magnus probably had a quilt and a spare pillow, made sometime in the last thirty years by another New York student who'd passed them down on graduation day. His walls were probably covered with cheery cards and pictures people had made for him, or even actual wallpaper, if he'd wanted it enough. His furniture would be polished warm wood, with warded locks on the drawers and cubbyholes. Maybe he had a keep-fresh larder box; he certainly had a proper desk lamp. His pens never disappeared on him.

I could go and find out. Magnus would be in his room by now; it was close to curfew. I could force my way in and tell him I knew what he'd tried to do to me, and then I could shove him into the dark—not like Todd had done Mika, not all the way in, just enough to make clear that I *could* do it; that anytime I wanted to, I could push him in and take his lush, comfortable room all for me, since he and his enclave buddies thought that was a reasonable thing to do to another human being.

I had my hands clenched again, and I had almost forgotten Aadhya was there, and then she said, abruptly, "Did—El, did *you* take out the maw-mouth?"

It was like having a bucket of just-melted ice thrown all over me. My eyesight actually fuzzed out a bit, going dim: for a moment I was back inside the maw-mouth again, the horrible pulsing wet hunger of it, and I lunged for the middle of the room and threw up into the floor drain, heaving up wet chunks of my half-digested dinner burning with stomach acid. The feeling of them in my mouth made me heave again, sobbing in between rounds. I kept going until I was empty and for a while afterwards. I was vaguely aware that Aadhya was holding my hair back out of my face: my plait had come undone. When I stopped, she gave me a cup of water, and I rinsed and spat over and over until she said, "This is the last of the jug," and then I made myself sip a little, trying to wash the last bile back down my throat.

I crawled a few steps back from the drain and eased myself against the wall with my knees pulled up and my mouth wide open, trying not to smell my own breath.

"Sorry," Aadhya said, and I raised my head and stared at her. She was sitting on the floor just a little way from me, cross-legged with the jug in her hands. She was in her pajamas already, or what passes for that in here, a ratty pair of too-small shorts and long-sleeved top let out with cheap mending, like she'd got herself ready for bed and had been about to get in and then instead she'd come to ask me—ask me—"You did, didn't you," she said.

I wasn't in any state where I was going to think through what the right answer was, or what it would mean to tell her.

I just gave a nod. We sat there for a bit and didn't say any-thing. It felt like a long time, but the curfew bell didn't ring, so it couldn't have been. I still couldn't think at all. I just sat there existing.

Eventually Aadhya said, "I started on a mirror for next quarter. I asked Orion what he did to the pour to make it come out so great, and he said he didn't do anything special. He's not really a great alchemist, anyway. He's just doing it, you know? Then I remembered you used some kind of incan-tation after the enchantment. So I tried to find it, except all I found was this section in my metals handbook that said using incantations to smooth the pour is stupid, because that's try-ing to force your will onto the materials against their nature, and almost nobody can do it unless they're really powerful, so you shouldn't bother trying. It didn't make any sense any-way. You're an incantations-track junior, but you got assigned a magic mirror? That doesn't happen."

I gave a snort, more than half a snuffle: my nose was run-ning. It happens to *me*.

Aadhya kept going, talking faster; she sounded almost angry. "That phase-control spell—you said you burned through it in a couple hours after dinner. Meanwhile the se-niors who are thinking about bidding, they're all discussing if they can learn it in time for graduation. Besides, that whole book is a crazy big deal. Luck like that doesn't happen. You had to do something really horrible to get it, or really amaz-ing. And you were so wiped out Sunday—and Todd wasn't hallucinating, no way. A maw-mouth is the only thing that would have freaked him out that hard. He could *survive* any-thing else." Then she asked, "Where'd you get the mana?"

I didn't want to talk. My throat was really sore. I reached over to my little box and opened it and showed her my crys-

tals; the two cracked ones and the dull drained ones next to
the primed empties and my last nine full crystals. "Push-ups,"
I said briefly, and shut the box again and put it away.

"Push-ups," Aadhya said. "Sure, why not, push-ups." She
let out a bray of a laugh and looked away. "Why aren't you
telling anyone? Every enclave in the world is going to be
drooling over you."

The half accusation in the words made me angry and want
to cry at the same time. I got up and got my little half-full jar
of honey off my shelf. I take it to meals every weekend for the
chance of a refill, but it's hard to get, so I use it sparingly. But
this called for it. I whispered Mum's throat-soothing charm
over a small spoonful and washed it down with the last lukewarm swallow of water in the glass before I turned back to
Aadhya and stuck out my hand down at her, mockingly.

"Hi, I'm El. I can move mountains, literally," I said. "Do
you believe me?"

Aadhya stood up. "So you do a demo! You should've done
one freshman year, just asked some enclavers to spot you the
mana. They'd be fighting to have you on their teams—"

"I don't *want* to be on their teams!" I yelled hoarsely. "I
don't want to be on their teams at all!"

Chapter 9
UNKNOWN

I LOVE HAVING existential crises at bedtime, it's so restful. I lay awake for at least an hour after the final bell, staring furiously at the blue flicker of the gaslight by the door. Every five minutes or so I told myself to unclench my hands and go to sleep, with no effect. I tried to get up and get a drink of water—Aadhya felt bad for me being mental, I suppose, so she'd gone with me to the loo so I could refill my jug—and I even tried doing some maths homework, and I still couldn't fall to sleep.

I've been bellowing at Mum about joining an enclave ever since I was old enough to work out that when enclave wizards from as far away as Japan are turning up at your yurt for advice, it probably means that they would be happy to have you in-house. After the scratcher attack, she even went to visit one. She wouldn't look at London, but she tried this old place in Brittany that specializes in healing. She picked me up from school that afternoon and said, "I'm sorry, love, I just can't," and only shook her head when I demanded to know why. I told her flat-out I was going into an enclave after I graduated if I could get one to take me, and she just looked sad and said, "You'll do whatever's right for you, darling, of course." Once—I still feel a bit sick about it remembering—when I was twelve, I even screamed at her in tears and told her if she loved me she'd take us to an enclave, and she just wanted something to get me so nobody would blame her and it wouldn't hurt her perfect reputation. Three mals had tried for me that afternoon.

She kept a calm face on with me, but then she went back to the trees and cried herself sick where I couldn't see her, or at least where I couldn't have seen if I hadn't gone after her to scream at her even more. When I saw her sobbing I went back to the yurt and threw myself on the bed crying and determined to *let* the next mal that came along take me, as I was such a horrible daughter. But I didn't do it. I wanted to live.

I still want to live. I want Mum to live. And I'm not going to live if I try to go it alone. So I should show off and make clear to all the enclavers that I'm available to be won: a grand prize up for grabs to the highest bidder, a nuclear weapon any enclave could use to take out mals—to take out another enclave—to make themselves more powerful. To make themselves safe.

That's all Todd wanted. That's all Magnus wanted. They wanted to be safe. It's not that much to ask, it feels like. But we don't have it to begin with, and to get it and keep it, they'd push another kid into the dark. One enclave would push another into the dark for that, too. And they didn't stop at safety, either. They wanted comfort, and then they wanted luxury, and then they wanted excess, and every step of the way they still wanted to be safe, even as they made themselves more and more of a tempting target, and the only way they could stay safe was to have enough power to keep everyone off that wanted what they had.

When the enclaves first built the Scholomance, the induction spell didn't pull in kids from outside the enclaves. The enclavers made it sound like a grand act of generosity when they changed it to bring us all in, but of course it was never that. We're cannon fodder, and human shields, and useful new blood, and minions, and janitors and maids, and thanks to all the work the losers in here do trying to get into an alliance and an enclave after, the enclave kids get extra sleep and extra food and extra help, more than if it was only them in here. And we all get the illusion of a chance. But the only chance they're really giving us is the chance to be useful to them.

But why should they do anything else? They don't have any reason to care about us. We're not their children. We're the other gazelles, all of us trying to outrun the same pack of lions. And if we happen to be faster than their children, more powerful, their children will get eaten. If not while we're in here, when we get out, and we decide that we want some of the luxury they have tucked into those enclaves for ourselves. If we're too strong, we might even threaten their own lives. So they shouldn't care about us. Not until we sign on the dotted line. That's only sensible. You can't blame people for wanting their own kids to live. I understand it, every last bit of it.

And I wanted to want in. I want to have a daughter one day, a daughter who will live, who won't ever have to scream alone in the night when monsters come for her. I don't want to be alone in the night myself. I want to be safe, and I really wouldn't mind a little bit of comfort, and even a taste of luxury now and then. It's all I've been hungry for my whole life. I wanted to pretend that all of that was fair and okay, like Orion bleating how we've got the same chances.

But I can't pretend that, because I didn't grow up in that

lie, so I don't actually want in. I don't want that safety and comfort and luxury at the cost of other kids dying in here. And sure, it's not like that, it's not some simple equation like me in an enclave means kids are dying in here; the kids will go on dying in here anyway, whether I'm in an enclave or not. But just because it's a forty-sixth-order derivative equation or something doesn't mean that I can't work out which side of that equation is the guilty one.

And I've probably known it all along, maybe even before I got here, because otherwise Aadhya's right, I should have just blown the bloody doors off in my freshman year and shown everyone back then. Instead I've spent three years putting it off and coming up with convoluted plans for how I was going to arrange my dramatic revelation and meanwhile, at the first chance I got, I just started being as rude as I could to every enclave kid who crossed my path. I'd certainly done my very best to chase *Orion* off. If he wasn't a towering weirdo who liked that in a person, I'd have succeeded. And now Aadhya saying, "I won't tell," like she was making me a promise, and I'd said, "Thanks," instead of saying *No, no, tell everyone!*

But if I'm not joining an enclave, I really don't want anyone to know, after all. If people in here find out I destroyed a maw-mouth, some of them are going to look up that same journal article I read on the subject and understand what I am, what I can do. I could certainly stop being angry at Magnus then, because probably half of the enclavers would start trying to take me out. Especially if any of them pick up a whisper of my great-grandmother's prophecy. And I still want to live.

Filled with all these cheery and relaxing thoughts, I passed a comfortable night in which I slept perhaps three hours all broken up with marvelous nightmares of being back in the maw-mouth and wide-awake bursts of gnawing anxiety in which I contemplated my odds of making it out of here alive all on my own with my nine remaining crystals against a whole graduation hall full of maleficaria. There was a side of gnawing hunger, too; I'd thrown up most of my day's food. My throat was still sore and painful the next morning, and my eyes were gummy.

Aadhya had been knocking on my door in the mornings on the way to the loo. I half expected her not to come that morning, but she called round, and then Liu poked her head out and called, "Will you wait a moment?" We stopped at her door while she grabbed her toothbrush and flannel and comb, so I didn't even have the worry of whether we were going to talk about the things I didn't want to talk about. As we walked, Liu and I talked about our history papers instead, and in the bathroom Aadhya and I took first watch while Liu grimly attacked the mysteriously appearing snarls in her waist-long hair. She was having to pay back three years' worth of great hair days all at once. Malia is great for your looks, right up until it really really isn't.

"I need to cut this all off," she said out loud, with gritted teeth. It was the sensible choice, and not just for saving time on hair care: you don't want to offer any mals a convenient handhold. Almost everyone in here shares the same fabulous hairstyle: half grown out after having been shingled as short as possible, as quickly as possible, the last time you had a chance to use a pair of proper scissors or hair clippers. Bringing a pair of bad ones that close to vital bits like eyes and throats is a very iffy proposition. If you'd like to know the hard-and-fast rule for telling whether a pair has gone to the bad, so would all of us. There's a senior named Okot from Sudan, one of the maintenance-track kids, who blew most of his induction weight allowance on a battery-powered electric razor and a hand-crank charger. He's made an absolute killing loaning it out to people over the years, and at the start of this year, he promised it to a group of five freshmen, who've spent all their free time since building him mana for graduation. Now he's in an alliance with three enclavers from Johannesburg.

Going fully shaved like that is popular if you can afford it. Dreadlocks are unfortunately not a great idea thanks to lock-leeches, which you can probably imagine, but in case you need help, the adult spindly thing comes quietly down at night and pokes an ovipositor into any big clumps of hair, lays an egg inside, and creeps away. A little while later the leech hatches inside its comfy nest, attaches itself to your scalp almost unnoticeably, and starts very gently sucking up your blood and mana while infiltrating further. If you don't get it out within a week or two, it usually manages to work its way inside the skull, and you've got a window of a few days after that before you stop being able to move. On the bright side, something else usually finishes you off quickly at that point.

So the very longest anyone usually lets their hair get is shoulder-length; mine only ever gets a couple inches longer than that because no one goes out of their way to let me know when they've got hold of good scissors. Even most enclavers won't bother to grow their hair. Liu's hair had been a power statement, an announcement of her family's growing strength for anyone who met her. But without malia, it was probably going to be too much of a liability for her to maintain.

Aadhya threw me a quick look to make sure I was still attending, then broke bathroom silence. "Are you serious?"

"Getting there!" Liu said, letting her arms drop for a rest, panting.

"I'd buy it off you," Aadhya said. "I could make you something of your choice next term, first quarter."

"Really?" Liu said.

"Yeah," Aadhya said. "It's long enough to string the sirenspider lute I'm making."

"I'll think about it," Liu said, and went back to combing the tangles out of her hair with more enthusiasm. Aadhya went back to watching. She wasn't entitled to an answer right then: bathroom and table company is important, but it's not like an alliance. And if Aadhya wanted Liu's hair, there would be other kids who'd want it. Enclave kids in artifice track, making themselves top-notch weapons for graduation, and some of them with extras or maybe even an alliance slot to offer in trade.

I thought about it hard while I took my turn in the shower. Aadhya was even more clearly my best shot for an alliance at this point. She was the only person who knew what I had going, and she at least wanted me for bathroom company. But I still was a long way from being a good bargain for her. I certainly wouldn't have picked me in her place: if she pulled off a sirenspider lute during the first half of next term, she was sure to get at least a dozen alliance offers from enclavers. Nobody else in here was going to have a sirenspider instrument: they're too large to bring inside, except maybe a tiny flute or something, and wind instruments aren't a great bet for graduation. You need your breath for casting incantations and running and optionally screaming. With a prize like that, she might even get one of those guaranteed placement offers, like the one Todd and his crew had dangled to get the valedictorian. Enclaves favor applications from kids who have been allies with their kids, but they don't actually take everyone.

I was increasingly sure to get zero alliance offers from enclavers, and apparently I wasn't going to take them if they did come. I couldn't even offer Aadhya the strategy of putting together a solid small team that one of the more loserish enclaver kids would pick to get them out. If I wanted her to even think about taking the chance of going with me, I was going to have to score a lot of points between now and New Year's.

So when we were all done and waiting at the meeting point for two more kids to walk to breakfast, I said casually, "Liu, I was just thinking. Do *you* need the phase-control spell?"

They both looked at me. Liu said slowly, "My family could really use it, but . . ." But they weren't rich enough to put her in the running. She was on her own in here almost as much as we were; she'd got a box of hand-me-downs from an older cousin who graduated six years ago, but that was it, and it had been passed to her through a kid who had graduated in our freshman year, who had agreed to be the go-between in exchange for getting to use the stuff until Liu came in.

"You could bid your hair," I said. "Aadhya's running the auction for me, she gets a cut."

It meant losing out on one of five bids, and on top of it, I'd be making Aadhya an even more appealing target for enclavers to recruit for their own alliances. A sirenspider lute strung with wizard hair would be really powerful. But it was also a chance I couldn't pass up: Aadhya would owe me for this, and—

"Or you could give it to me," Aadhya said to Liu, abruptly. "And El could give you the spell. And we'd have the lute for graduation. You could write some spells for it, and El can sing."

I just stood there dumbly staring at her. Liu looked more

than a little surprised, and she had a right to be. That *was* alliance; that was an alliance offer. You don't give things to other people in here. When you lend somebody a pen for one class, that's ink gone, ink that you'll have to replace by going to the stockroom. They have to pay you back for it. That's why you know you're dating if you don't have to pay it back. But you can break up with someone you're dating. You can't break up with your allies unless they do something exceptionally horrible, like Todd, or you all agree to split up. If you ditch an ally, even a weirdo loser girl that everyone hates, nobody else is going to offer you a slot. You can't possibly trust someone to watch your back in the graduation hall if you can't trust them to stick with you during the year.

Liu looked at me, a question: was I making the offer, too? I couldn't even make myself nod. I was on the verge of crying again, or possibly vomiting, and that was when an unholy shriek went off right by my right ear, putting half the world on mute, and the charred and twisted remnant of some mal that I suppose had been about to bite flew past me and described a lovely curve through the air to smash into an unidentifiable heap of cinders and ash on the floor.

"Are you not paying attention anymore on *purpose* now?" Orion demanded, coming up from behind me. I flipped him off with the hand that wasn't clamped protectively over my abused ear.

So that left the offer just sitting there through breakfast, and we couldn't talk about it, either, not in front of other people. It would be like snogging at the table: there are people who'd do it, but I'm not one of them. But I couldn't stop thinking about it, especially because I could see Liu thinking about it, too: she watched the kids who came by to take a look at the phase-change spell with a different eye. Not just idle curiosity, or getting a sense of the market, but like she was considering what their bids might be worth to her, what might come in that she'd be able to use. It had been clever of Aadhya actually to make the suggestion now, before the bidding happened: if we did go in together and let people know about it, some of the bids would be tailored to have useful things for the two of them, our alliance as a whole, not just for me personally.

At least, it had been clever of her to do it now, if she were going to do it at all, which I still couldn't really get my head round. But Aadhya didn't show any signs of having second thoughts; she ate a hearty breakfast, chatted up the kids coming by for the auction—a lot better than I did—and talked about her shield holder project and the spares she'd made, which obviously got Liu to prick up her ears even more.

I couldn't guess which way Liu would jump, though, and the offer had clearly been for a three-way alliance. But if she didn't go for it, I decided abruptly, halfway through breakfast, I'd ask Aadhya if she'd try to find another third person to go in with us, or agree to aim for alliance without sealing the deal right away, provisional terms. That was the opposite of a power move on my part, but she already knew I didn't have a lot of other options, so sod it.

It felt strange to have that thought, like it didn't belong in my head. It's always mattered a lot to me to keep a wall up round my dignity, even though dignity matters fuck-all when the monsters under your bed are real. Dignity was what I had instead of friends. I gave up trying to make any at about a month into our first year. Nobody I asked for company ever said yes unless they were desperate, and nobody ever asked me. The same thing has happened to me at every school I've ever gone to; every club, course, activity.

Before induction, I'd had some faint hope things would be different in here; maybe it wouldn't happen with other wiz-

ards. It was a stupid hope to have, since I'm not the only wizard kid who went to mundane schools by a long shot—if you
aren't in an enclave, the sensible choice is sending your kid to
the largest mundane school you can find, because maleficaria
avoid mundanes. Mundanes aren't exactly invulnerable to
mals—a scratcher can shove a giant foot-long claw through
your belly whether you've got mana or not—but they have
one extremely powerful protection: they don't believe in
magic.

You'll say loads of people believe in all sorts of codswallop
from the Snake Goddess to theologically questionable angels
to astrology, but as someone who spent her formative years
among the most determinedly credulous people in the world,
it's not at all the same thing. Wizards don't have faith in
magic. We *believe* in magic, the way mundanes believe in
cars. No one has deep discussions around a bonfire about
whether a car is real or not, unless they've taken more drugs
than usual, which is, not coincidentally, the condition of most
mundanes who *do* encounter mals.

Doing magic in front of someone who doesn't believe in it
is loads harder. Worse, if their disbelief trumps either your
certainty or your mana, and the spell doesn't come off, you'll
probably have trouble the *next* time you try and cast it,
whether the unbeliever's still there or not. Do that a few
more times and you'll stop being able to do magic at all. In
fact, it's entirely possible there are loads of unknowing potential wizards out there, people like Luisa who could hold
enough mana to cast spells, only they've been raised mundane and so they can't, because they don't *know* that magic
works, which means it doesn't.

And if you're a mal, and therefore only exist because of
magic in the first place, you effectively have to persuade a
mundane that you exist and function in the world, contrary

to all their expectations, before you can eat them. In fact, one time towards the end of my secondary school career, an excessively ambitious yarnbogle tried to come after me in gym class; the teacher caught sight of it, was absolutely convinced it was a rat, and whacked it triumphantly with a cricket bat. When she stopped whacking, it was in fact indistinguishable from a smashed rat, even though I couldn't have killed a yarnbogle with a cricket bat if I hammered on it all day. The reward's not worth the risk, considering that mundanes contain essentially no flavor or nutritional value from a mal's perspective, and so they keep well away. Which is why lots of wizard kids get sent to school with mundanes.

But Mum really does live in the back of beyond by wizard standards—too far from any enclave to conveniently work for them or trade with them—so I was the only wizard kid I knew, and at the time I tried telling myself that the reason mundanes didn't like me was they sensed the mana or something. But no. Wizard kids are just kids, and they don't like me, either.

And all right, as of five days ago, I had Orion, but Orion was too weird to count. I was reasonably sure that my one tried-and-true method of being aggressively rude wasn't actually how normal people made their friends. But maybe I got to count Aadhya and Liu as friends, now. I wasn't sure, and what did it mean if I could? It wasn't accompanied by nearly the warm triumphant glow of achievement I'd always imagined as part of the experience. I suppose I was still waiting for someone to give me the tatty friendship bracelet I'd never got at the Girl Guides. But someone holding out an *alliance,* offering to watch your back and go out of their way to save your life, that was on such a different scale that I'd obviously missed some intermediate steps.

It got me wondering about Nkoyo, too, while I walked to

languages with her and her friends. I didn't have any doubts about Cora and Jowani: neither of them liked me any more than they ever had. But the very contrast made me think maybe I could at least call Nkoyo friendly, if not a friend. I took my courage in both hands and asked her, as casually as I could manage, as if I didn't care very much about the answer, "Do you know any groups revising for the Latin final exam?"

"Yeah," she said, casually for real; as far as I could tell, she didn't even think about the answer. "Some of us are getting together work period on Thursday in the lab. The ticket is two copies of a decent spell."

"Would that fire wall I traded with you work?" I said, struggling to match her easy tone, as if of course I was welcome, if I could meet the fee—

"Oh, that's loads better than you need," she said. "More like a utility spell. I'm bringing one for restoring papyrus."

"I've got a medieval one for tanning leather," I said. That was actually a section of a larger spell meant for binding a cursed grimoire that would siphon off a bit of mana from every wizard every time they cast one of the spells inside: a very clever technique for creating a mana-stealer that would go unnoticed. But the leather tanning worked perfectly well on its own, too.

Nkoyo gave a shrug and a nod, *sure why not,* and we were at the door of the language hall. All four of us took turns putting our homework from yesterday into the marking slot, a thin postbox slit set in the metal wall at the door. We'd timed it quite well: you don't want to be dropping off your homework when there's a proper crush of people coming in, because then you can end up boxed in if something jumps out of the slit. You also don't want to be dropping it off really early, because something's much more likely to jump out of the slit then. But if you hand something in even ten seconds past the start of the lesson, it's late, and you'll get marked down.

Getting marked down in languages means you get assigned remedial work that's just the same stuff you've already done, for days or even weeks sometimes. That might not sound like a punishment, but as we're all studying languages to *learn spells,* it's absolutely brutal. The next time you ask for a spell, you'll get one that has material you theoretically should be up to, but don't actually know, and you won't be able to move on past it until you get through your stupid remedial backlog and finally reach whatever lesson you were at before.

I handed in my Arabic worksheet and then sat down at a booth to open the waiting folder and discover my fate, which turned out to be *three* Arabic worksheets, along with a vicious quiz in Classical Sanskrit that was labeled as taking twenty minutes but actually needed the entire lesson. I had barely finished enough of the questions to get a pass mark when the warning bell rang. I had to scribble my name on the sheet, pile all my things into my bookbag, and carry it awkwardly with my arm wrapped around it like a basket just to get in the line to stick the quiz into the slot before the final bell. I'd have to get the three worksheets done tonight instead, eating into my mana-building time, which I didn't have enough of to begin with.

Even that couldn't wreck my mood, which had been whipsawing so aggressively lately that I was beginning to feel like a yo-yo. I'd got used to my ordinary level of low-grade bitterness and misery, to putting my head down and soldiering on. Being happy threw me off almost as much as being enraged. But I wasn't in the least bit tempted to refuse when I got to the writing workshop and saw Liu looking around: she had the neighboring desk saved *for me.* I took myself over and got my bag down between our chairs: with someone on the other side who wouldn't object, I'd be able to steal a few moments here and there to sort it out.

I sat down and got out my current project, an extremely bad villanelle in which I was carefully avoiding the word *pestilence,* which was trying so hard to shove its way into every stanza that I was sure that if I actually wrote it down, the whole thing would turn into a tidy evocation of a new plague. I'm probably the only student who tries to prevent my writing assignments from turning into new spells.

I worked on it for the first five minutes before I belatedly thought that I might want to talk to Liu, if we were friends now. "What are you working on?" I asked her, as dull as small talk can get, but at least it had the benefit of an obvious answer.

She glanced sidelong over at me and then said, "I have a song spell passed down from my great-grandmother. I'm trying to write English lyrics for it."

Translating spells is basically impossible. It's not even reliably safe to do something like take a Hindi spell, rewrite it in Urdu script, and pass it along to someone else to learn. That would work three times out of four, but the fourth one would really get you. Song-spells are the only exception. But you don't exactly translate them; it's more that you write a new spell in the new language, but set to the same music and on the same theme. It's often harder than writing a new spell from scratch, and most of the time it still doesn't work, the same way most writing assignments don't successfully turn into a spell. Sometimes you just get a pale imitation of the original spell. But once in a while, if the new spell is good on its own, you get an almost doubled effect out of it: whatever your new spell does, and a significant part of whatever the original spell did. Those can be really powerful.

But more to the point for me, that was exactly along the lines of the alliance Aadhya had suggested this morning. Liu added, "Do you want to hear?" and held out a tiny music player, the kind with no screen that play for a million hours on a charge. Even so, the only way you can get battery power in here is by hand-cranking, and you could use that kind of work to generate mana instead, so you don't spend it for nothing. I put in the headphones and listened to the music— no lyrics, which was just as well, since I did *not* have time to start Mandarin right now. I hummed along with it under my breath, tapping my fingers on my leg to try and beat it into my head. Even wordless, it still had the feel of a spell to it, subtle but building. I don't know how to describe a spell song as opposed to an ordinary song; the best I can do is that it's like holding a cup in your hand instead of something solid all the way through. You get a sense that you can put power into it, and how much. This one was deep, a well going far down instead of a cup, something you could drop a coin or a pebble into and hear an echo coming back a long way. I took out the headphones and said to Liu, "Is it a mana amplifier?"

She had been watching me intently. She gave a start and then said, "You can't have heard it," which meant it was a family spell they weren't trading yet; they were probably saving it to exchange for some other piece they'd need to build an enclave of their own.

"I haven't," I said. "It just has that feel."

She nodded a little, her eyes on my face thoughtful.

We walked to history together afterwards and sat next to each other at the uncomfortable desks. The history classrooms are all scattered round on the cafeteria floor, reasonably high up. The worst part of history is that our assigned textbooks are incredibly boring, and there aren't booths like in the language labs, so you can hear every single noise everyone else is making, whispers and coughs and farts and the endlessly squeaking desks and chairs. Up at the front there's always this droning flickery video lecture going on that you have to strain to hear, ninety percent of which is completely useless and doesn't matter even to our grades except for a few random bits that show up for enormous points on quizzes. All the sections are either before lunch, so you're starving and it's hard to focus, or after lunch so you're ready to fall asleep. I always take before lunch, because it's safer, but it's a slog.

Having someone next to me, actually *with* me, made class at least a hundred times more bearable. We traded off watching the lecture and taking notes in fifteen-minute chunks, and worked on our final papers in between. We'd already exchanged translations of our source materials, and I could see her using the ones I'd given her, so they'd been useful. Liu's were good, too. I didn't have to try to think well of her just because she'd maybe put up with me.

Liu takes history in English so she can use it for her language requirement and get more class choice flexibility, so we've been in most of the same sections. But we'd almost never sat next to each other before. A couple of times, if she had to get supplies and came a bit late, and it was a choice of me or someone poorly and coughing, or the boy who puts his hand in his pants all class long—he tried sitting next to me once and once only; I stared straight at him with all the murder in my heart and he stopped and took his hand out—she'd take me. But most of the time she'd walk over with whoever she'd sat with in the previous class: there are a dozen other Mandarin-speakers doing English history who were fine letting her sit next to them, even if they got a vague whiff of the malia.

There wasn't a whiff to be had today. She hadn't started

using it again, I could tell. She still had color, and a shine to her eyes, but it was more than that: she just seemed softer, more pulled-in, a snail mostly tucked into a shell. I wondered if that was an aftereffect or if it was just *her*: probably her, since that's what Mum's meditation spell does. It didn't really line up with the malia use. Her family might have pushed her to do it: strategically there was good sense to it, and once she'd come in with a basket full of sacrifices, probably all her weight allowance dedicated to that, she'd have been hard-pressed to do anything else.

I didn't ask her what her new plan was, if she had one. It wasn't like she'd been openly using malia, and we weren't allies yet, so that was the kind of question that could cause alarm, particularly coming from the supposed girlfriend of the local maleficer-slaying hero. She might be in a tough position for graduation now, for that matter, if she didn't go back to it. She wouldn't have been storing mana along the way if she'd been planning all along to get a big chunk of malia out of her remaining sacrifices.

Which didn't make her a great choice for me to ally with, but I didn't actually care. I wanted her, I wanted Aadhya, and not just because I didn't have another option. I wanted this thing here between us, walking to lunch together after a morning working hard side by side, a small warm feeling that we were on the same team. I didn't just want them to help me live. I wanted for *them* to live. "I'd like to," I said to her abruptly, on the way to the cafeteria. "If you do." I didn't need to tell her what I was talking about. I knew she was thinking about it, too.

She didn't answer for a moment, and then she said softly, "I'm pretty behind on mana."

So I was right: she'd decided not to go back to malia, and

now she was reasonably screwed. But—she'd said so. She wasn't letting us sign on with her under false pretenses. "Me too. But we won't need as much with that spell of yours, and the phase-control spell," I said. "I don't mind if Aadhya doesn't."

"I can't cast the spell yet myself," Liu said. "My grand-mother . . . My mom and dad are working really hard, they take jobs at enclaves a lot. So my grandmother raised me. She gave me the spell to bring, even though she wasn't really sup-posed to. It's an advanced spell, only a few really strong wiz-ards in our family have got it working. But I thought . . . if I managed to translate it, maybe it might get easier."

"If you can't get a translation working by the end of next quarter, I'll drop some of my other languages and pick up Mandarin," I said.

She looked at me. "I know you can sing, but it's really hard."

"I'll be able to cast it," I said positively. Mana amplification is more or less a prerequisite for any of the monstrous spells I have, even with the loads of power they require to begin with. I've never got hold of anything nearly so useful as an incantation that separates out the amplification step enough that I could tease just that piece of the spell away from the bits with all the screaming and death, but the process is hap-pening along the way.

She took a deep breath and nodded. "Then . . . if Aadhya's okay, too . . ."

She didn't go on. But I nodded, and we just looked at each other for a moment, walking down the corridor, and Liu smiled at me, just a little tentative wobble at the corners of her mouth, and I was smiling back at her. It felt strange on my face.

"Want to work on the history paper after lunch?" I asked. "I have a carrel in the library, in the languages section."

"Sure," she said. "But isn't Orion going with you?" And what she *didn't* mean by that was whether Orion was going to be there for her to hang out with; she just meant, was there enough room for all three of us.

"It's a monster of a desk," I said. "It'll be fine, we'll just grab a folding chair on the way," but actually after lunch Orion said to me hurriedly, "I'm going downstairs, I've still got some stuff to do."

"Are you saying that because you've got some stuff to do, or because you'd rather lurk below than endure even modest amounts of human interaction?" I asked. "Liu's not going to be a twat around you." I firmly didn't offer to ditch her for his sake: we weren't *actually* dating.

"No, she's fine," Orion said. "I like her, she's fine. No, I've got stuff to do."

He didn't sound very convincing, but I wasn't going to point that out. He didn't owe me excuses. I shrugged. "Try not to dissolve yourself in acid or anything."

Liu and I had a great work session: we blazed through almost half our history papers. "I've got a group project down in the lab after dinner tonight, but I'd do work period again tomorrow," she told me as we left. I nodded, aglow with the thought that maybe I'd ask Aadhya or even Nkoyo to come up with me after dinner instead. I had *people,* in the plural, that I could ask to join me in the library, and even if they said no, they weren't really saying no, they were only saying not this time. It almost made me happier when Aadhya did cry off when I asked her at lunch, because she said she wanted to do some artifice work in her own room, and I could believe her; it wasn't just an excuse.

"But stop in before bedtime," she said. "We could go for a snack bar run, if you've got credit," and Liu and I nodded: we'd all had a chance to think it over, it was time to talk about it, to decide if we were going ahead.

I hugged the feeling to me all through afternoon classes, and I didn't even let it be spoiled when I saw Magnus and Chloe talking to Orion outside the cafeteria at dinner, asking him to come to the library with the New York crew afterwards. "Bring El," she was even saying, asking him to serve me up for the next attempt on a silver platter.

"I can't, I'm—going to the lab," Orion said.

"The lab, huh?" Magnus said. "Not a room?"

Orion did sound like he was making up an excuse, but Magnus shot a look over at me that made clear what he thought was getting covered up. Orion just said, obliviously, "Huh? No, not a room," about as convincing as before.

"Yeah, okay," Magnus said. "*Galadriel* going to be in the lab with you?"

"Afraid not," I said, with a snap: if he was going to be asking about me, I felt every right to intrude on the conversation. "I'm working on a paper."

"You want to join us in the library, El?" Chloe actually said to me outright. "We've got room at our table." A sure sign of the magnitude of their desperation: enclave kids didn't ask you to join them. At most they told you that you were welcome, with enormous condescension. Magnus himself looked highly annoyed by the necessity.

"No," I said. Then I went on into the cafeteria without saying bye to them, and Orion actually left them to catch up to me in the line.

"You can't tell me that Chloe was trying to get you to suck up, just then," he said.

"No, it was a pure and generous offer straight from her heart," I said. "Meant to go straight to mine, too. That crawler last night didn't go after me randomly."

"Oh for—right, they're being nice, so now they're trying to murder you, for no reason," Orion said. He had the gall to sound exasperated. "Are you kidding me? You want me to come after all and protect you from the evil schemes of Chloe Rasmussen?"

"I want you to shove your entire head in the mash," I told him, and vengefully scooped up both of the last two sausages in the steam tray. But I gave him one at the table. It wasn't his fault he'd grown up in a hive of entitled and murderous wee-vils.

I was fairly gobsmacked when, after all that, Chloe actually had another go at me in the library: she intercepted me in the reading room on my way into the stacks. "Still not in-terested," I told her icily.

"No, El, listen," she said. I walked away from her and into the incantations aisle, but she actually came in after me and grabbed my arm. "Look, will you quit being a bitch for *five seconds*?" she hissed, which was rich coming from her, and then she added, "It's not—don't go to your carrel."

I stopped in the corridor and stared at her. She wouldn't look me in the face. She had a vaguely hunted and half-guilty expression, actually, glancing back over her shoulder towards the reading room. We were in dim light, but probably at least partly visible from the New York corner. I could see Magnus there on one of the settees.

"Just—come sit with us, okay?" Chloe said. "Or go to your room or something."

"How long will my room be safe? Surely that's going to be Magnus's next clever idea." I was constructing a very detailed fantasy of marching over there and flattening his nose for him: a good punch straight down from above would do it, and have a really satisfying crunch. "Or maybe not: I suppose he'd be worried about getting Orion with it, too. That would be quite the goal, taking him out yourselves while going to all this trouble just to stop me poaching him."

Chloe flinched. "Have you said yes to Dubai?"

"I haven't been asked to Dubai! I fixed a chair in their corner because I'm looking to pick up a few measly words of Arabic. And if I had been asked and said yes, it wouldn't justify you lot trying to murder me with crawlers!" I added through my teeth, because Chloe had the nerve to look relieved.

"What? No! We didn't—" Chloe obviously realized halfway through her sentence that denial wasn't going to work, and shifted tacks. "Look, Magnus thought you were a maleficer. The crawler only had a malia-siphon spell. As long as you weren't a heavy-duty maleficer, the worst it would do was make you a little bit sick."

She made it sound like a noble defense. I stared at her. "I'm *strict mana.*" Chloe stopped with her mouth agape at me, shocked like the possibility hadn't even occurred to her. I'm sure it hadn't, to any of them. That crawler had been about to turn into a shiny new mal. When you make a construct with the ability to collect power on its own in any way, that's what you're asking for. You can wag your finger at it and tell it to be good, but if ever it can't get power from approved sources, the odds are at least fifty-fifty that it'll start taking it from anywhere it can get it. And since Magnus had made this one with the secret hope in his heart that it would drain evil-me dry, I was reasonably certain its odds were a lot higher. And then it *would* have killed me.

Chloe agreed with me, for that matter; she'd gone sickly pale, for good selfish reason: when a construct goes malicious, one of the first people it heads for is its maker, and anyone around them who might have contributed to its creation. It creates a tidy vulnerability that helps the construct suck out *their* mana. Not that I felt particularly sorry for her. "What's the present waiting at my desk, a box of jangler mites?" I demanded.

She swallowed and said, a little tremulously, "No, it's—it's an unbreaking sleep spell. He and Jennifer were going to put a hypno spell on you and ask you questions . . ."

"Assuming that nothing ate me before they got there."

Chloe did have the grace to look ashamed. "I'm so sorry, I really am. We've been arguing about it all week—most of us didn't think it, everyone's just really worried . . . But—if you're strict mana, that's—great, that's *amazing*," she informed me earnestly—yes, so amazing how her mate had nearly killed me by accident!—and carried right on from there. "Honestly, even without knowing that, most of us already wanted to recruit you. Knowing you're strict mana, I can just say it, five of us will vote you straight in, and Orion would make six. That's a majority. You can have one of the guaranteed places, and—"

"Thanks ever so!" I said, incredulously. "After having a pop at me, twice?"

She stopped and bit her lip. "Magnus will apologize, I promise," she said after a moment, as if she thought we were negotiating, as if she thought—

Well, as if she thought that I'd like a guaranteed enclave slot in New York City, which was more or less everything I'd ever desperately wanted and had spent most of the last six years strategizing to get, and here she was holding it out without even a single string attached.

And what I felt, because I'm me, was violently irritated, not at her but at Mum, who wasn't even here to look at me with that shining warm smile in her whole face that she gets once in a very rare while when I've made her really happy. Like the time when I was twelve and we had an enormous fight about cheating, because I didn't see why I shouldn't just take the last bit of life out of this bird I'd found dying in the forest anyway, and I stormed away and then came back to the yurt very grudgingly an hour later and told her even more grudgingly that I'd just sat in the trees with the bird until it died, and then buried it. I hated having to tell her, I hated how happy it made me seeing her face glow. It felt like *giving in*, and I hated giving in more than anything.

And I hated it just as much now when Mum wasn't here but I could see her face anyway, her happiness that I wasn't going to take what Chloe was offering me, the priceless unattainable thing I'd declared with enormous firmness I intended to get. Except I couldn't take it. It was so obviously rubbish after Liu saying quietly, *I'm behind on mana.* And not even because she and Aadhya wanted me, and Chloe only cared about clinging to Orion. They were just the better deal. When they were offering an alliance, they were offering their lives. They were offering to go all-in, asking me to do the same. Chloe didn't have a thing on the table by comparison.

"I don't want an apology," I said resentfully. "I'm not coming to New York."

Chloe's face went stricken. "If—Are you going to London?" she asked, her voice shaking. "Is this—is this because of Todd? He's going to be kicked out, obviously, no one in New York would—"

"It's not Todd!" I said, irritated even more, because she hadn't the slightest right to an answer, only she sounded like I was stabbing her with knives. "I'm not going to any enclave."

Chloe was starting to look bewildered. "But—are you and

206 ♦ NAOMI NOVIK

Orion just—" She couldn't even come up with something to finish the sentence.

"*We* aren't doing anything. I don't even understand why all of you are freaking out this way. Not that it's any of your business, but I'm *not* dating Orion, and even if I were, two weeks ago he didn't know my name. And you're ready to offer me a guaranteed slot? What if in a month he's taken up with a girl from Berlin?"

I thought that at least would make her back off, but Chloe didn't look at all comforted. She had an odd, confused wobbling sort of expression, and then abruptly she said, "You're the only person Orion's ever actually hung out with."

"Right, sorry, I forgot that your kind aren't allowed to associate with the plebeians."

"That's not what I mean!" she said. "He doesn't hang out with us, either." Which was a bizarre thing to say, given I'd seen him hanging out with her almost nonstop for the last three years, and my face must have shown it, because she shook her head. "He knows us, his mom told him to look out for us, but he doesn't—talk to any of us. He has to sit somewhere at meals and in classes, so he sits with us, but he doesn't say anything unless you ask him a question. He never comes and just hangs out, not with anyone—not here, not in our rooms; he doesn't even study with anyone! Except with you."

I stared at her. "What about Luisa?"

"Luisa was constantly begging him to let her follow him around, and he didn't shove her off because he felt sorry for her," Chloe said. "He still avoided her whenever he could. I've known him since we were born, and the only reason he knows my name is that his mom drilled him with flash cards in second grade. Even when we were kids, all he ever wanted to do is hunt mals."

"Yes, how could Candy Land possibly stack up against mal-hunting?" I said, incredulously.

"You think that's a joke? When we were in *preschool,* a suckerworm got into our classroom. The teacher found out because Orion was in the corner laughing, and she asked him what was so funny and he held it up in both hands to show us. It was thrashing around with its mouth going, trying to bite. We all screamed and he jumped and pulled it into two pieces by accident. All of us got sprayed with its guts." My face screwed up involuntarily: ew. She grimaced in memory. "He was doing gate shifts by the time he was ten. I don't mean he'd be assigned, it was his idea of fun. Magistra Rhys, he's her only kid, all our lives she was constantly dragging him to our places for playdates, to get him to make friends, and the whole time he was over, he'd just try to find ways to sneak out and go down to the gates so he could jump any mals that came in. He's not—*normal.*"

I laughed, I couldn't help it. It was that, or slap her. "Would you say he's got negativity of spirit?" I jeered.

"I'm not being mean!" she said tightly. "You think we didn't want to like him? I'm *alive* because of him. The summer when I was nine, we had a lyefly infestation in the city. Not a big deal, right?" she added, in a self-deprecating sort of way, as if she were almost ashamed to complain of anything so trivial. "The older kids had to stay inside while the council figured out what to do, but the lyeflies weren't bothering any of us under eleven. I was at the playground across the street from the enclave when I got a mana spurt."

I've read about mana spurts in the cheery "As Your Mana Grows" pamphlet that Mum pushed on me, but I've never experienced one myself. The capacity to hold mana does ex-pand in sudden jumps for most of us, but you don't get over-

whelmed with a surge of mana when you haven't got enough
of it to fill the capacity you already have. Chloe had obviously
been in a different situation.

"I was playing—" she shaped an enclosed space with her
hands, "—under the slide, with a couple of friends. No mundanes. And the lyeflies, the whole swarm, they all just came
for me. They started gnawing through the shield my mom
made me wear. There were so many—" She stopped and
swallowed. "My friends screamed and ran out. I couldn't do
anything. It felt like mana was coming out my nose, my
mouth, my ears. I didn't remember a single spell. I still have
nightmares about it sometimes," Chloe added, and I believed
her. She'd wrapped her arms around herself without even
thinking, her shoulders hunched in. "Orion was walking
around the playground edge, just kicking pebbles, not playing with any of us. He ran right in and burned them all off
me. I thought he was the most amazing person in the entire
world."

I was trying ferociously hard to hang on to being angry,
but it was hard going. I didn't *want* to give her any sympathy.
The one time a swarm of lyeflies came through the commune, when I was small, Mum had to sit up all day and night
holding me tight in her lap, singing a shield over us without
stopping until they gave up and flew onward, and if she'd lost
her voice, we'd both have died. Chloe had an enclave to hide
in, and a shield with enclave power behind it, and surely if
Orion hadn't come to her rescue, one of the grown-up child-
minders would have dashed right over to help. It was the one
thing that had happened to her, the one bad thing, not the
first of a thousand bad things. But—I couldn't help but be
with her in it: nine years old with mana erupting through
you, being swarmed by a cloud of lyeflies, feeling them gnaw-

ing their way to your flesh—I was hunching up myself, hearing a scratcher clawing at the wards on my threshold.

But fortunately for my spleen, Chloe was going on urgently from there, saying, "I spent months after that, following him around, trying to be his friend, asking him to do things together. He always said no unless his mom made him. And it wasn't just that he didn't like me. *All* of us have tried. Some of our parents even told us to, but that's not why, we didn't do it to suck up to the Domina in waiting or anything. It was for *him*. We all knew he was special, we were all grateful. But it didn't even register. He wasn't being a snob or anything, he's never mean or rude, I just—didn't matter to him. Nobody ever mattered to him before."

She waved a hand up and down over me, and she sounded so very sincerely bewildered. "Then he talks to you once, and all of a sudden he's making excuses for following you around. One day he's got to help you fix a door, the next he thinks you're a maleficer, then he's got to help you because you're hurt. He sits with you at lunch, he even comes to the library when you ask him. You know how many times I've tried to get him to come to the library? He came with us twice, the first week of freshman year, and I don't think he's come up here since. We even heard he did your *maintenance shift* with you! So yes, we *are* all freaking out. We weren't arguing over whether or not it's worth giving you a guaranteed spot. If Orion actually liked someone, none of us would think twice, nobody in the whole enclave would. We've only been arguing whether or not you're a maleficer who's *doing* something to him."

She finished up this litany and stopped defiantly, as if she was waiting for me to yell at her, but I just stood there, disappointing as usual. I was too *something* to speak. Not angry, exactly. I'd been angry at Magnus when I'd thought he was trying to murder me to hang on to Orion in all his strategic value, filthily and remorselessly selfish. Oh, how I'd enjoyed all that sweet crisp righteous anger, my favorite drug: I'd nearly ridden the high straight into murder. This sensation felt murky as sludge by comparison, thick with exhaustion.

I'd already worked out that what Orion wanted was someone who didn't treat him like a shining prince; I just hadn't understood why. Now I understood so well it made my stomach hurt. Chloe, Magnus, all of them, probably everyone in their entire enclave, had come up with this story that Orion was some kind of inhumanly heroic monster-slayer, who loved nothing more than spending all day and all night saving all their lives, who didn't give a thought to his own happiness. They'd made up that lie because of course they desperately *wanted* that from him. Oh, they'd have been happy to cosset him and flatter him and give him the best of everything in return—why not, they had it to give, that didn't cost them anything. They'd gladly hand that priceless enclave spot to me, to any rando girl Orion so much as smiled at; they'd probably have taken Luisa in just because he pitied her. Cheap at the price.

They were desperate to keep him in the exact same way that everyone back at the commune wanted to get rid of me. He was living the same garbage story I was, only in mirror image. Trying so hard to give them what they wanted, trying to fit himself into the beautiful lie they'd made up about him, staring obediently at flash cards his mum made so he could be polite to them. But of course he couldn't be friends with them. He could tell, surely, that they only wanted to be his friends as long as he stayed in the lie. Chloe with her big eyes telling me how *wonderful* he was, how they'd all *tried so hard*.

But I couldn't just be angry at her. Obviously I wanted to

scream at her and set her whole enclave on fire, but that was just habit. What I really wanted, what I wanted with frantic desperate hunger, was to *change her mind,* the same way I wanted to change everyone's mind about me. I wanted to grab her and shake her and make her see Orion—*me*—for five seconds as a person. Only I knew I wasn't going to get what I wanted, because that *would* cost her. If Orion was a person, he didn't owe it to her to keep wearing that convenient little buzzer on his wrist, just in case she or any of her actual friends needed help, for nothing in return. If he was a person, he had as much right as she did to be scared and selfish, and she was supposed to pay back everything he gave her. She wasn't interested in that deal, was she? She wasn't going to come running if *he* needed help. She'd be running the other way.

Her expression faded into uncertainty as I went on standing there: probably hearing the faint rumble of storm clouds in the distance. "Right," I said, through a sour throat. "Of course I've got to be a maleficer. Surely there can't be any other reason he'd prefer my company to you absolute doorknobs." Chloe flinched back. "Keep the enclave seat for someone who wants it. But ta very much for saving me the pleasure of having your friends poke through my head. In return, I'll let you in on my secret handling technique. I treat Orion like he's an ordinary human being. You might all try it yourselves and see how you get on, before you go to any more trouble on my account."

Chapter 10

GROGLER

I DIDN'T TRY to find somewhere else to work. I knew I wasn't going to get a thing done. I just shouldered past Chloe and went for the stairs, and I ran down the whole way to our res hall, although I knew better. Over the weekend, everything had started to warm up for graduation, oil pumping to lubricate the big gears in the core; they were coming loose, helped along by a bit of preliminary rocking. The stairs were shifting along with them, like glacially slow escalators that might reverse direction at any time. And I paid for being careless: a couple of stairs up from the landing, there was the start of a putrid opalescent slick, a remnant of something that had been killed just recently, and I stepped onto it too fast, skidded, and had to throw myself onto the landing in a hard tumble to keep from going headfirst onwards down the stairs.

I was limping down the corridor to my room when I realized I was going past Aadhya's door. I paused, and after a moment, I slowly knocked. "It's El," I said, and she cracked the door, made sure it was me, then saw the blood.

"What happened?" she said. "You want some gauze?"

My throat was tight. I was almost glad for falling down the stairs. Who cared about changing Chloe's mind? "No, it's not worth it, it's just a scrape," I said. "I was just stupid, I tripped coming off the stairs. Come with me to the girls'?"

"Yeah, sure," Aadhya said, and she walked with me and kept watch while I rinsed off my bloody elbow and my bloodier knee. My gut was aching all over again. I didn't care.

Liu got back shortly after we had finished, and the three of us climbed the stairs—more cautiously—up to the cafeteria. The main food line and the tables were locked away behind the movable wall, and we could smell the smoke of the cleansing fires going back there—self-clean ovens have nothing on mortal flame—but there were a few dozen kids around waiting their turn at the snack bar. That's a glorified term for what it is, a bank of vending machines that take tokens. Each of us gets three a week. I actually had almost twenty saved up: the risk of coming without other people isn't worth the boost of calories, unless you've had a few days in a row of really bad luck at meals and are starting to feel light-headed or sluggish.

You don't get to choose what comes out, of course. The items are rarely contaminated, as they're all things in packets, but they're usually aged, and sometimes inedibly ancient. Once, I got a military ration from World War I. I'd come up that time because I *was* feeling light-headed, so I was hungry enough to open it, but even then I couldn't bring myself to risk anything but the biscuit, and by biscuit I mean the kind of hardtack they sent on yearlong sea voyages. Today I got a bag of off-brand crisps, a packet of mostly crumbled peanut butter crackers, and the prize, a Mars bar only three years past the sell-by date. Liu got a bag of salted licorice, which is inexpressibly vile but you can swap it with the Scandinavian kids for almost anything, another packet of crisps, and a slightly questionable box of cured meat. Aadhya got a small packet of halvah, a completely fresh salmon onigiri dated this very morning, amazing, and a whole tin of chestnut spread so large it clanged the whole machine when it came down.

"Let me try and get something to put it on," I said, and put in another token: when you use a token you've saved for a while, usually you get something particularly good or particularly bad. This time I was in luck: out came the glorious orange plastic of a packet of Hobnobs.

We got our little paper cups of tea and coffee from the lukewarm urns and went back to Aadhya's room to share the lot. She had tapped the gas line of her room lamp to build herself a little Bunsen burner, which we used to boil the meat in an alchemy beaker while we wolfed down the onigiri, and then ate Hobnobs slathered with chestnut spread and topped with halvah and crushed peanut butter crackers. When the meat had cooked long enough, we ate it with the crisps, a feast finished off with celebratory slices of Mars bar. Aadhya sat at the desk, working on the belly of her lute, and Liu and I sat on the bed and worked on our papers.

We didn't talk very much: none of us had time to waste. But we'd said enough, and shaken hands. While the meat had been cooking, I'd gone to my room and come back with crystals for each of them. After we finished the food and it was getting on a bit, I began on my mana-building crochet, and Liu sat down on the floor and did yoga. Aadhya did sudoku puzzles. When the first bell rang, we went to the bathroom together, and after we had our wash, we went to the stretch of wall between the boys' and girls' bathrooms and wrote our three names there together: Liu wrote our names down in Chinese characters, and I did us in Hindi and English. We weren't the absolute first set, but close to it: there were only three other alliances already written up, nobody I knew. On our way back, Liu waited by her door until I got to mine, we both waited until Aadhya was at hers, too, and we waved to each other before we went inside to bed.

I slept really well. I don't usually remember dreams, which is probably for the best all things considered, but that morning I woke up just before the bell and while I was lying there in bed I had a vague half dream of Mum sitting in the woods looking at me worried. I said out loud, "It's all right. I'm all right, Mum, I'm not joining an enclave. You were right," and I didn't even mind saying it, because I didn't want her to be worried, and she was still worried, reaching out to me with her mouth moving silently, trying to say something. "Mum, I have friends. Aadhya and Liu and Orion. I have friends," and in the dream my eyes were blurry and I was smiling, and I woke up still smiling. It's supposed to be impossible to communicate with anyone inside the Scholomance, because if message spells could get through, so could some kinds of mals, so I wasn't sure if I'd really seen Mum, but I hoped so. I wanted her to know.

It's not that I was suddenly in charity with the whole world or anything. I saw Chloe coming out of her room as I went back to mine after washing up, and I did manage to get angry again. Orion wasn't at the meeting point, and Ibrahim said he hadn't seen him in the boys' that morning, either. I had been absolutely determined that I was never going to wait for him, but with indignation hot in my belly, I said, "Save us two seats, all right?" to Aadhya and Liu, and I went and banged on his door, loudly. I did it once more before I got back the sound of some thumping around, and he opened it without the slightest precaution, shirtless and with his hair sticking up, to blink at me bleary and haggard.

"Come on, Lake, breakfast won't eat itself," I told him, and he mumbled something incoherent and then turned back in, shoved his feet into his trainers and got a T-shirt off the floor, dropped it again—there was an enormous blue stain down the front—got a different T-shirt off the floor, pulled it over his head, and staggered off to the loo.

"Did you get high or something last night?" I asked in curiosity as we finally made it up the stairs: I'd had to catch him and give him a shove to get him onto the cafeteria landing, after he'd previously tried to turn off both onto the alchemy lab landing and the sophomore res hall landing.

Whipping up recreational substances *is* a fairly popular pastime for alchemy-track kids, but Orion said, "No!" in wounded tones like I'd insulted him. "I didn't get a lot of sleep." He emphasized the point by yawning so widely that he looked like he was about to unhinge his jaw.

"Right," I said skeptical. We can all deal with routine sleep deprivation by the end of freshman year, because by then the ones who can't have been winnowed out. "Too much saving the world to do? Go and sit down with Aadhya and Liu, I'll get you a tray."

I wasn't even that hungry myself today, thanks to our snack bar orgy the night before, so I kept the porridge for myself and let him have the egg and bacon butty I'd been able to snag. But he had to be poked, and then ate it with his eyes half closing, not responding even when Ibrahim asked him a direct question. He put his head straight back down after wolfing down the sandwich.

Aadhya and I had been discussing the demo I was going to do in shop class today; she paused, eyeing him, and asked, "Is he high or something?" Orion didn't register any protest this time.

I shrugged. "He said not. Just no sleep."

Fortunately he was in language lab first thing this morning, so I was able to shepherd him along and get him tucked into the booth next to mine. He promptly put his head down on the desk and fell asleep to the sweet lulling murmur of voices singing of violent death in French. There was only a single worksheet in his folder, dead easy, so I filled it in for him. He looked a bit more functional when I shook him awake at the end of class. "Thanks?" he said uncertainly when he saw the worksheet, but he got it and mine to the slot and managed to submit them without cutting off his own fingers or anything.

"You're welcome," I said. "Are you going to be all right getting to your next lesson?"

"Yeah?" he said, in even more doubtful tones.

"Do you need to be walked?" I asked, eyeing him.

"No, I don't need—what are you doing?" he burst out.

"What?"

"Why are you being this nice?" he said. "Are you mad at me for something?"

"No!" I said, and was about to inform him that I was a decent human being and nice quite regularly or at least once in a while, and it wasn't a sign I was angry, and then I realized that actually he was right, only it was his useless enclaver friends I was angry at; I was feeling *sorry* for him. Which I would have hated myself, with a violent passion. "Am I allowed to be in a good mood occasionally, or do I need to register this madness with the authorities first?" I snapped instead. "Go on and fall into the rubbish chute if you like. I'm off to the workshop." He looked relieved as I huffed off away from him.

The shop is never fun this near to graduation, and today was no exception: the floor trembled approximately every fifteen minutes, and it was so hot in the room that some of the boys were taking off their shirts. Almost anyone who could had finished off their final projects and was skipping class, so it would normally have been very thin of company, but a reasonably big crowd had shown for my demonstration. Aadhya sorted everyone out for best views, prioritizing seniors: what she really wanted was to get five seniors with top bids and then do a second auction after the term ended and the five original buyers were gone.

Meanwhile, I did a careful and slightly painful stretching routine to raise a bit of mana—the slight pain helped—and then I picked up the piece of wood that I was going to work with. I didn't want to waste the effort, so I was using the demo to start on the chest I'd promised the sutras I would make to hold them. It was going to be only just large enough to hold the one book: aside from conveying how special they were to me, I needed it to be light enough for me to carry out of the graduation hall next year. Aadhya and I had worked out a design that would end up shaped like a slightly larger version of the book itself, only carved of wood, and she'd given me a really nice piece of purpleheart wood to make the spine.

"I'm going to use the spell to liquefy the lignin in the wood, so we can bend it into a curve," I told everyone, and passed around the wood so they could all make sure it was real and actually the perfectly straight and solid piece of half-inch-thick wood that it appeared to be. When it got back to me, I held it in my hands, visualized, and recited the incantation. Aadhya had told me lignin was just the bit in the walls of wood cells that makes them hard, and I'm guessing it wasn't a huge amount of stuff that had to be changed, but even so, it was amazing how little mana the spell needed. It didn't even consume half of what I'd raised, and the wood literally went pliable in my hands. I bent it over the wide steel pipe we were using to shape it, and Aadhya and I clamped it into place; then I used the spell to make the lignin solid again. We unclamped it and just like that, the plank was a tidy curve; the spine of the sutras nestled into it beautifully. The whole thing took only a few minutes.

Everyone was murmuring and excited as we passed the curved plank around. For the second demo, Aadhya used an engraving tool and carved a little design in the very top of the plank, then set up a tiny funnel with a strip of silver out of her supply stash. I turned the silver liquid, and she poured it into the design. I even experimented a bit: I tried turning it back solid in a continuous process, just as it landed in the carving, so that it wouldn't overflow the edges. It worked brilliantly.

People started asking if I'd show them something more, and I didn't see any reason not to: I still had some mana left. Aadhya and I were trying to decide what we should do, and then a senior girl in the alchemy track suddenly came up with the idea of trying to turn some *nitrogen* liquid, straight out of the air around us. That could obviously be amazingly useful, although we weren't sure what would happen with the nitrogen after I did it: wouldn't it just instantly evaporate away again? But everyone was so excited about the idea that a couple of senior boys volunteered to climb up on a bench to get one of the metal canisters from the high shelves along the wall, if we let them keep whatever was left inside after. I agreed; that was fair when they'd be the ones sticking their heads that close to the ceiling without knowing if there was going to be any real return.

The first one climbed up, and then the next round of grinding vibrations hit, except this time it didn't stop; instead it got worse, a lot worse, almost graduation-day bad, and things started falling off the walls and shelves and then even the stools started falling over. The boy on the bench had crouched down for balance already, but he had to jump for it, grabbing for his friend's hand just in time as three of the canisters came crashing down on the table. One popped open and a writhing mass of baby copper-gnawers came spilling out on the floor, like the unwanted prize in a shell game.

But we were all running for the door by then. Thankfully I had never taken the book-sling off. I grabbed the newly inlaid spine of my chest on the way, and Aadhya and I made it out into the corridor in the middle of the pack of fleeing kids. We all dashed for the stairs. Getting to higher ground is the sensible thing to do when there's a disturbance from below, so of course I saw Orion go flying past the stairwell heading downward instead. The only place down from here was the senior dorms, and the stairs past that were the ones that would soon be opening up to the graduation hall.

"Lake, you utter wanker, go *up!*" I yelled, but he had already gone; he didn't even break stride. I clenched my jaw and looked at Aadhya, who stared back at me, and then I said grimly, "Can you take this?" and ducked my head out from under the sling.

"He's going to be fine!" Aadhya said, but she was grabbing the sling from me as she said it. She even took the purple-heart piece.

"No, he's not, I'm going to bash his head in with a brick," I said, and then we were in the stairwell and I fought my way out of the current running upstream and headed down after him. The grinding felt a lot worse as soon as I was out of the crowd; the stairwell walls were actually vibrating so much they were humming out loud. "Orion!" I yelled again, but there was no sight of him, and he probably couldn't have heard me over the sound.

As I wasn't myself a noble hero with a limitless store of

mana and all the sense of an unvarnished deck chair, I went down slowly and cautiously. Nobody came up past me: it was the middle of the school day, and this close to end of term the seniors were only in their res hall after curfew anyway. The grinding was even louder after I passed their landing: it was clearly coming from the bottom of the stairs, and I was horribly sure that I was going to find Orion down there with it.

I was nearly down to the next turn in the stairs when he came flying back up towards me, literally: he'd been thrown bodily through the air. He smashed into the wall and fell almost exactly at my feet, gasping. He stared up at me puzzled, and then a gigantic jellyfish-translucent tentacle came groping up around the corner, feeling for him, and he sat up and slashed at it with the thin metal rod he was clutching in his hand. If you would like to envision the dramatic results, get a very large bowl, fill it with jelly, take a toothpick, and very gently press it into the surface and lift it away. If the indentation stays for longer than a second, you've had more of an effect than he did.

Orion looked at the rod with a confused and betrayed expression: it had to be some artifact that had switched off. The tentacle was going straight for his arm in return. I had to reach out and touch it—I used the very tip of my left little finger—and shock it with the electrical-charge spell I'd got from Nkoyo. It recoiled long enough for me to grab Orion by the arm and help him scramble to his feet, and also to drag him up a few steps. Then I met resistance. "No, I have to—" he said.

"Get your brains beaten out against the stairwell?" I snarled at him, and pulled his head down as the tentacle lashed back over our heads.

"*Allumez!*" he said, and the rod burst into blazing white-hot flames between us. It nearly took off my eyelashes. I fell back on my bum and skidded down the stairs all the way round the next turning myself, where I got an absolutely beautiful view down the staircase into a horrible mass of writhing jelly tentacles at the very bottom. They had got themselves wound around everything that could be gripped, every inch of the railing and into the vents. They were straining to the utmost to pull the rest of whatever the mal was through a tiny cockroach-sized gap in the lower bottom corner of the stairwell. Which meant it was effectively trying to rip the staircase open. I couldn't remember ever noticing on the blueprints what was on the other side of the staircase wall over here, but at the moment, there was a *graduation mal* on the other side, which meant that somehow there was a path for mals to make it up here from the hall, despite all the wards and barriers along the way, and the staircase was our last line of defense. If this one made it through, all its friends would follow. It would effectively start graduation early. Except, since the senior hall hadn't been separated from the rest of the school yet, the waiting mals would instantly come pouring up for *all* of us.

After my first moment of pure *aaiiugh,* I noticed the deflated blobs littering the bottom of the stairs and howled, "No, wait!" but it was too late. Orion had just sliced off the tentacle still bashing at his head. The enormous chunk of the end fell down, sizzling, and the rest recoiled down to the mass, where it pressed the cut end into the middle of the knot, turning into a lovely bowed curve, and split itself elegantly into *four* tentacles, each already starting to swell into the size of the original one, and all of which went grabbing for more things to yank on.

Orion staggered down and pulled me to my feet. "Get out of here!" he said, and was about to sail right back into it. I had to grab his hair and *yank.* "Ow!" he yelled, and nearly took my arm off with the flaming sword. "What are you—"

"It's a grogler, you brainless cod!" I yelled at him.

"No, it's a hyd—oh shit, it's a grogler," Orion said, and just stood there for a dazed, gaping moment. Which we had to spare, since the grogler was currently ignoring us in favor of continuing its straining efforts to rip open the delicious extra-large snack pack for itself and every other mal down in the graduation hall.

"How aren't you dead yet?" I said, bitterly. To be fair to Orion, not that I felt like being fair to him, the grogler was so big that you couldn't see the thin pink cords running through the center of the tentacles, or the big red knot that was presumably somewhere in the middle of that mass. It had likely broken a million tentacles just bashing them against things, long before Orion had got himself down here. Groglers aren't known for patience or long-term strategy, but apparently sufficient hunger was sufficiently motivating. "Well?"

"Um," he said. "I'm thinking."

"About what?" I said. "Freeze it, why don't you!"

"I don't have a good freezing spell!"

"What do you mean, you don't have a good freezing spell?" I said, glaring at him. "You're from *New York.*"

He looked guilty and muttered, "I can't get mana out of the mals if I freeze them."

The whole stairwell trembled around us.

"Who cares!" I said. "Get mana out of the next one!"

"So I haven't *learned* any!" he yelled.

"Oh, for the love of the Great Mother Goddess," I said, with all the heartfelt disgust I could produce, which that phrase itself induces in me to begin with, and I grabbed my crystal and started to put together a picture in my head while

I tapped into my already badly depleted store of mana: in the shop, the senior girl had been telling me that nitrogen was more than half of the air, so I envisioned it condensing into a solid shell over the grogler's skin, just a few millimeters thick.

"What are you doing?" he said. I ignored him completely; my gut hurt like crazy from falling down the stairs, enough to bring tears to my eyes, and my scraped elbow and skinned knee stung, too, and it was an immense effort to keep my focus. He gave me up as a bad cause and ran down the stairwell and started grabbing tentacles one after another, pulling them loose from their grips and putting binding spells on them, trying to squash the whole thing into a single ball while it bulged out in one direction and another like a giant angry amoeba.

"I'm ready," I croaked.

"What?" he said, through gritted teeth, as he wrestled another tentacle into the mass.

"Get back from it!" I said louder, through gritted teeth. Orion glanced back at me, and the tentacle managed to half pull free and thump him, knocking him halfway up the stairs. Good enough to get him clear, and well deserved. I chanted out the phase-control spell, and tried to make the nitrogen in my vision liquid.

I'm reasonably sure I was successful, since the mana certainly went somewhere: half my laboriously refilled crystal, gone in a gulp. I guess the nitrogen did boil away again instantly, because there was no visual effect; maybe a faint whoosh of coldish air moving, but that was all. Except for one minor detail: the grogler's skin instantly frosted over, and then cracked up all at once like the surface of a pond in spring. The whole thing collapsed, the liquidy guts inside all spilling into a single giant puddle that drained away through the grating at the bottom of the stairs, going down in a brief whirlpool with a final loud gurgling slurp. The only thing left behind was the tiny core tentacle that had wriggled through the corner of the stairwell in the first place, like a spider plant budding off. *That* looked exactly like the classic illustration in the third chapter of the freshman-year textbook, iridescent jelly around a neon-pink vein. It pulled itself right back through the hole like a piece of spaghetti getting sucked up.

Orion sat up. "Hah!" he croaked out, like *he'd* done it, and looked up the stairs at me triumphantly.

"Lake, I hate you more than words can possibly express," I told him, fervently, and sat down and leaned against the wall and wrapped my arms around my aching belly. He got up a little sheepishly and filled the hole in the wall with some putty out of his pocket, did a quick make-and-mend, and then he came over and I think was about to try and carry me. I gave him a death glare and made him just help me up instead.

And after all that, he was yawning again even before we were at the senior hall landing, like he didn't have a drop of adrenaline running through his system. I was in more than minor pain and I still felt at least ten times as alert as he looked. I eyed him as we limped onwards. "Why *are* you this wiped out? Have you been having really incredible night- mares or—" But I was figuring it out even as he darted a half-guilty look towards me. "You moron, you've been staying up patrolling? Because of that pathetic murderous gob whining at you?"

Orion wouldn't meet my eyes. "He wasn't wrong," he said, low.

"What?"

"The mals in the graduation hall," he said. "It wasn't just the grogler. They must've forced a hole through the wards, down there, and now they're all trying to make it through into the school. It's worse at night. I've mended that same wall seven times so far—"

"And you haven't slept in fifty-five hours, which does explain why you spent ten straight minutes hacking tentacles off a grogler," I said.

"It was twice as big as any grogler's supposed to be!" he said defensively. "I thought it was a hydra-class mal!"

"A justifiable mistake right up until you've hacked off the first tentacle," I said. "How many had you done, seven? And you were still going strong when I got there. If it *had* yanked the stairwell open, no question you'd have earned an assist." His mouth went into a hard line, and I could feel his body tense with the desire to go storming away from me, which he'd probably have done, except at the moment it would've involved dragging me right along with him. "What's the point of this exercise exactly? Even if you're really set on going out in a blaze of glory, you won't get one if you go down at the start of the inundation."

"Will you stop? I don't care about *glory!*" he said. "I just— it's my fault! You told me it was. I screwed with the principle of balance, and—"

"Oh, now you're ready to accept the basic laws of reality," I said. "Shut up, Lake. We all know you don't get anything for free. Nobody complained when you were saving their lives, did they?"

"Only you," he said, dryly.

"I'll remember to be really smug about that as I'm getting eaten by the graduation horde," I said. "You've been white-knighting as hard as you can for three full years. You're not going to fix the consequences by white-knighting a little bit harder over the course of a single week. *That's* the principle of balance, too."

"Well, you've convinced me. I guess I'll just go take a nap, then. That's going to help a lot," he said, with a wealth of sarcasm.

I glared at him. "It would beat helping a grogler rip open the school." He scowled back at me. And then yawned again.

Chapter 11
SENIORS

L UNCH WAS almost over by the time we got back up. Everyone was in the cafeteria as usual despite the earlier panic in the shop: very few things are allowed to interfere with getting food, and the horrible grinding and vibrations had stopped, anyway. Aadhya and Liu had saved us seats, and even some food on their own trays, even though it meant they'd been sitting at an almost empty table by the time we got there. Keeping two seats open for kids who hadn't even made it to the cafeteria before the line closed was a lot, especially when there was a potential disaster going below. I even had to be grudgingly glad for Ibrahim, who had actually stuck it out with them even after most of his friends had made excuses and ditched for other tables. But he took care of that sentiment fast.

"It couldn't have just been an ordinary grogler," he said positively, after we filled them in. "It must have been some new kind of variant." Because otherwise his darling Orion might have made a stupid mistake, which was obviously inconceivable. If I'd had any food or any breath to spare, I'd have thrown some at him. As it was, I was too sore.

Thankfully, there were some people of sense at the table, who focused on the most important bits. "How exactly have you been patching the damage in the stairwell?" Aadhya asked Orion. "Just make-and-mend?"

"Yeah," Orion said tiredly. "With my dad's filler recipe." He stopped shoveling in leftovers and took out the lump of putty and showed it to her.

Aadhya took a bit of it in her fingers and stretched it into a square, holding it up to the light and then pushing down onto the table, folding it a few ways and kneading it, rolling it out and coiling it up again before she gave it back to him. "Don't get me wrong, this is amazing stuff, but it's still generic. And you've done a lot of separate repairs?" She shook her head. "There's no way that's going to hold through the end-of-term rotation. Honestly, I'd worry it'll come apart as soon as the first-tier gears engage this Sunday."

"We're not going to make it to Sunday if the mals down there keep pounding on it," I muttered from where I was barely clearing the surface of my mash. I was giving serious thought to just licking it up like ice cream instead of sitting up again to get a utensil that I would have to use muscles in my body to move from the plate to my mouth. "We're going to have to find a way to hold them back long enough to fix the damage properly. And we'll need some ridiculous number of people helping to raise the mana for it."

"Remember when the alchemy lab got damaged?" Ibrahim said to Orion earnestly, over my head. "We need to make an announcement, and recruit people to raise enough mana to fix the damage."

I said, without moving or changing volume, "Ibrahim, I'm

going to harvest your internal organs in your sleep." I saw his hands on the table twitch.

"But we can't," Liu said. I did haul my head up for *her* input. "We can't let the seniors find out at all."

"Huh?" Orion said, but I propped my elbows on the table and put my hands over my face. She was right, of course. The seniors weren't going to help us. If a hole opened up to the graduation hall before the senior dorms were closed off, the seniors went from being the whole buffet to the toughest and most stale entrées on the menu. If they knew it was a possibility, that the wards had weakened that much, they'd probably go down there and start hitting the stairwell themselves, so what if they were throwing the rest of us to the wolves? They'd all give themselves Todd's excuse: it was understandable, they didn't have a choice, it was Orion's fault. It didn't even need to be all of them who'd do it. Just enough.

We all knew it. Even completely knackered, Orion got it himself after a moment and stopped eating, hunched over the table. None of us said another word for the next ten minutes, until the senior bell rang. After they were all out of the room, I said, "How do we do it? How few people can we get away with telling, and still get it fixed?"

The best solution we came up with was trying to turn the iron wall of the stairwell into steel, in place. "So I recognize this is a crazy idea, but just as a starting point," was the encouraging way Aadhya suggested it. "What if we go down to the bottom of the stairwell with a portable crucible and a whole bunch of carbon. We light it up, and then El uses the phase-control spell to melt in just a little bit of the iron from the damaged wall, the size of a quarter, not big enough to let something really dangerous get through. I have a spell process to infuse carbon into iron, to turn it into steel. I'll do that to the melted iron, and then she can put it back solid again. We could do it in a running cycle, the way you were doing it with the silver during the demo," she added to me. "And if anything squeezes through one of the holes we make in the wall while we're working, Orion can take it out."

That was a wildly ambitious plan, only as far as any of us could see, the only other option was to make new walls in the shop in pieces, tote them down to the stairwell, and ask the mals nicely to stay back while we swapped them in. After first asking all the seniors nicely to stay out of the shop for the next three days, while we recruited about ten artificer-track students to make these new walls in the first place.

"How much mana would this take?" Ibrahim said.

"Shedloads," I said. "The phase-control spell is unbelievably cheap for what it does, but it's not *free*. Melting down an entire wall of solid iron isn't going to be like doing a tiny bit of silver or picking a single chemical out of a piece of wood. Fortunately, we've got a solution." I turned and looked at Orion pointedly.

He blinked back at me. "I don't know if there will be enough mals coming through for me to keep feeding you mana the whole time?"

"Just take it from your enclave power-sharer," I said. "You put enough in, they can't complain, surely."

"Well—I could ask Magnus—"

"Wait, what?" I said. "Why would you have to ask anyone?"

He paused for a weird moment, and then he swallowed and said, "I don't . . . I have a hard time paying attention to . . . if I have open access to the power bank, I'll just use it. So my sharer's got a block." He tried to sound casual about it, but he was looking away.

None of us said anything. Ibrahim looked utterly horrified. It was a shocking feet-of-clay moment for him, I suppose: Orion Lake, blocked from his own enclave share because he didn't have basic mana control. That's like admitting you wear nappies because you wet yourself now and again.

Only in this case, it was more like he was being forced to wear a nappy and wet himself now and again so all of *his enclave mates* could go on happily enjoying the mana he was pouring into their share, the streams of mana those greedy selfish bastards were milking out of him every time he took out another mal. I wanted to rip the power-sharer right off his wrist and go and chuck it at Chloe's head and tell her that Orion was right not to care about a single one of them, and we *were* going it alone, I was taking him to live in a yurt in Wales when we got out of here, and every last wizard in New York could set themselves on fire and cry about it.

I couldn't speak because I was so mad. And annoyingly, I'd underrated Ibrahim again; he was actually the one who broke the silence and said, "But—aren't *you* the one who—I heard you get mana from the mals—"

Orion shrugged a little without meeting anyone's eyes. "Everyone puts in mana. It's not a big deal. I can get some whenever I need it."

"But," Ibrahim said.

"Later," I told him, and he looked over at me and I assume gathered from my expression that yeah, it was an absolute mountain of rubbish that I wasn't going to let stand five seconds longer than it needed to, once we weren't all a few days away from even more sudden and unpleasant death than normal. He subsided, and I said to Orion, "Not Magnus. We'll ask Chloe."

CHLOE'S BRILLIANT INPUT on our plan was, "But wait, why don't we just put in a maintenance request?"

She said it as if that was a completely reasonable and obvious suggestion, and Orion actually rubbed his face and looked over at me a bit sheepishly, like oh, he hadn't considered that option, he really should have had more sleep. We went in for a round of staring around at each other with equal degrees of *what sort of moron are you* expressions, and then I said, "Does that ever actually work for you?"

"What do you mean?" Chloe said. "Of course it does. I put in requests all the time."

It shouldn't've been a surprise. The maintenance request form, which I haven't bothered filling out since second half of freshman year, has a box for your name. I had assumed they were all just going straight into a bin, and we got assigned to repair work by random and malicious chance, but now I realized of course the forms went into a box instead, somewhere in the hidden janitorial rooms that only the maintenance-track kids know about, and they fished out requests made by, for instance, New York enclavers, and saw to it that those got handled. In fact, after a brief moment, it *wasn't* a surprise, and I went right on past it. "Right, have you ever put in one at graduation time?"

"No!" Chloe said, like I'd insulted her. "I know we're not supposed to put in unnecessary maintenance requests at midterms and finals. But I think this qualifies as life-threatening damage!"

"It certainly does qualify," I said. "It's especially life-threatening to anyone who goes down there to fix it, which is why you won't get any maintenance-track kids to do it for you. They'll give you half an hour of their time to patch your desk lamp, Rasmussen; they won't face down the graduation horde on your behalf just because you ask nicely. Not to mention the *seniors* are probably the ones who dole out the shift assignments. So are you going to help us or not?"

Chloe did come round, especially after I made several very sharp and pointy remarks about Orion's contributions to the New York mana supply, which I suppose conveyed the extent of my desire to take Orion's power-sharer and throw it with great force at her head. She did have one useful suggestion, namely, "Shouldn't we try this out first?" even if it came from the unflattering direction of doubting that we were competent enough to actually manage the process.

What she really wanted to do was to ask in a half-dozen other New York kids, including Magnus, all of whom had many close senior friends. She only agreed to hold off temporarily after we agreed to do a practice run. I think she expected it wasn't going to work, and we'd have to give in to her afterwards. Whatever her reasons, I was just as glad for the practice, as long as she was putting up the mana.

We got together in the shop the next day, during work period, and Chloe gave me and Aadhya each a power-sharer. When I clasped it round my wrist, I tugged experimentally and got a line of mana that felt roughly like a hose being fed by the Atlantic. I'd already known that the enclavers had access to gobs of mana, loads more than the rest of us, but I hadn't realized how *much* more. I could've razed a city or two without even making a dent. I had to work really hard not to just start pulling it down as wildly as if I didn't have any basic mana control of my own. I couldn't help but tell that I could've filled every crystal I had, twice over, with a few good gulps.

Orion trotted round the supply bins to collect up all the materials for us, with about as much hesitation as usual. He was less exhausted this morning; I'd made him go to bed early last night, on the grounds that whoever was going to get munched during the night was going to get munched just as much along with everyone else in the school on Sunday if he couldn't keep the mals off us while we worked.

"I still think it would be a really good idea for us to get some more people in on this," Chloe said, looking around nervously. The shop was completely deserted: after yesterday's excitement, no one was risking it down here unless they absolutely had to go to class, and anyway, I doubt she'd ever been in the shop with less than ten kids around her. Ibrahim and Liu had come along with us to stand watch—well, Liu was standing watch, and Ibrahim was trailing Orion around the room trying to chat with him—but that was it.

"Ready?" I asked Aadhya, ignoring Chloe; then I spoke the phase-change incantation and pushed the first few inches of the bar of wrought iron we were testing with—left over from some failed project, presumably—into liquid form. Aadhya had the crucible heated and waiting, right underneath it, and as soon as the metal ran in, she sprinkled in the soot with her free hand, in a smooth pattern, frowning in concentration as she made them merge. Then she gave me a quick nod, tipped the crucible over the edge of the rod where the iron had been, and I shoved the metal back into a solid form.

It did go solid. However, only just *barely* solid. The blob of metal plonked down on the workbench surface, sizzled violently, melted a hole straight through and fell down towards the shelf underneath, smashed a hole through a stack of panes of glass, set the tarp that was covering them on fire, melted through the second shelf, fell to the floor, melted straight through *that,* and was gone.

There was some yelling and flailing—I may have done some myself—before Aadhya grabbed four of the powders she'd asked Orion for, clapped them together, and threw them onto the cheerfully spreading fire. Once that was out, we all gathered and peered down at the hole nervously. It went all the way through what turned out to be an uncomfortably thin floor. All I could make out in the darkness down there, at least from a cautious distance, was one very rusty pipe running past, with a circle of five antique vials, the kind of artifice you only see anymore in museum pieces, turning round and steadily doling out drops of different alchemical substances into an opening in the top of the pipe.

"Do you think any of the mals will try and get in through *there?*" Ibrahim said.

"Let's fix it and not find out," Aadhya said. "Orion, can you get some more—" and then we all belatedly noticed that Orion couldn't get anything, because he wasn't standing with us: he was at the doorway busy killing a slipslider that had come to investigate our yelling with a dream in its heart, or at least its digestion.

"Yeah?" he said, coming back, breathing only a little hard, after tossing what was left of the slipslider back out into the hall: when it had tried to squirm out of his grip by dumping its outer layer, he'd grabbed the half-shed skin, pulled it back over the head, and tied it in a knot and kept it that way until it strangled. That wasn't how you were *supposed* to kill them, but it seemed to have worked fine.

It was just as well that we were practicing. It took me several tries to learn how to convince the metal to go back into a *really* solid form, not to mention back into the specific shape that it had started in, but even once I had, it still wasn't coming out right. I didn't melt any more holes through the floor, but I left a dozen contorted lumps of metal that didn't really look like steel stuck firmly to the surface of the table.

Chloe said suddenly, "Hey, if it's steel, don't you need to fold it?"

It turned out her dad was an artificer, too: that's how he and Orion's dad knew each other. Aadhya looked it up in the metallurgy textbook she'd brought and discovered she was right. "Right, okay, you need to envision the final shape being made up of like one thin layer folded back and forth on itself, like puff pastry or something, instead of a solid block."

Using that mental image got me a substance that seemed approximately right. But it became even harder to work out the right pace for me and Aadhya to go so that we could convert the iron in a continuous process. About half of the iron rod ended up in tidy one- or two-inch separate sections scattered around the table.

And then we hit our stride, swapped out six inches in a row without stopping, and suddenly it was easy, as easy as the wood, as easy as the silver. Aadhya actually laughed out loud. "Oh my God, this is amazing!" she said, holding up the rod, half of it new steel bright and shining, patterned with wavy lines, right up to the hard edge where it met the old blackened iron. "Just look at this, this is *so cool*."

I couldn't help smiling myself, and even Chloe looked a little reluctantly impressed when we all passed around the rod. "All right, we'll do the wall repair in work period tomorrow," I said. We packed up a huge sack of soot, which is one ingredient not at all in short supply around here, and headed back upstairs.

But as soon as we got into the stairwell, we heard voices coming from below. It made even less sense for anyone to be down there in the middle of the day after yesterday's festivities. Orion paused and turned down the stairs, going quietly, and when I followed him, everyone else did, too, even Chloe, who threw a half-desperate look at the stairs going sensibly up, but wasn't going to go it on her own.

Footsteps started coming back upstairs towards us as we reached the senior dorm level. I grabbed Orion and pulled him off the landing; everyone followed. We all huddled in the dark of the res hall corridor as three seniors went past going up: kids I didn't know at all, talking in low voices, ". . . one really good hit to those repairs," floating out to us as they went. We didn't really need to hear any more of the conversation.

"Or, hey, I just had an idea, we could fix the wall right now," Aadhya said, as soon as their steps faded out of earshot.

"Yes. Now would be good," Ibrahim agreed, hushed, as we all nodded. "Now is an excellent time."

"You guys can take some extra mana from the pool, to do makeup work for missing class," Chloe even volunteered.

We went down to the bottom of the stairs and started in on the work. We could see where the seniors had picked at a few of Orion's patches already, testing them. Even without help, there were a bunch of visible strain lines and bulging deformations in the walls, like something had been pounding on them from the other side.

Aadhya fired up the crucible, got a handful of soot, and I started in on the outer wall: iron into the crucible, steel back out. I hadn't lost the rhythm; the change rolled along just as easily as in the shop. I just kept going and was about halfway along the wall when Aadhya said, "I'm sorry, I need a break," and I looked round to see that she was almost sagging. She put down the crucible and dusted her hands off the bag of soot, then sat down hard on the next-to-last step with a whoof of breath.

"I wouldn't say no," I said, and sat down next to her, although I felt fine, myself, except for being thirsty. Liu offered us a drink from her water bottle, and I could've finished the whole thing alone. Even my gut wasn't hurting very much anymore. It occurred to me that I might have helped the healing along by pushing it a little yesterday: Mum's healing spells tend to work with your own body, so if you do something that gets your own system doing things like sending over more white blood cells and building replacement muscle, the magic picks up, too. It had been only a little more than a week, so the flax patch was definitely still working in me.

The new wall panels looked starkly different next to the old ones, bright with the wavy patterns stretching all over: actually pretty. But Chloe was frowning at them from where she was sitting on the stairs next to Ibrahim. Orion was going back and forth restlessly, up the stairs and back, running a hand over the surface of the remaining old bulged wall panels, peering at the joins. Chloe looked over at him and then at me and Aadhya, a puzzled expression starting, and I thought she was about to say something, but then instead she turned and looked up the stairs and then said urgently, "Guys, I think they're coming back."

We all stood up. The footsteps above slowed down as whoever it was realized in their turn that someone was down here. When they finally came around the corner, it was in a tight knot ready to fight: two tall boys in the back with both hands poised and ready to cast incantations, a girl and a boy in the front crouching slightly, each with shield holders on their outside wrists, and another girl in the sheltered middle position holding the hilt of a fire whip. Those are horribly versatile because they have kinetic power on top of flame. If you're good, you can wrap it around things and burn them off, or whip the end back and forth and knock mals—or people—to either side to clear a path. A smart, well-designed

graduation alliance team, one that had probably been practicing together for months. When we're all mixed up in the
cafeteria just busy stuffing in food, there isn't always a big
visible difference between the seniors and the rest of us, but
here with us opposite them, it was painfully clear just how
much difference a year made.

Except Orion moved instantly to stand in front of us all: it
looked a little silly, just skinny him confronting them, but he
said, "Something you were looking for?" with his hands
clenched, and they all hesitated. He nodded when they didn't
say anything. "Maybe you guys should go back upstairs.
Now."

"That's new steel," the girl in the front row said abruptly:
she was looking past Orion at the wall. "They're replacing
the panels."

"You're Victoria, from Seattle, right? I'm Chloe from New
York," Chloe said suddenly to the girl in the middle, trying
for a chatty tone that was spoiled by a substantial nervous
wobble. "There's damage to the stairwell, it's letting in mals
from the graduation hall. That's what Todd Quayle had that
complete breakdown over. We're just fixing it. Orion didn't
want any more of them getting in to hurt anyone."

Victoria from Seattle wasn't buying. "Sure, he wants to
keep them waiting down there to hurt *us*," she said. "So hey,
Orion, are you planning to attend graduation this year and
help us out with this horde you've whipped into a frenzy?
People were saying you took out a grogler the size of a truck
yesterday. Who knows if we'll even be able to *move* down
there."

"You'll still have better odds than a newly inducted freshman, since your own plan seems to be break the wards wide
open and let them all come pouring in," I said. "And that will
be the end of the whole place. The mals will go nesting in the

res halls and probably break the scouring equipment up here like they did down there. The death rates will double or more. Don't any of you mean to have kids of your own?"

"I'm going to worry about living that long first, thanks," Victoria said. "All of you can go back upstairs now and figure out where you want to be. We're opening up this wall."

"No, you're not," Orion said.

"Think you're going to stop us?" she said, and even as she was saying it, she flicked the fire whip. The whole thing flamed up instantly and the end whacked Orion into the wall hard, then went coiling up around him fast from ankles to neck. "I've got him. Hit the walls, just bash them with anything," she said, a little tightly: Orion was thrashing in the coil like crazy, and she needed both hands to hold him, but he was definitely not getting out of there anytime soon. "Lev, make sure you have that yanker ready," she added, and I realized they were all wearing belts with a small hook symbol on them: they'd set up a spell hooked to some other place in the school along a straight line, a few flights up, so the second they did manage to break through, they'd trigger it and be yanked straight back to their safe point before the mals started pouring in.

"Yeah, I've got it," Lev said, the boy in the front row, and Chloe screamed and ducked as the boys in the back row started lobbing good old-fashioned fire blasts at the still-damaged panels, flames splashing over the surface and raining sparks down on us.

"Orion!" Ibrahim yelled, and dashed for him: he cast a shield spell on his hands and started fumbling at the coil to try and pull it loose, but the fire whip was too strong; it kept burning through his shield quicker than he could have any effect.

Liu called out in Mandarin and put up a shield over us, a

good one: it flexed with the impacts, letting the fire run down in little streams. It wasn't big enough to cover the whole wall, though, just the three of us. "The wall!" she said. "Can you fix the parts they're hitting before they break through?"

Aadhya looked at me. There were a thousand spells in my mouth ready to go: I could have killed all five of them with a word, or for variety's sake I could have imprisoned their minds and made them my helpless slaves. I wouldn't even have to pull malia to do it: Chloe had hunkered down behind a shield of her own, but the power-sharer was still wide open, mana flowing like a river. I could have made them fix the wall for us, and even wash the floor after. If only I could have scrubbed my mind clean as easily when it was through.

"We'll have to do the whole rest of the wall at once," I told Aadhya, grimly. "Can you open that crucible bigger?"

Her eyes popped. "If you take down the whole wall, *something's* going to come in!"

"If it does, our senior friends are going to yank away, and then Orion can get it for us," I said. "Will the carbon-mixing part work in a single go?"

Aadhya swallowed, but she nodded. "Yeah, the process has a diminishing—yeah," she said, cutting off her own instinctive explanation. She grabbed her crucible and gave the end a quick hard flip, snapping it open to full size. "Ready." I stood up and pointed at the wall, and pulled down all four of the remaining panels into a sloshing pool of iron.

So far while we'd been working, nothing had tried to come at us at all. When I took down the rest of the panels, the reason for that became quite horrifyingly clear. One of the seniors' fire blasts shot through the sudden opening and splashed beautiful shimmering reflections all over the smooth, armored plate atop the argonet head that was completely filling up the space of a maintenance shaft on the other side. It had its eyes closed, apparently taking a peaceful nap before it got back down to the business of breaking in. One little talon, roughly a foot across, was resting atop a ladder. It must have had a tight squeeze of it, getting up. The sides of its head were streaked with familiar iridescent goo: it had evidently used the grogler as lubrication.

"Oh my God," Chloe said faintly. The argonet cracked open first one and then six and then all nine of its eyes as it realized that dinner had been served early, and it started to pull itself inside.

"Lev!" one of the other boys yelled, and there was a sudden hard popping of air as he triggered the yanker and they were all bungeed back up the stairs—all five of them, including Victoria with her fire whip. It stretched out for a moment, but she must have kept concentrating on it, because instead of breaking, it also yanked *Orion,* who was still coiled up, and Ibrahim, who was still trying to pull coils away, right along with them. A few moments later, I heard Ibrahim scream faintly from somewhere above: he'd probably let go and fallen out of the yank.

Chloe shrieked, "Put back the wall! Put back the wall!" and then turned and ran up the stairs. Aadhya had already emptied the whole bag of soot into the crucible and was stirring desperately, but the steel wasn't quite ready yet. The argonet was squirming its huge taloned hand up and through the opening, reaching to grab her before its elbow even got clear.

Lucky for us all, Chloe hadn't shut off the mana supply. I pointed my hand at the argonet and recited a forty-nine syllable curse that had been used a few thousand years ago to disintegrate the guardian dragon of a sacred temple in Kangra by a group of maleficers who wanted to claim the temple's supply of a mysterious arcane dust. The dust turned out to be the powdered shed scales of the dragon, which was information that you'd think the priests might have shared more widely in order to prevent just that sort of misguided attempt.

The argonet looked puzzled as its talons started to crumble. I don't think it understood that it was disintegrating, so it kept trying to get in. Fortunately, my spell picked up steam quicker than the crammed-in argonet could move, so by the time it got its head thrust into the opening in place of its vanished arm, the disintegration was coming up its neck. I was even able to reach up and pluck one fist-sized tooth, gone loose and wobbly, right out of its mouth just before the spell swept up over the rest of the jaw.

Aadhya and Liu came to the edge of the hole and stood staring down it with me, open-mouthed, Aadhya clutching the long handle of her stirrer. The line of disintegration kept going down and down the body crammed into the shaft, revealing far more than anyone needed to know about the internals of an argonet. Then Liu gasped and said, "Quick! Quick!" and I realized, right, as soon as the cork disintegrated out of the bottleneck—

Aadhya whirled around and went back to work on the carbonization. Liu stood to one side of the opening, tense, putting her shield spell over the top of the shaft. A few moments later, she gave a yelp of horror: a small flock of shrikes hadn't waited for the argonet to dissolve all the way: they'd devoured themselves a path *through* its body. They came flying up the shaft, whacked against Liu's shield like sparrows flying into a too-clean window, and immediately started pecking at it violently with their iridescent-gleaming beaks.

We couldn't do anything but keep working. Aadhya yelled, "Ready!" She levitated the crucible to the top of the opening and tipped it over, and as the liquid metal came pouring out, I called out the phase-change spell again and shoved the metal back into a single massive sheet, seamlessly stretched from one edge of the remaining wall to the other.

One shrike just managed to poke a big enough hole in Liu's shield to wriggle itself through, and it darted through the final gap as I sealed up the wall, leaving a tail feather stuck in the seam. Aadhya was panting for breath, but she started to gasp out a shield spell of her own that would probably have been too late to keep one of us from losing at least a pound of flesh, but the shrike was flying so fast that it didn't bother to backwing to come at us: instead it kept on going right up the stairs towards the open buffet above, chirping with excitement.

That was a bad choice: brief seconds after it had vanished, while we were gaping after it, still shaking with adrenaline, its fading chirps suddenly broke off in a loud shrilling cry and then stopped. A really awful scraping and rattling noise was coming back in its place, getting louder and louder. Before we could pull ourselves together to do anything, Orion came whipping around the corner, surfing down the stairs on a steam tray, and took all of us out like ninepins.

On the bright side, the new steel wall held up very nicely. It had taken on the faintly soapy feeling of warded artifice: the repair had integrated into the school's overall protection spells and the damage was fixed. I could say so with great confidence, because my cheek was squashed up against the metal so hard that I could literally feel the shrieks and wails fading away as the rest of the waiting mals got chased back down, and the low *gronk-chunk-gronk*–noise of some kind of protective mechanism going down below.

"Ow," Liu said, next to me.

"Yeah," Aadhya groaned, and flopped off us. She'd had to fling herself in our direction to avoid getting knocked into her own still-hot crucible and burnt to a crisp. She sat up and looked at it in dismay: the right corner had been completely accordioned against the wall. "Oh *man*."

"Um, sorry," Orion said, standing over us. He was clutching the dead shrike in one hand and the badly dented steam tray in the other. *He* had been on top. "I got here as fast as I could."

"Lake, one of these days I'm going to kill you," I said, out of the side of my mouth that wasn't jammed into the wall.

"So," Liu said to me, a little tentatively, as we limped up the stairs. Orion was behind us lugging the full-sized crucible—it couldn't be folded up again—and continuously apologizing to Aadhya, who knew how to milk an advantage and was undoubtedly going to come out of this with more than enough supplies to repair her crucible, as well as the shrike corpse, which Orion had already given to her. The beak would likely go into her sirenspider lute, and I'd already given her the argonet tooth for the tuning pegs. It was going to be monstrously powerful by the time she was done. "Your affinity—"

"Just think about the 'love me and despair' version," I said.

"What?" Liu said.

"'All shall love me and despair,'" I said. She was eyeing me very dubiously. "Galadriel? In Lord of the Rings?"

"Is that the movie with the hobbits? I've never seen that. Is that where your name is from?"

"Liu, I'm so glad we're friends," I said, partly because it felt like a safe opportunity to say the word out loud. If she didn't want it to be true, it could just be a joke. But actually I meant it with great sincerity on both fronts. I've never seen the films, either. Mum read me the books out loud from beginning to end once a year from when I was born, but she was disappointed by the violence of the movies and wouldn't let me see them. Everyone *else* in the commune has, though. I've heard a lot of clever remarks on the contrast.

But Liu gave me a brief, shy smile. "I have the idea," she said. "But . . . no malia." It wasn't really a question.

"No," I said, with a deep, gusty sigh. "No malia. At all. I can't . . . do it just a little." I looked over at her, meaningfully.

Her eyes widened a moment, and then she looked down and put her arms around herself, rubbing her upper arms. "No one can," she said, low. "Not really."

Chloe actually met us coming down. She had run up to the alchemy floor and got Magnus and two other New York kids out of their lab section and they'd recruited basically the entire class to come and help. Either that or they'd bet on having a big crowd around them for trying to get to the gates and escape. Her total astonishment when she saw us and blurted, "Oh my God, you're alive!" would have been insulting if she hadn't sounded half glad about it.

The crowd, all of whom desperately wanted to know what had happened, was so big that none of them found out anything for a while, as they couldn't hear our explanations over the babble of other voices asking the very same questions. I finally had to cup my hands over my mouth and shout, "The stairwell is *sealed*. Nothing is coming up!" which answered the most urgent one for most people and calmed things down.

"What happened with the argonet?" Chloe said to me, as we all started moving back upstairs en masse: nobody was going back to their lessons at this point, and it was almost dinnertime by now. She swallowed and added, in a rush, "I'm sorry that—I figured I should get help—" without actually meeting my eyes.

"Liu put a shield up, and Aadhya and I got the wall fixed in time," I said, and didn't tell Chloe it was okay, which I'm sure she wanted me to. I'd been right about her not wanting the deal. She'd run away exactly the way that every enclave kid ran away when bad things showed up, letting their entourages take the hit. That was why they had the entourages, and the kids in those entourages were doing it because they were desperate for a way out at graduation, and they had nothing else to offer that would get an enclaver to recruit them. So they made shields out of their bodies, and if they lasted all the way to graduation, at least the most dedicated of them would be offered filler spots in enclave kids' alliances. And that wasn't okay, and she could work out for herself it wasn't okay.

She didn't ask me for the comforting lie again. She just said, "I'm really glad you're all right," quietly, and then fell back in with Magnus.

Chapter 12

THE GRADUATION HORDE

THE BELL FOR DINNER hadn't rung yet; the line wasn't open. But we were such a big crowd that we didn't even need to worry the way you normally would if you tried to go to the cafeteria alone while classes were still in session. We got six tables together and did perimeters and checks on all of them, and sat down to wait for the food to be served, sharing gossip instead.

"What happened to our senior friends?" I asked Orion.

"Hiding out somewhere in the library, I guess," Orion said. "I managed to get out of the yanker spell on the landing on this level, but they kept going up the stairs."

"They'll be back downstairs trying to bash through your work ten minutes after dinner," Magnus said. He and Chloe had taken seats at our table. He was talking to Orion only, though; English might inconveniently leave the pronoun ambiguous, but in this case the *your* in *your work* was very clearly intended to be singular. "We should call a tribunal on them."

However many literature classes might try to sell you on *Lord of the Flies,* that story is about as realistic as the source of my name. Kids don't go feral en masse in here. We all know we can't afford to get into stupid fights with one another. People do lose it all the time, but if you lose it for any length of time, something hungry finds it and you, too. If anyone tries to organize anything especially alarming, like a gang of maleficers, and other kids find out about it but don't have the firepower to stop it on their own, they can call a tribunal, which is just a pretentious word for standing on a table in the cafeteria at mealtime and yelling out that Tom, Dick, or Kylo has gone over to the dark side and asking everyone to help take them down.

But that's not *justice*. There's no hand of the law that comes down to ceremonially spank you if you've been bad. Todd was still around, going to classes, eating; presumably sleeping, although hopefully not very well. If someone's giving you a hard time, that's your problem; if you're giving someone a hard time, that's their problem. And everyone else will ignore any situation that's remotely ignorable, because they've all got problems of their own. It's only worth calling a tribunal if you can reasonably expect that everyone else in the school is going to instantly agree that there's a very clear, very imminent threat to their lives from the person you're accusing.

Which wasn't the case in this situation. "The seniors will be on *their* side," Aadhya said, since Magnus apparently needed it said.

He didn't like it at all. I imagine he had always blithely operated on the assumption that he could call a tribunal if ever he saw an imminent threat to *his* life, and naturally everyone would agree: like Chloe and her maintenance requests. "The seniors can't take the whole rest of the school," he said defensively. "And they can't afford a fight the week before graduation anyway."

"We can't either," I said. "What's it going to get us? Those five kids are graduating in a week. Do you want to punish them for wanting to improve their odds at someone else's expense? I could think of some people in our year who'd do the same." He gawked at me, shocked that I'd even hint at a parallel.

Orion didn't weigh in himself; he was getting up from the table. The line had just opened, and we all headed in for the reward of virtue, namely being first into the buffet loaded with fresh hot food. Orion checked the line ahead of us all, taking out a couple of mals on the way, and we all came out with our trays crammed full. Nobody talked for the rest of dinner: it was probably the best meal any of us had eaten in a year, even the enclavers, if not in the last three years.

The rest of the school came in round us. Perhaps halfway through the meal, our ambitious group of seniors even warily came back down from the library: they'd got tired of waiting for the general screaming and slaughter to begin, I suppose. They stared at us from the door and then slowly headed to the line themselves after a quick discussion. They were in for a lot of hostile looks along the way, as by then everyone knew what they'd tried to do. But Aadhya had been absolutely right: none of the hostile looks came from the other seniors. In fact, by the time they came out, room had been made for all of them at prime tables, and they ate with other seniors watching their backs, the sort of thing you do for someone who's at least taken a shot at helping you.

"They *are* going to try and do something," Magnus said, throwing a hard look at me. "If the new wall is going to hold, they'll hit the other stairwells. And if we don't make it hurt, all the seniors are going to help."

"No, they won't," Orion said quietly. He put his hands on the table and started to stand up, but I was ready for it; I kicked him right in the back of the knee, and he gave a sharp, loud gasp and fell back into his chair clutching at it, panting. "El, that freaking *hurt!*" he squalled out.

"Yeah? But did it hurt like getting pasted into a wall with a steam tray?" I said through my teeth. "Just put the theatrics to rest for once, Lake. You're not graduating early."

The half of our table that had begun glaring at me turned to stare at Orion instead, and he was red and obvious by then. Anyone's welcome to graduate early: you just make sure you're in the senior dorms when the curtain comes down. It's about as good an idea as skipping out on school entirely, but you're welcome to do it.

Orion's mouth had gone mulish. "I'm the one who's set them up—"

"And you'll also be the one who's set us up, if you starve the mals of half this year's graduating class," I said. "How is that better? Even assuming you don't just get yourself killed."

"Look, even if the seniors don't break the stairwells open, the *mals* are going to break them open. If not now, then next term, probably next quarter. If they've got hungry and desperate enough to start hitting the wards, they'll keep at it. I'm not planning to just get the seniors out. I'm going to cull the graduation mals."

"The gates are open for half an hour at most. Even if Patience and Fortitude don't do you in, you can't possibly kill enough mals in that time to do anything but open up some space for the little ones to grow," I said. "Or were you planning to take up permanent residence? You'd get quite hungry living in the graduation hall, unless you want to start *eating* mals instead of just sucking out their power. I know you're just waiting for us to put your statue up, but that's no reason to carry on like a slab of solid rock."

"If you've got a better idea, I'm listening," he shot back.

"I don't need a better idea to know yours is completely rubbish!" I said.

"*I've* got a better idea." It wasn't anyone at our table talking: Clarita Acevedo-Cruz had crossed over to us and was standing at the end of our table. I'd never spoken to her before, but we all recognized her anyway: she was the senior valedictorian.

In the early years, the school used to post academic rankings frequently. There are four enormous gilt-edged placards on the wall of the cafeteria, one for each class with our graduation year on top in shining letters, and at the end of each quarter, the names would march elaborately onto each one in order. However, the practice encouraged bad behavior, such as murdering the kids doing better than you. So now it's only the very final senior ranking that's put up, at New Year's, and the rest of the placards stay blank. And all the kids who are going for valedictorian—and no one gets it without deliberately going for it—do their best to hide their marks. You can guess who's trying by how much intensity they put into their schoolwork, but it's hard to know for sure how well they're doing. The kids who get anywhere in sniffing distance of valedictorian almost have to have massive egos as well as the drive of champion thoroughbreds, and if they aren't also mad geniuses, they're such brutally hard workers that they've made up for it.

Clarita hadn't just made valedictorian, she'd played it so close to the vest that nobody had even suspected she was in the running. She had even picked up the occasional spare shift from maintenance-track kids who needed some free time, so most people assumed she was in maintenance track herself. Including the twenty kids who'd ended up directly below her in the rankings, having spent their own academic careers in savage and occasionally violent rivalry, snooping on each other's exams and sabotaging each other's projects. After the list had finally gone up with her name at the top, the news had gone buzzing round the school for days. The thing everyone had said was some variation on, "That dull girl from—" and insert a random Spanish-speaking country. She was actually from Argentina, where her mum did occasional maintenance work for the enclave in Salta, but it took about two weeks before the accurate information finally worked its way around, because hardly anyone knew anything at all about her. Until then, she'd been easy to overlook: short and thin and hard-faced, and she'd always worn—deliberately, in retrospect—dull beige and grey clothing.

It was a brilliant strategy. Even if she had only made top ten in the end, the surprise of her showing up out of nowhere would've made her look better than someone who'd visibly been going for the top spot the whole time. Three and a half years of hiding your light under a bushel, doing the odd maintenance shift on top of your classwork, without ever once bragging about a mark on a project or an exam— that was more discipline than most teenagers have when marks are the only thing in school you care about. Well, apart from surviving.

Her discipline had paid off with a guaranteed spot in New York. Nobody cared if you were dull if you could cast six major arcana workings in a row, which she'd done for the final project in her senior seminar. We all knew about that, too, because after the rankings finally went up, she'd mounted a binder on the wall next to her door with literally every mark she'd received in the past three and a half years, so anyone could come and look through it and see them in detail, possibly to make up for all the bragging she hadn't done before then.

Too bad for her that she was now also stuck with Todd on

her team. Orion hadn't wanted to talk about it much, but I'd gathered that Todd's dad was indeed high up on the enclave council, and despite what Chloe had promised me in the library, the other New York seniors on his team were apparently reluctant to ditch his darling boy. Very likely he had control of at least one or two of the better defensive artifacts they were planning to use. And Clarita didn't get a vote, unless she wanted to ditch the entire alliance herself—along with her guaranteed spot, which she wasn't going to be able to replace this close to graduation.

But being saddled with Todd wasn't her fault, and none of us needed any incentive to take her seriously. Everyone at the tables nearby had stopped whispering and was straining over to listen to her. "I've worked out the numbers," she said to Orion. "There're records in the library of inducted students and graduated students. You've saved six hundred lives since you started school." The quiet spread further out, followed by a ripple of whispers as people repeated the information. I'd known he was saving ridiculous numbers of us, but I hadn't known it was *that* much. "More than three hundred just this one year. That's why *we're* all hungry, not just the maleficaria. The food trays aren't supposed to be empty if you get here before the bell rings."

Orion stood up and faced her, his jaw tight. "I'm not sorry."

"I'm not *sorry*, either," she said. "Only a bastard would be sorry. But that is the mana we have to pay back. There are nine hundred seniors left. An ordinary year, half of us can expect to get out. But if we alone have to pay back all the lives you've saved this year on top of that, we're talking less than a hundred survivors. It's not fair for our class to bear that burden."

"So we should let the mals into the school?" Chloe said. "Then you all make it out, the freshmen all die, and they *keep* dying until the school gets shut down completely so they can do a full extermination on the place, if they even can. How is that fair, either?"

"Of course it's not," Clarita said cuttingly. "If we got out that way, over your bodies, that's malia whether or not we took the hit for it directly. *Most* of us don't want that." She didn't actually turn and glare at Todd across the room, but the emphasis didn't escape any of us. I would've been furiously angry with him in her place: three and a half years slogging to the very top of the mountain, and this was what she'd got for it. Not only did she have to worry about just how expendable Todd was going to consider *her*, she was going to come out with her reputation attached to him. Everyone would always think of her as the valedictorian who'd chosen to stick with a poacher, however little choice she really had.

"*I* don't want it," she added. "But we also don't want to let you buy your lives with ours. That's what I hear seniors saying. Not, let's rip open the school, but why don't we make you, your class, graduate with us. Your class are the ones Orion has saved the most." Chloe flinched visibly, and a lot of the other kids at our table tensed. "So? Are you all willing to do that, graduate early, to save the poor little freshmen? If not, you can stop"—she waved a hand in a spiraling circle, making a gesture of drama—"about how evil we are because we don't want to die. It doesn't help anyone. We know what we have to do, if we don't want to pay it back with blood. We have to pay it back with *work*."

Clarita turned back to Orion. "There're more than four thousand of us in here right now. Ten times more wizards than built the Scholomance in the first place. We've got a little more than a week. All of us put in work, build all the mana we can, and you go down into the graduation hall and use it to fix the scouring machinery down there. And that will clear the hall before we graduate, enough that our class doesn't all have to die. Because we'll have paid back the debt together." She had to raise her voice to finish: a wild babbling of conversation had erupted throughout the entire room.

Her plan certainly had a nice sound to it. If you put aside the challenge of *getting* to the cleansing equipment downstairs, the challenge of repairing it wasn't insurmountable at all. We wouldn't have to invent anything new. The detailed blueprints for the whole school that are on display everywhere include the engines that generate the walls of mortal flame for cleansing. The best artificers would be easily good enough to create replacement parts, and the best maintenance-track kids would be easily good enough to install them.

You could really hear in the changing pitch of voices in the room that everyone was beginning to get *excited* about the idea. If we did get the cleansing fires running in the graduation hall, it wouldn't just be the seniors this year who saw the benefits. There would be fewer mals in the school for years, and the cleansing might run again for our graduation, and the sophomores, too.

Unfortunately, you can't, in fact, put aside the challenge of getting to the equipment. It broke for the first time back in 1886. The first repair crew—the original idea the enclaves had for school maintenance was that paid crews of grown wizards would pop in through the graduation gates every so often and come up, ha ha—anyway, the first crew sent in didn't come back out again and also didn't repair a thing. The second and much larger crew did manage to get the equipment repaired, but only two of them made it back out, with quite the alarming tale to tell. By then, the graduation hall was already home to our senior resident maw-mouths and several hundred exceptional horrors—the kind smart enough to realize that once they wriggled in through the gates, they could just lie around the hall and wait for an annual feast of tender young wizardlings. And the cleansing failed again in 1888. There were wards protecting the machinery, but somehow the mals kept getting through. They didn't have anything to do all year but sit around down there bashing on things, I suppose.

There were enough recriminations flying among the enclaves by then that Sir Alfred himself personally led in a large crew of heroic volunteers to install what he insisted would be a permanent repair. He was the Dominus of Manchester— he'd won the position for having built the school—and was generally agreed to be the most powerful wizard alive at the time. He was last seen going screaming into Patience or possibly Fortitude—witness accounts differ about which side of the gate the maw-mouth in question was on—along with about half of his crew. His "permanent" repair got dismantled again three years later.

There were a few more attempts by groups of desperate parents with graduating children, but they all just ended up with the parents dead and no repairs done. Manchester was in chaos with its Dominus and several of its council dead, enclavers all over the world were howling. People were talking about abandoning the school entirely, except then they'd be back to where they began, with more than half their children dying. In the midst of that, London enclave more or less organized a coup, took the Scholomance over, then doubled the number of seats—the dorm rooms became significantly smaller—and opened the place up to independent students. Rather in the same spirit as the seniors who wanted to bring our class along for graduation.

And it worked splendidly. The enclaver kids do make it out alive almost all of the time—their survival rate usually hovers around eighty percent, a substantial improvement over the forty percent chance they've got if they stay home. There are so many weaker and less protected wizards around them, and even in the graduation hall, the mals can't catch *all* the salmon swimming upstream. And that's the best solution that all the most powerful and brilliant wizards of the last century and more have been able to come up with. Not a one of them has tried to repair the scouring machinery since.

But every excited and happy and pleased face in the room, everyone looking admiringly at Clarita, the genius who'd come up with this plan, wasn't questioning for a single moment the idea that Orion was theirs to put on the hook to somehow make it happen. Not even Orion himself, who I could see was about to nod to her as his own surprise cleared out.

I shoved my chair back with a deliberate scrape and stood up before he could do it. "Were you planning to ask nicely at some point?" I said loudly. Clarita and Orion both jerked round to stare at me. "Sorry, just wondering whether a *please* might ever enter into this brilliant idea of yours that depends completely on Lake here serving himself up in all our places. He's saved six hundred lives, so now he's meant to save more to make up for it? Can anyone here tell me even one time that he's ever had any reward for saving any of us?" I swept a look around the room that was furious enough that the handful of kids who made the mistake of looking me back in the face all flinched and dropped their eyes. "He's never asked me for a thing, and I'm up to eleven by now. But right, he's to go down to the graduation hall, all on his own, and fix the cleansing machinery. One hand for the work, and the other to fight off the mals, I suppose? It seems a little awkward. How exactly is he meant to do the repairs anyway? He's not artificer track, he hasn't so much as done a single maintenance shift."

"We'll build him a golem—" Clarita started.

"Right, a golem," I said with contempt. "Because the powers that be never thought of trying that, surely. Don't even open your mouth in my direction, you overgrown lemming," I snapped at Orion, who glared back, having in fact been just about to open his mouth. "No one is going to survive going in there alone, not even you, and a golem isn't going to get it sorted before you're overrun. That's not heroism, it's just suicide. And after you're dead, we'll all be back here—only once you're gone, the seniors will be in a rather better position to decide for the rest of us what we're doing about it," which sent a low murmur going round.

Clarita had her thin mouth pressed even thinner. Yes, that particular angle had absolutely been in her head, and she hadn't liked me dragging it out into the open. "Maybe you're right," she said. "If he needs help, we could have a lottery of people whose lives he's saved to go in with him. Maybe *you* should go, since you're up to eleven."

"I can do it on my own," Orion put in, unhelpfully. "I can hold the mals off a golem."

"It'd fall apart before you get halfway across the hall. And that's right, *I'll go*," I added to Clarita, who frowned; she'd obviously been looking to make me back off. "But we're not going down there alone just to get eaten for our trouble, and we're not having any lottery, either. If this is meant to *work*, it's got to be seniors going, and the best seniors at that. And then we really have got a chance to do the repair, if we have Orion keeping the mals off, and the whole school's mana behind us."

I don't actually know whether Clarita had even meant her proposal as anything other than a clever hail-Mary attempt that would at worst get rid of Orion. But hope is good strong drink, especially when you can get someone else to buy it for you. A bunch of the seniors from the Berlin enclave were whispering urgently among themselves; when I finished, one of them stood up on the bench at their table and said loudly in English, "Berlin will guarantee a place to anyone who goes with Orion!" He looked over at the Edinburgh and Lisbon tables, near theirs. "Will any other enclaves make the same promise?"

The question went racing around the room, being translated into a few dozen languages as it went, senior enclavers quickly huddling together to discuss, and one after another someone from almost every enclave stood up to sign on. Which changed the equation rather dramatically. The top students had all spent their Scholomance careers trying to make exactly that deal with the enclavers: their help fighting mals on the way out, in exchange for a home on the other side of the gates. And most of them *hadn't* got guaranteed spots for their trouble. The top three, yes, but the rabble below that were having to content themselves with alliances and hope, unless they'd tried for guaranteed places at small enclaves, and even that would only have been available to the top ten students. That was why the competition for valedictorian was so savage.

And meanwhile the maintenance-track kids had all made a different kind of deal: the best of them would likely get homes, but they'd done loads of scut work already, and they'd be doing it for the rest of their lives. It was really their kids who'd get to be enclavers, not them. An offer like this meant a chance for *them*, a chance they'd given up on in freshman year.

Anyone could have told you which seniors were thinking about it and what enclave they wanted to live in, just by watching which table their heads turned to watch. There were a lot of them. Clarita herself was looking narrowly, not at the New York table, where one of the senior girls had stood up to announce that they were in, but at the table on the fringes where Todd was still sitting with his pathetic entourage of freshmen.

ALL OF US GO into the last week of school—*hell week* has a whole new meaning in here—with fairly detailed plans, even if we're not graduating. Aside from final exams and papers and projects, and the increasingly excited maleficaria, all of whom are reaching their peak, it's also the most active trading time. The seniors are all selling off every last thing they own that they aren't using to get out of the graduation hall; everyone else is selling off things they don't need anymore, or that they can replace with something better from a departing graduate. Everyone who can afford to stockpile goods or mana for the end-of-year trading is running around in a frenzy making substantial deals; everyone who can't is also running around in a frenzy trying desperately to find any opportunity they can to at least make small ones.

I'd been looking forward to a bit of success, for once. Aside from the auction Aadhya was going to run for me, I'd already traded some mercury to an alchemy-track sophomore in exchange for his half-burnt blanket, since he'd got a replacement from a senior in return for a tiny vial with three drops of a vitality potion. I'd be able to unravel it and crochet myself a desperately needed new shirt while I was building mana.

Which might sound like a ridiculous thing to be worrying about at this time of year even under more normal circumstances, when every hour brings a new maleficaria eruption, sometimes literally, like the shrieker blooms that came bursting out of all the sinks in the nearest girls' bathroom on Friday morning. But any other time of year, a new shirt would cost me six snack bar tokens, assuming I could get one at all instead of having to sacrifice half my own blanket and sleep partly uncovered, which at best guarantees you the same lacerating ekkini bites the poor or rather lucky sophomore had in a wide band above the top of his fraying and stained tube socks, and at worst gets you stung by a numbing scorpion and eaten alive. If you don't do well enough in the end-of-year trading, you're getting yourself into a potentially fatal hole.

Of course, now I was instead in the midst of planning to get myself into a much *more* potentially fatal hole, namely the graduation hall. The bright side—no, sorry, the side with a very faint hint of phosphorescence—was that I wasn't going to have to sit a single exam. I'd already done with shop, and Liu had offered to wrap up my history paper for me; Chloe had organized a dozen alchemy-track kids to finish my and Orion's final lab assignments, and that otherwise useless trombone Magnus had commanded people to take our maths and language exams for us. The school will come after you if the work doesn't get done, but it doesn't care in the slightest if you cheat. I didn't even go to any of my last classes on Friday, except to stop by Maleficaria Studies, in possibly a morbid spirit, and stare at the giant mural of the graduation hall. The one relief it gave me was that at least I wouldn't have to go anywhere near the maw-mouths this time. The machinery was all the way at the opposite end of the hall from the gates.

I spent the rest of the day making arrangements instead. "I *will* get the book chest done for you, I promise, soon as we're done with this nonsense, which isn't nearly as important as you are," I told the sutras, stroking the cover in apology, before handing them over to Aadhya: she was going to be booksitting for me. "I just have to help save everyone's lives, that's all." Possibly a bit over the top, but better safe than sorry. The book had kept itself out of circulation for more than a thousand years, with probably dozens of enclave librarians and hundreds of independent wizards fishing for at least some of the spells in it. It was still almost unbelievable that I'd got it at all, and now that I'd actually used the phase-control spell, I was even more desperate to get on with translating the rest of it. "Aadhya's going to look after you so well. I promise."

"I will," Aadhya said, accepting it carefully with both hands. "Absolutely nothing's going to happen to the book while you're gone. I'll do some work on the spine of the case, make sure it's sanded down just right to fit." She went through a big show of putting a folded strip of silk against the back of the sutras, tucking the engraved purpleheart against that, and wrapping the whole thing back up in the satchel that I'd just taken it out of, before putting it under her pillow. She rested a hand on it and said without looking at me, "El, you know there are a lot of seniors who are willing to take a shot now that the enclaves are putting up guaranteed spots."

It was something between an offer and a request. I wasn't just me anymore. I was El, in alliance with Aadhya and Liu, our names in a line on the wall next to the nearest bathroom, underneath the lamp. That wasn't a little thing. It was everything, and everything to me. And if I went down to the graduation hall and didn't come back out, I was binning our alliance along with myself. So Aadhya had a right to push, to say that maybe I shouldn't be taking the chance, not just with myself but them.

But I wasn't just taking a jaunt down there for my own amusement. I'd got myself into this making a play for all our lives, and in some sense, being in alliance with me meant that they were supposed to back me, arguably to the point of coming along themselves. On graduation day, at best you have fifteen minutes between the first step into the hall and last step out the gates. You don't sign on with someone if you aren't willing to swerve when they yell, "Go left!" By saying anything, Aadhya was practically inviting me to ask her and Liu to come.

I hugged my knees to myself on the bed. I wanted to take the excuse, badly, and bail myself out. There was even some tiny whimpering selfish part of me that would desperately have liked to take Aadhya up on the other side of her offer. Of course I wanted her and Liu at my back, not a bunch of seniors I didn't know, who had an excellent strategic reason to ditch me if things went badly. But I wasn't going to put them on this line with me. I was reasonably certain I *wasn't* coming back, and neither was anyone else. Ten, maybe fifteen kids, jumping into the graduation hall alone to fix the machinery? One in a hundred odds, at best. Better to have stayed in Wales, after all.

So I told Aadhya, "I can't let Orion go it alone with all the worst piranhas of the senior class. Someone's got to watch his back for him. They'll let him save their skins, and then they'll cut him off the yanker and leave him down there so he does have to graduate with them. He won't be paying attention to anything but the mals."

I suppose the seniors really might have tried something like that. But I wasn't really worrying about that possibility. If we actually got the machinery fixed, the seniors would probably garland Orion with laurel: they'd all be graduating through a cleansed hall, with guaranteed enclave spots. But it was plausible enough to serve as an excuse, an excuse for me to go, and her and Liu to stay behind.

And I had to go. Because Orion was going, and I couldn't do anything about that. He'd have gone down without even a golem, the git. The only thing I could do for him, which Clarita had helpfully spelled out, was go along and give him a fighting chance. He had one now because we were going with a dozen seniors, and top seniors at that, who actually could do the repair work. And I'd only got that for him by throwing myself on the line.

I wasn't the shining hero of the school. And yeah, everyone thought I was dating Orion, but they didn't think I was in love with him. They thought I was *using* him, and clever me for doing it. People expected the worst of me, not the best; when I'd volunteered to go along, I'd made it seem like something that wasn't completely effing insane. In their heads, if I was going, it was because I'd made the cold hard decision it was a good bet, at least for a loser girl with no prospect of getting into an enclave if she lost Orion.

We all have to gamble with our lives in here, we don't get a choice about that; the trick is figuring out when it's worth taking a bet. We're always looking to one another for signals and information. Do *you* think that's the best table to sit at? Do *you* think that's a good class to take? Everyone wants to jump on any advantage. Me saying I was going meant that at least one presumed-to-be-rational person thought she had a sliver of a chance of making it out, and then the enclave kids had sweetened the pot. That's why there were now more volunteers than places, because I'd put my finger on the scales.

If I took it off again now, who knew how many seniors would start to have second thoughts? They might decide that actually I was playing a double game of my own: maybe I was just trying to wipe out a dozen of the top seniors, and delay the rest of them long enough to stop them from either smashing open the school or dragging my class along with them to graduation. That would've been clever, now I thought of it, and surely the geniuses coming along had thought of it, too, and were keeping a wary eye on me to see if I bailed out at the last minute.

Clarita was going; so was David Pires, the still-resentful salutorian, saluditorian, whatever you call the number two besides "not the valedictorian," which was in fact exactly what I was inclined to call him. He was an incanter also, and he hadn't spent his academic career hiding his light under a bushel; he'd spent it informing everyone who talked to him for so much as thirty seconds that he was going to be valedictorian, and brandishing his every mark like a trophy. He'd told *me* back in my freshman year, when I'd accidentally knocked over one of his precariously balanced stacks of books in the reading room. He'd yelled at me and demanded to know if I knew who he was, which I hadn't until then, and didn't much care to afterwards. And he was going, as far as I could tell, because he wasn't satisfied with the guaranteed enclave spot he already had coming in Sydney; he wanted to be able to pick and choose. Getting close to valedictorian does require a muscular ego, but his was on steroids.

After the first wave of volunteering, that boy from Berlin had rounded up a couple of other senior enclavers from the bigger places, the ones we all had in our heads as the most powerful kids, and we'd huddled up in the library—Orion included for obvious reasons, my own presence tolerated—to discuss the situation with Clarita and David and the third obvious candidate, Wu Wen. He was actually ranked only fifteenth overall in the senior class, and also made the discussion require more translation, because he was the only one there who didn't know a word of English. He had copped out and claimed Mandarin was his native language so he could take Shanghainese—his actual native language—for his languages requirement. And he'd all but flunked the coursework for that. In fact, he'd barely squeaked through every course he'd taken that *wasn't* shop or maths.

Since literally everyone else in the top twenty had almost

perfect marks on everything and fought it out with extra-credit work, that gives you an idea of the kinds of marks he got on his artifice projects. He already had a guaranteed spot in Bangkok enclave, but he'd volunteered to come with Orion the instant that Shanghai enclave put one on the line.

I didn't have any part in the planning, except to annoy the senior enclavers even more by insisting that we weren't going until the morning of graduation day itself. "Don't be ridiculous," the boy from Jaipur enclave informed me coldly. "You can't leave your rooms until morning bell, and graduation is two hours later. We need to allow more time than that. What if something goes wrong?"

"Then we're all dead, and everyone left in the school has a worse-than-usual time of it for the next few years until things balance out. Shut it, Lake," I added to Orion, who was opening his mouth to say that actually he was ready to go this evening, or something else similarly dim. "Sorry, but you don't get to keep a tidy murder plan in reserve in case we don't succeed."

That could've turned into more of a fight, except Clarita and David and Wen weren't on the enclavers' side of it anymore—they weren't going to be enjoying the benefits of any reserve plan if we didn't make it back. Wen even suggested that the more time we had to build the parts and practice installation, the better.

Apart from that, though, the plan was fairly obvious anyway. We needed a group of artificers and maintenance-track kids who'd build the parts and do the repair, and we needed a group of incanters to shield them while they did it. And Orion would be our offense, dashing out from behind the shield at every opportunity, hopefully taking out enough mals to let us keep the shield up for long enough to get the work done. The alchemists were out of luck, if that's what you want to call it. In this case, the machinery was going to need maybe one liter of the common school lubricant, which the maintenance kids brew for themselves in massive vats.

"I have a shielding spell we can use," Clarita offered a bit sourly, which I understood after she got it out and grudgingly shared it with me and David: she'd written it herself, and I'd never seen anything like it. There are plenty of shielding spells that you can strengthen by casting them through a circle, but you still have to funnel the power through a primary caster, and if that one person goes down, so does the shield. Clarita's shield spell was fundamentally designed to be cast by multiple people, to cover a group. It wove between English and Spanish, and read almost like a song, or a play with different roles for each caster: there were lines and verses that we could cast either solo or together, chaining them together one after another, so we could all take a breather now and then, and the lines weren't even nailed down: you were allowed to improvise as long as you kept the same basic rhythm and meaning, which is a massive advantage when you're in a combat situation and you can't remember which adjective you're supposed to use.

It was undoubtedly a wrench to hand over a spell that valuable to other people for nothing. She'd probably have got into an alliance on the strength of it even if she hadn't had anything else to offer. My own best shielding spell is top-notch, but it's a purely personal shield. And everyone else already has it, as Mum invented it, and she gives her spells out freely to anyone who asks. There's a wizard who comes to the commune once a year and collects up her new ones and sends out copies to quite a lot of subscribers. *He* charges. I've yelled at Mum for just giving him the spells, but she says he's providing a service, and if he wants to charge for it that's his concern.

"Four incanters, you think?" David said, looking up narrow-eyed from the bottom of the page before I'd even finished reading a quarter of the way down.

"Five," Clarita said, with an unflattering look at me, even though another person meant diminishing returns: the bigger an area we had to shield, the more mana we'd need to use, and the harder it would be for Orion to keep mals from hitting the shield in the first place. But I kept my mouth shut; I wasn't going to convince any of them to rely on me by telling them that I was brilliant.

The next incanter down the list, number five, already had a guaranteed spot from Sacramento and wasn't as loony as Pires, so he wasn't volunteering to go along. But number seven was Maya Wulandari, a languages-track girl from Canada, who had both English and Spanish, but not the guaranteed spot in Toronto that she badly wanted. That's one of the few enclaves with the remarkably civilized practice of allowing any new recruit to bring their entire family in with them, which in her case meant that her little brother and sister would come here as enclavers.

Those enclaves are all unusually picky, though. If she'd been top three, the Toronto enclaver kids could have offered her a guarantee; top ten only got her an alliance and a promise of serious consideration. She could've taken a guaranteed spot for herself somewhere else; instead she'd taken the gamble that when she got out, she'd be able to persuade the enclave council that she and her family were a good choice to bring in. And now she'd taken a different gamble: she'd talked to the Toronto kids about the guarantee, and they'd agreed that even if she didn't make it back from what we were with excessive drama now calling *the mission*, they'd consider the spot hers—and her family would get to come in.

The next incanter down the rankings who'd volunteered

and had both Spanish and English was Angel Torres, at lucky number thirteen: also not good enough to get a guaranteed spot anywhere, after three and a half years fighting tooth and nail for every mark; he was one of the nose-to-grindstone workhorses, the kind who sleep five hours a night, get ten extra spells a week down in their books, and do extra-credit projects in every lesson.

That made five of us. Wen ran over the list of volunteers and picked out five artificers and ten maintenance-track kids, ignoring the rankings entirely. The senior enclavers all peered over his shoulders while pretending to be casual, paying close attention to which names he passed over and which ones he immediately put down. Expert information about which artificers and maintenance-track kids coming out are the best is both hard to get and extremely valuable, not so much in here, but for any enclave recruiting new people. He went for Mandarin-speakers, obviously, so I didn't recognize any of their names myself except for Zhen Yang, a maintenance-track kid who had come in already bilingual and done the same thing as Liu: took her maths and writing and history classes in English so she could avoid taking any language classes and get more time to do shifts.

Everyone else in school spent hell week in the usual mix of panic and frenzy, with a special side order of building shared mana for the mission, three times a day, after every meal. All the bigger enclaves have a large mana store in the place, built over generations, which the enclavers get to pull from: they keep them hidden somewhere in the upper classrooms or the library and only the seniors from each enclave know where they are. Ten of the biggest enclaves contributed power-sharers to our little team—Chloe gave me back the same one as before, from New York—and in return, everyone poured mana into their battery packs. There were rows of kids doing push-ups in the cafeteria like it was a military training exercise and they were all being punished.

Our group spent it in the workshop, also in panic and frenzy. The artificers had the worst of it, obviously; they had to do most of their work in advance, and the rest of us ferried in their meals and raw materials and also protected them from the five-daily mal attacks that came at our heads, which I suppose was good practice at that. Clarita did get a bit less hostile to me after the first time we all cast her spell together successfully, in a practice session on Wednesday. That might sound like the hour was late, given that graduation was on Sunday, and it was, but that was also probably as good as we could possibly have hoped for. Casting a single spell with a circle of people isn't like going to a yoga class with an instructor who encourages you to all go at your own pace; it's like learning a choreographed dance with four people you barely know for an aggravated director who yells at you if you put a toe out of line.

We were all looking round at the shield, pleased with ourselves, when the big air shaft overhead exploded open and a hissingale the size of a tree came writhing down at us: it literally wrapped us up completely in pulsing snaky limbs and started trying to rip us apart, without noticeable success. I confess I yelped, which mortified me because none of the seniors so much as paused for a second. They'd all spent the last six months doing obstacle-course runs in the gym; you could probably have crept up to one of them sleeping and exploded a balloon next to their heads, and they'd just have killed you before they opened their eyes.

David Pires just said, "Got it," and stepped out of the spell, leaving the rest of us to hold the shield; he drew a deep breath for what I'm sure would've been a really impressive casting, except before he could start, Orion ripped apart the hissingale like he was pulling open a stage curtain, and dragged the limp mass of it off us.

By Friday, when the five of us put the shield wall up, it felt roughly as strong as the major school ward we'd repaired down in the stairwell. And even as we were all congratulating ourselves, the repair team all screamed out loud and started jumping up and down hugging each other. After about five minutes of us yelling furiously for them to tell us what was going on, Yang and the other English-speaker—Ellen Cheng, from Texas—explained that Wen had just figured out a way to separate the parts into three collapsible pieces. They'd be able to build them up here and install them in under five minutes.

All the seniors on the team suddenly realized that we had *decent* odds to get through this alive, and if we did, they would emerge from the Scholomance as shining heroes, with guaranteed spots to any enclave they wanted. By the time graduation day was upon us, the maintenance kids were actually savagely competing to see who could do it the quickest: to keep the shield as tight as possible, only the four fastest of them were going—two to do the work and two spares, in case the rest of us couldn't keep all the mals off them—along with Wen and Ellen and Kaito Nakamura, who were coming in case it turned out we needed some unexpected part.

It was just as well we had some cause for optimism, because otherwise, I'm fairly certain that at least half of our group would have balked when we got to the sticking point— namely, the way down.

The whole point of the school's design is to keep the bit we're in completely separated from the bit with the gates. If it were easy to get down, it would be easy to get up. The maintenance shaft we'd seen on the other side of the stairwell wall, packed full of argonet, wasn't even on the blueprints. Not even the maintenance-track seniors had any idea where it would come out, or for that matter if it would be safe for *us* to go through whatever wards were on there to keep the mals out. They *thought* it would be all right, because presumably it had been built for those professional maintenance crews who'd been meant to be coming in here to fix things, but they couldn't find a word about it in a single one of their manuals, even the old ones.

That was even sensible: if everyone forgot about it and didn't think it was there, it would stop being there, more often than not, and that would be one unnecessary point of vulnerability closed up. The mals in the graduation hall had probably dragged it back into existence through their collective starving desperation to find a way to get up at us. And now it was our only way of getting down to them: climbing into the dark, with who knew what down there waiting.

When the morning bell rang on graduation day, Orion came and got me, and we went down to the senior res hall and met the rest of the group in the landing. Wen gave us each a belt hook for the yanker spell that would hopefully get us out alive; the anchor end was already secured to the drain in Todd's old room, the one right across from the landing. The thirteen of us all marched the rest of the way down to the bottom of the stairwell, and the head of the maintenance team, Vinh Tran, carefully unrolled a maintenance hatch over my beautiful new steel wall, using a squeegee to make it come out smooth. It just looked like a big flat poster of a metal trap door at first, but as he smoothed it back and forth, murmuring some kind of incantation under his breath, it began to look like part of the wall. He took a thick brass handle out of his pocket, inserted it into the small, round black circle at one end, and pulled the hatch open in one quick motion, jumping back with one hand ready for a shield.

He didn't need it: nothing came out. Orion went over and stuck his head in with a light on his hand—literally all the rest of us cringed—and then he said, "Looks clear," pulled back in, and climbed on through, feet first.

Even with our fearless hero leading the way, no one was in a hurry to be the *second* person into the hole. There were a bunch of glances traded round, which after a moment predictably started to coalesce on me. I didn't wait to be prodded; I just said, "Well? Let's get on with it before Lake gets too far ahead," and pretended to be perfectly sanguine about dropping myself down a very long, nasty oubliette.

We all know that the school is enormous, we have to slog around the place morning until night. But knowing it as you trudge up to the cafeteria isn't the same as knowing it when you're climbing down an endless ladder through a shaft so narrow your back is pressed against the other side and your elbows keep hitting the walls. A person isn't near as big around as an argonet, but the shaft had apparently shrunk down since then, hopefully on the way to disappearing again. It was stiflingly hot, and the walls were vibrating around us with the shifting of the gears. The gurgle of liquid running through pipes on the other side rose and fell, never steady enough to turn into white noise. The only light was the dim glow filtering up from Orion's hand.

The loud chomping noise we'd heard after the wall repair hadn't started again. After I'd climbed down the first thousand miles of ladder, I paused and leaned back against the wall to catch my breath and give my arms a break, and after I was there panting for a bit, not more than a few seconds, I heard the first part of the sound start up, not very loud. Exactly at the height of my neck, a panel in the wall, only about a centimeter high, started to slide open.

I'm not an idiot; I didn't just sit there. I hurriedly started climbing down once more, and the wall closed up again, so I never actually saw what would have come out, but I'm confident that it was the artifice responsible for keeping the shaft clear. It wouldn't have been anything as simple as a swinging blade, either: it was smart enough to aim for the point of highest vulnerability on whatever was climbing through, which is quite the trick, *and* it could tell human beings from mals, at least well enough to let us through. I tried not to take it to heart that it seemed to have entertained doubts about me.

I didn't pause again. After another century of climbing, a light abruptly bloomed below my feet, and I let out a very quiet but explosive sigh of relief: Orion had got out the other end, and the lack of instant howls and gnashing meant it was moderately sheltered. I heard a few similar sighs come out in the shaft above me, too.

I dropped out of the shaft into a narrow chamber with its walls and floor covered in almost a solid centimeter of powdery soot, and stinking of what had to be fairly recent smoke. I had the strong suspicion that we were standing in the remains of whatever hopeful mals had been crowding into that shaft behind the argonet, after their encounter with the repaired artifice. I hate this school more than anyplace in the entire world, not least because every once in a while, you get forcibly reminded that the place was built by geniuses who were trying to save the lives of their own children, and you're unspeakably lucky to be here being protected by their work. Even if you've been allowed in only as another useful cog.

That's all I was, me and everyone else on our team: the fourth repair crew sent into the graduation hall by the enclavers to try and save their kids. Except for our one hero, who was already going over the walls in full hunting mode, his eyes intent and bright, a small witchlight in one hand shining on his silver hair and pasty skin, which was already getting finely speckled with black as he felt around, smearing through the soot, presumably for a hatch. Although I have no idea why he thought there would *be* a hatch: anyone sent here would presumably have brought a maintenance hatch with them, and leaving one permanently would have been a stupid vulnerability. The more likely result was he'd make a noise and wake the mals up to our presence. Not that he was concerned; he was so intent on finding a way through that when I poked him in the shoulder, he even absently batted my hand away. So I flicked his ear instead, which recaptured his attention, and when he glared at me, I glared right back and pointed up into the shaft at everyone else still climbing down, and he got a sheepish sort of look and stopped to wait with me.

The room was oddly shaped: narrow and long, and slightly curved along its length: I realized after a moment we had to be inside the exterior wall of the school. A lot of the maintenance access points I've caught sight of over the years have been in those kinds of in-between spaces, not shown on the blueprints. I expect maintenance-track kids keep track of them the way I keep track of library books.

Vinh was the next one out of the shaft. He instantly went to the inner wall with a little silver ear-cup that he carefully put against the metal in a few places, roughly halfway down the wall, listening. By the time everyone else was down, he'd found a spot he liked. He wiped the soot away, then got out a cloth and a tiny dropper bottle; he put three drops on the cloth, and when he rubbed it over the wall in a small circle, the metal shimmered and went the murky-transparent of one-way glass, and we each took a turn to crouch down and peer through to see what we were in for.

I've been dragged to rugby games on the regular throughout my childhood. Most people consider that you're not properly Welsh if you don't have a passionate interest, so of course I aggressively refused to care, but every once in a while Mum would get invited for free and then insist on my coming along for the experience. Once, we even went to a game in the national stadium in Cardiff, one of the biggest in the world: seventy thousand people yowling *Gwlad! Gwlad!* all together. That was roughly the scale of the place, only we were the ones going onto the field, and the crowd were going to try to eat us.

The enormous central column of the school's rotating axle actually looked small where it pierced the hall. There were patches of greasy black-stained metal exposed where various mals and spells had torn away some of the once fancy marble cladding. Thin bronze columns ran up the outer walls and then spoked in over one another to make a ceiling like a bicycle wheel overhead. The marble had crumbled away from between many of them, exposing the metal beneath, and there was one really massive gaping hole across the ceiling that looked like an unpleasant amount of structural damage. Also there were strips of sticky-gleaming nets woven between most of the bronze bars and to the central column, at all sorts of heights, like someone had draped up some elaborate bunting that had all fallen down: the sirenspiders were undoubtedly hiding somewhere above waiting to pounce.

But we were lucky: the mals had clearly given up on getting up through the shaft. Now they were all jockeying for positions, clustered up to the big sliding walls on either side of the hall, which would open up when the senior dorm came down. Outside our little crawl space, the field was clear, and Vinh silently pointed our eyes toward a pair of huge cylinder shapes against the wall, armored, with pipes and cables coming out, and two large glass sections in the middle: our destination. We had a mostly wide-open path straight to the machinery.

It had been built—sensibly—in the most deserted area of the room, directly opposite the gates. The official graduation handbook warns strongly against retreating into that area, even temporarily or to cast a more complex working. It might look extremely tantalizing and safe, but there's a reason that mals don't hang out there waiting: it's a bad idea, as is anything else that takes you out of the main herd of fleeing students. If you can do an evocation of arctic light, freeze everyone along your path into place, and zoom out before they thaw, all right. But if you can do that, you can probably do something else that doesn't require seven minutes of highly interruptible casting time. As a general rule, anyone who doesn't stay with the pack just gets snagged for dessert when they finally do make their run, because everyone else has gone one way or another and they've got the full attention of the room.

Like we were about to, which was a cheery thought. The mals weren't directly in our way, but there were still so *many* of them, clawing and scrabbling over one another to get higher up in the pile, obviously so starved they had no caution left. It was awful to look at the seething mass of them, the awful of walking in the woods and stumbling across a swarm of ants and beetles and rats and birds all devouring a dead badger. Victoria from Seattle had been right to worry about not having to move. When the seniors got dumped into that frantic mass, they'd be ripped apart in moments from all sides in a frenzy. They looked pretty grim when they stood back up from their turn peering through the spyhole.

At least that made it obvious we really did have to carry on with the plan. There wasn't any discussion. We all got in line behind Orion, and Vinh opened up another hatch, carefully rigged to the end of the yanker spell, so it would close and then peel away behind us as we shot back through.

I can't say much for actually going out into the graduation hall. It wasn't *as* bad as going into a maw-mouth? Also, what we were doing was so insane that the mals didn't react to us immediately. The ones at the walls were too busy struggling with each other, and the rest were the weaker opportunists, huddled in dark corners defensively until there was a lucky chance of a meal. And the real monsters were quiescent in their places: Patience and Fortitude both at the gates softly murmuring to themselves, snatches of nonsense songs and whimpers like a drowsing baby, their eyes almost all closed and tendrils idly pawing the well-cleared space around them.

Our original plan had been to make a run for the machinery, Orion fighting the mals off us as we ran, and put up the shield when we got there. But when nothing leapt at us right away, Clarita just started walking instead, slowly and methodically with her body held straight. We all fell in behind her. The mals against the walls did start picking up their heads and peering at us, but since no one had ever been this stupid before, they couldn't immediately make sense of us. Unfortunately, there are heaps of mals that don't have enough brains to try to make sense of anything, just the equivalent of noses to tell them there are tasty bags of mana in their vicinity. A handful of small scuttling things started towards us, making raspy clicking noises against the floor.

That was enough to get some of the more hollow-sided chayenas to get up out of their sleeping pack and investigate us, thin drips of violet drool leaking out of the sides of their jaws as they began to pad in our direction. We all started to walk more quickly, and then the enormous hole in the dome turned out not to be an enormous hole but an enormous nightflyer that let go of the ceiling and came gliding down towards us. Orion said, "Okay, *go*," his sword-thing illuminating, and we all pelted away.

The chayenas charged after us instantly. They're one of the more stupid crossbreeds: from cheetah to hyena by way of water buffalo and rhinoceros and probably a couple others you can't tell by looking. They were smashed together in the days of colonial glory by some idiots setting up an enclave in Kenya who wanted more of a hunting challenge. An independent alchemist who lived with the local mundanes was annoyed. She took on some work from the enclavers so they'd let her come and go, and then she quietly enhanced the chayenas with the charming additional feature of a paralytic bite and let them all loose. That was the unpleasant and gory end for the enclave, but the chayenas survived, and now are sometimes bred deliberately as the equivalent of guard dogs. They're arguably not mals; if you raise one properly, it won't kill you for your mana even if it's hungry. Mostly they don't get raised properly, since the goal is in fact for them to kill intruders for their mana. Mum always gets wound up about their mistreatment.

At the moment, I felt something other than sympathetic. I'm in fair condition when I haven't recently had a gut wound, but I haven't spent the last six months doing wind sprints in the gym. I was at the end of our group. With the power-sharer on my wrist, I had the mana available to kill a whole continent's worth of chayenas, much less three mangy half-starved ones, but if I turned to cast at them, I'd end up separated and surrounded, and even if I managed to fight my way over to everyone else, I'd blow enormous amounts of our shared mana, which we needed for the repair work.

But the first chayena was already clawing at my personal shield, and if I waited any longer, one of them was going to get its teeth through it. I had chosen my place to turn, just past a scrap heap of marble and bones, and then Ellen tripped over a broken tile on the floor and went down not two steps ahead of me. Momentum carried me past her, and I didn't turn back: there wasn't any point. Her scream had already cut off into a dying gargle, and I knew better than to make it real by looking around. As long as I didn't look, she didn't have to be dead, and I didn't have to have feelings about Ellen, beaming at me two days ago while she told me we were going to make it. I couldn't afford feelings right now.

I made it to the machinery and fell into line next to David. The crowd of mals packed up against the walls was turning towards us like some enormous singular blob of a creature, humping itself around and flowing over the ground. The ones that had been at the back were racing for us as fast as they could go, trying to take advantage of their unexpected lead, while the ones that had been up at the front were trying to take it back. Clarita had already started casting. I called out my lines in turn, and we put the shield wall up, even as the repair team yanked off the polished brass that covered the machinery: all according to plan.

That of course was when Wen said something in Mandarin that I was unhappily certain was very profane.

And look, to defend myself, there'd been really excellent cause to be suspicious of the seniors, and going close to graduation was only the reasonable thing to do as a result. That said, in retrospect, odds were that the seniors still wouldn't have been able to carry out an effective backup plan even if we'd gone the night before instead, and allowing a little more time for things to go wrong might in fact have been a better idea. I'd just been completely certain that if they'd gone more wrong than that, we'd all be dead anyway.

I should have been right about that. We *would* have been

dead under any normal circumstances. We were in the middle of the graduation horde, all alone. We did have the mana of the entire school pouring into us, so we could probably have held Clarita's shield up against them for twenty minutes of violent pounding. And then we'd have run through the mana, and the shield would have gone down, and they'd have shredded us all.

But normal circumstances weren't what we had, because we had Orion.

It was a truly atrocious experience: standing there just holding up a shield, listening to the repair team clanging away desperately behind us, when I had no idea what the problem was or how long it was going to take to fix it. None of us on the shielding team did; we'd lost Ellen, and Zhen hadn't come along, as she'd been the fifth-fastest in the repair run. The only way we could have got an explanation right then would've involved getting Vinh to tell us about it in French, and at the moment he was kneeling on the ground with his entire torso shoved into the machinery, yelling muffled boomy information that sounded extremely urgent back out to Wen and Kaito, who were frantically ripping apart one of the pieces of artifice that they'd spent so much time putting together in the shop. I deeply regretted not having made time for Mandarin.

But the whole time, Orion went on performing nonstop heroics, pouring fresh mana into us with every mal he slaughtered. The idea had been that he'd stay behind the shield and foray out whenever something especially dangerous came at us, or threatened to take down the shield. But he hadn't come back even once to take a drink of water. He just stayed out there completely exposed and went on killing them in front of our faces. And I had nothing to do but stand there like a block, just doing my part to keep the bloody shield going, which was barely an effort because almost none of the mals were making it past him to hit us. We might have been watching him on telly through a safe, thick pane of glass.

The mals actually *backed off*, at a point. I'm not really sure how long it had been, it could've been ten minutes or a hundred years; it certainly felt like a hundred years. Orion was gasping for breath, his hair dripping and massive sweat stains all down his back, with a ring of deflated, stabbed, incinerated, shredded, and otherwise dispatched mals in a clear semicircle round him, a good foot wide, and the assembled maleficaria on the other side making a wall of glowing eyes and drooling jaws and glinting metal. The scavengers were the only ones still in motion: there were half a dozen, each scooting away happily with the remains of one of Orion's kills. The others all just held their positions for a good minute before one of them finally tried again, and even then, it didn't go for *him,* it tried to go round him and went for us.

As soon as that one darted round, another dozen came at once, each one trying to take advantage of Orion's distraction. But we held the shield up against them without any problem, at least not any problem for me, right up until David Pires abruptly went down. I caught a glimpse of his gone-grey face: I think he was dead even before he toppled forward out through the shield. I hope he was dead. Four different mals instantly got hold of him, and the next moment another ten piled on. Orion lunged in that direction, but by the time he got there and the mals all scattered before him, there was literally nothing left, not even a smear of blood: David might have evaporated.

A hundred mals took advantage of this new opening and came at us, and Orion couldn't stop the whole wave all at once: they came crashing into the shield, just as it was weakened. A lot of spells cast by more than one person fall apart instantly when anyone goes. Clarita's had a much better failure mode, the way a conversation can survive when someone leaves the room as long as the other people keep talking. We'd even practiced keeping it up when one of us dropped out. But we hadn't practiced after holding it for a century of constant attacks, and Maya, who'd been standing between me and David, gave a choking strangled gasp and dropped her part, too, pulling her hand out of mine and staggering a few steps back to collapse into a huddle on the ground, her hands pressed flat against her chest.

Clarita was already calling out David's next line, her voice strained; I came in on Maya's part after and reached out and grabbed Clarita's hand to close the line: only three of us left now, with Angel Torres on her other side. The shield wavered for a moment like haze above a summer road, and a gigantic suckerworm the length of a decently sized truck erupted explosively out of the crowd of mals and hurled itself right towards us. It smacked onto the shield like a lamprey directly in front of my face, round Sarlacc-toothed maw full of phosphorescent teeth glazed in neon pink, all of them working to get a hold on the shield so it could start twisting itself round to drill a hole through.

The shielding spell was a conversation, so I summoned up the memories of all the ways people made clear to me that I wasn't welcome to join theirs: cold shoulders and deliberately dropped voices. I fixed the idea in my mind as if David and Maya weren't really gone out of it, they'd just turned away a bit so the suckerworm couldn't hear enough of what they were saying to join in, because it wasn't wanted and should shove off, and it helped that it hurt me to think about it; I whispered David's next lines through my teeth and shoved more mana into the shield on a burst of anger, and the suckerworm lost its hold and slid down to the ground. Instantly seven smaller mals leapt on its back and tore it apart.

Clarita jerked her head to stare at me, but right then behind us Vinh gave a yowl of triumph and pulled himself out. We couldn't look round, but I heard the whole repair crew performing the final chant, the first familiar thing they'd done. The mana surge that poured through them was so massive that I could feel it against my back, a crackle like static electricity, and then Vinh and Jane Goh shoved the cover back on over the machinery with a loud clang, and the repair crew were turning and grabbing our shoulders, the sign that they were ready. *"Allons, allons!"* Vinh was yelling, but we didn't really need the command. Kaito was helping Maya to get up and grab on, and I started shouting like a madwoman, "Orion, get over here! Orion! Orion Lake, that means *you,* you tragic blob of unsteamed pudding, we're *going. Orion!"* and if you think that should've been enough, when he was literally two feet away from me at the time, I agree with you profoundly, except it *wasn't.* He didn't even have the excuse that he was in the middle of a hard fight, because actually he had just cleared another temporary ring around himself and was just crouched and *waiting.*

Thank goodness there were other sane people round; Angel on Clarita's other side bent down and grabbed a small hunk of broken marble off the ground with his free hand, and threw it at Orion with, well, quite frankly all the skill of a four-year-old, managing to hit his shoe a little bit. That was enough to get Orion to whip around instantly and blast *Angel*—fortunately we still had the shield up—and then his eyes widened for an instant as he realized what he'd just done, but he had to keep going around again to take out the

two mals that jumped him in the opening. "Lake, you absolute spanner!" I yelled furiously, but thankfully his head didn't
empty out again that quickly; he just killed the two mals and
finished turning, ran over to us and grabbed Angel's out-
stretched hand, and then Wen triggered the yanker on his
belt.

I'd never actually ridden a yanker spell before. If you think
bungee jumping off the world's highest cliff sounds like the
best time imaginable, you'd find it a cracking time. I personally did not. I screamed shrilly the whole way as the yanker
dragged us at extremely high speed through the horde of
monsters, the last remnant of our shield bowling them out of
our way, and all the way back up the painfully narrow maintenance shaft, banging us back and forth. I screamed even
louder for the really special part when we flew out through
the landing and into Todd's room and, thanks to our collective momentum, *overshot the edge.* Half of us hung suspended
for a moment just out in the open void, the yawning impos-
sibility of it beneath us, around us, and I would have started
screaming in a whole new way, but then the yanker went taut
again, snapped us back in through Todd's room, and dumped
us all into the middle of the senior dormitory corridor.

If my brain had in fact been rewritten so I couldn't communicate with anyone, I couldn't have told the difference at
the moment. I was just sunk on my knees on the floor shaking, arms wrapped over my gut, and my whole face feeling
like it was made of plastic that had melted partway off my
bones. Doors were clanging all around us up and down the
hall, seniors running past in groups, some of them throwing
us startled looks but not slowing down at all, and at first I
didn't pull myself together enough to realize—

"*Graduación!*" Clarita said, and she and Angel and Maya all took off different ways, Maya stumbling and clammy blue but still going, melting into the crowd; the whole repair crew were running also: going to their allies.

Orion grabbed my shoulder, and I squawked in alarm: it was like having pins and needles shooting through my body. "We missed the bell!" he shouted over the pandemonium.

I nodded and staggered to my feet and followed him, dodging seniors; he plunged back into the stairwell ahead of me just as I heard someone shout, "El! Orion!" I paused: Clarita was standing in the door of a room just visible at the curve of the corridor, and she beckoned. "You're not going to make it before the cleansing starts! Don't be crazy!"

I hesitated, but Orion was already disappearing up the stairs two at a time, and I shook my head at her and ran after him. It wasn't a very good decision. Orion had vanished out of sight, and I had to stop after only a little while to catch my breath, clinging to the vibrating railing; the stairs were moving back and forth like the pitching of a boat and my stomach was going with them. I forced myself back into motion, and Orion suddenly reappeared and grabbed me by the arm and started hauling me upwards with him. I didn't even snap at him, just wrapped one arm tight around my gut to squash the pain in, and let him keep me from falling over as I staggered up alongside him.

But a scrabbling noise was building before we even reached the landing for the workshop level, and as we made it, a wave of tiny mals came squeaking and squirming and hopping towards us out of the corridor, in such complete flight that they didn't even stop to try and munch on us; other waves came fleeing both up and down the staircase, all of them running in opposite directions, bowling each other over and turning into a scrabbling horde. I made a grunting effort and got myself the last few steps onto the workshop landing, panting, but the noises of the mals were being drowned out by the rising roar, like a campfire someone had rigged up to an amplifier, coming from both above and below, and the stairs were filling up with sharp-edged shadows in the brightening light. Orion stood still gripping my arm, frozen, then dragged me into the shop corridor instead. But there wasn't anywhere to run to. Ahead of us, the wall of mortal flame, blue-white, was already filling the corridor from floor to ceiling like a whispering, crackling curtain, broken up by the shadows of mals being caught and incinerated in the waterfall of it, leaping dark shapes in final agonies and small construct mals coming apart in clatters as their power got sucked out of them. Bursts of static electricity came spider-crawling ahead of it over the panels and floor tiles as it swept towards us.

Orion's breath was coming in short wavery gasps. I hadn't seen him afraid down in the hall even once that I'd noticed, but mortal flame isn't a mal: it consumes mals, it consumes anything in its path that has mana or malia to burn up. Combat magic isn't any use against them; you can't *fight* it. But to do him credit, he didn't panic, even if he was staring down the one and only thing that he was actually afraid of; he just stood there staring at it sort of blankly, like he couldn't quite believe this was happening to him.

I straightened up and shut my eyes, getting ready to start casting, and then had to push him off; he was trying to grab hold of my hand, which I needed rather urgently right then. "What are you doing?" I said, trying to get loose: he was being stupidly persistent about it. Yes, I really sincerely hadn't any idea: whatever was Orion doing, trying to hold hands with me in the moment of what he thought was his imminent demise, and then as soon as I spared it that much of a thought, the answer became so obvious that I felt like a complete idiot. "You *are* dating me?" I yelled at him, in a fury, and he turned around with his face screwed up in pinched determination and grabbed my face and *kissed me.*

I kneed him with as much energy as the situation called for, since I also needed my voice, and then pushed him down to the floor so I could turn back to the onrushing fires and conjure up my own wall of mortal flame, just in time to put it around us as a firebreak.

Chapter 13
MORTAL FLAME

I T GOT VERY HOT inside our dubious shelter, but the protection didn't need to last long. The cleansing wall rolled past us in less than a minute and went on its merry devouring way along the corridor. I dismissed my own wall—it was a bit resistant about being unconjured without getting to actually consume anything, but I managed to shove it away—and we were left there alone in the newly scorched corridor, with the faint charred-mushroom smell of burnt maleficaria coming out of every vent.

I kept standing resolutely upright and staring after the wall of flame that had passed as if I thought any moment now it might come back. It wasn't going to: the end-of-year cleansing is quick and thorough. The walls of mortal flame start in pairs and sweep away from each other towards the next one down the corridor, all of which are placed and timed so they don't leave any places to hide. The same time the wall had been going past us, the two walls in the stairwell had met on the landing. They'd both winked out, and the wall that had swept over us was probably finishing up a little further down the corridor. However, I was much more inclined to watch for a wall of mortal flame coming back than I was to look down at Orion, since I'd have to see his expression and might have to actually say words to him at that point.

Then I nearly went over as the whole place began to heave and surge beneath my feet. The walls and floor outside the ring where my protective wall had been were all still scorching-hot, so I had to crouch inside the tiny space with him, both of us clinging to each other with one arm and holding out the other like a clumsy two-headed surfer trying desperately not to topple over and sear ourselves on the heated walls. At least I couldn't have heard anything he tried to say to me. The gears were going, a hundred times louder than when I'd been safely tucked inside my room for graduation, and the stairway outside began to really move, squealing horribly. The familiar landing of our own res hall ground slowly into view and then continued on to vanish further below; it was all the way out of sight before the stairs locked into place again with a heavy clanging thump, and the grinding noise stopped.

A moment later all the sprayers turned on at once, and the corridor instantly filled with clouds of steam. We were left sopping-wet in a humid cloud of fog so thick we could barely see or breathe for a moment, but the walls were already baking off the moisture, and the hollow roar of the drain vacuums began to suck up the excess, leaving just the drowned-rat pair of us gasping in the middle of a sparkling-clean corridor. The end-of-term bell clanged away, and faintly echoing in the stairwell I heard doors clanging open in the dormitories above and below.

Beneath our feet, a more muffled grinding was still going: that was the senior dorm level winding the rest of its way to the bottom. If the cleansing machinery had run, down there

Clarita and Wen and the others would come out into a nearly empty graduation hall, scorched from end to end by an even bigger wall of mortal flame. Some smaller mals would have hidden under larger ones, or under debris. Some of the siren-spiders could probably have made it, thanks to their shells. Patience and Fortitude would have survived, too; it would have taken a solid week of a direct bath in mortal flame to wear those away. But their thinner tendrils would all have burnt up, and the eyes on their surface. The seniors would be able to go straight for the gates, all of them.

Or maybe it hadn't worked after all, and the seniors would instead be dumped into a starving horde that had been stirred up like a nest of wasps and was waiting for them with open jaws. We wouldn't know one way or another, not until next year. When it would be our turn to go. We'd made it to our senior year, the one in two odds we'd beaten so far. Only our chances had been modified by Orion, changing the house rules under us, and when he took hold of my shoulders, I didn't shove him off again.

"You saved my life," he said, sounding baffled about it. I gritted my teeth and turned to look back at him, ready to inform him he wasn't the only one who could be useful on occasion, except he was staring at me with an absolutely unmistakable expression, one I'd seen fairly often in my life: men occasionally aim it at my mum. Not the kind of expression you're thinking of; men don't lust after Mum in a leering kind of way. It was more like looking at a goddess, accompanied by thinking that maybe you might get the goddess to smile at you if you, I don't know, proved yourself sufficiently worthy, and I'd never once imagined anyone pointing anything remotely like it at me.

I had absolutely no idea what to do with it, other than possibly knee Orion again even harder and flee. That was really appealing the more I thought about it, but I didn't get the chance; instead *he* shoved *me* to the floor, straight into a half-frozen and half-scalding puddle, and fired off half a dozen targeted blasts over my head to destroy a small pack of gorgers who had evidently survived in the ceiling inside the pocket of safety I'd created, and were now jumping down to have us for a celebratory feast.

Which was exactly the moment when a dozen people came off the landing, just in time to see me on the floor at Orion's feet, him standing heroically over me, his hands full of glowing smoke and the scorched and smoking corpses of the gorgers in a neat circle around me, just as the last one came thumping down.

READER, I RAN the fuck away.

It wasn't difficult; everyone wanted to talk to Orion, to hear how he'd done it, how he'd slaughtered the mals and fixed the machinery and saved the seniors—I was fairly sure that by the end of the day, no one would remember that there had actually been any team involved at all, much less that I'd been on it. If I'd wanted to stay with him, I'd probably have had to wind both my arms around his waist and cling like a really determined ivy, but the crowd moved me away without any effort on my part at all.

All I had to do was make sure that I was getting pushed off in the right direction to do what any sensible person does at the end of term: I went straight for the workshop, where I had two shining minutes all to myself before anyone else got there. The supply containers are all purged completely and refilled from scratch at end of term, so I didn't even have to worry about mals. There were five forging aprons hanging by the big furnace, made of some heavy flame-resistant fabric; I grabbed the one that looked closest to Aadhya's size, spread it out on a workbench, and started loading it up.

I went for book chest materials first, because if you have a particular project firmly in mind, and you sacrifice an opportunity like being first into the shop after a resupply, you're more likely to find what you need. Straight away I scored another four pieces of purpleheart, two bars of silver for the inlay, a set of heavy steel hinges, and a coil of titanium wire that I was pretty sure I could use to make a spelled wire that would hold the lid in place however open I wanted to leave it. I even found a little section of an LED lightstrip. Spellbooks are mad for electronics; if you make a book chest that lights up when you open it, you're almost guaranteed never to lose a book unless you're really careless.

Other people started turning up just as I finished piling that up on the apron, but even then I had another good couple of minutes to grab miscellaneous things before I had to start worrying about protecting my haul, since all of the new arrivals went straight for the materials that are really valuable for trade, like titanium rods and bags of diamond chips. I decided not to compete: instead I thought about what Aadhya might need for her lute, and I found a bag of fine metallic wire, a packet of sandpaper, and two enormous bottles of clear resin. I bundled it all up and carried it out with me just as the crowd really started to arrive.

I went the other way down the corridor from the shop, to the opposite landing all the way on the other side of the school. I didn't want to have to fight my way through the adoring crowd that was probably still clogging up the one where Orion was, and anyway since our floor had rotated, it was entirely possible that the other landing would now be closer to my own room, and all sorts of other perfectly adequate excuses. The stairs are crowded at end of term with everyone running all over the school madly for supplies, but going down to the senior dorm room wasn't as bad. There wasn't anyone below us anymore.

Our res hall itself was positively civilized. Anyone still there had missed the best shot for supplies, so mostly it was just enclavers who didn't need to go to the effort; they were enjoying hot and relatively carefree showers, or just hanging out in the freshly cleansed corridor chatting in groups. Some of them actually nodded to me as I went by, and one girl from Dublin said, "You got a forging apron, lucky girl! Would you swap for it?"

"It's for Aadhya, ninth room down from the yellow lamp," I said. "I'm sure she'll be glad to hire it out."

"That's right, I saw you written up, best of luck," she said, with a congratulatory nod, exactly as though I was a fellow human being or something.

I got my haul back to my room, which I entered pretty warily, since I hadn't been there to barricade the door against mals trying to flee the mortal flames in the corridor. Mana was still flowing handily through the power-sharer on my wrist, and I didn't have the least compunction using it to cast a Revelatory Light spell. I went over every last corner of my room with it, including under the bed, which I pushed onto its side. Just as well: I spotted a mysterious cocoon tucked very carefully inside one of the big rusty springs, waiting to become an unpleasant surprise. I tipped out the jar of nails and screws on my desk and put the cocoon inside it. Maybe Aadhya would be able to do something with it, or I could sell it to some alchemy-track student.

I found a few more handfuls of vermin-class maleficaria on the shelves among my textbooks, and while I was dealing with them, one small scuttler jumped off my desk where it had been hiding behind the papers. It had no ambition for a meal at the moment; it just ran straight for the drain in the middle of the floor. I tried to zap it, but it was too fast and I missed. It dived between two bars of the grating, energetically wriggled its rear with the gleaming stinger, and squeezed through before I could think of anything else to throw that wouldn't have melted down a large section of the floor or possibly killed anyone walking past in the hall. Oh well. That's how the whole place would get thoroughly infested again by the end of the first quarter; there's not much to be done about it.

I'd just tiredly tipped my bed back over with a big clang when someone knocked on the door. I killed the Revelatory Light instantly; my impulse was to pretend I was somewhere else, on the moon maybe, but the light had surely been visible on the other side of the door through the cracks, and anyway I'd literally just made an enormous thumping noise. I steeled myself and went to the door, and cracked it open with several possible remarks going through my head, none of which turned out to be relevant, since it was just Chloe. "Hey," she said. "I saw the light. I heard you and Orion made it out, I figured I should see how you were doing. Are you okay?"

"I'd say I'm as well as could be expected, but I don't think anyone had any right expecting me to come out alive, so I suppose I'm actually better," I said. I took a deep breath, made the effort to let go of the freely flowing mana, and unclasped the power-sharer band and held it out to her.

She hesitated and said tentatively, "You know—if you change your mind about the spot—"

"Thanks," I said, shortly, without pulling it back, and after a moment she reached out and took it.

I thought that would be it, and I'd have liked it to be. Chloe had clearly just taken a shower and had her damp dark-blond hair back from her face in two thin silver clips; it was in a neat bob that someone had surely cut for her lately, and she was wearing a blue sundress with a twirly skirt and a pair of strappy sandals, the kind of outfit not even an enclaver would risk wearing past the first month of term. It didn't have a single stain, and it wasn't even much above the knee; she couldn't have worn it until this past year or it would've been hanging off her.

Meanwhile I was in the more threadbare of my two shirts, which hadn't been improved by my recent adventures, my dirty, patched combat pants with the thick belt holding them up and the two strips I've sewn onto the bottoms to make them longer, and the ragged six-year-old Velcro sandals I'd had to trade for midway through sophomore year when I definitively outgrew the pair I'd come in with. I'd gone for a too-big pair at the time, but by now they were on the last inches. My hair was mostly hanging out of the ragged plait I'd done before going down into the hall. Not to mention I hadn't showered in the last four days, unless you counted getting drenched to the skin in the corridor purge. And I don't care about dressing up, I wouldn't even if I could, but the contrast made me feel even more like I'd recently been dragged backwards through an entire hedge maze.

But Chloe didn't say a polite goodbye; she just stood there in my doorway turning the power-sharer over in her hands. I was about to excuse myself to go and fall into my bed for twelve hours or so, and she blurted, "El, I'm sorry." I didn't say anything, because I wasn't clear on what she was apologizing for. After a moment she said, "You just—you know, you get used to things. And you don't think about whether they're good. Or even okay." She swallowed. "You don't *want* to think about it. And nobody else seems to, either.

"And there's nothing you can see to do about it." She

looked at me, her whole soft face and clear eyes unhappy. I shrugged a little. "Because there's not meant to be anything you can do about it."

She was quiet, and then she said, "I don't know anything I can do about it. But I don't have to make it worse. And I—" She was a collection of fidgets suddenly, looking away and licking her lips, uncomfortable. "I lied. In the library. We weren't . . . we weren't really worried that you were a malefi-cer. We wanted to be worried about that, because we didn't like you. We'd all been talking about how you're so awful and rude, how you were trying to use Orion to make everyone suck up to you. Except it's the total opposite. That day Orion introduced us, I acted like all I needed to have you be my friend was to let you know that I was willing to let you talk to me. Like I'm so special. But I'm not. I'm just lucky. *Orion's* special," she added, with a huff that was trying to be a laugh and didn't quite manage it. "And he wants to be your friend because you don't care. You don't care that he's special, and you don't care that I'm lucky. You aren't going to be nice to me just because I'm from New York."

"I'm not nice to anybody, really," I said grudgingly, feeling squirmy inside being on the other end of her speech; it was too much of a real apology.

"You're nice to people who are nice to you," she said. "You're nice to people who aren't fake. And I don't want to be fake. So—I'm sorry. And—I'd like to hang out sometime. If you wanted."

Yes, because just what I wanted was to make a friend of a rich enclave girl so I could routinely rub my face around in all the luxuries I couldn't have, all of which were in fact quite nice even if they didn't measure up to the things I'd chosen in their place. And if Chloe Rasmussen turned out to be an ac-tual decent person and a real friend, that would mean the things I didn't have weren't necessarily incompatible with the things I really cared about, and how exactly I was meant to put that together without being discontented all the time, I didn't see, only I was reasonably certain that saying *no and on your way now* would in fact make me rude and stuck-up after all, just in a quixotic and contrary way.

"Yeah, all right," I said, even more grudgingly, and the only good thing that came of it was that then, finally, after she smiled at me a little shyly, she said I looked tired, she'd go and let me rest, and then she did go, so I could shut the door and flop myself down on my bed and sleep like the dead I somehow miraculously wasn't.

There was another knock on my door some time later, and I heard Liu say, "El, are you awake?" I'd been asleep, but the alert on my door had woken me, and I got up for her and Aadhya. They'd brought me some lunch down from the cafeteria. I gave Aadhya the forge apron and the supplies I'd found for the lute. They'd both got decent supply hauls, if not as amazing as the one I'd managed, and Liu had picked up some good notebooks and spare pens for me while she'd been picking some up for herself.

"Do you want to tell us about it?" Liu said, after I'd finished wolfing down the food and had sprawled back out on my bed.

"The machinery was broken in some different exciting way that took them more than an hour to fix," I said, staring at the ceiling. "We lost one of the artificers on the way in, and Pires keeled over doing the shield, and we got back late and got caught on the shop floor during the cleaning and Orion kissed me," which I hadn't actually meant to say, but it came out, and Liu gave a squeak of excitement and covered her mouth.

"But how did you get clear of the cleaning fires?" Aadhya said, deadpan, and Liu shoved her knee and said, "Stop that! Was it nice? Is he a good kisser?" and then blushed bright red and burst into giggles and covered her face.

I would probably have been the same color if I could have managed it. "I don't remember!"

"Oh, come on!" Aadhya said.

"I don't! I—" I groaned and sat up and put my face against my knees and finished in a mutter, "I kneed him and shoved him off me so I could cast a firebreak," and Aadhya laughed so hard she fell off the bed while Liu gawked at me, totally stricken on my behalf.

"'I'm not dating Orion at all, we're just friends,'" Aadhya wheezed from the floor without even getting up, mimicking what I'd told her and Liu the night before we'd shaken on our alliance: I hadn't wanted them to come into it on false pretenses. "You fail at dating so hard."

"Thanks, I feel loads better," I said. "And I wasn't wrong! *I* wasn't dating *him*."

"Yeah, that's fair," Aadhya said. "Only a boy would date somebody for two weeks and not mention it to them."

We all kind of sniggered together for a bit, but after we settled back down, Liu said, tentatively, "Do you *want* to?" Her face was serious. "My mother told me it was a really bad idea."

"*My* mom told me that all boys are carrying a secret pet mal around in their underwear, and if you get alone with them they let it out," Aadhya said. We both shrieked with laughter, and she laughed, too. "I know, right? But she did it on purpose, she told me to pretend that was true, the whole time I was in here, because it would *be* true, if I let a boy get me pregnant."

Liu gave a shiver all over and wrapped her arms around her knees. "My mother got me an IUD."

"I tried one. I got massive cramps," Aadhya said grimly.

I swallowed. I hadn't bothered; it had seemed the least likely of my many worries. "My mum was almost three months gone with me at graduation."

"Oh my God," Aadhya said. "She must have *freaked.*"

"My dad died getting her out," I said softly, and Liu reached out and squeezed my hand. My throat was tight. It was the first time I'd ever told anyone.

We sat quiet for a bit, and then Aadhya said, "I guess that means you'll be the only person ever to graduate twice," and we all laughed again. It didn't feel like tempting fate, just then, to talk about graduating like something that was going to happen.

I lay back down to rest until dinnertime, half drowsing while we talked about plans for the first quarter, how much mana we thought we could build. As Liu scribbled down budget numbers, I couldn't help but think wistfully of the power-sharer; I rubbed my fingers around my wrist where it had been. I almost couldn't blame Chloe, anyone from New York. All that mana just flowing at your fingertips, so much you couldn't see the end of it. I hadn't been able to feel the work behind it. It had felt as free as air. I'd had it for only a few hours and I already missed it.

I kept almost falling asleep again and then rousing back up. I wasn't sure why; Aadhya and Liu would have understood, and even watched over me and woken me up for dinner. "We should think about what else we could use, and anyone else we might want to recruit," Aadhya said. "I might be able to finish the lute early enough to make some more things first quarter. We should go through each other's spell lists, too."

Liu said softly, "There's one more thing I have," and then she got up and went out the door, and I realized abruptly with strong indignation that the reason I kept starting up was that I was *waiting* for another knock. I glared at the door. And a few minutes later there was another knock, but it was just Liu coming back with a small box in her hands. She sat down on the floor with crossed legs around it and opened the lid and brought out a little white mouse. It wriggled its nose and squirmed around over her fingers, but didn't make a dash for it.

"You have a familiar!" Aadhya said. "Oh my gosh, it's so cute."

"He's not a familiar," Liu said. "Or he wasn't. I'm just starting to . . . I have ten of them." She didn't meet our eyes: it was an all but open admission she'd been going for the very unofficial maleficer track. Nobody brings in ten mice and feeds them out of their supplies for any other reason. "I have an affinity for animals."

Which was probably why her parents had made her do it, I realized: they'd known she'd be able to keep her sacrifices alive. And also why she'd hated it so much, even after three years, that she'd decided not to go back to it.

"And now you're making him a familiar?" I asked. I don't know exactly how that works. Mum has only ever had spontaneous familiars: once in a while an animal arrives in our yurt that needs looking after, she helps it, and then it hangs about and helps her for a while before it drifts away again to being an ordinary animal. She doesn't try to keep them.

Liu nodded, stroking the mouse's head with a fingertip. "I could train one for each of you, too. They're nocturnal, so they can keep watch while you sleep, and they're really good at checking food for anything bad. This one brought me a piece of a string of enchanted coral beads two days ago. His name is Xiao Xing." She let us hold him, and I could feel the mana at work in his tiny body: he already had a kind of blue shimmer over the surface of his eyes and if you looked at his fur from a sharp angle, and he sniffed at us curiously, unafraid. After we each stroked him for a bit, Liu put him down and let him just roam around the room; he scampered around sniffing at things and poking his head into places. He got up on the desk and then turned wary right near the spot where the scuttler had been hiding; he ran away from it fast, back to Liu, until she checked it for him and showed him it was clear; then she patted him and praised him and gave him a little chunk of dried fruit out of a bag she had tied to her waist. He climbed into the front pocket on her shirt and sat there nibbling on it happily.

"Could you train the rest for other people?" I asked, watching him, utterly entranced. "You'd get a lot in trade." I'd never had much time for animals before, once Mum trained me out of wanting to dissect them; I mainly ignored the dogs on the commune and was ignored in turn. I've never even liked cute cat videos. But I hadn't quite realized how starved I was of seeing anything alive and moving that wasn't trying to kill me. Familiars aren't common here: it's really expensive in terms of weight to bring them in, and painfully hard to take care of them inside. When your choices are to feed yourself or feed your cat, you feed yourself, or else the next mal gets you and the cat, too. But mice are cheap enough to feed that it wouldn't be that difficult. I just hadn't thought of it as something I'd want.

"Yes, after I train one for each of my cousins," Liu said. "They'll be here tonight."

It took me by odd surprise again, being reminded of something that you already know but that doesn't seem true yet: We were seniors now. It was our last year. Tonight was induction.

"Can we come pick one out now?" Aadhya said. She was as mesmerized as I was. "Do they need anything? Like a cage?"

Liu nodded, getting up. "You'll need to make something enclosed so they can hide during the day while you're out and they're sleeping. But come and choose one now. You have to play with it for at least an hour every day for a month or so before you take it. I'll show you how to give them mana: you have to put it into the treats you give." I swung my feet off the bed and got on my shoes, and then Liu opened the door and we all jumped back, because Orion was standing right outside like a creeper. He jumped himself, so it wasn't that he'd actually been planning to ambush me; I could only guess that he'd been standing there working himself up to knocking.

"I'll come and take a look now, Liu," Aadhya said loudly. "I can figure out how to put together a good enclosure." She pushed Liu—who was blushing again and trying not to look at Orion—ahead of her and out the door past Orion, and then from behind his back she made a wild pointing motion towards him and exaggeratedly mouthed words that I had no trouble recognizing as *SECRET PET MAL,* so I had to fight not to go squawking with hysterical laughter into my pillow. They vanished down the corridor.

Orion looked as though he would have liked to run away, which I would have sympathized with, except at least he *could,* since he wasn't already inside his own room. He'd showered, changed clothes, got his hair cut, and even *shaved:* I eyed his newly smooth jawline with suspicion. I really had absolutely no intention of going out with anyone at school. Forget pregnancy; the last thing I needed was the *distraction.*

He was already generating more than enough distraction in my life even when I didn't have to wonder whether kissing was going to happen anytime he was in my vicinity.

"Look, Lake," I said, just as he blurted, "El, listen," and I heaved a sigh of deep relief. "Right. You just wanted to tick it off before you died."

"No!"

"You *don't* actually want to date me, do you?"

"I—" He looked baffled and desperate and then said, "If you—I don't—it's up to you!"

I stared at him. "It is, but that's my part. Your part's not up to me. Or are you actually trying to further develop this bizarre loser form of dating where you never actually get round to asking the other person what they think of the idea? Because I'm not helping you with it."

"For the love of—" He dissolved into a strangled noise of wild irritation and shoved both his hands into his hair: if it hadn't just been mostly shingled close, it would've been standing up like an Einstein mop. Then he said flatly, without looking me in the face, "I'm trying not to get kicked out of your life," and I got it, embarrassingly belated. I had Aadhya and Liu, now, and not just him. It was like all that mana at my hands, something so vital you could get used to it so fast you'd almost forget what life had been like without it—until it went away again. But he didn't. He didn't have anybody else; he'd never had anybody, the same way I'd never had anybody, but now he'd had me, and he wanted to lose that about as much as I wanted to trade him and Aadhya and Liu for an enclave seat in New York.

Of course, he was still being inexcusably stupid about it. "Lake, if I *did* want to date you, I wouldn't want you to date me just because I commanded you to as the price of admission," I said.

"Are you just trying to be dense?" He glared at me. But I glared right back, indignantly, and then in the tones of someone speaking to a dim pony, he said, "I'd want to. If you want, I want. And if you don't want, then—I don't want."

"That's the general idea of the thing," I said, getting wary all over again: that sounded alarmingly like he did want. "Otherwise it's just stalking. Are you *asking*? And I'm not kicking you out of my life no matter what!" I added, although I hadn't any idea what I'd do if he did ask. "I kicked you out of my *way* downstairs because I had the odd notion that you'd prefer your life saved, which I'd like to point out for the record I've now done in turn."

"I'm pretty sure I'm up to thirteen at this point, so you've got a way to go," he said, folding his arms over his chest, but it didn't really have the right effect: he looked too thoroughly relieved.

"We needn't quibble about numbers," I said, loftily.

"Oh, I think we *do* need," he said, and then just when I was about to relax, thinking I'd steered us back into safer waters, he dropped his arms again and his face went open and a little pale, leaving scared pink standing out on the edges of his cheekbones. "El, I'd—I'd like to ask. But not—in here. After we—if we—"

"Don't even try. I'm not getting *engaged* to go out with you," I said rudely, shoving in before he could drag us back onto the shoals. "If you're not asking now, that's sufficient unto the day! If we make it out of here alive and you slog across the pond to come ask me, I'll decide what I think of it at the time, and until then, you can keep your Disney movie fantasies," *and your secret pet mal,* my brain unhelpfully inserted, "to yourself."

He said, "Okay, okay, fine!" in a tone one-tenth irritation and nine-tenths relief, while I looked away, trying to stop my mouth contorting around the laugh I was having to fight desperately to keep in yet again: thanks ever so, Aadhya. Her mum was a genius, actually. "Can I ask you to meet for *dinner* in an hour?"

"No, you twit," I said, as if I hadn't just forgot about it myself. "It's induction. We've got half an hour at best." He immediately looked sheepish, although to be fair to us, we'd definitely had the weirdest graduation day ever. I grimaced and looked down at myself. "I ought to shower. And put on my slightly less filthy top."

"Do you want another one?" he said, a little tentatively. "I've got spares."

Our conversation had made clear that he didn't need the slightest encouragement, but caution warred with my fairly desperate longing for another T-shirt, which even the one glimpse I'd had into his room had been enough for me to say with perfect authority he had far too many of for his own good. "Yeah, all right," I said, with an inward sigh. At least the whole school was already completely certain we were dating.

I WAS ABSOLUTELY RIGHT about Orion needing no encouragement: the shirt he brought me had the Manhattan skyline on it in silver glitter, a single spot marked out roughly halfway along the island with a rising swirl of colored glitter, presumably the enclave location: not at all meaningful or claim-staking in any way. I'd have thwapped him across the head with it, except it was clean, and in fact smelled faintly of washing powder: he'd probably had it wrapped up somewhere in a drawer waiting for his senior year. At least it gave me the excuse to abandon him for the girls' bathroom instantly so I could put it on, a clean top over clean showered skin: bliss.

He had waited for me outside, and we collected Aadhya and Liu from her room. I peeked into the big tank she had the mice in. Aadhya's was already marked with a bright-pink dot that she'd put on with a highlighter. "You can pick yours tonight," Liu said.

The stairs felt odd when we started up because they weren't moving anymore: like getting off a ship after you've been on the water for a long time. The gears had all settled back into place, and there was only the faint ticking of the minor machinery, more or less just keeping time until the end of next year. Everyone was going upstairs in a big tidal flow together, so it didn't even take long to climb to the cafeteria and join the waiting crowd.

The food line hadn't opened yet, and about half the tables were folded up against the walls to leave a big open space cleared in the middle, with wide aisles leading to it from each of the stair landings. Up above was the brand-new res hall, same as the old res hall, more or less literally, just waiting for the brand-new shivering freshmen to be dropped inside.

We'd cut it a little fine. Induction started moments after we got there: we could feel the faint ear-popping sensation of so many bodies displacing volumes of air, one after another, and it was followed almost immediately by the loud clanging and scraping of doors being slid open, up on the freshman dorm level. Unless you're one of the monstrously unlucky few like Luisa, you've been told over and over what to do the second you arrive, no matter how vomitous or shell-shocked you are: you get out of your room and run straight down to the cafeteria. The freshmen came streaming in through all four doors, a few of them holding paper bags that they were throwing up into even as they kept staggering along. Induction is about as much fun as a yanker, and it takes longer.

In ten minutes or so, they were all shaking and huddled in

the middle of the cafeteria. They looked so tiny. I hadn't been one of the tallest kids when we came in, but I couldn't remember ever being that short myself. We had all gathered around them, keeping an eye on the ceilings and the drains, pouring them glasses of water carefully. Even the worst people will come out to protect the new inductees. Selfishly, if for no other reason; as soon as the freshmen calmed down and drank some water, they started calling out our names: they had letters from the other side, especially if they were enclave kids.

I knew there wouldn't be one for me. We weren't close to any other families with wizard kids: the couple of times Mum tried to arrange for us to play together when I was little didn't go amazingly well. And she wouldn't have been able to pay someone to give up some of their allotment to bring me a letter. The only thing she had to barter that would be worth as much as a gram's allowance to another wizard would've been her healing, and she doesn't charge for healing. She told me she wasn't sure she'd be able to get me anything, and I'd told her it was all right.

But even knowing, I would have been there anyway, and this time I even got to enjoy it vicariously. Aadhya was given a letter by a black girl with her hair in a million braids—each one with a tiny enchanted protection bead at the end, really clever idea. Liu brought over her cousins to introduce them to me, two carbon-copy boys with bowl cuts who bowed really politely like I was a grown-up, and I suppose I was, to them: they were a head and a half shorter than me, with soft round-cheeked faces. Their parents had probably been all but force-feeding them like geese in preparation.

And then a boy with a voice that hadn't quite finished breaking called, uncertainly, "I've got a note from Gwen Higgins?" I didn't hear it the first time, but there was a little lull after, as people heard it, and he said it again.

Aadhya had come over, bringing both her letter and the black girl, from Newark, whose name was Pamyla—one of the reasons parents will have their kids spend a tiny bit of their precious weight allowance on a letter is that they know they'll get an automatic older friend on the other side in return. "Do you think it's *that* Gwen Higgins? Does she have a kid in here?" Pamyla said to Aadhya, sounding hopeful.

Aadhya just made a shrugging expression. Liu was shaking her head. "If she does, they're keeping quiet; everyone would be on them for healing magic, I guess."

Then the boy said, "For her daughter Galadriel?" and both of them—along with the handful of other people around who'd been paying enough attention to hear him—gave me a double take, and then Aadhya shoved me in the shoulder, indignantly. Several other people were having a furtive look around the cafeteria like they thought maybe there was some *other* girl named Galadriel in the place. I gritted my teeth and went over. Even the kid looked doubtfully up at me.

"I'm Galadriel," I said shortly, and held out my hand: he put a tiny little thing almost like a shelled hazelnut into my palm, probably not even the weight of a single gram. "What's your name?"

"I'm Aaron?" he said, like he wasn't completely sure. "I'm from Manchester?"

"Well, come on," I said, and gave him a jerk of my head, leading him back past a bunch of staring faces. There wasn't really an escape from them, though: Aadhya and Liu were eyeing me themselves, Aadhya with a narrowed look that suggested I was in for another good long lecture as soon as she got me alone. I introduced Aaron to the others a bit grudgingly, and he and the other three freshmen started talking; Liu's cousins both spoke English without the slightest hitch, and as fluently as either he or Pamyla did. Aadhya had a small sheet of enchanted gold leaf in her letter: she showed it to us gleefully. "I'll put this round the argonet-tooth pegs, on the lute."

Liu had an almost flat postage-stamp-sized tin crammed full of a fragrant balm that she let us each use a tiny touch of, dipping the tips of our pinkie fingers in and rubbing it on the bottom edge of our lower lip. "It's my grandmother's poison catcher," she said. "It lasts a month or so if you're careful about brushing your teeth. If you feel your lip tingle when you start to put something in your mouth, don't eat it."

And all of that was what induction meant to everyone. A tiny infusion of hope, of love and care; a reminder that there's something on the other side of this, a whole world on the other side. Where your friends share whatever has come to them, and you share back. Only that had never been induction for me. It was the first time I'd ever been on the inside of it, and my eyes were prickling. I had to fight not to put my tongue out and lick the balm over and over.

Orion joined us with his own mail already in his hand, a fat envelope and a small bag, and whispered to me in a cheerful singsong under his breath, "Busted," slinging his arm around my neck and grinning at me. I made a face at him, but I couldn't help smiling a little myself as I carefully unrolled my very own letter—a single tiny strip of onion skin so thin it was translucent, which had been rolled up into a bead not much bigger than the ones Pamyla had on the ends of her hair. It had faint folding lines scored along the length, one every inch: marks for tearing the sheet into pieces to eat. When I held it to my mouth and breathed in, I got the smell of honey and elderflower: Mum's spell for refreshment of the spirit. Even just that one breath of it was good; I swallowed down a hard lump of happiness that warmed my belly as I brought the strip down again to squint through it. Mum's writing on it was so small and faint that it took me a second to puzzle out the single line.

My darling girl, I love you, have courage, my mother wrote, *and keep far away from Orion Lake.*

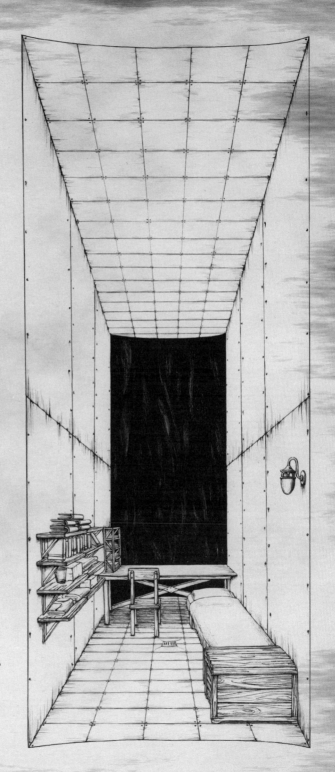

Galadriel's Dormitory Room

Chloe's Dormitory Room

Acknowledgments

I owe endless debts to Sally McGrath and Francesca Coppa: allies in the graduation hall.

Thanks also to the many other beta readers who cheered me on, especially to Monica Barraclough, and to Seah Levy, Merry Lynne, and Margie Gillis, who also put me up through the frantic homestretch run of writing. Katherine Arden wrote alongside me and let me lose myself in her own work when I needed to step out of the Scholomance now and again.

And to my tireless agent, Cynthia Manson, and my editor, Anne Groell, for telling me who this book was for (PS: Anne, I still don't believe they're in their thirties), her associate editor, Alex Larned, and the entire wonderful team at Del Rey Books, the best partners that an author could hope for, including in particular David Moench, Mary Moates, Julie Leung, and Ashleigh Heaton, and with special thanks for so many years of enthusiasm and support from Scott Shannon, Keith Clayton, and Tricia Narwani.

I am also so grateful to the PRH rights team, especially Rachel Kind and Donna Duverglas and Denise Cronin, and the many brilliant editors abroad that I've had the good fortune to work with thanks to their efforts, and in particular on this one to Ben Brusey and Sam Bradbury in Penguin Random House UK.

The Scholomance posed some unique visual challenges to the imagination, and I'm so lucky to have had help realizing the details of my world from David Stevenson at Del Rey, and the work of several brilliant artists, including Elwira Pawlikowska, my own assistant Van Hong, and Miranda Meeks, as well as Sally McGrath's brilliant work on the Scholomance website.

And finally and always and most to Charles and Evidence: thank you for loving me, for being proud of me, for holding me and holding me up.

About the Author

NAOMI NOVIK is the acclaimed author of the Temeraire series and the award-winning novels *Uprooted* and *Spinning Silver*. She is a founder of the Organization for Transformative Works and the Archive of Our Own. She lives in New York City with her family and six computers.

naominovik.com
Facebook.com/naominovik
Twitter: @naominovik
Instagram: @naominovik

About the Type

This book was set in Dante, a typeface designed by Giovanni Mardersteig (1892–1977). Conceived as a private type for the Officina Bodoni in Verona, Italy, Dante was originally cut only for hand composition by Charles Malin, the famous Parisian punch cutter, between 1946 and 1952. Its first use was in an edition of Boccaccio's *Trattatello in laude di Dante* that appeared in 1954. The Monotype Corporation's version of Dante followed in 1957. Though modeled on the Aldine type used for Pietro Cardinal Bembo's treatise *De Aetna* in 1495, Dante is a thoroughly modern interpretation of that venerable face.

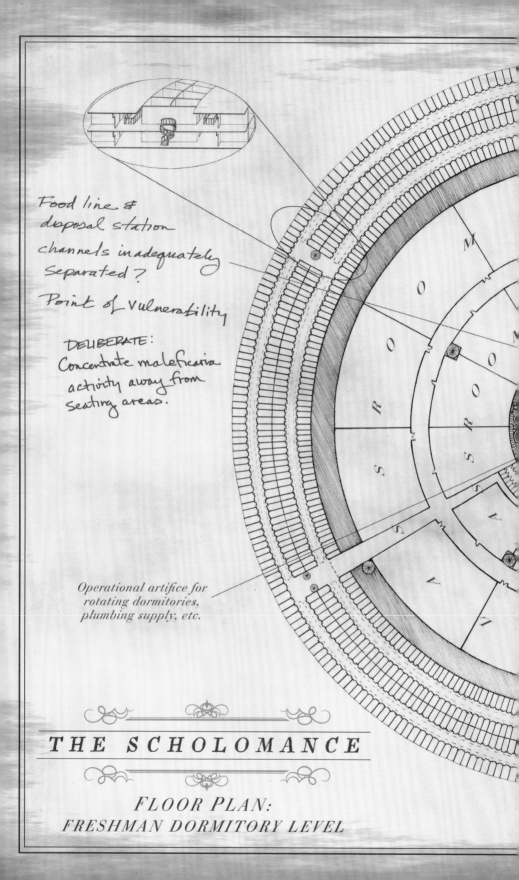

Food line & disposal station channels inadequately separated?

Point of vulnerability

DELIBERATE: Concentrate maleficaria activity away from seating areas.

Operational artifice for rotating dormitories, plumbing supply, etc.

THE SCHOLOMANCE

FLOOR PLAN:
FRESHMAN DORMITORY LEVEL